THE WINTER BELL

THE WINTER BELL

BROOKWOOD MYSTERIES
BOOK 4

JORDAN JACE

To Alice—my partner in love, words, and wonder.

Thank you for believing in every story, and for sharing this beautiful journey of writing together.

CONTENTS

FOREWORD

When the Winter Bell of Brookwood falls silent for the first time in nearly a century, the entire town feels its absence. Shops open late, voices drop to whispers, and an ancestral hush settles like frost over every doorstep. For generations, the bell has tolled on the Winter Solstice—a sound of promise, peace, and continuity. But when it fails to ring, it awakens long-buried secrets and rekindles stories the town vowed never to tell.

Marley Taylor, still discovering her role as the keeper of her aunt's beloved bookshop, is drawn deeper into Brookwood's mysteries when she stumbles upon a half-burned note: "If the bell does not ring, the vow was broken." From that moment, Marley senses that something sacred has been paused—not only in the town's traditions but in its very soul. Each clue she uncovers pulls her further into a haunting ancestral riddle: the legend of Amelia Colvin, the "veil bride" who never wed, and whose unfinished vow has bound Brookwood in silence for nearly a century.

Damien Hawthorne, the archivist and historian whose sharp intellect is matched only by his guarded heart, joins

Marley in unraveling the truth. At first, he searches for rational explanations: mechanical faults, forgotten maintenance, natural decay. But as every practical lead collapses, Damien is forced to admit that the silence is more than mechanical—it is personal, spiritual, and impossibly intimate. Together, Marley and Damien follow a trail of spectral fragments: a sealed ribbon box in the bakery attic, Elijah Callahan's lost journal, music boxes that whisper hidden words, and lace gloves left like offerings at Marley's door. Each artifact weaves them closer to Amelia's forgotten story—and closer to each other.

As Brookwood prepares for its Winter Ball, Marley wrestles with how much of Amelia's truth the town is ready to hear. Is Brookwood strong enough to face the reality that its beloved traditions are rooted not in joy, but in sacrifice and silence? And as Damien receives an offer that could be a great opportunity—but away from Marley—he must decide where his true calling lies: in preserving history abroad, or in living its unspoken vows here in Brookwood.

What begins as a hushed anomaly becomes a test of faith, love, and courage. The bell's silence reveals itself not as absence, but as a crucible. Marley and Damien stand at the threshold of choice: to let Brookwood retreat into silence, or to risk everything by speaking Amelia's truth aloud. When the bell rings again—unbidden, clear, and resonant—its sound restores more than tradition. It restores memory, unity, and the hope of new vows written in the present.

The Winter Bell is a story of ancestral promises and contemporary reckonings, where love becomes a vow as sacred as history itself. Steeped in romance, mystery, and the shimmering magic of winter, this fourth installment of the Brookwood Mysteries is both a revelation and a renewal.

Readers will find themselves swept into a world where forgotten brides leave whispers in the snow, music boxes carry the songs of the departed, and the courage to speak truth becomes the greatest vow of all.

Perfect for fans of heartwarming small-town romance, generational mysteries, and stories that blend history with the supernatural, The Winter Bell delivers on every page: an emotional love story, a pulse-quickening mystery, and a community's journey toward healing. It is a novel of vows broken and vows restored, of presence over promise, and of love that rings true—even when the bell does not.

Step into Brookwood this winter. Listen closely. The silence has a story to tell.

PROLOGUE

The cold came early that year.

By late November, Brookwood's streets bore the weight of silence as much as snow. The lamps along Main Street glowed against frost-rimmed windows, but fewer people lingered in doorways or clustered in shopfronts. Even the laughter of children had softened, muffled beneath scarves and unspoken questions that had begun to circulate since the Chapel bell had failed to toll.

The Winter Bell.

For eighty-eight years, it had marked solstice and ceremony, births and vows, departures and funerals. Its tone—deep, sonorous, and unwavering—was the heartbeat of the town. And yet, when the first dusk of Advent descended, the bell rope had hung slack. No sound. No chime. Only absence.

Marley Taylor felt that absence in her very bones.

She had walked alone through the snow-powdered square, scarf tight against her throat, journal pressed beneath her arm like a talisman. Each step sounded too loud, echoing against cobblestones that should have been cushioned by the bell's resonance. Her mind, ever attuned to the memory of Brookwood, caught on the oddness: how the snowflakes seemed to fall slower in silence, as if time itself hesitated.

The bell was not broken. She knew that instinctively, the way one knows the difference between illness and refusal. Objects remembered. The Winter Bell had a memory of its own, and tonight it withheld its voice like a vow unkept.

She paused before the meetinghouse door. For decades, the people of Brookwood had gathered here to hear the bell call them to attention, to bind them in community. The wood was worn by countless hands, its iron hinges sturdy despite years of weather. Marley placed her palm flat against the door and felt—not the cool grain of oak—but a stillness heavy with absence.

Inside, the rope dangled untouched, its fibers coiled like a serpent unwilling to strike. The rafters loomed above, shadows dancing where the lanterns flickered. She was not alone. Damien Hawthorne stood across the hall, as though the silence had summoned him, too.

No lantern in his hand, no book tucked beneath his arm this time. Only his presence—tall, steady, eyes shadowed with the same realization she carried.

"It didn't ring," he said.

Marley nodded, her throat tight. "Not once. Not in eighty-eight years."

They stood there, the quiet pressing against them like a living thing. Damien reached for the rope, lifted it once, then let it fall. No echo followed. No reverberation of bronze through wood and stone. Only the reminder of what had been withheld.

"It's not broken," Damien murmured. His voice carried the certainty of someone who had handled ancient manuscripts, who had pieced together lost genealogies and forgotten archives. He knew the weight of memory. "It's refusing."

The word hung between them. Refusing.

Marley exhaled slowly. "Then we have to ask what vow it's holding hostage."

Their eyes met, and for a moment she felt both the fragility and the inevitability of their connection. Since the lighthouse had drawn them together, since the echoes of earlier mysteries had tested them, she had come to know Damien as more than a scholar or a companion. He was an anchor. Yet anchors, too, could tether or hold one back.

The bell waited above them. Silent. Expectant.

Together, they climbed the narrow spiral stair, their hands brushing once on the railing. Neither pulled away. The air grew colder the higher they ascended, as though the tower itself guarded its secret.

Lantern-light revealed the bell at last.

Bronze darkened by decades, edges nicked by storms and resonance, its lip heavy with history. Around the crown, letters caught the light: *Veritas in Silentio.* Truth in stillness.

Marley brushed her gloved fingers across the inscription. She had passed beneath this bell countless times, but she had never noticed the words. Perhaps they revealed themselves only when silence demanded attention.

"Stillness reveals truth," Damien translated, his voice quiet. "That was Aurelia's language, too."

"She wrote it in light," Marley whispered. "Here it's written in sound—or in the absence of sound."

The silence vibrated like a note held just beyond hearing. Marley closed her eyes, letting the hush speak. For an instant she almost heard laughter—faint, distant—as if from another decade. The shuffle of footsteps ascending these very stairs. The sharp intake of breath before vows spoken. Then, abruptly, absence. A void where promise should have lived.

Her eyes opened. Damien watched her, his gaze searching, steady.

"You heard something," he said.

"Not words. A space. A missing piece." She touched the inscription again. "A forgotten bride."

Damien frowned—not at her intuition, but at its weight. "Then it isn't mechanical. It's memorial. The bell remembers a promise broken. And it won't ring again until we find who was left standing in silence."

Marley's breath caught. The Keeper of Memory role she had inherited from her aunt had already drawn her into the depths of Brookwood's forgotten vows. But this—this was different. This was not an archive bound in paper and ink. This was a silence that reached through generations.

She turned to Damien. "Then we have to listen harder than ever before."

He nodded, though she could see the unease in his shoulders. Duty weighed on him as much as it did on her. His daughter, Sophie, his obligations to the town—those roots ran deep. And Marley, though tethered to Brookwood now, still carried the restlessness of someone who might be called elsewhere.

The bell loomed above them, unyielding. Below, the town slept, unaware that its next mystery had already begun.

They descended the stair in silence, carrying the absence with them like an artifact. Outside, the square lay washed in moonlight, cobblestones shining silver. Marley pulled her scarf tighter, the cold sharp against her skin.

At the fountain, she paused. "Do you ever wonder," she

asked softly, "whether choosing to hold memory means choosing not to hold anything else?"

Damien looked at her fully, his expression stripped of all the guardedness he so often wore. "All the time," he admitted. "I wonder if being Keeper of Memory means you'll leave when I need someone to stay. And I wonder if my roots will keep me here when you're called elsewhere."

The words cut deeper than the cold. Marley wanted to promise, to soothe. But Keeper of Memory meant truth first. And truth was: she didn't know.

"We don't have to answer tonight," she whispered. "Stillness first. Listening first. The truth will speak between the memories."

He nodded, accepting. His hand brushed hers—light, fleeting, no claim, no demand. Just presence.

Behind them, the bell tower remained silent. Ahead, the lighthouse beam swept across the water, steady, eternal.

Between them, Brookwood slept, unaware that silence had already opened the next chapter.

And Marley, with Damien beside her, understood: the Winter Bell would not toll again until its story was told.

THE FOLLOWING MORNING, Brookwood awoke to a silence heavier than frost.

The sun rose pale over the Harbor, its light caught in the ice along the rooftops. The bell tower cast its shadow long across downtown a mute sentinel. Even the gulls seemed reluctant to cry, circling above without the usual racket. Word had already spread through the town like fire through dry grass: the Winter Bell had not rung.

Marley stood at the window of the bookshop, notebook open, pen idle in her hand. Across the street, shutters opened hesitantly, faces peeking out as though afraid to find the silence waiting for them. She watched as Councilor Lorraine Gearhart, who had lived through wars and blackouts, crossed herself at the sight of the still rope dangling from the tower. Mrs. Bennett, the baker, hesitated before sweeping the steps, as though unsure if commerce should proceed on a day that felt unmoored.

The bell's absence had not only unsettled the evening before—it had shifted the cadence of the town itself.

Damien arrived just after eight, boots crunching on ice. He carried no books, no stack of archival notes. Only a thermos of coffee in one hand, and in the other, the key to the tower.

"Are we the only ones who aren't pretending it's a mistake?" he asked as he stepped inside, brushing snow from his shoulders.

Marley closed her notebook. "Everyone else is hoping it's rust, or wind, or neglect. But you and I both know objects don't neglect. They remember."

Damien's gaze lingered on her face, as if weighing whether to challenge her or to admit he agreed. He unscrewed the thermos cap, poured coffee into its lid, and offered it to her. The heat bit her cold fingers.

"You really think it's memory?" he asked.

Marley took a sip, let the bitter warmth settle in her throat. "Last night, I could almost hear it. Not sound— absence. A missing vow. A bride who never stood at the altar."

Damien lowered himself into one of the shop's chairs, rubbing his hands together. "So what does that make us? Investigators of silence? Or mourners for a promise never kept?"

She set the cup down. "Both."

The word settled between them. Both. The way she and Damien existed now—partners in unearthing Brookwood's mysteries, but also two people caught in the fragile space between companionship and something more. Their lives pressed against each other like two panes of glass: separate, yet always reflecting back the other.

The bell's silence had forced them into yet another threshold.

Marley rose, tugged her coat tighter, and reached for her satchel. "If the bell remembers a broken vow, then the archives will hold the evidence. We'll start there."

Damien hesitated before following. "And if the archives don't give us the answer?"

"Then we listen harder."

They crossed the street together, the air sharp with cold. A hush seemed to follow them, as if the entire town were waiting for their verdict. Lanterns still burned in some windows, though daylight had already broken. It was an old ritual—candles in the window until the bell rang again. But today, those flames looked less like tradition and more like pleading.

Inside the archive, dust lingered thick as ever, though Marley felt its quiet differently now. Each creak of the wooden floor sounded amplified. Each shuffle of paper resonated like a footfall in an empty hall. The bell's refusal had attuned her ear to absence, and she couldn't unhear it.

Damien pulled volumes from the shelves: parish records, town council minutes, family registries. His hands moved with the efficiency of someone who had spent his life coaxing secrets from old ledgers. Marley moved slower, running her fingers along spines, pausing to read inscriptions in margins.

It wasn't long before she found it.

A scrap of paper slipped between two hymnals, brittle with age. Half-burned, its edges blackened. In faded ink, the words: *If the bell does not ring, the vow was broken.*

Her heart jolted. She turned the fragment over, but no signature, no date. Only the stark declaration, preserved as though waiting for this silence.

"Damien," she called softly.

He crossed the aisle, and when she placed the note in his hand, his jaw tightened. "Where was this?"

"Between hymnals. As if someone meant for it to be found, eventually."

He studied the burn marks, tracing them with his thumb. "Someone tried to destroy it."

"Or hide it until the right time," Marley countered.

They locked eyes again. Neither needed to say aloud what they both understood: the bell's silence wasn't an accident. It was an echo of something unfinished.

Marley leaned back against the shelf, the paper fragile between them. "Who was the bride?" she whispered.

Damien shook his head slowly. "That's the question, isn't it? And maybe the reason the bell refuses to ring."

For a long moment, they stood in the archive's stillness, listening not to sound but to what had been denied. The silence stretched, becoming less absence and more presence. A vow broken. A bride forgotten.

And somewhere in that stillness, Marley felt the pull of her calling sharpen: the Keeper of Memory was not only guardian of books and words. She was steward of silences, too.

Damien exhaled, steady but weary. "If we're going to unravel this, we need to begin where every vow begins—the families. The Colvins, the Callahans, the old lines tied to the solstice ceremonies. Someone remembers, even if they won't speak it aloud."

Marley folded the burned scrap carefully into her notebook. "Then we'll ask."

Outside, the square lay waiting, its silence now tinged with expectation.

THEY BEGAN WITH THE BAKER.

Brookwood's bakery had always been a place of warmth: loaves stacked high, ribbons tied around seasonal cakes, the air rich with cinnamon and sugar. But today, when Marley and Damien stepped inside, the scent seemed subdued. Customers spoke in hushed tones. Even the oven's crackle felt muted.

Mrs. Bennett glanced up as they entered. Her eyes darted to the tower visible through the frosted window before settling back on Marley. "You're here about the bell."

Marley nodded. "We're trying to understand."

The woman hesitated, then disappeared into the back room. When she returned, she carried a box—dusty, tied with a faded ribbon. She set it on the counter with a care usually reserved for relics.

"This was in the attic," she said. "My grandmother told me never to open it. Said it belonged to someone whose name we weren't meant to speak."

Damien untied the ribbon slowly, lifted the lid. Inside lay pressed flowers, brittle with age, satin ribbons yellowed by time, and at the bottom, a sealed envelope. The paper bore a name written in a hand so delicate it seemed ready to vanish: *Amelia C.*

Marley's chest tightened. She reached for the envelope, breaking the seal with trembling fingers. Inside: a torn marriage license and a folded poem titled *The Bride in the Snow.*

The words blurred in her vision. Amelia. A bride. A wedding that had never taken place.

Damien read over her shoulder, his voice low: "This was meant for the Winter Solstice."

Mrs. Bennett shivered. "My grandmother said the bell once tolled for a wedding that never happened. After that, she never spoke of it again."

Marley closed the envelope carefully, her mind racing. The bell's silence had not emerged from nowhere. It was remembering Amelia. A promise broken at the altar.

Damien placed the box back on the counter, his expression unreadable. "Thank you," he said simply.

Outside, the cold struck sharper. Marley clutched the envelope to her chest, feeling the weight of words unspoken, vows unfulfilled. The bell loomed above them, its silence now heavy with a name.

Amelia.

THAT EVENING, Marley sat by the bookshop's fire, the poem spread open on her lap. The words were spare but haunting, written in a voice both tender and resigned:

She waits where snow and silence meet,
A vow unspoken, incomplete.
Her breath, a cloud that fades away,
Her bell un-rung, her vow astray.

Marley traced the lines with her finger. The forgotten bride had not simply been abandoned—she had been left to wait in the silence, her vow stranded in the winter air.

Damien entered quietly, his presence filling the room the way the lighthouse beam filled the harbor. He glanced at the poem, then at Marley. "Amelia Colvin," he said, naming her fully now. "The bride the bell remembers."

Marley looked up, the firelight flickering across her face. "And the silence won't end until we bring her story back into the open."

Damien sat across from her, leaning forward, elbows on his knees. His eyes carried both admiration and hesitation. "Are you ready for what it might cost? For what it might mean for us?"

She held his gaze. The silence between them was answer enough.

The bell's refusal was not only Brookwood's mystery—it was theirs, too.

And somewhere in the distance, though no hand touched the rope, Marley thought she heard it: a faint, withheld note, waiting.

SNOW FELL HEAVIER as the week closed in, blanketing Brookwood in a hush that matched the silence of the bell. Streets narrowed beneath drifts. Footpaths vanished under layers of white. The town seemed smaller, compressed by winter and absence.

Yet beneath the quiet, tension stirred.

Marley walked the square at dusk, boots crunching, scarf drawn tight. The fountain was half-frozen, water gurgling beneath sheets of ice. Windows glowed warm with candlelight, though the flames flickered as if uneasy. The townsfolk kept to routine—shops opening late, closing early—but their eyes gave them away. Conversations faltered. Laughter thinned. The silence of the bell had seeped into them, unsettling the very rhythm of breath.

She stopped beneath the tower. Snowflakes clung to the

stone, softening its edges, but the rope still hung slack. Her fingers itched to pull it, to demand the bell give voice, but she knew better. You cannot force sound from something that refuses.

"Thinking of climbing it alone?"

The voice came from behind. Damien emerged from the shadows, coat dusted with snow, lantern in hand. He looked tired, as though sleep had eluded him.

Marley managed a faint smile. "I've done worse."

"Worse than confronting silence?" He came to stand beside her, his breath clouding the air. "The bell doesn't yield to force. It yields to truth."

His words echoed what she already felt. Still, standing beside him, she admitted aloud what pressed in on her: "I'm afraid, Damien. Not of the silence itself, but of what it means. A vow broken. A bride forgotten. If the bell refuses because memory refuses, then it won't ring until we lay bare something this town has hidden for nearly a century."

Damien lifted the lantern higher, its light catching on the rope. "Then we find it. Together."

For a moment, that word—together—anchored her. But beneath it lurked the other silence between them: the question of whether together meant now, or always. She pushed the thought aside. One mystery at a time.

THEY CLIMBED the tower again that night, lantern swinging, steps creaking beneath their weight. The air inside was colder than the snow outside, as though the silence had leeched warmth from stone.

At the top, the bell loomed—bronze darkened, inscription gleaming faintly. *Veritas in Silentio.* Truth in stillness.

Marley touched the words once more, her gloved fingers trembling. Closing her eyes, she let the silence settle around her, pressing against her skin, filling her lungs. And in that stillness, she heard it again—not sound, but the ghost of sound.

Footsteps. Laughter. The intake of breath before vows spoken. Then, abruptly, absence. A broken promise.

Her eyes flew open. "She was left waiting," she whispered. "At the altar. Alone."

Damien stepped closer, his brow furrowed. "Amelia."

"Yes." Marley's throat tightened. "The bride in the snow."

The silence seemed to thrum in agreement, vibrating against the rafters. Damien reached out, brushing her hand with his. "Then the bell is not silent—it's remembering. Refusing to ring for joy when it remembers sorrow."

Marley met his gaze, the truth settling heavy between them. "It won't toll again until her story is told."

They stood together, lantern light flickering across their faces, the weight of history pressing down. For the first time since the bell's silence, Marley felt certainty: the Winter Bell demanded not repair, but remembrance.

DAYS STRETCHED INTO NIGHTS, and the snow deepened. Marley and Damien spent their hours in the archives, in attics, in whispered conversations with townsfolk reluctant to remember. Pieces surfaced—burned notes, torn licenses, old poems, half-told stories. Each fragment pointed back to Amelia Colvin. A bride who had prepared for vows that never came.

One evening, Marley sat by the fire in the bookshop, poem in her lap, journal open beside her. Outside, the storm howled, rattling shutters. Inside, silence pressed heavy, punctuated only by the crackle of wood.

Damien entered quietly, snow dripping from his coat. He carried something wrapped in cloth. Without a word, he set it on the table, unwrapping it carefully. A music box.

Marley's breath caught.

"I found it in your aunt's locked drawer," Damien explained. "Another one, different from the first."

He wound it gently. The melody spilled into the room—slower, discordant, but hauntingly familiar. Marley froze. She had heard it before.

"The Bell Bride's Waltz," she whispered. "My aunt told me the legend as a child."

The music filled the space, weaving itself into the silence, tugging at memory. Marley closed her eyes, and in the notes she could almost see it: a woman in a gown trimmed with bells, walking down an aisle lined with snow, her hands trembling as she reached the altar. And there— nothing. No groom. No vows. Only the bell refusing to toll.

Her eyes snapped open. "This was her song. Amelia's."

Damien's expression darkened. "Then every fragment, every silence, every absence—it all leads back to her. The bell remembers her vow, broken, and it will not speak until we give her voice."

Marley's chest ached. She reached for the music box, holding it close as though it were a heartbeat. "We'll tell her story. We'll listen until truth reveals itself."

Damien leaned forward, eyes intent. "But Marley... what happens when the truth changes everything we think we know about this town? About us?"

The firelight flickered between them, shadows dancing. Marley met his gaze, her voice steady though her heart trembled. "Then we choose truth anyway."

For a moment, neither spoke. The music box wound down, its final note lingering like breath held too long. Silence returned—but it no longer felt empty. It felt charged, alive. Waiting.

THE NEXT MORNING, Brookwood awoke under a sky the color of pewter. Snow lay heavy on rooftops, and the fountain in the square had frozen solid. People moved slower, their steps cautious, their voices subdued.

Marley and Damien walked together through the hush, carrying the music box between them. As they neared the bell tower, townsfolk paused, watching. They didn't speak, but their eyes followed, hope mingled with unease.

At the foot of the tower, Marley stopped. She turned to Damien. "We're not just solving a mystery, are we?"

He shook his head slowly. "No. We're unearthing a vow. And vows always carry a cost."

Together, they climbed once more, the lantern casting long shadows. At the top, Marley set the music box on the stone ledge beneath the bell. She wound it carefully, and the melody began again—soft, trembling, discordant.

The bell loomed above, silent.

Marley closed her eyes, letting the music weave into the stillness. She imagined Amelia standing here decades ago, veil trembling, hands clutching flowers that would never be exchanged. She imagined her waiting, breath clouding the air, as silence swallowed her vows.

When Marley opened her eyes, tears blurred her vision. She reached for Damien's hand, gripping it tight. "She never left," she whispered. "Her vow froze here, bound in silence."

Damien squeezed her hand back, steady as ever. "Then

it's our task to thaw it. To let truth ring where silence has lingered."

They stood together, the melody fading, silence swelling. The bell did not move. But for the first time, Marley sensed it wasn't withholding—it was listening.

And in that listening, she felt a shift. Not sound, not yet. But possibility.

The Winter Bell would not remain silent forever.

When they descended, the townsfolk had gathered. No one spoke, but all eyes turned toward them. Marley carried the music box in her arms, Damien walking close beside her. She met their gazes one by one, then lifted her voice.

"The bell has not rung," she said, "because it remembers. A vow was broken, a bride forgotten. Until her story is told, the silence will remain."

A murmur swept through the crowd, some gasping, others crossing themselves. But no one laughed. No one dismissed her. The truth, once spoken, had a weight too real to ignore.

Marley looked back at the tower, its shadow long across the snow. She felt Damien's presence beside her, solid, grounding.

The Winter Bell waited.

And so did they.

1

———

THE BELL THAT STAYED SILENT

The town of Brookwood had always measured its winters not by calendars or clocks, but by the toll of the Winter Bell.

Each December, when the longest night drew near, the community gathered in the square beneath the tower. Lanterns lined the cobblestones, candles glowed in every window, and children clutched hands as elders told stories of vows kept and promises renewed. The bell's chime was the ceremony's heart—one resonant note that marked the balance between darkness and light.

On this night, the tradition was no different. Families pressed close together, scarves pulled high, breath rising in clouds. Snow fell in steady flurries, coating hats and shoulders, softening the edges of lantern light. The meetinghouse doors stood open, the bell rope hanging ready.

Marley Taylor stood among them, journal tucked into her satchel, her gaze lifted to the tower. As Keeper of Memory, she had inherited the role of watching, recording, preserving. Tonight should have been no different—only a note in the archive, another solstice observed. But even before the rope was pulled, she felt it: the silence had already settled, waiting.

The elder chosen to ring the bell stepped forward, gloves removed despite the cold. His hands, lined with age, closed around the rope. The crowd hushed, every face tilted upward.

The elder pulled.

The rope strained, wood groaned, but no sound followed.

No toll. No echo.

Only silence.

A ripple passed through the crowd, sharper than the wind. The elder tried again, tugging harder this time, his body shaking with the effort. Still, nothing. The bell, which had tolled without fail for nearly a century, refused to sing.

Marley's breath caught. Around her, whispers rose.

"It hasn't missed a solstice since my mother was a girl," Councilor Gearhart murmured.

"Not since before the Depression," another elder added, his voice thick with disbelief.

Children clutched their parents' arms. Lantern flames flickered as though unsettled. The silence stretched, no longer empty but weighted, heavy as stone.

Marley looked upward, snowflakes drifting slow against the black sky. For a moment, it seemed to her that time itself had slowed—the flakes hovering midair, pausing in their descent. The hush was so complete she could hear the creak of leather boots shifting, the faint scrape of a child's mitten against fabric.

Her heart thudded, loud in her chest. The bell had not rung. And in that silence, something more than ritual had been broken.

. . .

THE CEREMONY DISSOLVED IN MURMURS. Elders gathered near the rope, arguing in hushed tones. Some insisted it was rust, others blamed the cold. A few shook their heads, muttering prayers. Families began to disperse, their steps hesitant, as though leaving too quickly might shatter something fragile.

Marley lingered in the square, her gaze still fixed on the tower. Damien Hawthorne found her there, his daughter Sophie tugging at his hand. He looked tired, the kind of tired that came not from work but from worry.

"It didn't ring," he said simply.

Marley nodded. Her breath clouded the air. "Eighty-eight years, Damien. Not once has it missed."

He exhaled, steadying Sophie with his free hand as she slipped in the snow. "Maybe it's nothing. Mechanical. A frozen hinge."

"Objects don't neglect," Marley murmured, repeating the truth that had anchored her since childhood. "They remember."

Damien studied her face, but said nothing more. He turned his attention to Sophie, bundling her scarf tighter. Still, Marley saw the unease in his eyes—the same unease that coiled in her chest.

The bell's silence was not an accident. It was a refusal.

And refusals always meant something remembered.

THAT NIGHT, Marley returned to the bookshop, lighting a single lantern on the counter. The streets were quiet, snow blanketing sound. She sat by the window, journal open, pen poised. But for the first time in years, she struggled to write. What could words capture of silence that felt alive?

Instead, she stared at the tower beyond the frosted glass.

The rope had been left hanging, untouched. Moonlight caught its fibers, silver against shadow.

She closed her eyes, and in the hush she almost heard it: faint laughter, footsteps on stone, a breath before vows spoken. Then, nothing. A void where sound should have been.

Her pen trembled against the page. She wrote a single line: *The bell that stayed silent remembers what we forgot.*

She didn't know what it meant. Not yet. But she knew where it would lead.

Morning brought no explanation.

The town buzzed with speculation. A contemporary blacksmith was called to provide an inspection and in consultation claimed the clapper must have cracked. The print shop operator insisted it was frost. Children whispered about ghosts. The elders, however, remained solemn, repeating that the bell had never failed, not even in blizzard or blackout.

Damien arrived at the bookshop mid-morning, coat dusted with snow, a bundle of papers in hand. "Parish records," he explained, setting them on the counter. "If something sacred was broken, the archives will tell us."

Marley raised an eyebrow. "You don't believe it's mechanical either."

He hesitated, then shook his head. "I've seen hinges frozen. I've heard bells crack. This... was neither. It pulled, Marley. It strained. But it refused."

Her breath caught at the word. Refused. Exactly what she had felt.

They spent the day combing through the records, side by side at the long oak table. Ink smudged their fingers, dust clung to their sleeves. The air grew heavy with the smell of old parchment and the weight of unspoken questions.

By dusk, Marley leaned back, rubbing her temples. "Nothing. Marriages, deaths, births. But no mention of silence. No mention of refusal."

Damien tapped a finger against one record. "Look here. Winter Solstice, 1936. A wedding scheduled. Amelia Colvin. But no record filed after."

Marley leaned closer. The space where a license should have been signed remained blank.

Her pulse quickened. "A vow unkept."

He met her gaze, steady, unblinking. "And maybe the reason the bell won't speak."

Outside, the snow fell slower again, as if time hesitated at the edges of silence.

LATER THAT NIGHT, Marley stood once more at her window, journal open to a fresh page. She wrote the date—December 21st—and then, slowly, the words: *The Winter Solstice ceremony began as tradition. But the bell never rang.*

Her hand paused. She added: *The snow fell slower, as if the silence had bent time itself.*

She closed the journal, the weight of it heavy in her lap. The bell had refused. The town had murmured. Time had faltered.

And Marley knew the mystery was only beginning.

THE MORNING after the failed ceremony, Brookwood felt altered.

Snow still fell, lanterns still burned in windows, the smell of bread still drifted from the bakery. Yet every detail carried the weight of unease. The absence of the bell's toll had unsettled the town's rhythm the way a missing heartbeat unsettles the body.

Marley walked through the square with her satchel slung over her shoulder. Each footstep crunched louder than it should have, echoing against stone facades. She noticed people speaking in lowered voices, as though they feared being overheard by the silence itself.

At the fountain, two elders huddled together, their canes propped in the snow.

"It hasn't missed a solstice since before I was born," one muttered. "Not since before Roosevelt."

"Before the Depression," the other corrected, shaking his head. "Even in the storm of '52, when half the roofs caved in, the bell rang."

Marley lingered near them, her pen scratching notes against her journal. The words carried the weight of truth repeated too many times not to matter: *It has never missed. Not once.*

She turned as Damien approached, his collar turned up against the wind. His expression bore the same tightness she had seen last night—a mixture of curiosity and worry.

"They're already writing it into rumor," he said quietly. "Some say the rope's cursed. Others whisper about an omen."

Marley closed her journal. "And what do you say?"

He met her gaze. "That it matters. More than people want to admit."

They walked together toward the meetinghouse. The door creaked when Damien pushed it open, revealing the rope still hanging slack in the hall. Lanterns had been extinguished, leaving only pale daylight filtering through the windows. The silence inside was thicker, heavier, as though the tower itself was guarding its secret.

Marley touched the rope. Its fibers felt rough beneath her fingers, familiar, unbroken. She pulled once, gently. Nothing. The bell above remained mute, unmoved.

Damien crossed the hall to inspect the mechanism. He peered upward, eyes narrowed. "No rust. No cracks. No ice in the wheel." He stepped back, his breath leaving a white cloud in the cold air. "It's intact. It should have rung."

Marley's pulse quickened. "But it refused."

Damien turned, studying her with the look he reserved for moments when her instincts reached beyond the evidence in front of them. "You believe it chose silence."

"I believe it remembers," she replied, her voice steady. "Objects remember. And this bell remembers something broken."

For a long moment, Damien said nothing. Then, quietly: "If that's true, then we're not dealing with mechanics. We're dealing with memory."

She nodded. The thought was both terrifying and clarifying.

THEY LEFT THE CHAPEL AGAIN, the hush clinging to them like frost. Marley's steps slowed as she noticed the snowflakes drifting through the air. They didn't fall with their usual weight and rhythm. Instead, they seemed suspended, pausing midair as though time itself hesitated.

Damien followed her gaze. "What is it?"

"Do you see?" she asked. "The snow. It's slower. Like the silence is bending time."

He squinted, watching. At first he said nothing, then his shoulders stiffened. "I see it. Just for a breath—but I see it."

Marley wrote the observation quickly into her journal: *The snow fell slower in the silence, as if time itself was hesitating.*

Damien read the line over her shoulder. "If the bell holds time, or bends it, then its silence isn't only absence. It's disruption."

She closed the journal. "Which means it will keep disrupting until we uncover why."

BY MIDAFTERNOON, the town gathered at the archive. Word had spread that the Keeper of Memory and the historian were searching records. Elders filed in, their faces solemn, their hands wrapped around canes and scarves. Younger residents lingered at the door, whispering about omens and curses.

Marley and Damien spread ledgers across the oak table. Parchment yellowed with age, ink faded but legible. Each page carried the weight of lives cataloged: births, deaths, weddings, losses.

Marley traced her fingers down columns of names. "Every solstice recorded. Every chime of the bell noted. Except..." She stopped, her finger landing on an empty space. "Here. 1936. A wedding scheduled. Amelia Colvin. But no record afterward. No certificate filed."

Damien leaned over, brow furrowing. "A missing marriage record."

She nodded, the truth heavy in her chest. "A vow unkept."

Around them, elders murmured. Some shook their heads, whispering of family names better left buried. Others muttered prayers beneath their breath.

One elder, Councilor Gearhart, stepped forward. Her

voice shook as she spoke. "My grandmother told me of that year. A bride left waiting in the snow. No vows spoken. No bell rung. After that, no one dared speak her name."

Marley's heart clenched. "Amelia."

The name seemed to hang in the air, as though even memory itself held its breath.

Damien's voice was low, almost reverent. "The bell remembers her. And it refuses to ring until she's remembered, too."

Silence fell again, thicker now, wrapping the room in its grip. Marley felt her role pressing down on her shoulders: Keeper of Memory was not only about preserving the past, but about restoring what had been erased.

She closed the ledger carefully, her hands steady despite the tremor in her chest. "Then we begin with her."

THAT EVENING, Marley returned to the bookshop exhausted. The fire crackled in the hearth, casting shadows along the walls. She sat at her desk, spreading the ledger and her notes across the surface. The ink blurred in the low light, but she wrote anyway, her hand moving quickly: *The bell remembers Amelia. A vow unkept. A silence that bends time.*

The door creaked open. Damien stepped in, his coat damp from snow, his eyes weary but alert. He carried something wrapped in brown paper.

"I stopped at the bakery," he explained. "They found this in their attic."

Marley unfolded the paper carefully. Inside lay pressed flowers, ribbons yellowed by time, and an envelope sealed with wax cracked by age. The name written across it in delicate script made her chest tighten: *Amelia C.*

Her breath caught. "It's hers."

Damien nodded, watching her closely. "Open it."

Marley broke the brittle seal with trembling fingers. Inside, a torn marriage license fell onto the desk, along with a folded poem titled *The Bride in the Snow.*

She unfolded the paper, reading aloud in a voice barely above a whisper:

She waits where snow and silence meet,

A vow unspoken, incomplete.

Her breath, a cloud that fades away,

Her bell un-rung, her vow astray.

The words sent a shiver down her spine. She looked up at Damien, whose expression had grown grim.

"It was her wedding," Marley said. "Planned for the Winter Solstice. But it never happened."

Damien's jaw tightened. "And the bell has never forgotten."

For a moment, they sat in silence, the poem lying between them like a wound reopened. The fire popped, sparks rising. Snow whispered against the windows.

Finally, Damien spoke. "Then the bell won't toll again until we bring her story to light."

Marley nodded, her hand brushing the fragile page. "And we will. We have to."

Outside, Brookwood lay hushed under snow, the bell tower looming silent against the night sky. Lanterns flickered in windows, small flames of hope against the darkness.

But above it all, the Winter Bell remained mute, remembering a bride whose vows had been swallowed by silence.

And Marley, with Damien beside her, understood: this was only the beginning.

.　.　.

THE TOWN DID NOT SLEEP EASILY in the nights that followed.

Each evening, lanterns were lit in windows as ritual demanded, but the flames quivered as though uneasy in their glass. Families gathered closer by their hearths, their conversations lowered, as if even firelight could not protect them from the absence pressing in from the bell tower. Children asked questions parents could not answer. Elders avoided eye contact, unwilling to speak the truths their memories held.

For Marley and Damien, the silence was more than ritual disrupted—it was the opening of a wound.

ON THE THIRD night after the failed ceremony, Marley stood alone outside the chapel, her scarf pulled high against the cold. Snow muffled the cobblestones, making her footsteps ghostlike. The bell tower loomed above, its bronze mouth hidden in shadow. She tilted her head back, staring upward, waiting for a sound that refused to come.

The square was empty except for Damien, who emerged from the shadows with his usual quiet steadiness. He carried no lantern, only his presence, and that was enough to fill the space between them.

"You shouldn't be out here alone," he said softly.

"I couldn't sleep," Marley replied, her breath clouding the air. "It feels as though the whole town is holding its breath, waiting. How do you sleep when silence has weight?"

Damien stepped beside her, his gaze following hers to the tower. "You don't. You endure."

They stood together, watching snowflakes drift. Marley noticed it again—that strange pause, the way flakes seemed suspended midair before resuming their descent. "Do you see it?" she asked.

Damien nodded, his jaw tightening. "Time falters. As if the silence bends it."

Her chest tightened. "Then the bell isn't just refusing. It's reshaping."

He turned toward her, eyes shadowed but steady. "Which means we can't treat this as a curiosity. It's not folklore. It's not only history. It's alive, Marley. Whatever vow was broken, it's still binding us."

The words struck her like the toll of a bell that should have sounded. For the first time, she felt the full weight of it —not just a mystery to be solved, but a responsibility they could not set aside.

THE FOLLOWING MORNING, Marley sat at her desk in the bookshop, the torn marriage license and poem spread before her. The fire hissed quietly, but its warmth did little to ease the chill in her bones. She traced the delicate script of Amelia's name again and again, as if by touch she could summon her voice.

Damien arrived with his usual quiet knock. He stepped inside, his coat dusted with snow, his eyes tired from nights of searching records by candlelight. He set a small bundle on the counter—newspaper clippings bound with twine.

"From the archives," he explained. "Announcements, obituaries, notices. Nothing about the wedding itself. Only silence where her story should be."

Marley untied the twine, spreading the brittle papers. Births, deaths, sales of land. A Winter Solstice festival advertised in bold print. But nothing of Amelia Colvin. The absence screamed louder than words.

She exhaled, frustration heavy in her chest. "It's as if the town erased her."

"Or buried her," Damien corrected. He leaned against the counter, his arms folded. "But the bell hasn't forgotten. And it won't let us forget either."

Marley looked up at him, her eyes weary but sharp. "Do you feel it too? That this is more than memory? That the silence is alive, demanding something from us?"

He held her gaze, and for once he didn't hide behind analysis or hesitation. "Yes. I feel it. And I think we're the only ones who can answer it."

The fire crackled, filling the silence between them. For a moment, Marley allowed herself to imagine what it would mean—two lives bound not just by affection or circumstance, but by a vow they had not made yet could not ignore.

Her pen hovered over her journal. She wrote: *This silence is not emptiness. It is insistence.*

By EVENING, unease rippled more visibly through the town. Businesses closed early. The bakery's loaves sold out faster than usual, as though people feared scarcity. Parents hurried children indoors. Even the lighthouse's steady beam, sweeping across the water, felt different—less guiding, more warning.

Marley and Damien walked together along the frozen riverbank, snow crunching beneath their boots. The world felt suspended, the horizon blurred into pale fog.

"Do you ever wonder," Marley asked quietly, "why the bell chose now? After eighty-eight years, why tonight?"

Damien's breath clouded the air. "Because silence waits until someone is listening. And you, Marley—you're Keeper of Memory. You hear what others ignore."

She swallowed hard, turning her gaze to the river. His words warmed her even as they burdened her. Being Keeper meant carrying weight others had set down. But it also meant she wasn't free to turn away.

They stopped near the old covered bridge, its arches dusted with snow. Marley leaned on the railing, her fingers cold against the stone. "What if this silence doesn't just mark a broken vow?" she whispered. "What if it demands something of us now? A vow renewed? A vow carried forward?"

Damien stood close enough that she could feel the heat of him in the freezing air. "Then we'll face it together."

Her throat tightened at the word. Together. She wanted to believe it, but part of her feared the silence would demand more than either of them could give.

Still, when she looked into his eyes, she saw no hesitation. Only steadiness.

And for the first time since the bell had refused, she felt hope—not certainty, but hope—that silence might yet yield truth.

LATER, back at the bookshop, Marley lit a single candle and sat at her desk. She opened her journal to a fresh page and wrote:

The bell refused. Time faltered. Silence has become memory alive.

She paused, pen trembling, then added:

Damien believes we are bound to its demand. I believe he is right.

She closed the journal, extinguished the candle, and sat in the dark. Through the window, she could see the bell tower looming, its shadow long across the snow. She felt

Damien's presence even in his absence, as though their breaths had synchronized with the silence itself.

The Winter Bell had not rung. But it had chosen them.

And as Marley drifted into uneasy sleep, one truth echoed in her mind: this silence was not merely history—it was a mystery that demanded devotion, not only from her, but from them both.

2

FROST IN THE AIR

By the fourth day after the Winter Solstice ceremony, Brookwood had settled into a hush that felt less like weather and more like decree.

Shops opened late, their windows glowing with light but their doors hesitating to swing wide. Evelyn, arranged the tables at the café with deliberate slowness, as if the rhythm of regular customers had been broken. At the bakery, loaves vanished before noon, but the usual hum of conversation—the laughter, the gossip—remained absent. Even the children on their sleds shouted softer, their joy subdued by something they couldn't name.

The silence of the bell had extended its reach, weaving into every corner of daily life.

Marley noticed it most as she walked down Main Street, notebook tucked beneath her arm. She paused before the tailor's shop, where a half-finished dress lingered on its mannequin. The tailor, who usually hummed while he worked, sat quietly behind the counter, his lips pressed tight, his eyes darting once toward the tower as though expecting reprimand from stone.

She moved on, and at every corner she felt it again: hesitation, restraint, the world muted. The hush had become a second winter, one layered not with snow but with unease.

At the square, Marley stopped beneath the fountain. The water had frozen solid, mid-cascade, as though even it obeyed the bell's silence. She drew her gloves tighter and tilted her face upward. Snow fell, slow and deliberate, each flake pausing in descent before landing.

It was then she felt it—not just quiet, not just absence, but disruption.

Something sacred had been paused.

It rippled through her like a note withheld, vibrating in the bones more than the ears. It was ancestral, older than Brookwood itself. A vow broken, yes—but also a rhythm unspooled.

She pulled her notebook from her satchel and wrote: *The silence is not only absence. It is suspension. A sacred pause.*

When she returned to the bookshop, she found Damien already there, his coat discarded, his sleeves rolled up. Spread across the oak table lay a scatter of diagrams and records: architectural sketches of the tower, repair ledgers from decades past, lists of expenditures for rope and wheel.

He looked up briefly, his expression tight with concentration. "If the bell is refusing, I have to rule out what it isn't. No crack in the clapper, no rust in the mechanism, no evidence of ice freezing the wheel."

Marley set her notebook beside his papers. "And?"

"And nothing," Damien admitted. He leaned back, rubbing his temples. "Every test I've run says it should work. By every mechanical measure, the bell is intact."

Marley sank into the chair opposite him. "Which means it's not mechanical."

Damien's jaw flexed. "Which means it's something else. But I can't put that into a ledger. I can't present silence as evidence."

She studied him, the crease in his brow, the weariness in his eyes. "You've built your life on what can be proven. But sometimes proof isn't in what is—it's in what refuses to be."

He gave a small, humorless laugh. "You sound like your aunt."

"I'm supposed to," Marley replied softly. "Keeper of Memory means inheriting not just the archives, but the listening."

He lowered his gaze to the diagrams. "Then what does the listening say?"

Marley hesitated, then spoke the truth. "That something sacred has been paused. And it won't move until we remember why."

The words hung between them, heavier than the hush outside.

THAT EVENING, Marley walked alone along the river. The banks were frozen, the water moving sluggishly beneath sheets of ice. The lighthouse's beam swept across the horizon, steady, but it felt distant—its rhythm belonging to another mystery, another vow. The bell tower loomed behind her, its silence pressing against her back.

She stopped at the old stone bench where her aunt used to sit. The cold seeped through her coat, but she remained, listening. The air carried no birdsong, no crack of branches, not even the hum of wind.

All she heard was suspension.

It reminded her of childhood nights when her aunt would pause in reading a story, letting silence stretch before revealing the next line. Only now, the line never came. The story remained unwritten.

Marley closed her eyes. "What are you waiting for?" she whispered to the air.

No answer came. Only the weight of pause, as though the world itself were mid-breath.

She opened her eyes and scribbled in her journal: *The town waits. The air waits. I wait. The silence demands memory returned.*

WHEN SHE RETURNED to the shop, Damien was still awake, pouring over records by lamplight. His hair fell into his eyes, his hand smudged with ink. He glanced up, his expression softening when he saw her.

"You should rest," Marley said gently.

"So should you," he replied, without looking away from her.

She smiled faintly, setting her journal on the counter. "The difference is, I'm not trying to prove silence into numbers."

He exhaled, weary but wry. "You're right. But I don't know how else to approach it. My whole life has been about evidence."

Marley stepped closer, resting her hand lightly on the table beside his. "Then maybe this mystery requires both. Evidence and listening. Ledger and memory."

Their hands brushed. Neither moved them away.

Damien looked at her, his eyes shadowed but steady. "Then we'll need each other."

Marley swallowed, her heart tightening at the truth of it. "Yes. We will."

The silence pressed in, but this time it didn't feel empty. It felt like the beginning of devotion.

THE HUSH DEEPENED with each passing day, and Brookwood grew stranger in its rhythm.

Marley noticed how people seemed to tread more carefully on the streets, their boots quieter, their conversations briefer. It wasn't just reverence—it was fear dressed as respect. Even the animals mirrored it: dogs barked less, horses stamped less, birds lingered in trees as if reluctant to cut the stillness with song.

It wasn't only absence of sound—it was a pressure. A hush that insisted on itself.

MARLEY MOVED through it as Keeper of Memory, her senses sharpened. She visited the square each morning, standing beneath the bell tower, her scarf drawn tight. Snowflakes fell around her, slow and deliberate, as if dragged through an unseen resistance. She watched the way they lingered in the air, each one pausing like punctuation before completing its descent.

It felt ancestral, deeper than weather.

In her journal she wrote: *The silence is not emptiness. It is pause. The world mid-breath, waiting for a vow to be remembered. It is disruption—not of sound, but of order itself.*

That thought chilled her more than the frost. If the bell could bend rhythm, it wasn't merely symbolic. It was a keeper in its own right, demanding balance.

She began to feel it in her own body: her heart skipping,

her breath catching at odd intervals, as though even her pulse had fallen under the bell's refusal.

DAMIEN, meanwhile, poured himself into evidence.

By the fifth day, he had exhausted the parish ledgers, engineering schematics, and even municipal repair logs. He climbed the tower with rope in hand, inspecting every hinge, every bolt. Marley followed once, watching him in the dim light as his hands traced the mechanisms.

"The wheel turns freely," he muttered, his voice echoing in the chamber. "The clapper swings without obstruction. No fracture in the crown. Bronze intact, no sign of warping. The rope holds weight. By every rational measure, it should ring."

Marley stood at the base of the bell, her gloved hand brushing its cold surface. "But it doesn't."

Damien's jaw tightened. "That's what I can't reconcile. There's no failure here. Nothing I can write into a report. Nothing I can point to and say, 'Here lies the fault.'"

Her gaze lifted to the inscription etched into the crown —*Veritas in Silentio.* Truth in stillness. She whispered it aloud, the Latin rolling off her tongue like prayer.

Damien looked down at her, his brow furrowed. "Do you believe the inscription is literal?"

"I believe it was warning us," Marley replied. "That stillness reveals what we refuse to face."

Damien descended the stair, his boots echoing against stone. He stopped before her, close enough that she could see the ink smudges on his fingers from days spent combing records. "I want to believe this has a mechanical cause. But I can't deny what I've seen—or what I've felt. When the snow slows, when the town breathes differently... it feels like the silence itself is alive."

Marley held his gaze. "Then stop trying to cage it in ledgers. Let yourself hear it."

His lips parted as if to argue, but no words came. At last, he nodded once, reluctantly, as though conceding not to her but to the weight of the hush itself.

THE TOWN, too, began to admit unease.

At the bakery, Marley overheard whispers. One customer murmured that her dreams were filled with footsteps climbing stairs that never ended. Another confessed that she heard faint ringing in her ears each night, though no sound had been struck.

At the café, an elder leaned close to Marley, his voice trembling. "When I was a boy, my grandfather told me the bell once tolled twice in a day—once for a wedding, and once for a death. He said it marked vows, not just hours. Be careful, child. If it refuses now, it means something we cannot afford to see."

Marley carried these whispers back to the bookshop, where Damien sat hunched over blueprints of the bell's construction. She laid her notes beside his diagrams.

"These are not failures," she said softly. "They're disruptions. The silence is weaving itself into dreams, into the rhythm of lives. That isn't mechanics. It's memory."

Damien rubbed his brow, his fatigue visible. "Then why do I feel compelled to keep searching? Why do I need to prove what we both already sense?"

Marley smiled faintly, though her eyes softened. "Because proving is what you've always done. And listening is what I've always done. Maybe the bell requires both."

He studied her face for a long moment, then leaned back in his chair. "If that's true, then we're bound together in this whether we're ready or not."

Her heart skipped, not only from the words but from the weight behind them. She opened her journal and wrote: *Damien persists in proof. I persist in listening. Together, perhaps, we might unearth the vow silence demands.*

THAT NIGHT, a storm rolled in. Snow thickened, wind howled against shutters, but even in the storm, the hush prevailed. The town did not feel the chaos of weather—only its own breath held longer.

Marley sat by the fire, the poem *The Bride in the Snow* resting on her lap. She traced the faded ink, feeling Amelia's absence like a presence beside her. She thought of the bell as not broken, but grieving. Waiting.

Damien sat across from her, his notes scattered. His hair was disheveled, his eyes rimmed with weariness, but he looked at her with an honesty he rarely allowed himself.

"I've exhausted every rational cause," he admitted quietly. "I've tested, measured, recalculated. And still— nothing. It should ring. But it doesn't."

Marley lifted her gaze from the poem. "Because it's not refusing you, Damien. It's refusing us. All of us. Until we face what was broken."

He closed his eyes briefly, exhaling. When he opened them again, the weight of surrender was in his voice. "Then the answer isn't in the gears. It's in the vow."

Marley felt the words strike her heart with both relief and dread. She closed the poem gently, her hands steady. "Then we begin not with ledgers, but with memory. With listening to what silence is still carrying."

Damien leaned forward, elbows on his knees, his gaze steady on hers. "Then we begin tomorrow. Together."

And in that vow—not spoken in ceremony, not tolled by bronze, but whispered in the hush—they bound themselves to the mystery the bell demanded.

BY THE END of the week, the silence had become more than a fact—it had become folklore in the making.

Marley felt it in every conversation she overheard, every wary glance she caught. The hush was no longer confined to streets and shops—it had seeped into the marrow of Brookwood. People moved as though watched, careful not to disturb something ancient and unseen.

She walked through downtown at dusk, notebook pressed to her chest, the air sharp against her lungs. The fountain glistened with frost, its frozen spouts bent like silent mouths. Snowflakes drifted slow, heavy, pausing mid-descent as if the world itself were unsure whether to continue.

She closed her eyes.

And the resonance came.

It wasn't sound, not exactly. More like a pulse beneath the skin, a rhythm felt in bone. The silence wasn't empty. It was ancestral, alive, carrying memory like a current. She thought of her aunt's words—*objects remember*—and understood more deeply than ever before. This bell wasn't withholding by accident. It was holding time itself, pausing it until the forgotten vow was remembered.

Her breath hitched. She wrote quickly: *The pause is ancestral. Not the town's alone, but a memory older, deeper. The silence is insisting we attend to what we left undone.*

When she looked up, Damien was there, as though the hush itself had drawn him to her.

THEY WALKED TOGETHER toward the bookshop, boots crunching in the snow. The streets were quiet, but not with peace. Windows glowed faintly, shadows moving inside homes where families gathered close. It struck Marley how much Brookwood felt like a village under siege—though the invader was not storm or famine, but silence.

Inside the shop, the fire warmed the air, but Damien kept his coat on, pacing before the hearth. His shoulders were taut, his expression harder than usual, as if something pressed against him from within.

Marley set her notebook on the counter, watching him. "You've been different since the bell refused."

He stopped pacing, his gaze catching hers. "Because it's no longer only about the bell."

Her brows furrowed. "What do you mean?"

Damien crossed the room, lowering himself into the chair opposite her. The firelight caught the edges of his face, shadowing his eyes. He leaned forward, elbows on his knees, his voice low and unguarded.

"At first, I told myself it was mechanics. Something I could measure, explain, repair. That's how I've lived my whole life—sorting mystery into evidence. But this... Marley, I've tested every angle, every gear. It should ring. By all reason, it should ring. And yet it doesn't."

His hands clenched together, then loosened. "And I realize now, it's not only refusing the town. It's refusing me. I feel it when I stand beneath it—that silence isn't absence. It's confrontation. It's asking me something I don't know if I can answer."

Marley's breath caught at the rawness in his voice. She had seen Damien thoughtful, stern, frustrated—but rarely vulnerable. The silence had shaken him, not just as a historian, but as a man.

She spoke softly. "It feels personal."

He nodded once. "Yes. Personal. As if it's not just about Amelia or the past, but about me. About us."

The fire popped, filling the pause. Marley's pulse quickened, her throat tight. She wanted to ask—*us how?*—but feared the answer. Instead, she reached across the table, laying her hand lightly over his.

For a moment, neither moved.

"The bell is demanding truth," Marley said, her voice barely above a whisper. "And truth is always personal."

Damien turned his hand, his fingers brushing hers, anchoring them both. His eyes met hers fully now, stripped of the distance he so often carried. "Then we can't treat this as just an investigation. We have to give it more. We have to give it ourselves."

The words lingered between them, heavy with implication. Marley felt her chest tighten, not with fear, but with inevitability. Keeper of Memory. Historian of proof. Bound together, not only by the bell's refusal, but by what the silence demanded of them.

LATER THAT NIGHT, Marley sat by the fire alone, her journal open. She wrote:

The town grows restless, whispering of curses and vows. But beneath superstition lies truth: the silence is not passive. It is a hand pressing against our chests, demanding we listen. Damien feels it too. He admits the search is no longer only intellectual. It is personal. The vow broken is becoming our vow to restore.

She paused, pen hovering, then added: *I fear what this will cost us. Yet I also feel—perhaps for the first time—that we are not merely preserving memory. We are living it.*

She closed the journal and leaned back, staring at the flames. Outside, the hush held steady, pressing into every corner of Brookwood. The bell remained mute, its bronze crown catching moonlight like a watching eye.

And Marley understood that silence was no longer the absence of sound. It was the presence of demand.

The Winter Bell had refused.

The town had bent beneath its hush.

And she and Damien had crossed a threshold. What lay ahead was no longer curiosity, but devotion—a mystery not only to be solved, but to be lived.

3

____

WISHES UNDONE

The fire in her aunt's old hearth had long since gone cold, but Marley still liked to sit there. The apartment, inherited with the bookshop, was filled with fragments of her aunt's presence—pressed flowers tucked between pages, a faded shawl draped over the chair, ink bottles clouded with dust. On this night, as snow piled thick against the windows and the hush of the bell pressed deeper into town, Marley lit a lantern and crouched before the fireplace.

The ashes had not been disturbed in months. She stirred them idly with the poker, more out of habit than curiosity. But when the metal nudged something firmer than soot, she leaned closer.

A scrap of paper, edges blackened by flame.

Carefully, she plucked it out, brushing away ash. The words were faint but legible, written in her aunt's unmistakable hand:

If the bell does not ring, the vow was broken.

Marley's breath caught. The paper trembled in her fingers, fragile with age, singed nearly to nothing. Why had her aunt tried to burn it? Why had she kept it at all?

She pressed the scrap flat against her journal, tracing the words with her gaze. Her aunt had been Keeper of Memory before her—meticulous, reverent, unwilling to destroy anything of importance. If this note had been consigned to fire, it meant one of two things: it was too dangerous to keep, or too demanding to ignore.

Her heart thudded. She copied the words into her journal, the ink stark against fresh paper: *If the bell does not ring, the vow was broken.*

She closed her eyes and whispered the line aloud. In the hush of the cottage, it sounded less like text and more like invocation.

The vow. Always the vow.

By morning, Marley carried the half-burned note with her into town. She tucked it into her satchel beside her journal, determined to press the townsfolk for answers.

At the bakery, she lingered near the counter after purchasing her bread. Mrs. Bennett, who had always been warm, shifted uneasily when Marley asked if she'd ever heard of a vow tied to the bell.

"I wouldn't know about that," the woman said quickly, her hands tightening around the loaf she wrapped. "Superstition. Nothing more."

Her eyes betrayed her, flicking toward the tower visible through the frosted window. Marley recognized the look—refusal.

Marley returned to the square, frustration heavy in her chest. The bell tower loomed above, mute and unyielding, as though amused by her failure. She pulled the half-burned note from her satchel and read it again, the words sharper now: *If the bell does not ring, the vow was broken.*

But whose vow?

As DUSK FELL, Marley turned down the narrow lane toward the metaphysical shop, owned by Hazel. Hazel's memory ran deep as her roots. Her shop smelled of rosemary and smoke, its shelves lined with jars of dried leaves and tinctures that glowed amber in the lamplight.

Marley placed the note on the counter. "Do you recognize this?"

Hazel studied it for a long time, her lined face unreadable. At last, she said, "Your aunt should not have burned it. But I understand why she tried."

Marley's pulse quickened. "What does it mean?"

The woman looked toward the window, where snowflakes lingered in their descent. Her voice lowered, weighted with caution. "It means what it says. The bell tolled for vows, not for time. And when it refuses, it remembers the vow that was broken."

Marley leaned forward. "Whose vow?"

Hazel's gaze returned to her, sharp as flint. "Do not expect the town to speak freely. Silence is safer. But there was once talk of a bride. A veil bride, they called her. Promised to someone, bound by families, but never wed. She stood waiting while the bell remained silent."

Marley felt the words strike her chest like frost. "The veil bride," she repeated softly.

Hazel nodded. "A bride veiled not for ceremony, but for erasure. Her name was hidden, her story buried. But the bell does not forget. It tolls for memory, even when people will not."

The lantern flickered, shadows stretching long across the jars. Marley swallowed hard, slipping the note back into her satchel.

"Do you know her name?" she asked.

Hazel shook her head. "Names hold power. Hers was taken. But if you listen to the silence long enough, it may return."

THAT NIGHT, Marley sat by the fire with her journal open, the half-burned note beside her. She copied Hazel's words: *A veil bride. Promised, but never wed. Buried by silence. Remembered only by the bell.*

The fire crackled, sending sparks into the chimney. Outside, the town lay hushed beneath snow, every window glowing faintly against the dark. But Marley felt the silence pressing harder now, more insistent. It was no longer content to linger as background. It was demanding.

She touched the fragile scrap of paper again, feeling its edges crumble under her fingers. Her aunt had tried to burn it, to end its demand. But memory refused to die.

The bell's hush was no longer only absence. It was accusation.

And Marley knew she would not rest until she uncovered the truth of the veil bride.

THE FOLLOWING MORNING, Marley carried the half-burned note with her like a weight. She had slept little, her dreams filled with images of veils dissolving into snow, of footsteps climbing the tower stairs but never reaching the bell. Each time she woke, the words returned like a whisper against her ear: *If the bell does not ring, the vow was broken.*

She tucked the note into her satchel beside her journal and set out into the square. The air was brittle, sharp with frost, yet the hush was thicker than the cold.

At the post office, she tried again. "Have you ever heard of a wedding the bell refused to bless?" she asked Mrs. Keene, the postmistress, sliding a letter across the counter.

The woman's hands stilled on the stack of envelopes. Her eyes darted briefly to the tower's shadow stretching across the square before she pressed her lips into a thin line. "I sort letters, not stories."

Marley waited. The silence grew taut, but the woman never looked up again. The answer was refusal.

At the welder's training facility, she found a similar wall. "Elders say the bell never failed until now," Marley began. "But what if it refused before? For vows broken?"

The welder's continued on with their task more dilligent than necessary. Sparks flew, filling the silence with angry light. "Steel bends under force," one if them said gruffly from under a mask. "Bronze cracks. But bells don't choose. Don't ask me to pretend they do."

His jaw was tight, his eyes shadowed. Marley recognized it—not disbelief, but fear disguised as dismissal.

When she returned to the bookshop, Damien was waiting at the table, a ledger open before him. His expression was unreadable, though the ink on his fingers and the weariness in his eyes revealed the hours he had spent searching.

"I've checked every marriage record I can find," he said without preamble. "All accounted for except one—Amelia Colvin. We already knew that. Nothing else missing. Which tells me the silence isn't about oversight. It's about erasure."

Marley sank into the chair opposite him, pulling the

half-burned note from her satchel. She laid it between them. "And it was deliberate. My aunt tried to destroy this. Others are refusing to speak. Damien—they're afraid."

He studied the scrap for a long moment, his jaw tightening. "I've seen this before. Not here, but in archives abroad. When a community cannot face its wound, it buries it. But burial doesn't erase—it festers. The silence isn't only the bell's, Marley. It's theirs. Collective."

Her chest tightened. "Then the town itself has become part of the vow. Keeping it hidden."

"Or keeping it buried," Damien replied. His eyes lifted to hers, steady but shadowed. "Which means uncovering it won't just stir memory. It will stir resistance."

Marley exhaled slowly, feeling the truth of it settle heavy in her bones. "Then we'll have to listen harder. Push deeper. Even if they'd rather we didn't."

THAT AFTERNOON, they walked together through Brookwood, snow crunching beneath their boots. The hush was thicker now, its pressure felt in every lowered voice, every shutter drawn early. Children played, but their laughter was subdued, almost wary.

At the café, they overheard whispers.

"Did you hear? Someone said she found a note in the ashes."

"A note? Or an omen?"

"Better not ask. Best to leave it quiet."

The words silenced quickly when Damien and Marley stepped inside, as though the very air conspired to keep them out.

Marley turned to Damien as they left. "Do you see it? How they stop speaking the moment we appear?"

"I see it," he said grimly. "It's not coincidence. The silence isn't just in the bell—it's in them. A conspiracy of quiet."

Marley wrote the phrase down as they walked: *A conspiracy of quiet. The town colludes with the silence, burying what it cannot bear to name.*

As DUSK FELL, they visited Moon & Morrow again. Hazel met them with her usual sharp gaze, her hands stained with herbs. She eyed the note when Marley placed it on the counter once more.

"You've been asking questions," Hazel said flatly.

"Of course I have," Marley replied. "I'm Keeper of Memory. If there was a vow broken, I need to know whose."

Hazel's mouth thinned. "And what if the name brings more harm than silence?"

Damien stepped forward, his voice quiet but steady. "Then harm has already been done. Silence hasn't healed it. It's only left it festering."

Hazel's eyes flicked between them, measuring. At last she spoke, her words slow, deliberate. "There was talk, long ago, of a bride veiled not for honor, but for concealment. A veil bride. Promised, but never wed. Bound by families who thought vows could bend truth to their will. When she refused—or when he did, depending on which tale you believe—the bell refused too."

Marley's breath caught. "Do you know her name?"

Hazel shook her head once. "Names were erased. But memory isn't so easily undone. That's why the silence lingers."

She pushed the note back toward Marley. "Be careful, child. The veil bride's story is not only hers. It belongs to those who silenced her, and they will not welcome its return."

THEY LEFT MOON & Morrow in silence, the air biting cold. Snowflakes lingered midair, suspended as though listening.

Damien stopped beneath the tower, his breath clouding. "She's right. This isn't only about Amelia, or the veil bride, or whoever she was. It's about the town itself. They've built their lives on forgetting. If we unravel this, we unravel them."

Marley tilted her head back, staring at the bell. Bronze caught the moonlight, inscription gleaming faintly: *Veritas in Silentio.* Truth in stillness.

Her voice was quiet but resolute. "Then it's time the truth spoke."

Damien looked at her, something unguarded in his eyes. "Even if it costs us their trust?"

Marley met his gaze steadily. "Keeper of Memory doesn't serve trust. It serves truth."

The hush pressed tighter, as though the bell itself approved.

THAT NIGHT, in the bookshop, they sat side by side before the fire. The half-burned note lay between them, fragile and accusing.

Damien leaned forward, his hands clasped, his voice low. "This search is no longer about curiosity for me. It's not only intellectual. The silence presses on me, Marley. I feel it in my chest, in my pulse. As though it's demanding not only remembrance, but something personal. Something I owe."

Marley's heart tightened. She had felt it too—that the

hush wasn't only collective, but intimate, pressing into her bones, demanding devotion.

She reached for her journal, writing slowly: *The silence is no longer only history. It is alive. It is demand. Damien feels it too. We are no longer observers—we are participants.*

She closed the journal, her hand brushing his. For a moment, the silence between them felt less like burden and more like vow.

The Winter Bell had refused. The town had colluded. But Marley and Damien had chosen.

They would not collude.

They would remember.

The night after leaving Moon & Morrow, Marley lay awake in her appartment, the silence pressing harder than the weight of blankets. The half-burned note rested on her nightstand, its words a brand against her mind: *If the bell does not ring, the vow was broken.*

Her aunt had tried to destroy it. The townsfolk refused to speak of it. Hazel had only hinted. But Marley could no longer ignore it.

The veil bride was not a rumor. She was truth suppressed.

And Marley could feel her—like a thread pulled through time, tugging against the present. The silence was not absence but presence, vibrating in her bones, as though demanding to be carried forward.

She rose before dawn, wrapping herself in her cloak, and stepped outside. Frost clung to the cobblestones, lanterns still burning faintly in windows. She walked to the square, stopping beneath the tower. Snow fell around her, slow and deliberate, pausing mid-descent.

Closing her eyes, she whispered: "Who were you?"

The silence pressed back. Not emptiness—resistance. As though the veil bride herself lingered, bound not in body but in memory.

Marley opened her eyes and wrote in her journal by lantern light: *The vow was broken, but not erased. The silence is her voice. The veil bride waits in the pause.*

By MIDMORNING, Damien arrived at the bookshop. His face was drawn, his steps heavier than usual. He carried no ledgers, no blueprints—only the weariness of someone who had confronted truth he could not rationalize away.

He dropped into a chair near the fire. "I've been thinking about what Hazel said. About the veil bride."

Marley closed her journal. "And?"

His gaze met hers, stripped of distance. "If we break this silence, Marley, we won't just be restoring memory. We'll be tearing open a wound the town has spent nearly a century trying to keep closed. There will be a cost."

Marley sat opposite him, her hands folded in her lap. "I know. But what's the alternative? To collude with silence like everyone else? To let her remain veiled even in death?"

He exhaled, running a hand through his hair. "You speak of collusion. And you're right. I've seen it before—communities building entire traditions on forgetting, because remembering would fracture them. But the fracture is already here, Marley. It's in the bell. It's in the snow that won't fall right. It's in the way no one can meet our eyes."

Marley's chest tightened at his words. "Then we have no choice. Keeper of Memory doesn't mean choosing safety. It means choosing truth, no matter the cost."

Damien's jaw flexed, his eyes darkening with thought. "And you believe I'm part of that choice?"

"Yes," she said simply.

For a long moment, he looked at her, the firelight flickering across his features. Then he nodded, slow, resolute. "Then we take the first step together."

THEY DECIDED to begin not with elders or officials, but with memory itself—the remnants hidden in places others had overlooked.

That afternoon, they returned to the bookstore. The fireplace still smelled faintly of ash, the note's absence lingering like smoke. Marley knelt by the hearth again, brushing soot aside, searching for anything more.

Damien crouched beside her, his hand steadying the lantern. "If she tried to burn one note, there may have been others."

Marley sifted carefully through the ashes. At first, nothing but blackened debris. Then—another scrap, smaller than the first, crumbling as she touched it. She lifted it carefully, the words barely visible: *veil bride... silence will keep...*

Her breath caught. "She knew. She carried the story. And she tried to bury it."

Damien's hand brushed hers as he steadied the fragment. "Not bury. Protect. Maybe she thought destroying it would end the demand. But it didn't."

Marley felt the truth of it settle in her chest. The silence had outlived even her aunt's attempt at erasure.

She placed the fragment carefully into her journal, pressing it between pages. "Then it's our turn to carry it."

· · ·

THEY LEFT the bookshop and walked through the square. The air felt heavier, as though the bell tower itself watched them. Townsfolk glanced up as they passed, conversations stalling mid-sentence. It was subtle, but unmistakable: the conspiracy of quiet tightening.

Damien leaned close, his voice low. "They know we're asking. And they don't want us to continue."

Marley met his gaze, her own steady. "Then we must."

AT TWILIGHT, they climbed the bell tower. The stairs groaned beneath their boots, lantern light throwing shadows along the walls. When they reached the chamber, the bell loomed above, its bronze darkened by time, inscription gleaming faintly: *Veritas in Silentio.*

Marley approached it slowly, her hand brushing the cold surface. She whispered the words aloud: "Truth in stillness."

Damien stood beside her, his voice quiet. "Perhaps the first step is naming her. Even if no one else will. Perhaps memory needs us to call her back."

Marley's throat tightened. "The veil bride."

The hush deepened, vibrating against the rafters.

She closed her eyes, imagining her standing there decades ago—veiled, waiting, silenced. Her chest ached with the weight of it. She opened her journal and wrote: *We name her, even without her name. The veil bride waits in the silence, and the bell holds her vow.*

Damien placed his hand gently over hers, steadying the page. "Then tonight, we vow too. To uncover her truth. To break this silence, no matter the cost."

Marley looked up, meeting his eyes. In the flicker of

lantern light, she saw not only resolve but devotion. His words were not just for the bell—they were for her.

She closed the journal, her hand brushing his. "Then let this be our first step. A vow to remember."

Together, they stood in the hush, their breaths visible in the cold air. The bell remained silent, but its silence felt different now—not refusal, but witness.

The first vow had been broken. But another had just been made.

WHEN THEY DESCENDED into the square, the town lay hushed beneath snow. Windows glowed faintly, doors barred early. The fountain was frozen, the cobblestones slick with frost. But Marley felt something shift inside her—a new rhythm beneath the hush, the faint beat of a vow spoken in stillness.

She turned to Damien as they walked toward the bookshop. "We've taken the first step. Now the silence will demand the next."

He nodded, his expression solemn. "And we'll answer it. Together."

The bell tower loomed behind them, shadow stretching across the square. Above, snowflakes lingered mid-descent, suspended like breath.

The Winter Bell did not ring.

But its silence had been heard.

And for Marley and Damien, the mystery was no longer only history. It was their vow now—a vow to reclaim the promise the bell remembered.

4

───────

THE BAKER'S RIBBON BOX

Snow powdered the bakery awning in a clean, white scallop the morning Marley returned with Damien to ask for the attic key. The town had woken to hushed streets again, doors opening late, voices pitched lower than their owners realized. Even here—Brookwood's warmest room in winter—the clatter of trays and the clink of teacups had softened, as if every sound understood it was entering sacred ground.

Mrs. Bennett—, cheeks pink from the ovens—wiped her hands on her apron when they stepped in. She'd watched Marley and Damien cross the square from the window. Waiting not with suspicion, Marley thought, but with the resignation of someone who knows a hidden thing has ripened past secrecy.

"You're here for what I showed you before," Mrs. Bennett said quietly. "I shouldn't have sent you away with only a glimpse. It's not a thing to be half-remembered."

Marley nodded. "Not anymore."

Mrs. Bennett reached beneath the counter, drew out a ring of keys with a brass one shaped like a flower. "The attic's been shut for years. My grandmother said: 'Lock it, leave it, let it sleep.' I think we've slept too long."

They followed her through the warm heart of the bakery. Loaves crackled softly on their cooling racks. Spiced buns shed sugared dust. Even here, the hush had weight; even sugar seemed to know it was trespassing. Mrs. Bennett led them to a narrow door behind the flour bins, worked the flowered key into the lock, and lifted a trap ladder that creaked like an old violin's first note.

"Take the lantern," she said to Damien. "The pull-chain up there sticks."

They climbed single file into the air of another century —dry boards, the lemon-salt smell of old ribbon, winter light pressed thin through a row of tiny dormers. Mrs. Bennett's grandmother had been a saver of beautiful things: hatboxes nested like Russian dolls; gilt picture frames with nothing to hold but dust; a stack of handbills for winter dances that once promised waltzes until the bell's last chime.

In the middle, exact as memory, sat the decorative box Mrs. Bennett had only dared open halfway the first time: green silk moiré, edge-piped in gold braid, a tiny clasp in the shape of a bell. The sight of it tightened Marley's throat. She remembered the dream from two nights ago—veils becoming snowfall, footsteps reaching a stair that never ended. She knelt beside the box and waited for her pulse to steady.

"May I?" she asked.

Mrs. Bennett came to her knees opposite. "With care."

Damien knelt close, lantern cupped in one hand, ledger tucked under his arm out of habit he hadn't yet shed. "I'll record everything," he said, almost to himself. "Placement, condition, lettering." The man who had tried to prove the bell's silence into bolts and gears had surrendered to listening—but he still catalogued. Marley loved him for both.

She slid the bell-clasp open. The lid lifted on a soft exhale of silk and dust.

Inside: satin ribbons, dozens, wound and tied into loops —a winter's palette of pine and cream, cranberry and holly, a few faded to old-rose and icicle. Between them lay two pressed bouquets in tissue, petals thin as paper prayers: white hellebores (Christmas roses), sprigs of rosemary for remembrance, a ring of cedar needles stitched with thread that had browned with time.

Beneath the ribbons and flowers lay an envelope sealed long ago, its wax cracked at one edge. The handwriting on the front was delicate, all curve and restraint, and familiar from Marley's nights in the archive: the hand practiced by girls taught to write without taking up space.

Amelia C.

Her name landed like a toll that refused to be heard.

Mrs. Bennett put her fingers to her mouth as if to keep a breath from escaping. "The day I found it," she whispered, "I told myself it was a keepsake, nothing more. But look at the colors. Green and white, and those"—she pointed to a narrow woven braid—"those are winterberry strands. We use them on solstice cakes."

Damien set the lantern so the light pooled inside the box. "Allow me?" he asked. When Marley nodded, he eased the envelope free with two fingers, laid it on the silk. He angled the lantern to read the faint impression in the brittle wax. "A bell and vine."

"The same motif we've seen in old handbills," Marley said. "The old winter vow."

The envelope crackled when Damien teased its flap

open. He tipped the contents into Marley's hands: a folded document, its corner torn clean as if the rip itself had been one careful decision; and a single sheet of foolscap that carried the hush of a voice pressed between pages for decades.

Marley unfolded the document first. Even before she smoothed it flat she knew its weight—the thin legal paper, the places where ink sits on the surface like breath on a window.

"Marriage license," Damien murmured, already reading along with her. He pointed to the printed lines. "County of —" He paused. "The date."

Marley felt the room pull tight around that line. **December 21, 1936.** The longest night. The town's oldest rite. The night the bell was bound to bless what would bind the town in return.

Her eyes dipped to the signatures. Groom's name, partly scrawled. Officiant line, blank. Witness, blank. And the corner—torn away exactly where a license would be countersigned and sealed.

Mrs. Bennett's voice thinned. "That's where my grandmother always stopped the story. 'A paper torn is a promise not made,' she'd say. She never told me whose."

Marley folded the license and set it gently on the ribbons. Her fingers shook when she lifted the poem. As she unfolded it, the attic's small windows seemed to draw in the day, holding it at the edges so the words could float in their own light.

The Bride in the Snow
She waits where snow and silence meet,
A veil of winter at her feet.
The bell holds breath, the town holds time,
A vow unspoken, out of rhyme.

She wears the cedar, rosemary's thread,
For what is kept and what has fled.
The night is long, the lanterns low—
The bell says nothing. So: she knows.

The last stanza carried a different hand; the letters looked hurried, as if the poem had been copied into the envelope by someone with cold fingers. A second script, perhaps—someone who chose to carry the words out of a room that had turned cruel with silence.

Damien bent closer. "A duet of hands," he murmured. "One neat, one pressed by circumstance. Either way, the voice is hers."

Marley looked back to the cedar loop in the box, stitched in that uneven thread. *For what is kept and what has fled.* The poem wasn't a lament; it was a record. A ledger of a night the town had tried to unwrite.

She turned the poem over. A faint graphite notation clung to the corner—two initials, **E.C.**, and a single word, **soon**.

"Elijah Callahan?" Damien asked, barely audible.

Marley felt the outline of a story gathering like winter light: a promised union between families who thought they could train the bell to bless their arrangement; a bride who stood in cedar and winter rose and heard — not the expected chime, but the refusal of bronze to witness a lie. The silence had not disgraced her. It had defended her.

"Amelia planned to marry on the solstice," Marley said, voice steadying as she set each piece into the only order that honored them. "This was a Winter Bell union. The colors, the flowers, the date, the envelope marked with a bell and vine. But something unraveled between license and vow. Something that made the bell withhold."

Mrs. Bennett wiped her eyes with the heel of her palm.

"It would be like our town to keep the ribbons and burn the truth."

Damien's pen clicked softly. He had set the ledger on his knee almost without meaning to. "Pressed flower composition, cedar loop, rosemary: remembrance; hellebore: winter's purity; colors keyed to solstice." His voice warmed around the details. "A rite prepared with intention."

Marley lifted one of the cream ribbons. The silk whispered over her glove like a breath. She pictured Amelia's hands doing what Marley's now did—counting loops, checking cut lengths, arranging the cedar ring on the table by the window, then flattening the ribbons with the side of her palm to tame their will. All the ordinary, tender labors that mean *we will show up for this vow with our hands before we show up with our words.*

Everything was ready except consent.

Marley lowered the ribbon into the box and let that thought sit inside her where the hush had lived for days. "She didn't leave the town," she said. "The town left her. Then covered the door with a story of its own."

Mrs. Bennett nodded once, sharp. "That sounds like us."

They packed nothing back as it had been. They cataloged gently, lined each item in fresh tissue, slid stiff paper beneath the hellebores so their petals wouldn't crack, tucked the marriage license in a sleeve Damien cut from a bread-wax wrapper. Before Marley folded the poem, she read the final stanza again and realized the last line had been altered—one word pressed darker where a lighter word lay beneath.

"The bell says nothing. So: she knows."

"So she knows what?" Mrs. Bennett asked.

"That the truth doesn't need an audience," Marley answered. "Only witness."

They closed the lid. Marley held the box a moment longer, palms on moiré silk, as if the warmth of her hands could substitute for the warmth withheld that night. Then she passed it to Mrs. Bennett.

"Will you let me keep it at the bookshop for the night?" Marley asked. "I'll write a catalog entry and make a proper protector for the letter. Then it should come home to you until we decide together what to show the town."

Mrs. Bennett looked from Marley to Damien and back again. The grief in her eyes did not belong to her alone; it belonged to the women who had stitched cedar with their careful, practical hands because someone asked them to dress a ceremony they knew wasn't true.

"Take it," she said. "And bring me back a copy of whatever you write. My grandmother would want it written right."

On the ladder down, Marley paused and listened. Not for sound this time, but for the change in the hush—the way the air sometimes lifts when a sealed room is finally opened. The bakery below sent up the faint tick of cooling loaves. The town outside kept its conspiracy of quiet. But beneath it, something old leaned closer to the present.

On the street, the snow fell in those same suspended commas, and the tower's shadow parceled out the square. Damien shifted the box in his hands and walked beside Marley without speaking. He didn't need to ask if she'd seen what he had; the story was already threading them into its weave.

At the bookshop counter, Marley set the box down as if she were setting a child to sleep. She opened her journal to a clean page and wrote the first line of the catalog, the first line of Amelia's return:

Decorative moiré box (green silk with bell clasp), attic of Mrs.

Bennett's Bakery. Contents: solstice ribbon palette; pressed helle-bore, cedar, rosemary ring; envelope addressed to "Amelia C." containing torn marriage license (Dec 21, 1936) and poem "The Bride in the Snow." Condition: fragile but legible. Significance: preparation for a Winter Bell union that did not proceed.

She underlined the last four words. Then she wrote another sentence, not for the ledger, not for any archive but her own:

The bell says nothing. So: she knows.

Marley capped her pen and looked up at Damien. "We were right," she said. "It was the solstice."

He didn't smile. The news wasn't joy. It was gravity finding its center. "Then the bell's silence isn't a riddle. It's a protest."

"And a promise," Marley added. "That truth waits, even if it has to wait in winter."

Outside, the lighthouse threw its steady, far light across black water. Here, in the bookshop's circle of lamplight, Marley felt the two keepers of Brookwood—the light and the bell—finally agreeing on something: the way forward would be through witness, not excuse. Through the hand that writes, not the hand that hides. Through a vow that would not let itself be spoken until it was real.

Marley slid the poem into a sleeve and laid it beside the license. "Tomorrow," she said, to Damien, to the ribbons, to the town that had built itself around a silence it did not deserve, "we begin to give her back her name."

The bell did not toll. But for a breath long as winter, the snow seemed to fall without hesitating.

THE MORNING after cataloging the bakery box, Marley returned to the bookshop early. The fire in the hearth had not yet settled into a steady flame, and her ink was still cold in the well. She placed the green moiré box in the center of the oak table, its silk catching the weak daylight that seeped through frosted panes.

She opened it again with the same care she had used in the attic. The pressed hellebores, the cedar ring, the torn license—all lay where she and Damien had left them. But today they seemed louder, as though each object hummed with the weight of witness.

She touched the ribbons first. Their silk whispered against her fingers, releasing faint, ghostly scents of cedar and starch. She imagined Amelia choosing each color, smoothing each loop, preparing them not as decoration but as declaration. Then she touched the poem, her finger pausing on the line that still echoed: *The bell says nothing. So: she knows.*

Her throat tightened. She whispered aloud, "Amelia, we are listening now."

The silence pressed in, dense but no longer cold.

Damien arrived later, shaking snow from his coat. He looked more awake than he had in days, though lines of fatigue still marked his face. He set his satchel on the table and leaned over the box.

"Couldn't sleep?" Marley asked.

He gave a wry smile. "I've been thinking about the initials. E.C. They could stand for Elijah Callahan. The Callahans were one of Brookwood's founding families. If he was the groom—"

"And the marriage failed before the vows were spoken," Marley finished, her pulse quickening. "Which would explain the town's refusal to talk. A family like that—powerful, proud—they would rather bury the truth than admit their son left a bride veiled in snow."

Damien nodded, his jaw tightening. "And they succeeded for nearly a century. But the bell didn't collude. It remembered."

Marley studied him for a moment. "You sound less like a skeptic every day."

He exhaled. "Because skepticism won't answer this. Not anymore."

THEY DECIDED to seek out others who might have fragments of the story. Marley suggested starting with Councilor Gearhart, whose grandmother had lived through the 1930s.

The elder welcomed them into her parlor with tea and shawls. Her eyes, sharp despite her years, darted immediately to the box Marley carried.

"That belonged to Mrs. Bennett's grandmother," Councilor Gearhart murmured. "I wondered how long it would be before someone brought it back into daylight."

"You knew about it?" Marley asked gently.

Councilor Gearhart stirred her tea slowly. "I knew it existed. But in those days, children were told only what kept them quiet. My grandmother whispered once, on a winter night, that the bell refused a vow. She never said whose. I learned to stop asking."

Marley leaned forward. "Did she ever use the phrase 'veil bride'?"

The elder's spoon froze mid-stir. Her lips pressed thin. "Yes. She said Brookwood had one, and we'd do best never to speak of her. That to name her was to invite the bell's silence back."

Damien's voice was steady. "But the silence is already here."

Councilor Gearhart's eyes lifted to his, sharp and unflinching. "And so are the costs of stirring it. Be careful, Mr. Hawthorne. You have roots here. Your daughter has roots here. Some of us would rather you not tangle them with ghosts."

Marley's chest ached at the veiled warning. But she met the elder's gaze steadily. "Roots don't die when they touch truth. They deepen."

THEY LEFT the parlor with the box heavier in Marley's arms, though its weight had not changed. Damien walked beside her, silent until they reached the square.

"She's right about one thing," he said finally. "If we push further, we'll be stirring not only memory but families who built their lives on burying it."

Marley stopped beneath the tower, the bell looming above. "Then let them be stirred. We've already vowed to remember."

Damien studied her face, snowflakes catching in his hair. "I don't fear the truth. I fear what the town might do to protect its silence."

Marley's throat tightened, but her voice was steady. "Then we'll face that cost together."

He held her gaze a moment longer, then nodded. "Together."

THAT EVENING, back at the bookshop, Marley prepared her catalog entry with fresh ink and careful script. She described each ribbon, each flower, each detail of the license and poem. Damien read aloud from his notes as she wrote, their voices overlapping like two halves of the same rhythm.

When they finished, Marley leaned back, exhaling. The catalog was more than record—it was resurrection. Amelia's name had been written into memory again.

Damien closed his notebook. "Tomorrow, we ask the Callahans."

Marley's pulse quickened. The Callahans were the town's most guarded family, their influence still woven through the council, the church, even the archives. To question them was to prod the very heart of Brookwood's silence.

But she nodded. "Tomorrow."

The bell's hush seemed to thrum approval, vibrating faintly through the walls.

And Marley knew the next step had already been chosen for them.

THE CALLAHAN HOUSE stood at the far edge of Brookwood, a manor of brick and ivy that carried the weight of generations. Its windows glowed faintly through the snow, a fortress of light against the gathering dusk. Marley tightened her scarf as she and Damien walked the path lined with blackened hedges, their boots crunching into silence.

Her chest ached with the sense of what waited inside. Not merely answers, but resistance—the sort born of pride and fear entangled.

Damien's jaw was set as they reached the heavy oak door. He raised his hand and knocked. The sound echoed like a muted drumbeat through the hush.

A servant answered, ushering them into the entry hall with reluctant politeness. The air smelled of cedar polish and old stone. Portraits lined the walls, Callahans from decades past, their eyes painted with the calm of those who believed their stories would never be questioned.

At the end of the hall, Edmund Callahan waited. His hair was white, but his posture unbent. He wore a dark suit as though every evening were a council meeting, and his eyes—pale and sharp—landed immediately on Marley's satchel, where the edge of the envelope she carried peeked out.

"You've been asking questions," Edmund said without preamble. His voice was controlled, but there was iron beneath it. "Questions best left in the ground."

Marley set her shoulders, stepping forward. "We found Amelia's marriage license. Torn, unsigned. And a poem she wrote, hidden in a box in the bakery attic."

A flicker crossed Edmund's face—something between anger and fear—but it vanished quickly. "Superstitious scraps," he said. "Not worth dragging through snow and rumor."

Damien spoke then, his voice even. "And yet the bell has refused to toll for the first time since the Depression. You know as well as I that bronze does not bend to scraps. It bends to memory. To vows broken."

The air in the hall seemed to tighten. The portraits loomed closer, their painted eyes cold.

Edmund's hands gripped the head of his cane. "Amelia Colvin is not a name to be spoken here."

"Then why does the silence still speak it?" Marley countered, her voice steady though her heart pounded. "Why does the bell remember when you would rather forget?"

For a long moment, Edmund did not answer. Then he turned, motioning them toward the study.

· · ·

THE ROOM WAS DIM, firelight flickering against shelves of leather-bound ledgers. Edmund stood by the hearth, his cane tapping once against the stone.

"My father arranged a match," he said at last, his voice quieter. "Elijah Callahan was meant to marry Amelia. The union would have bound our families, secured land, ensured prosperity. But Elijah—" He paused, his jaw tightening. "He refused her at the altar. Walked away before the vows. She stood waiting in the snow. The bell was pulled, but it made no sound. It was as though it judged us. Refused to bless what had already been broken."

Marley's throat tightened. She could almost see it: Amelia veiled, cedar and hellebore in her hands, standing beneath the tower as snow slowed around her. Waiting.

"And you silenced her," Marley said softly. "Erased her name."

Edmund's eyes hardened. "She left. Vanished. Some said she moved west. Others said she drowned herself. I never sought the truth. Some wounds heal only if left untouched."

Damien stepped closer, his voice low but firm. "No wound heals in silence. It festers. And the bell has carried it forward until now."

The old man's hands trembled slightly on his cane. "If you continue this, you will break what little peace remains. The Callahans still hold this town together more than you realize. Digging into Amelia's memory will unravel more than a vow—it will unravel Brookwood."

Marley felt the words land heavy, but she did not retreat. "Then let it unravel. The truth is not a thread to be cut—it is the fabric itself. Without it, everything is already fraying."

For a moment, Edmund's mask slipped. His eyes softened, grief flickering through the iron. "She was kind," he murmured, almost to himself. "Too kind for the way she was left. Sometimes I still hear her name in the snow."

The words struck Marley deep. She recognized them not as admission, but as confession—the kind whispered when silence no longer protects but accuses.

WHEN THEY LEFT the Callahan manor, the snow had thickened. The path back to town was muted, lantern light diffused in the haze. Marley carried the envelope tight against her chest, her breath quick and shallow.

Damien walked beside her, silent until they reached the edge of the square. Then he stopped, turning toward the tower looming above.

"She wasn't just abandoned," he said. "She was erased. And the town colluded in it."

Marley nodded, her throat tight. "The bell isn't silent because it was broken. It's silent because it refuses to bless a lie. It's judgment, Damien. Judgment that has waited almost a century."

The words hung between them, colder than the snow.

Damien looked at her then, eyes shadowed but steady. "If we bring this truth back, it won't only be Amelia we uncover. It will be every silence the town has ever kept. Every secret buried for the sake of peace."

Marley met his gaze, her own steady despite the ache in her chest. "Then we bring it back. Even if it costs us everything. Because the bell will not toll again until we do."

The hush deepened, vibrating faintly through the cobblestones. Marley felt it in her bones—the silence was no longer only history. It was a demand. A vow unfulfilled, a judgment waiting for answer.

She closed her eyes, the image of Amelia standing in snow rising again before her. Veiled. Waiting.

When she opened them, Damien's hand brushed hers, steadying. "We're in this together," he said.

"Yes," Marley whispered. "Together."

The Winter Bell loomed above, mute yet thundering in its silence.

And Marley knew the path forward was no longer theirs to choose. It had already been chosen by the vow broken, by the bride veiled, by the bell that remembered when all others had tried to forget.

5

MISTLETOE AT THE LIGHTHOUSE

The lighthouse rose from the cliff like a sentinel of stone and glass, its beam sweeping rhythmically across the frozen Sound. On this night, snow drifted in soft spirals along the coast, each flake catching the light before vanishing into dark water. Marley climbed the stone steps with Damien at her side, her breath clouding in the icy air, her heart thrumming with something heavier than the cold.

They had come not for the archives or the bakery or the tower, but for the rare silence that did not belong to judgment. Here, beneath the lighthouse's arch, the hush was gentler, carried by the sea instead of the bell.

A sprig of mistletoe had been hung in the arch's curve, tied with twine that swayed faintly in the wind. No one had claimed credit for it—it had appeared overnight, a small defiance against the weight pressing down on Brookwood. The town's children whispered that it was the lighthouse keeper's doing, or the work of lovers who sought to remind the town of vows still worth keeping.

Marley tilted her head back, looking up at the green

leaves and pale berries. "Do you think it was left for us?" she asked softly.

Damien's mouth curved, but his eyes carried their usual shadow. "If so, someone has more faith in us than we have in ourselves."

She turned toward him, her face half-lit by the lighthouse beam. "Do you doubt it? Us?"

His silence was not the bell's silence, but his own—a hesitation that had always been there between them. He reached up, brushing snow from his hair, and exhaled slowly. "I don't doubt what's here," he admitted. "I doubt whether we can carry it. You, with your calling to memory. Me, with my history of failing what I've loved."

Marley's chest ached. She wanted to speak, but the words caught in her throat. Instead, she reached up, fingertips grazing the mistletoe. The berries glistened pale as moonlight.

Damien's hand covered hers, steady, warm despite the cold. "Maybe it was left to remind us," he said quietly. "That some vows are still waiting to be spoken."

The moment hung suspended, fragile as the snowflakes pausing midair. Marley felt the weight of choice pressing in, the ache of devotion and doubt entangled.

But before either could cross the threshold of words unspoken, Damien's phone buzzed sharply in his pocket. The sound fractured the silence like glass.

He pulled it out, brow furrowing. "The archive," he said, glancing at the screen. "One of the volunteers."

Marley's pulse quickened. "At this hour?"

He answered, his voice low. "Yes?"

Through the wind, Marley could faintly hear the volunteer's voice—hurried, uncertain. Damien's expression shifted, sharp with surprise. He ended the call and turned to her.

"A journal was returned tonight," he said. "Left at the archive door. No name, no note. But it belonged to Elijah Callahan."

Amelia's fiancé.

Marley's breath caught, her eyes lifting toward the dark sweep of the lighthouse beam. "The veil groom."

Damien nodded grimly. "And someone wanted it found. The question is—who?"

The mistletoe swayed above them, silent witness to a vow that had been broken long ago.

And Marley knew: their night beneath the arch was no longer only theirs. The silence had summoned them back into its demand.

THEY DESCENDED THE STEPS QUICKLY, snow crunching beneath their boots, the lighthouse beam sweeping behind them. Marley felt the sprig of mistletoe burn in her memory as vividly as the journal that waited at the archive.

At the base of the path, she stopped, pulling Damien's sleeve. "Do you think this is coincidence?"

He shook his head. "Not in Brookwood. Not now."

"The bell refuses to ring, and suddenly Elijah's journal is returned? After all these years?"

His jaw tightened. "It means someone in town still carries the truth—and they've decided to hand us the key."

Marley swallowed hard, the weight of it pressing into her chest. "Or they've decided to hand us the burden."

Damien's gaze lingered on her, shadowed but steady. "Either way, Marley, we're the ones chosen to bear it."

She closed her eyes briefly, the wind stinging her face.

When she opened them, she nodded. "Then we follow where it leads. Even if it leads us into silence deeper than this."

Together, they walked back toward the square, the lighthouse beam sweeping one last time across the snow before vanishing into fog.

THE BROOKWOOD ARCHIVE sat at the edge of the square, its stone facade pale under the winter moon. Snow had gathered in shallow drifts against the steps, muffling their footsteps as Marley and Damien approached. Inside, a single lantern glowed near the front desk. A young volunteer—Edith—rose from her chair when she saw them, her face drawn with unease.

"It was just there when I arrived for evening duty," she said, pointing to a parcel on the counter. "Wrapped in brown paper, no name, no note. But when I untied it, I knew…" Her voice faltered. "It belonged to him."

Marley stepped forward, her breath catching. The journal lay on the desk, its leather cracked, edges frayed, a ribbon marker stained with something darker than age. She reached for it carefully, the weight of history pressing into her palms.

"Elijah Callahan," she whispered.

Damien stood close beside her, his expression unreadable, but the tension in his jaw gave him away. "The veil groom," he said softly.

Edith hugged her shawl closer. "I shouldn't keep the building open so late, but I thought—better it pass to the Keeper of Memory than linger here."

Marley nodded her thanks. She and Damien carried the journal into the reading room, lighting two more lanterns.

The long oak tables gleamed faintly in the glow, shadows gathering in corners where archives slept.

Marley opened the journal with reverence. The first page bore Elijah's name in firm, practiced script, dated 1935. Beneath it, his handwriting sprawled across the lines—at first neat, then slanting more as the entries deepened.

She began to read aloud.

December 10, 1935. Father speaks of alliance, of prosperity, of land made firm by marriage. He calls it legacy. I hear only chains.

Her throat tightened. She glanced at Damien, whose eyes darkened as he listened.

March 2, 1936. Amelia is kind. Too kind. Her voice like water smoothing stone. But kindness is not choice. They place her in my path as though love were a ledger to be signed.

Damien leaned back in his chair, exhaling slowly. "So it was true. He didn't choose her."

Marley turned the page carefully, the leather creaking.

October 14, 1936. She brought ribbons today, colors of pine and frost. She spoke of vows, of the bell that sanctifies. I saw the hope in her eyes, and I could not tell her: the bell cannot sanctify what I cannot give.

The words blurred as Marley read them. She could almost see Amelia's hands smoothing those ribbons, her face lifted with hope that Elijah could not match.

Damien's voice was quiet, almost detached. "He knew. Long before the solstice."

Marley touched the page, as if her fingers could reach across the years. "And yet he let it go on."

THEY SAT in silence for a moment, the only sound the

crackle of the lantern wicks. Snow whispered against the windows, muffling the world outside.

Damien broke the silence first. "Do you ever think about what might have been different if we'd spoken sooner? If we'd chosen instead of waiting?"

Marley's breath caught. His words were not about Amelia.

She closed the journal, pressing her palm against its worn cover. "I think about it every day."

Damien leaned forward, elbows on the table. His eyes, shadowed and steady, met hers. "I see Elijah's hesitation in myself. He let silence make his choices. And look what it cost her—look what it cost this town."

Marley felt her chest tighten. "You're not Elijah."

He gave a faint, humorless laugh. "No? I've spent years keeping my head down, convincing myself there would always be time later. For truth. For love. For vows that mattered. And now the bell refuses, as if to remind me that later doesn't come."

Marley's hand trembled against the journal. "Then don't let silence decide for you anymore."

The air between them vibrated, heavy as the bell's hush. Damien's lips parted, but no words came. Instead, he leaned back, running a hand through his hair, eyes closing briefly as though gathering himself.

At last, he opened them again, gaze steady. "Let's read on."

MARLEY OPENED THE JOURNAL AGAIN, turning to the next entry.

December 21, 1936. The snow fell like ash. Amelia waited at the altar, cedar and hellebore in her hands. I pulled the rope. The bell held its breath. It knew. It would not speak for me. I left before the silence could name me liar.

Her voice broke. She covered her mouth with her hand, tears blurring her vision.

Damien reached across the table, his hand covering hers. "Marley."

She looked up, meeting his eyes through the blur. "He left her there. And the bell chose her over him."

"Yes," Damien said quietly. "And the town chose him over her."

The truth pressed into the room like a weight, heavier than stone. The journal had not only confessed Elijah's refusal—it had revealed the bell's judgment. The silence was not accident. It was witness.

Marley closed the book carefully, her hands trembling. "This changes everything."

Damien nodded. "It changes nothing and everything at once. We knew the vow was broken. Now we have his own words. But the town..." His voice trailed off. "The town won't thank us for it."

Marley steadied her breath. "We're not here for thanks. We're here for truth."

The lantern flames flickered higher, shadows dancing across the shelves. Outside, the snow thickened, each flake pausing in descent as though the silence itself leaned closer to listen.

Marley pressed the journal to her chest. "Amelia's story will be told. Even if the town resists. Even if it costs us everything."

Damien's hand brushed hers again, steady, grounding. "Then we vow it now. No more silence."

The hush deepened, vibrating through the room.

And Marley knew—the bell had heard.

. . .

THE JOURNAL LAY open on the oak table, its final entry stark against the yellowed page. Marley traced the words with her finger, each letter heavy with consequence: *I left before the silence could name me liar.*

The weight of the sentence did not end on the page. It pressed into the room, into her chest, into the hush that vibrated faintly through the walls. The silence was no longer abstract—it was Elijah's confession echoing across decades.

Marley closed her eyes, and in the stillness she felt it: the resonance of Amelia's vow, unfinished yet enduring, tethered to the bell, to the snow, to the very air of Brookwood. The silence wasn't only remembering—it was demanding. It had been waiting, patient as frost, for someone to pick up what Elijah had dropped.

Her breath caught. "It's alive," she whispered.

Damien looked up from where he sat opposite her, his face shadowed by lantern light. "What is?"

"The vow. It didn't end with him walking away. It lingered. The bell held it. And now—it's asking us to finish it."

For a long moment, Damien said nothing. Then he leaned forward, elbows on the table, his eyes dark but unflinching. "Do you hear yourself, Marley? You're saying we're being asked to bear a promise that wasn't ours to make."

Marley met his gaze steadily. "And yet it's ours to answer. Otherwise, why would the silence keep pressing on us? Why else would Elijah's words find their way back now?"

The air between them throbbed with the bell's hush, heavy, undeniable.

. . .

DAMIEN ROSE ABRUPTLY and began pacing, his hand raking through his hair. "Do you know what terrifies me?" he asked, his voice rougher than usual. "That I am more like Elijah than I want to admit."

Marley turned in her chair to watch him, her heart quickening. "You're not Elijah."

He stopped, facing the shelves stacked with ledgers, his shoulders tense. "A man who kept silent too long. Who let indecision shape a life. I see his hesitation in myself, Marley. In every moment I should have spoken and didn't. Every chance I let slip past because I thought there would always be time later." He turned, eyes raw. "What if I carry the same flaw? What if silence is my inheritance too?"

Marley rose, crossing the space between them. She laid her hand gently on his arm. "The difference is that you're speaking now. You're naming the fear. Elijah never did."

Damien's jaw tightened. "But what if I fail you? Fail us?"

Her voice softened. "Then we begin again. Because vows aren't about perfection, Damien. They're about devotion. About refusing to walk away."

The hush deepened, vibrating through the archive like breath held. Marley felt the resonance stir in her bones, in the journal on the table, in the snow still falling outside.

"We don't have to repeat Elijah's silence," she whispered. "We can answer it."

THEY RETURNED to the table together. Marley placed her hand over the journal, steadying it. Damien mirrored her, his larger hand brushing hers as he laid it on the worn leather.

"This silence isn't only history," Marley said quietly. "It's judgment. And it won't lift until someone takes responsibility for what was abandoned."

Damien's eyes softened as he studied her face. "And you believe that someone is us."

She nodded. "Yes."

The lantern flames flickered higher, casting their shadows long across the shelves. For a moment, Marley felt as though Amelia herself stood beside them, veiled, waiting.

Damien exhaled slowly, his shoulders easing. "Then we vow it. To uncover the truth. To carry her memory. To finish what the bell began."

Marley's heart thudded, not with fear but with clarity. She placed her other hand on top of his, sealing the journal between them. "Then let this be the first step."

The silence shifted, no longer cold. It thrummed like approval, like witness.

LATER, as they stepped outside, the night pressed close. Snowflakes drifted slowly, suspended midair as though time itself had bent to watch them. The square lay empty, lanterns glowing faintly in shuttered windows.

Marley looked up at the tower, its bronze mouth hidden in shadow. "Do you feel it?" she asked.

Damien followed her gaze. "Yes. The bell is listening."

Marley's breath clouded the air. "Then we speak, not with sound, but with truth. With every step we take to uncover her story."

He turned to her, his hand brushing hers, steady. "Together."

The word landed like a vow itself, anchoring her against the weight of silence.

She closed her eyes briefly, imagining Amelia standing there decades ago—veiled, cedar in her hands, the bell refusing to bless a broken promise. But tonight, the hush felt different. Not refusal, but expectation.

The vow had not died. It had only waited.

And now, with the journal in their possession, with their hands joined against silence, Marley and Damien had chosen to carry it forward.

The Winter Bell did not ring. But for the first time since its refusal, Marley felt something shift. The silence was no longer merely judgment. It was invitation.

An invitation they had answered.

6

THE MUSIC BOX MELODY

The key was hiding where her aunt would have approved—in plain sight, disguised as tenderness. Marley discovered it at dawn, when the bookshop still wore the color of unbrewed tea and the street outside was all frost and hush. She had risen before the town again, drawn by that new, insistent current under the Winter Bell's silence. She lit one lamp, then another, and pulled the heavy ledger desk away from the wall until its back rasped against beadboard. Dust rose, faint as breath.

She had searched this desk after her aunt died, the way one searches the loved and familiar: opening every drawer, patting the obvious recesses, finding nothing she wasn't already meant to find. But the silence had made her notice the unremarkable—the way the left middle drawer never rested flush, how it barked her fingers as though resisting closure, how the scratched crescent near its lock matched, inexplicably, the arc of an old bell pull.

Marley slid the drawer out and set it on the rug. Inside: pencils shears-short, a spool of linen thread, envelopes addressed but never sent, a palm-sized smoothing stone her aunt used to press seals. Nothing conspiratorial, and yet—she felt the tug again, that second heartbeat under her own.

She thumbed the smoothing stone and felt it catch at a thread she had never seen. The drawer bottom lifted at the corner. Not broken. Floating.

She eased the false panel up. Beneath lay a narrow velvet-lined cavity and, tucked into its groove, a brass key as thin as a thought. Its bow had been filed into a tiny shape—the outline of a bell.

"Of course," Marley breathed, and love for her aunt hit her with the same ache as missing her.

The desk had three locks. Only one had never yielded—a small drawer to the right, where her aunt kept the kind of things she called *not yet*. Marley fitted the key. The lock turned with the quietest assent, an old permission granted at last.

Inside, wrapped in tissue and tied with green thread, rested a small walnut music box with a domed lid and feet like the paws of a sleeping cat. The wood wore the calm of a thing untouched for too long. When Marley lifted it, the weight felt familiar in her hands in a way that made the bridge of her nose ache.

She set it on the desk's cleared corner and untied the thread. The tissue unfolded, and the scent that rose was a century of drawers: lavender, paper, the metallic ghost of old keys. An etching curled under the lid's hinge—a ringed bell and vine, the same motif pressed into the wax that sealed Amelia's envelope.

For a long moment, Marley only traced the emblem with her thumb.

The brass crank waited at the side like a hand extended.

Marley glanced toward the covered front windows—the square still empty except for the tower's shadow pooling across its stones—and wound the crank three slow turns. The spring took the tension with a softened click. She let the lid fall back and the comb catch.

The melody rose, and the room changed around it.

At first, it was recognizably itself: three steps forward, lift, three steps back, turn—the ghost of a ballroom told by someone who believed dancing might persuade winter to relent. Notes dragged a fraction late. One tooth in the comb seemed to hesitate, then catch. On the third beat of every measure, the phrase slurred and settled, like breath fogging cold glass.

Marley gripped the edge of the desk. It was the same song. It wasn't the same at all.

"The Bell Bride's Waltz," she whispered, and the saying of it lifted a door that had not opened in years. Her aunt's voice came back—bedtime, lamplight, a quilt pulled high. *Once there was a bride who danced by the bell. When the bell chimed, she stepped. When the bell paused, she waited. The town thought she danced for them. But she danced for truth. That was why she wore cedar in her hair. So she would remember what to keep and what to let go.*

As a child, Marley had loved the image of a girl who danced in winter without freezing, who believed that the bell would never let her step alone. Later, as Keeper, she had discovered the story's edge. Still later, standing beneath the tower as it refused to sing, she had felt the edge turn and cut.

The waltz found its refrain again and then failed it—just a breath—delayed, nearly falling, somehow catching. The way the snow had been falling since the night the bell refused. The way time itself had moved as if recalling there had been a promise it should not repeat.

Marley let the melody circle twice more and then stilled

it with her thumb before the spring ended. The last note hung a fraction flat and then died obediently.

She pressed her hand to the music box lid, and the wood took her warmth. "What did you keep," she asked the room softly, "and what did you let go?"

The front door latch turned. Damien came in out of the cold, shrugging his coat off with the practiced care of a man who did everything as if not to wake something. The scent of wind and wool crossed the old lavender.

"I saw your lamp," he said, and then his gaze landed on the desk. "You found it."

"A key," Marley said. "Then a false bottom. Then what the silence wanted me to see."

He pulled a chair with his boot and sat. His eyes had that quickened-dark look they got when he stood between proof and wonder and would not choose a side, and his hands came to rest on his knees—as if he didn't trust them not to touch until she allowed it.

"Was it like the first?" he asked. "The one in the lighthouse ledger chest?"

"And like the other you found in my aunt's drawer," Marley said. She rewound the spring one careful turn. "Listen."

She let the comb catch again. Damien's head tilted toward the sound, the way he tipped his face toward the sea when the lighthouse foghorn rolled through his bones. He shut his eyes, counting silently. She had seen him count prayers this way and proofs.

"One-two-three... one—two—three—" he murmured, stopping on the delay. His fingers moved as if they wanted a pencil. "The third beat drags... no, it doesn't drag, it... yields."

"Yields," Marley repeated. The word fit the way a glove fit—when it was hers, not borrowed.

He leaned closer, peering into the box without touching it. "The cylinder's set a hair off. Look—there." He pointed with his knuckle, careful not to tap. "The pins are staggered irregularly through the third pulse. It isn't damage. It's design."

"Someone made it refuse," Marley said.

"Or made it remember how refusal felt."

They let the melody loop until the spring emptied, until the last note gave out like a tired child. Marley closed the lid, and the silence after it was shaped like the song—hollowed by absence, still ringing around its edges.

"My aunt told me the legend as a lullaby," Marley said. "She made it sound like a children's dance so I wouldn't hear the plea in it. The Bell Bride waltzes so the town remembers when to step and when to wait."

Damien's mouth turned, not quite a smile. "And now the town cannot step. Because it refused to wait when it mattered."

Marley lifted the box and weighed it again. "There are three," she said softly, counting without meaning to: the first from the lighthouse chest, the second you found in my aunt's locked drawer, and this one—hers. Each the same song, each altered by circumstance."

He nodded. "And each an argument. The first: how it ought to be. The second: how it began to break. This one... how it bears the break."

Marley set the box between them. Her aunt's key gleamed on the desk like a punctuation mark. "The slowdown—do you hear how it matches the snow?"

Damien's gaze flicked to the window, where flakes hovered before their chosen fall. "I do. And I hate that I do.

Because it means this is not just a metaphor I can put to bed."

"It means the bell has pulled time into witness. Even melodies will not lie."

He blew out a breath through his nose—a sound of surrender that wasn't defeat. "Let me take notes."

He opened his notebook and wrote what she had already learned about him: that when he could not reconcile a thing, he made a record and let the ink hold what his mind could not. He sketched the cylinder, counted measures, marked the delay. Marley stood and put on water for tea. The kettle's small sounds marked the room in a way that felt treasonously human.

Standing at the stove, Marley bent over her journal and wrote beneath the date: *Locked drawer yielded a second music box (walnut, bell-and-vine etching). Tune: "The Bell Bride's Waltz." Tempo altered. Third beat yields. The song remembers the pause the bell keeps.*

She added a second line, forward and plain, the sort of line she trusted when riddles threatened to turn itself into smoke: *Childhood legend now speaks as law.*

When she brought the tea, Damien had laid his pencil down and was just staring at the box as if he could make it volunteer the rest. His face, even in stillness, carried history the way the desk carried dust.

"Do you remember the story?" Marley asked. "The one my aunt told—the child's version."

"Vaguely," he said. "Enough to resent it. I never liked stories that asked children to behave for the sake of the town's dignity."

"She never told it that way," Marley said, a protest as small and absolute as a footprint. "It wasn't about behaving for them. It was about aligning yourself to what doesn't lie. The bell was a teacher, not a parent."

He considered that, and then lifted the lid again without winding. The comb gave one tired ping, the way a struck glass gives in sympathy to a note across the room. He flinched at the smallness of it and shut the lid again.

"What did your aunt call it?" he asked finally. "When you were small."

"The Bell Bride's Waltz," Marley said. The saying of it felt suddenly like saying goodbye. "She'd tap the rhythm on the quilt with two fingers, and she'd say—" Marley moved her fingers on the desk, an echo of that remembered tapping. "*Step, step—wait. Step, step—wait.* And when I got older, she changed the words. *Keep, keep—let go.*"

Damien closed his notebook and leaned back. "What do we keep?"

Marley ran a finger along the lid's edge, then rested her palm flat on the wood. "Amelia." The name came easily now. "We keep her name. We keep the protest of the bell. We keep the waltz that refuses to pretend." She held his gaze. "And what do we let go?"

He didn't look away. "The town's convenience. The story that protects us from the cost of truth. My habit of late confessions."

There it was: not yet a vow, but pointed toward one. Marley felt the bell in her bones sit up a little, like a watcher recognizing its own.

They drank their tea. The shop came awake in small ways—pipes clanked, the kettle sighed again, the floorboards remembered feet. Outside, the square brightened from pewter to pearl. Someone shoveled three careful paths —one from the bakery, one from the café, one toward the tower that stopped before the shadow touched their boots.

Marley rewound the box once more. She let the first strain of the waltz rise and then placed a finger lightly against the cylinder so the third beat faltered differently. It was a childish experiment, half-believing the song might forgive itself if given permission. The note smudged, argued, and resumed its wrongness with the stubbornness of fact.

"It won't lie for us," she said.

"Good," Damien said softly. "Then neither will we."

He stood, and before he could reach for his coat, the bell tower's shadow shifted across the window—just a breath, as if the sun had made a decision. The music box finished its phrase and fell still.

Marley closed the lid. The brass key lay on the desk between their cups, thin and bright as a thought that refuses to dull.

"Keep, keep—let go," she said again, and this time it didn't feel like bedtime. It felt like instructions.

BY MIDAFTERNOON, the snow had softened into a slow drift that seemed to hang in the air, its descent no swifter than the yield in the music box's third beat. Marley sat at the bookshop desk with the walnut box before her, the bell-shaped key resting beside her journal. She had filled three pages with careful notations—tempo alterations, the bell-and-vine etching, the remembered words of her aunt's lullaby. But none of it had released her from the weight of the melody still circling in her chest.

Damien had gone out to fetch bread and tea, promising to return before the square closed into its nightly hush. He had insisted she not leave the shop; that the music box, fragile as it was, should not be left unattended. Marley had agreed, though the truth was she wanted the solitude. She wanted to hear the song again without Damien's pen scratching beside her, without his restraint pressing like a second silence.

She wound the crank three turns, released it, and let the melody begin again.

Step, step—wait.

The notes spilled soft and steady, faltering where they must, circling where they had been told to circle. Marley leaned back in her chair, closing her eyes. The sound seeped into her bones, and with it came the memory of her aunt's voice.

Once there was a bride who danced by the bell. She wore cedar for memory and rosemary for truth. She danced so the town would know when to keep, when to let go.

As a child, Marley had fallen asleep before the end. Tonight she pressed herself to remember more. Her aunt's voice had lowered at that point, almost a whisper. *The bell bride waits for a partner who will not walk away. The bell bride waits for the vow to be spoken true.*

Marley opened her eyes, breath catching. That line had not been part of any published version of the legend. It had been her aunt's addition—or perhaps the part too dangerous to write down.

The music box's last note wavered and died. Marley rewound the crank with trembling fingers.

THE DOOR OPENED, and Damien stepped in, the scent of frost and bread clinging to him. He set a bundle of loaves on the counter and crossed the room, his gaze falling immediately on the music box.

"You've been listening again," he said.

Marley nodded. "It isn't only melody, Damien. It's

memory. My aunt told me words I'd forgotten until now. The bride waits for a partner who will not walk away."

Damien stilled, his hands braced on the table's edge. His eyes flicked to the journal, then back to her. "That's more than legend. That's Amelia's night in another tongue."

"Yes," Marley whispered. "She waited. He walked away. The bell refused to lie for him. And now the waltz remembers the refusal."

Damien's jaw tightened. "And it asks us not to repeat it."

She studied his face—the shadows under his eyes, the lines deepened by years of caution. "Is that what you're afraid of? Becoming Elijah?"

He hesitated, then nodded once. "I've thought it since the journal. He left her because silence was easier. And I've lived too much of my life letting silence decide for me. I don't want to see you standing in snow, waiting for me to speak."

Marley's throat tightened. She reached across the table, laying her hand lightly over his. "Then don't let silence decide. Choose."

The air vibrated with the hush again, as if the bell itself had leaned closer.

Damien closed his eyes briefly, then opened them with steadier resolve. "Then I choose this. I choose to carry the vow forward with you."

Marley's heart thudded, relief and fear twined together. She pressed her hand against the music box. "Then we've taken the first step."

THEY ATE IN NEAR SILENCE, the bread warm between them, the tea fragrant but barely touched. The music box sat between their cups like a third companion.

Afterward, Damien drew his notebook closer and began sketching. "There's more here than just a tune. Look at the yield—it's deliberate, not accidental. Whoever crafted this wanted the waltz to falter. To mark time differently."

"Like the snow," Marley said softly.

He nodded. "Like the silence itself. If the bell pulls time into pause, then this melody is its echo."

Marley leaned back, closing her journal. "And if it's echoing, then it's asking us to listen. To remember the vow not as story, but as demand."

Damien set his pencil down, rubbing his temples. "Which means we can't keep treating these discoveries as curiosities. They're instructions. And Brookwood has ignored them long enough."

Marley felt the truth settle like a stone in her chest. "Then we won't ignore them. We'll follow them. Step, step—wait. Keep, keep—let go."

The lantern flickered, shadows stretching across the desk. The music box gleamed in the dim light, its etched bell-and-vine motif catching the flame. Marley thought of Amelia, veiled and waiting, the bell refusing to speak. She thought of Elijah's confession, the journal abandoned at the archive. She thought of her aunt, hiding keys in plain sight, teaching lullabies that were warnings disguised as comfort.

The vow had never died. It had only waited.

And now, with each object returned, each melody remembered, it was calling louder.

THEY ROSE from the table together, Marley carrying the music box, Damien taking the lantern. They moved to the front window, where the square lay hushed beneath snow.

The bell tower loomed, its shadow stretching long and unbroken.

Marley set the box on the sill and opened the lid without winding it. The comb gave one faint, sympathetic ping, the sound so small it could have been mistaken for imagination.

But Marley knew. The bell had heard.

She turned to Damien, her voice steady despite the tremor in her hands. "We vow to finish what was left undone. To remember Amelia. To restore what silence tried to bury."

Damien lifted the lantern higher, its glow catching in his eyes. "And we vow not to walk away."

The hush deepened, no longer accusation but acknowledgment.

And Marley felt, for the first time, that the vow was no longer only Amelia's to bear. It was theirs now, bound to their hands, their voices, their devotion.

The Winter Bell did not ring.

But the silence answered.

That night Marley dreamed in steps.

Not words, not faces—steps.

The waltz circled her in the dark, each measure landing with the peculiar hesitation of the music box's slowed third beat. She was on the square, though it was not the square of her waking life but one folded in snow and silence. The bell tower loomed, its shadow stretched beyond the horizon. The town stood in rows around her, their faces veiled, their lips unmoving. Only the snow moved—and even that in fits and starts, drifting, halting, falling, pausing.

Marley's feet began to move of their own accord. Step, step—wait. Step, step—wait. The pause pulled her harder than the steps. It was in the pause that she felt Amelia beside her, veiled and waiting, cedar in her hair. It was in the pause that she felt Damien too, his hand steadying hers, his presence grounding the dance in more than memory.

When she woke, her hand was still stretched across the coverlet, palm open as though it had held someone's.

The music box sat on the nightstand, its lid shut. No one had touched the crank. Yet Marley swore she could still hear the faint echo of the waltz beneath the silence, like a heartbeat muffled by snow.

She sat up, breath quick, and reached for her journal. By lamplight she wrote:

Dream of the waltz. Square filled with veiled faces. Step, step —wait. Amelia beside me. Damien beside me. The vow is not past —it is asking for completion. The music box is guide, not relic.

She set her pen down and pressed her fingers to her temple. The line blurred between sleep and waking, but the certainty remained: the melody was showing her what came next.

At BREAKFAST, she told Damien everything. He listened in silence, bread untouched, his eyes darkened with the kind of focus that made Marley ache for the things he had spent his life keeping contained.

When she finished, he leaned back in his chair, exhaling. "It wasn't just a dream."

She shook her head. "No. It was instruction. A way forward. The waltz is more than memory—it's a map."

He rubbed his jaw, gaze fixed on the music box resting on the counter. "Then we need to read it as such. And that means admitting something I've tried not to say."

Marley's pulse quickened. "What?"

He lifted his eyes to hers, and for once there was no distance in them, no shield of restraint. "That I'm terrified, Marley. Not of the vow. Not even of the town's silence. I'm terrified of failing you the way Elijah failed Amelia. Of walking away when the vow demands I stay."

Her throat tightened, the ache sharp. She reached across the table, covering his hand with hers. "You're not him, Damien."

His voice was low, raw. "But I could be. Every instinct in me is to keep quiet, to hold back until I'm certain. That's how I've lived my life. And that's how he left her standing in the snow. What if my silence ruins this too?"

Marley shook her head, gripping his hand tighter. "The difference is that you're naming it. You're speaking where he never did. That's how we break the pattern. Not by pretending fear doesn't exist—but by refusing to let it choose for us."

The hush pressed around them again, vibrating faintly, as if the bell itself were listening.

Damien's shoulders eased. His eyes softened, steady on hers. "Then I vow it now. No silence between us. Not again."

Marley swallowed hard, tears threatening, but she nodded. "Then so do I."

They sat there for a long moment, hands clasped across the table, the music box between them like a witness.

LATER THAT AFTERNOON, they wound the crank again and let the waltz fill the bookshop. This time they didn't sit apart—they stood, side by side, and let the melody guide their steps across the worn rug. Step, step—wait. Step, step—wait.

Marley's heart raced, not with the fear of misstep but with the certainty that the dance itself was an act of memory. She felt Amelia in the pause, not as absence but as presence. She felt Damien's hand in hers, his grip steady, his vow held not in words but in the refusal to let go.

When the last note faltered and died, they stopped. The silence that followed felt less like judgment and more like expectation, as though the bell were waiting for them to understand.

Marley pressed her hand to the lid of the music box. "It isn't just playing back the past. It's teaching us how to move into what's next."

Damien nodded, his breath unsteady but his eyes alight. "Then the question is—where does the dance lead?"

Marley opened her journal and wrote beneath the day's date: *The Bell Bride's Waltz is not memory alone. It is map, vow, and guide. To follow it is to uncover the next step in restoring what was broken.*

She underlined the words three times.

Damien leaned over, reading them, then whispered: "Then we follow it. Step, step—wait."

And in that vow, in that shared resolve, Marley felt the silence shift again. Not accusation. Not only judgment. But recognition.

The bell had found its partners.

THAT NIGHT, as they closed the shop and barred the doors against the cold, Marley felt a quiet certainty settle in her chest. The vow was no longer just Amelia's, no longer just history. It was theirs now—bound to their steps, their voices, their devotion.

The Winter Bell did not ring.

But its silence no longer felt empty. It felt alive, guiding them forward, step by step.

And Marley knew: the waltz had only just begun.

7

CANDLES IN THE WINDOW

Brookwood's winter ritual was older than memory and older even than the council records that claimed to govern it. On the longest nights, each house lit a candle and set it in the window, a line of small flames binding the town against the cold. The bell usually tolled to open the vigil, its resonance rolling from tower to hearth, and then the light spread outward street by street until no pane was left unlit.

This year, the bell had refused. Yet as dusk fell, the townsfolk moved with practiced care, striking matches, trimming wicks, shielding flames with hands. The square filled with a hush less of reverence than of unease. One by one, window after window bloomed with light.

Marley left the bookshop just as the last grey drained from the sky. She pulled her cloak tight, journal tucked under her arm, and stepped into streets lined with firelit panes. The snow reflected each glow, scattering it into the hush until it seemed the town was stitched in golden thread.

She walked slowly, listening. In other years, the bell's opening peal had lent this ritual its rhythm—each flame kindled as echo. Now, the silence rang louder than any bronze. Still, the townsfolk performed their part, as though hoping the act itself might coax the bell into speech again.

Marley moved along Main Street, where the bakery's windows gleamed with three candles, their wax pooling like memory. Past the café, four flames burned steady against frost. The postmistress had set five on her sill, one for each child she had raised through winters.

Marley stopped at the end of the lane, her breath catching.

A house stood dark against the snow. Its windows were blank glass, reflecting the flames across the street but offering none of their own. The shutters hung still, as though waiting for hands that would never return.

The Colvin estate.

Amelia's house.

Marley stepped closer, boots crunching. The gate was unlatched, though the snow showed no footprints. She pushed it open, the hinges creaking into silence. The walk was drifted, the steps unshoveled. The windows stared back at her, dark and empty.

She pressed her palm to the frosted pane. It was cold, lifeless. No candle. No flame. No vow.

Her chest ached. The rest of Brookwood might collude with silence, but this absence was louder still. It was as if the house itself refused to participate, standing witness to the vow broken within its walls.

Marley opened her journal with trembling hands, the ink freezing in the night air. She wrote: *Every home lit a candle. Every window offered flame. Except hers. The estate stands dark, as though Amelia herself declined to join a ritual that failed her.*

The silence thickened around her, vibrating with judgment. She pressed her forehead briefly to the glass, then stepped back, throat tight.

"Amelia," she whispered. "We see you."

The words hung in the air, misting before her face, then vanished into the hush.

BACK AT THE BOOKSHOP, Damien was waiting at the long oak table, a stack of yellowed newspapers spread before him. He looked up as Marley entered, his expression grave.

"You were walking the lanes," he said.

"Yes." Marley pulled her cloak free and sank into the chair opposite. "Every home lit a candle. Except hers."

His jaw tightened. "The Colvin estate?"

She nodded. "Dark. Refusing."

He turned the newspaper so she could see the clipping pinned under his hand. The paper was dated *December 23, 1936.* Its ink had faded, but the words still carried the shape of scandal.

Wedding Ceremony Cancelled: Elijah Callahan Unaccounted For

Beneath the headline, the brief column explained that the marriage between Miss Amelia Colvin and Mr. Elijah Callahan had been "postponed indefinitely due to the unforeseen absence of the groom." No cause given. No statement offered. The last line was stark: *Guests were dismissed, and no further plans have been announced.*

Marley's stomach clenched. "They erased her. Even in the newspaper, they framed it as his absence—not her refusal, not her abandonment, not the bell's silence. Just... a postponement."

Damien's eyes darkened. "Which became permanent the

moment the bell refused. And yet they printed it as if it were nothing more than a scheduling error."

Marley pressed her palm to the clipping, the brittle paper crackling. "The town's ritual is to light every window so no one stands in darkness. And yet hers is dark still. Her story was never given flame."

The music box sat on the desk beside them, silent now, but its presence filled the pause.

Damien's voice was low. "Then it falls to us to relight it."

Marley nodded, her throat tight. "Yes. To place a candle in the window she was denied. To vow in her name what silence refused."

The hush pressed close, as if listening.

And for the first time, Marley felt not only judgment in its weight but also invitation.

THE NEXT MORNING, Brookwood smelled faintly of extinguished wicks and melted wax. The vigil had ended with dawn, but its residue lingered—trails of soot on windowpanes, half-burned stubs cooling in their holders, the quiet hangover of a night when the town had prayed with fire instead of words.

Marley and Damien stepped out into the square together, the newspaper clipping folded in Marley's satchel. The silence of the bell still weighed heavier than the hush of snow.

"Every window had a flame," Marley murmured, eyes roaming the tidy rows of houses. "Except hers."

Damien's jaw flexed. "And the clipping proves it wasn't just the vow that broke. It was the story they told about it. They rewrote her absence as his. They turned her witness into his convenience."

Marley touched the satchel. "We need to know who still carries that lie—and why they refuse to let her candle burn."

THEIR FIRST STOP was the bakery. Mrs. Ruth Bennett looked up as they entered, her hands dusted in flour. The shop was warm, the air thick with sugar and spice, but her eyes betrayed unease.

"You walked last night," Mrs. Bennett said, not a question but a recognition. "You saw the dark house."

"Yes," Marley answered. "Why did no one light her window?"

Mrs. Bennett set her hands firmly on the counter. "Because the Colvins are gone. No family remains. To light a candle there would be to claim her ghost."

Marley's throat tightened. "Or to honor her."

Mrs. Bennett's jaw worked. "And in this town, those two things are the same. Ghosts unsettle. We've lived long enough with silence. We don't need to invite it in."

Damien leaned forward, his voice even. "Silence is already in, Mrs. Bennett. The bell has seen to that. Whether you name her or not, she is here."

Mrs. Bennett turned away, brushing flour from her apron. "Then perhaps you should leave her where she is. Some truths don't warm—they burn."

BY MIDDAY, they had spoken with half a dozen townsfolk. Each one gave the same reply, though with different words: to light her candle was to summon the silence closer, to disturb the fragile truce they had made with it.

Back at the bookshop, Damien spread the clipping

across the table again. The brittle paper seemed smaller than the weight it carried.

"They lied to protect themselves," he said. "Elijah vanished, and instead of naming the vow broken, they published a postponement. As if she were the inconvenience. As if her waiting in the snow were not worth print."

Marley pressed her palm against the page, as if she could smooth out its distortion. "They called it postponement. But we know what it was. Abandonment."

She drew her journal closer, writing quickly: *The paper colluded. The town colluded. Amelia's absence was reframed as Elijah's. Her silence was made his. Her darkness was left unlit.*

Damien watched her, his eyes shadowed. "Do you see what this means? The bell isn't only judging Elijah. It's judging Brookwood. Every home that lights a candle while hers stands dark is complicit. Every vigil since 1936 has been a ritual of forgetting."

Marley set down her pen. "Then we must rewrite the vigil. We must give her the flame they denied her."

Damien leaned back, folding his arms. "And if the town resists? If they see our candle as provocation?"

Marley's voice steadied, her resolve hardening. "Then let it be provocation. Because silence is the greater danger."

The hush pressed closer, as though affirming her words.

And in that moment, Marley understood: the newspaper clipping was not only evidence. It was indictment.

THE SNOW WAS ALREADY FALLING thick by the time Marley and Damien reached the Colvin estate again. The house loomed dark, shutters closed, its windows reflecting only the faint flames of neighboring homes. The silence was so absolute that Marley could hear her own breath against the scarf at her lips.

She carried a single candle in her gloved hand, shielded by a glass holder. Damien walked beside her with the lantern, his jaw set with quiet determination.

"This isn't just about honoring her," Marley said softly as they stepped through the unlatched gate. "It's about forcing the town to face what it buried."

Damien nodded. "Then let's make it undeniable."

They climbed the unshoveled steps together, boots crunching ice, and stopped before the central window. Marley set the holder down on the sill, struck a match against the stone, and touched it to the wick. The flame caught instantly, flaring against the glass.

For the first time in nearly ninety years, Amelia's house had light in its window.

The glow was small, but in the hush of the square, it felt like a bell tolling.

It didn't take long for the first neighbors to notice. Curtains twitched. Doors opened. Within minutes, townsfolk were gathering at the edges of the square, faces pale in the snowlight.

Ruth Bennett was the first to speak, her voice sharp with fear. "What have you done?"

"We've done what should have been done all along," Marley answered, her breath steady despite her pounding heart. "We've given her the flame you denied her."

Murmurs rippled through the crowd. Some faces looked stricken, others angry, still others unreadable. Mr. Whitcomb pushed his way to the front, his eyes blazing. "You don't understand what you've risked. The bell is already silent. To provoke it further—"

"Provoking truth is not a sin," Damien cut in, his voice even but firm. "What you call risk is simply recognition. The silence has already judged us. We are only acknowledging it."

A woman Marley didn't know shook her head. "We've kept this peace for decades. Why stir it now?"

"Because peace built on lies is not peace," Marley said. "It's surrender."

The murmurs grew louder, the hush breaking under the weight of unease. Yet none dared cross the steps to extinguish the flame. The candle burned steady, its reflection glowing in the dark window.

THE CROWD DISPERSED SLOWLY, uneasily, until only Marley and Damien remained at the estate's gate. The candle's glow flickered faintly against the snow, fragile yet defiant.

Damien exhaled, his breath clouding the night air. "They're afraid, Marley. Afraid that if the silence is broken, everything they've built will collapse."

Marley met his gaze. "Then let it collapse. The bell is not asking for preservation—it's asking for truth."

He studied her for a long moment, then nodded. "Then this is the crucible. The silence isn't just memory. It's the test of Brookwood's soul."

They stood there together, watching the flame burn against the glass. The snow fell slower, as though time itself had bent once again into the waltz's rhythm: step, step— wait.

.   .   .

BACK AT THE BOOKSHOP, Damien unfolded the newspaper clipping once more. The brittle words seemed sharper now, almost cruel.

Wedding Ceremony Cancelled: Elijah Callahan Unaccounted For.

Marley pressed her fingers to the page. "They called it postponement. But it was abandonment. And by printing it, the town agreed to forget her. Every year since, the vigil has been incomplete. Every candle in every window has been lit against her darkness."

Damien's voice was low, steady. "And tonight we reversed it. We set her flame alight. The silence will not let us stop here."

Marley closed her journal with resolve. "Then we won't stop. We'll follow where it leads, no matter the cost."

The hush pressed close, vibrating through the floorboards, through their bones.

And in that vibration, Marley felt the truth settle deep: the Winter Bell's silence was no longer simply judgment. It had become the crucible in which the town itself would be tested.

The candle in Amelia's window burned on.

And Brookwood would never be the same.

8

AN UNEXPECTED OFFER

The letter arrived on a morning when the square still smelled faintly of candle wax and snow. Marley found it tucked beneath the shop door, heavy cream stock with a seal embossed in gold. She turned it over in her hands, uncertain whether to break the seal at once or leave it a mystery.

When she did open it, the words startled her into stillness.

Esteemed Keeper of Memory,

We at Hawthorne & Dempsey Historical Press have followed your work with admiration. Reports of your stewardship in Brookwood, particularly your careful cataloging of the Winter Bell's legacy, have reached our attention. We wish to extend to you a formal invitation: to author a memoir and cultural history of Brookwood's ancestral mysteries. We believe your unique vantage point will bring not only clarity but resonance to a wider world eager for accounts of truth long concealed.

The signature was in neat script—an editor whose name she recognized from shelves she had once shelved herself, back in the years when she thought publishing houses were far away citadels that never called upon people like her.

Her heart thudded. She read the letter twice, then three times, until the words began to blur.

A contract. A memoir. Her work, her town, her vow—bound not only in her journal but in print that might outlast them all.

SHE SET the letter on the oak table, smoothed her palms against its surface, and waited for Damien.

He arrived shortly after, brushing snow from his coat, his face drawn from lack of sleep. Marley rose to meet him, heart quick, letter trembling in her hand.

"This came this morning," she said, offering it.

He read it silently, lips moving faintly with each line. When he finished, his brow furrowed in thought. He read it again, slower. Then he looked up, a spark in his eyes she hadn't seen in weeks.

"Marley, this is extraordinary," he said. "A chance to preserve what you've uncovered. To give Amelia her name back in a way no one can erase."

Her throat tightened. "It feels like more than that. Like a calling."

Damien nodded. "And it is. You've been chosen for this. And you should take it."

His words steadied her, but something in his tone unsettled. A distance. A note that wasn't encouragement so much as release.

FOR THE REST of the morning, she drafted a reply—thankful, tentative, but willing. Damien kept busy at the far end of the table, his notebook open, pen moving in fits and starts. She caught him glancing toward the window more than once, eyes unfocused, as though already seeing a horizon beyond Brookwood.

When the kettle boiled, she poured two cups and carried one to him. "You've been quiet," she said gently.

He accepted the cup, nodding. "Just thinking."

"About the offer?"

He hesitated, then shook his head. "About work. Before Brookwood, I had opportunities... overseas. Archives in Prague, manuscripts in Jerusalem, a posting at the university in Leiden. I put them aside when I came here. But now..." He trailed off, staring into the steam rising from his cup.

Marley's chest ached. "You're thinking of going back."

His silence was answer enough.

THAT NIGHT, long after she had closed the shop, Marley sat alone at the desk, the music box beside her, the publishing letter spread across her journal. She touched each with one hand, as though weighing them.

The music box whispered of vows yet unfinished, of Amelia's silence demanding answer. The letter promised recognition, preservation, a future where the truth could be written into history rather than erased.

She should have felt only joy. Instead, unease threaded through her.

Because when Damien encouraged her, she had felt the distance in his voice. Because the way his eyes lingered on the horizon told her that the silence was not the only thing pulling at them now.

She pressed her palm to her forehead, whispering

aloud, "What if the vow is drawing us in different directions?"

The flame of her lamp flickered, shadows shifting across the walls. The bell tower loomed in her imagination, mute yet thundering.

Separate callings. One to write. One to wander.

Marley closed her eyes, listening to the silence. It gave no answer.

But she felt, with a certainty that tightened her chest, that the question itself was only beginning.

BY NOON the letter had already become rumor. Brookwood could keep a secret for eighty-eight years, but it could not keep news about its Keeper for more than a morning.

Marley decided not to hide. She folded the cream stock into her satchel and walked into the square, where the hush of the bell still threaded every errand with restraint. She began at the bakery because Ruth Bennett had a way of measuring truth like flour—by the handful, careful but generous.

Mrs. Bennett looked up from dusting sugar on rings of pastry. "I heard a whisper," she said without preamble. "Bring it out where it can see daylight."

Marley set the letter on the counter. Mrs. Bennett wiped her hands, read it once, then again. The sugar on her knuckles glittered like frost.

"A memoir," Mrs. Bennett murmured. "Your name on the spine. Our town in the pages. I'll bake a cake the day it's bound." Then her mouth tightened. "But say what you'll call what can't be softened. The Colvins, the Callahans, the bell that refuses to bless us. Will you print the town we were, or the one we told ourselves we were?"

"The one the bell remembers," Marley said.

Mrs. Bennett held her gaze for a long breath, then nodded. "Then bake I shall. And I'll bring the first slice to Amelia's window."

Word met Marley at every door. The postmistress beamed, pressing both of Marley's hands between hers as if sealing a prayer. "It's about time the world knew the right version," she said. At the tailor's, a needle paused in mid-air; he squinted at the letter, approval hidden behind caution. "Write," he said. "But stitch the seams strong. We live inside them."

At Moon & Morrow, Hazel rolled the seal between thumb and forefinger as if testing a tincture's potency. "Ink can call the living back," she said at last. "But it calls the dead too. Be certain which you want answering." She pushed the letter toward Marley. "Say yes. Then be ready to pay what yes requires."

On the way out, a teen who stacked kindling outside the smithy called, "Miss Taylor! Is it true you're writing a real book?" When Marley nodded, he flushed with the fierce hope of someone who had not yet been taught his town's preferred volume. "My friends and I will read it the day it's out," he blurted. "Even if they tell us not to."

"Especially if they tell you not to," Marley said, smiling despite the ache behind her eyes.

By afternoon the square felt pointed toward her, each shutter and shopfront a small, waiting face. Consensus did not arrive; the bell would have mocked it if it had. Instead, Brookwood offered what it always offered: a chorus out of key. Blessing braided with warning. Pride threaded with fear.

She brought all of it back to the bookshop where Damien waited, shoulders bent over a cluster of index cards he'd been arranging into maps of thought. He stood when she entered, his expression bright for her in a way that made the brightness itself feel like a resource he was budgeting.

"How bad was it?" he asked.

"Mixed," she said. "Which means honest."

He nodded. "Honest is better than easy." He reached for the kettle and filled it without asking how she took her tea; lately he remembered small things so precisely that the precision felt like a goodbye rehearsed in kindness.

While the water heated, Marley drew the bolt ledger toward her. "Would you...? There's a form letter the press enclosed. I should send a preliminary acceptance and ask for terms."

Damien took the paper, scanned it, and fetched his pen. He wrote with his usual clarity, the words neat as steps laid across thin ice. But when he handed the page back, his fingers lingered on the edge a fraction too long. Marley saw the hesitation travel through him like a shadow carrying news.

"Tell me," she said softly.

He looked at the window instead of at her. Outside, snow fell in the bell's odd rhythm. "The Leiden post reopened," he said at last. "A colleague wrote to ask if I'd reconsider. Six months. Ottoman manuscripts newly acquired. After... after the paper returned Elijah's journal, the university remembered my name." He tried to smile and failed. "Hawthorne is a credential in Europe. They don't care that I earned it here by learning how to listen."

Marley set the acceptance aside as if it were hot. "When?"

"A spring term," he said. "They need an answer before the thaw."

"The thaw," she repeated, and hated how the word sounded like parting.

He went on, voice low. "There's also an offer in Prague. A short fellowship. And a curator in Jerusalem sent a note that read like a prayer." He rubbed his brow. "I keep thinking—if I go, I could bring back what we need. Techniques, contacts, ways of forcing archives to yield. I could return with keys."

"You're also thinking you might not return," Marley said.

He didn't deny it. The kettle began to shiver. He took it from the flame, set it aside. Neither reached for the cups.

"When your letter came," Damien said, "something in me stood up. Not jealousy. Relief. As if the bell had found your path and mine at the same time. That's what frightens me. Separate callings can sound like broken vows."

Marley heard her aunt across years: *Keep, keep—let go.* Her thumb found the ridge of the music box key in her skirt pocket and pressed there hard. "I don't want to keep you from your work," she said. "And I don't want to let go of... this."

He finally looked at her. Silence drew a ring around them the way frost draws rings around leaves. "You once told me vows aren't about perfection," he said. "They're about devotion. Maybe devotion can survive distance." His mouth tugged at the corner. "Maybe it can even require it."

"But Sophie," Marley said. The name opened another quiet between them. His daughter had taken to the music box with grave concentration, had counted along to the third-beat yield like it was a code she might someday break.

"I've spoken with her," Damien said. "Badly. Haltingly. She said she doesn't want to move again. She asked if the bell would be angry if we left. I told her the bell isn't angry. It's patient." He swallowed. "I don't know if that was true. But it was kind."

"Maybe both," Marley said.

The door chimed. Councilor Gearhart tottered in on a hush of cold and wool. She took in their faces like a librarian scanning a margin note for panic. "I've come to say my piece," she declared, lowering herself into the chair by the fire. "On the letter. On the man. On the bell."

Marley tried to smile. "In that order?"

"In the only order that will do." Councilor Gearhart tapped the table. "First, the letter: say yes. I want to see the shelves hold a book that doesn't lie about us. Second, the man: if his feet need to walk, let them. If his hands return carrying what we need, bless them. If they don't return, bless them anyway. You aren't a gate to close on a person."

"And the bell?" Damien asked gently.

"The bell doesn't care where you stand when you hear it," she said. "Only that when it finally speaks, you don't pretend you didn't." She reached for Marley's hand, papery and fierce. "Child, you've been called to write what winter tried to erase. There's no smaller calling hiding behind that one. Take it."

She rose with effort. "That is all," she said, and left before they could thank her, as if gratitude were a luxury best saved for pages.

When the door shut, Marley laughed once—the kind that breaks out of a person like steam. "She always arrives like a verdict," she said.

"Or like a benediction," Damien answered.

The laugh died quickly. "Are you going to say yes?"

"I don't know." He pinched the bridge of his nose, then let his hand fall. "I know what I owe the vow. I'm trying to learn what I owe myself."

"Those aren't different," Marley said, and then softer,

admitting the bruise beneath her confidence: "They might be."

They stood in the bell's quiet, the two of them pulled by different tides that might, in the end, be the same sea. Outside, a child's mittened hand traced its own name in fog on a window before a parent lifted the candle to relight a wick that had guttered. The simple domestic act felt holy.

"Will they forgive me for writing it?" Marley asked, immediately ashamed of the question and needing its answer anyway.

"Some," Damien said. "Some won't. Forgiveness is a later thing. Truth is the now thing." He hesitated. "If I go—if— may I send you what I find? Story-shards, letters, fragments of other towns that survived their own bell?"

"You'd better," Marley said, and the crack in her voice was not a crack so much as a seam being reinforced from both sides.

Dusk took the square early. Damien lit the lamps one by one. Marley brought the music box to the counter and set it where she could see the door and the tower at once. She wound the crank and let the waltz thread the shop with its off-kilter courage. *Step, step—wait.* The third beat yielded, as if kneeling.

Damien's shoulders lowered. He came to stand beside her, not touching, exactly near. "Whatever I decide," he said, "I want you to hear this part aloud: I am not walking away."

Marley nodded, a breath she didn't know she was holding leaving her in a shiver. "Then I'll write it that way," she said. "Not as a goodbye, but as the chapter where the paths fork and keep running parallel."

He smiled with his eyes more than his mouth. "And sometimes cross back."

"Sometimes cross back," she echoed.

He left later than usual, coat collar up, head bent to the snow. She watched him pass the bell tower's shadow and pause—as if listening for a word spoken too low for anyone else. Then he moved on, his figure thinning into the winter light.

Marley sat with the music box and the letter and the town's mixed chorus and knew that a calling is just a vow spoken into some larger silence. The bell had not rung. The snow still paused on its third invisible beat. But her pen no longer trembled when she lifted it.

She wrote two sentences to end the day's ledger. One for herself: *I accept.* One for them both: *Neither of us walks away.*

When she blew out the lamps, the square answered with a scatter of window flames rising against the early dark. It was not unanimity. It was enough light to see by. And for now, that would do.

THE NEXT FEW days moved like snowdrifts—slow on the surface, but with a hidden shifting that threatened to bury them if they stopped paying attention.

Marley spent her mornings at the oak desk drafting fragments of what the memoir might become: descriptions of the candlelit vigil, Amelia's abandoned window, the slurred melody of the second music box. She wrote with the urgency of someone who knew history was not waiting politely but pressing its palm against the glass. Each sentence felt less like invention and more like translation— turning silence into ink.

The townsfolk continued to stop her in the square, their reactions splitting down the fault line she had come to expect. Some blessed her, offering recipes, letters, even old keepsakes to be folded into her work. Others warned her away with sharpened whispers: "Do not stir the ashes." "Don't give outsiders our bones." Their resistance told her as much as their offerings did. The town was fractured, and the fracture itself was part of the truth she had been asked to write.

Yet each evening, when she closed her journal and looked for Damien, she found him already leaning toward distance.

HE SPENT MORE time at the archive now, poring over ledgers not only of Brookwood but of shipping records, academic correspondences, bibliographies of archives abroad. He would return with ink on his cuffs and a gaze that seemed to stretch farther than the bell tower. When she asked what he'd found, he answered in careful pieces—never lies, but not fullness either.

One evening he brought home a stack of catalog cards. "I'm testing a classification scheme they use at Leiden," he explained, his voice too casual. "It might help us track which families left records during the year of Amelia's silence."

Marley nodded, but what she heard beneath the words was: *I'm already halfway back there.*

She tried to tell herself it was her imagination. That he was merely thorough, not absent. But imagination doesn't leave mugs cooling on the table untouched. Imagination doesn't make a man flinch when a child's voice in the square sings the wrong third beat of the waltz, as though echoing his own hesitation.

ONE AFTERNOON, she asked him directly.

They were cataloging by lamplight, the music box between them, its lid shut. The journal lay open to Elijah's confession. Marley put down her pen and said, "Damien, if you go, will you come back?"

He looked at her as though she had spoken aloud the question he had been trying to keep in ink rather than breath.

His throat worked. "I don't want to leave you with the vow alone. But I also don't want to trap myself where my hands can't do their work. My life before this was wandering through archives like a pilgrim through chapels. And now..." He gestured at the journal, the music box. "Now the pilgrimage has found me. But I don't know if it intends me to stay."

Marley's heart ached with the contradiction. "And what about me? About us?"

He closed his eyes briefly, then opened them. "That's the part I can't bear to answer. Because if I admit how much I want to stay, I might never allow myself to leave. And if I admit how much I want to go, I might break what's just begun to mend."

His honesty felt like both gift and wound.

Marley reached across the desk and covered his hand. "Then don't admit it yet. Just promise me you won't walk away in silence. That if you go, it will be spoken, not hidden. That you won't be Elijah."

Damien's fingers curled around hers, steady. "That I can vow."

THAT NIGHT she dreamed the waltz again, but this time the square was empty except for her. No veiled faces. No town. Just the flame in Amelia's window burning against the hush.

The music carried her through the steps until she realized someone was watching from beyond the tower's shadow. Damien, holding a suitcase, his outline blurred by snow.

She woke with tears on her cheeks and the music box's off-kilter rhythm still pulsing in her chest.

When morning came, she found Damien already gone to the archive. On the table lay a note in his careful hand:

Brookwood will not collapse if we name the truth. Perhaps neither will we. I will return before dusk. —D.

She pressed the note to her chest, then folded it into her journal beside the publisher's letter. Two callings, parallel, threatening to diverge. Both necessary. Both true.

She dipped her pen and wrote beneath: *The vow may not bind us to one place. It may bind us to one truth, carried wherever we go.*

The hush of the Winter Bell seemed to hum assent.

BY EVENING, Damien returned, coat dusted with snow, a bundle of papers under his arm. He placed them on the table without preface. "Passenger manifests," he said. "Trains leaving Brookwood Station in winter of 1936. One name is missing from every record: Amelia Colvin. She didn't leave on paper. Which means her silence is still here."

Marley's breath caught. "Then she never escaped. And neither will the vow until we finish it."

They sat together in the glow of the lamp, the flame reflecting in both their eyes. Marley felt the town pressing in around them—the candles, the windows, the whispers, the lies, the truths. She felt the bell's silence like a crucible, waiting to see if they would endure.

"Whatever happens," Damien said quietly, "whether I go

or stay, we can't let the silence divide us. The vow is larger than geography."

Marley nodded, her throat tight. "Then we won't let it. We'll follow it wherever it leads, together—even if together means apart for a while."

The music box sat between them. Marley wound it once, and the waltz began again, faltering on its third beat. Step, step—wait. The pause was not absence but instruction.

They listened. And in the pause, they both felt it: the vow was not pulling them apart. It was teaching them how to move.

The Winter Bell did not ring. But its silence thrummed with recognition.

9

SNOWFALL AND SEPARATION

The storm began at dusk, though its warnings had been whispered all day in the uneasy rhythm of the clouds. By the time Marley and Damien bolted the shop door, snow was already sweeping across the square, erasing footsteps as quickly as they were made. The wind pressed against the shutters like a hand that would not be refused.

The bookshop had weathered worse storms in its century of standing, but tonight its walls seemed to absorb more than weather. The silence of the Winter Bell still lingered, and in the rising blizzard Marley felt the echo of that refusal tighten around them both.

She stoked the fire, coaxing the flames higher, then carried her journal to the desk. Damien remained by the front window, arms crossed, watching snow climb the lampposts until their light became halos trapped in glass.

Neither spoke for a long while.

When Marley finally dipped her pen, the scratching of nib on paper sounded too loud in the hush. She wrote quickly—about the storm, about the letter from the publisher, about the candle lit at Amelia's window. Each word felt like a plank she was laying across a gap she could not yet name.

Behind her, Damien sighed and crossed to the back room. She heard him pull a chair across the floor, heard the familiar creak of his own notebook opening. The separation was not deliberate, yet it felt deliberate all the same. Two halves of the same silence, choosing different corners.

HOURS PASSED. The wind howled. Snow lashed against the shutters with the insistence of waves. Marley added wood to the fire, the warmth reaching her hands but not her chest.

She glanced toward the back room, half-expecting Damien to return, to share some discovery or even just to warm his hands by the fire. He did not. She imagined him bent over his notebook, pen moving in those neat, restrained strokes she had come to know.

The distance between them was not space—it was choice.

She bent again to her journal, and the words came slower now, tangled. She wrote: *Storm isolates. Damien in back. I at desk. We work as if in separate houses. Silence between us heavier than snow.*

She laid the pen down, throat tight.

SLEEP CAME in fits when she finally stretched out on the sofa, fire still burning low. The storm pressed itself into her dreams.

She was walking down an aisle carved of snow, lined with bells. Each bell swung without sound, their bronze mouths open in mute witness. At the end of the aisle stood a figure veiled in frost—a woman in a gown stitched with tiny silver bells that chimed without music as she moved.

Marley's heart raced. She stepped closer, certain it was Amelia. But when the bride reached the altar, the space where the groom should have stood was empty.

The silence rang louder than any toll.

Marley reached out, but the woman dissolved into snow, and Marley was left standing alone in a gown not her own, the bells sewn into her hem weighing her down.

She woke with a cry muffled in her throat, the fire still glowing, the storm still howling. The silence in the shop had not changed.

DAMIEN DID NOT STIR from the back room until morning. When he emerged, his eyes were shadowed, his hair tousled from leaning on his hand too long. He held his notebook against his chest, closed.

"You slept on the sofa," he said softly.

"I dreamed of her," Marley whispered.

He nodded, as though he had expected no other answer.

Neither reached for the other. The storm had done its work: they were snowbound not only by weather but by choice, each waiting for the other to cross the silence.

Marley pressed her journal shut. Damien kept his notebook closed.

And the Winter Bell, outside, remained mute—its silence now the crucible in which both their hearts were being tested.

THE STORM DID NOT relent by morning. Snow piled high against the door, sealing the shop like a tomb. The lamps burned longer than usual, their light a golden defiance against the grey. The silence of the bell pressed through the walls as if the storm itself were its accomplice.

Marley sat at the desk, her journal open to the dream she had scribbled down at dawn. Her handwriting was jagged, uneven—more the scrawl of a witness than a writer.

Aisle of snow. Bells swinging without sound. Bride in gown of silver bells. Groom absent. I stood alone at altar.

She traced the words with her finger, shivering. The image of the bride lingered: the way the bells had chimed without sound, the way her steps had seemed certain until they ended in absence.

Marley leaned back, closing her eyes. "Is this how Amelia felt?" she whispered. "Or is this how I will feel if Damien goes?"

The fire crackled, but no answer came.

IN THE BACK ROOM, Damien hunched over his notebook. His pen scratched steadily, though his hand trembled at times. He wrote not for history now, but for himself.

Brookwood holds me like a clasp too tight to open. Every discovery pulls me deeper, but each silence also reminds me I do not belong fully. I am keeper, but not of this lineage. Marley belongs. I borrow.

He paused, staring at the ink. Outside, the wind whistled against the shutters like a flute off-key.

He dipped the pen again.

If I stay, I become bound to her vow, bound to a silence not of my making. If I leave, I risk breaking what has only begun between us. But what is worse: to abandon her as Elijah abandoned Amelia, or to remain half-true to myself, resenting the cage of place?

His breath caught at the last line. He crossed it out violently, as if ashamed of the thought, then pressed his palm against the page to smear the ink.

MARLEY LEFT her journal and walked to the back room, drawn by the faint rhythm of his writing. She paused at the threshold, watching him bent over his notebook. His shoulders were tight, his head bowed, his pen moving as though wrestling with words too heavy to be spoken aloud.

She did not interrupt. She turned instead, returning to the fire. But the image of him hunched over his notebook burned behind her eyes.

She picked up the music box from the mantel and wound it once. The waltz filled the room, faltering on the third beat as always. Step, step—wait. The melody seemed almost mocking in its steadiness compared to the storm outside, compared to the uncertainty within her chest.

The tune drew Damien from the back room at last. He stood in the doorway, his notebook still in hand, his face shadowed.

"You dreamed again," he said quietly.

Marley nodded, still holding the music box. "A bride walked down the aisle. Bells in her gown. But when she reached the altar, there was no one waiting."

His expression flickered, almost a wince. "And you think it was Amelia."

Marley shook her head. "I think it was me."

The waltz stumbled on its refrain, then ended in silence. The storm filled the pause, snow hurling itself against the walls.

Damien crossed to the fire, staring into its flames. He

opened his notebook briefly, then shut it again before she could glimpse the words.

"What are you writing?" she asked softly.

He hesitated, then shook his head. "Nothing ready to be spoken."

Marley's chest tightened. "Then promise me you won't let silence decide for you. If you're thinking of leaving, say it. Don't let me stand at an altar of snow waiting for someone who never comes."

His jaw tightened, but he said nothing. He closed the notebook and set it on the mantel, as though even its weight was too much to hold.

MARLEY RETURNED to her journal after he left the room again. She dipped her pen and wrote with trembling hand: *Dream warns me. Altar empty. Damien withdrawn. Silence is not only in the bell—it is in us. The vow cannot be fulfilled if we repeat what Elijah did. Better a painful truth than an absent one.*

The ink blurred slightly as a tear fell onto the page.

She closed the journal, pressed her palm against the cover, and whispered aloud: "Don't make me Amelia."

The fire cracked, the storm raged, the bell tower loomed unseen but present.

And somewhere in the back room, Damien bent again over his notebook, writing words he could not yet bear to speak.

THE SECOND NIGHT of the storm arrived heavier than the first. Snow pressed against the windows, sealing the book-shop into its own world. The air felt dense, the kind of stillness that swallowed even the sound of firewood splitting in the hearth.

Marley sat at the front desk, staring at the darkened street through the frost on the glass. She felt as though the storm had taken up residence inside her, muffling her thoughts, slowing her pulse to the rhythm of the muted waltz that would not leave her chest. The aisle from her dream stretched before her still: bells swinging without sound, the altar waiting empty.

Behind her, Damien lingered in the back room again. She heard the steady scratch of his pen, the faint sigh each time he paused. The sound of his writing felt like distance embodied. He was here, yet already beyond.

She whispered to the windowpane, "This storm is us."

DAMIEN'S JOURNAL filled page after page that night. His hand cramped, but he refused to stop.

I write because speaking feels impossible. Marley deserves truth spoken, not written, yet my mouth betrays me each time I try. The bell has judged this town for its silence. Am I to be judged the same way?

He closed his eyes, pressing fingers to his brow. The storm's roar felt like an echo of his own confusion.

He dipped the pen again.

To stay is to bind myself to one place, one vow, one woman whose courage humbles me. To leave is to risk losing her, but to gain the archives that have called me since before I knew her. Both choices are devotion. Both choices are betrayal.

The ink bled at the word *betrayal*. He underlined it, once, then twice, as if forcing the page to absorb his torment.

What is a vow worth if it asks you to sever a part of yourself?

What is a calling worth if it demands you stand at an empty altar?

He slammed the notebook shut, chest heaving. Silence rushed in, louder than the storm.

MARLEY HEARD the thud and rose from the desk. She crossed to the back room, pausing in the doorway. Damien sat at the table, his notebook closed, his hands braced on either side as if holding the world steady.

She stepped forward. "Damien."

He looked up, and the shadows in his eyes told her more than words ever had.

"I dreamed again," she said. "The bride walked the aisle, but the altar was empty. It felt less like Amelia and more like me."

He flinched.

Marley drew closer. "I can't walk that aisle in silence, Damien. If you're going, say it. If you're staying, vow it. But don't leave me waiting for a bell that won't ring."

He shut his eyes briefly, then opened them. "I don't know how to choose. If I stay, I betray part of myself. If I go, I betray you."

Her throat tightened. "Then betray neither. Speak. Share the choice with me. Don't carry it alone as Elijah did."

The storm rattled the shutters. The fire snapped. The silence between them deepened until it felt like another presence in the room.

Damien rose, walked to the mantel, and picked up the music box. He wound it once, set it down, and let the waltz falter through the air. Step, step—wait. Step, step—wait.

He turned to her, voice raw. "This pause—it's what I am.

Always yielding, always delaying. I am afraid that if I vow to stay, I'll resent it. Afraid that if I vow to go, I'll lose you."

Marley crossed to him, placing her hand over the music box. The melody stuttered and died. "The pause is not absence. It's instruction. You don't have to choose silence. You only have to choose truth."

Damien's jaw tightened. "And my truth is divided."

Marley's hand trembled against the box. "Then let us vow not perfection, but devotion. If you go, you go with my blessing. If you stay, you stay with my trust. But I will not stand at an empty altar. I will not repeat Amelia's fate."

His breath caught. For a moment, neither moved. The hush of the Winter Bell pressed around them, vibrating like judgment.

Then Damien reached for her hand. His grip was strong, almost desperate. "Then vow this with me—no matter what paths call us, we do not walk away in silence. We speak. We remain bound by truth."

Marley swallowed hard, tears burning her eyes. "Yes. I vow it."

The storm howled louder, as if protesting their audacity. But the silence within the shop shifted, no longer crushing but clarifying.

The bell still refused to ring. Yet both knew they could no longer postpone the choice. The crucible had closed around them.

10

———

THE MISSING MARRIAGE RECORD

When the storm finally relented, Brookwood looked like a town erased and redrawn by a steadier hand. Plows carved narrow canyons through the drifts, leaving the square ringed with walls of white. The bell tower stood rimed in frost, its mouth dark, its silence somehow sharper in the sudden stillness.

Marley and Damien set out at first light, boots biting into snow that squeaked like old floorboards. They said little. Two nights of confinement had left their words careful, their devotion spoken—and yet the choice between paths still waiting like a sealed envelope. Work, for now, was the safer language.

"Registry first," Marley said, breath fogging the air. "Then the Colvin house."

Damien nodded. "If the town clerk's books survived the storm, they've survived everything."

The municipal building smelled of damp wool and furnace heat. Mr. Pollard—who had kept the records since men wore bowler hats to council meetings—met them at the counter with a towel around his neck and a pencil behind one ear. He blinked at their snow-stiff coats as if they were two figures stepped out of a woodcut.

"Storm didn't blow you off your questions, then," he said.

"Nothing does," Marley returned gently. "We need the marriage index for 1936. Winter quarter."

He eyed Damien, then Marley, then the bell tower visible through the high windows. "We lighting candles this morning or papers?"

"Papers," Damien said.

Fenley led them past a glass case of ceremonial gavels to the back room where ledgers slept in ranks—hand-stitched spines, leather worn soft. He lifted the volume labeled *Marriages, 1930–1939* and its thinner companion, *Certificates Filed.* The book creaked as he opened it, as if reluctant to winter again through old entries.

"Here's your December," he said, sliding the ledger under the green-shaded lamp.

Names marched in careful script: couples wed in kitchens and parlors and the little white church by the mill —names that echoed across generations in the café tally and the old cemetery's stones.

And then a gap.

Not a torn-out page—no violence. A space deliberately left blank between *Harrigan & Reed* and *Jansen & Pike,* its line ruled, its date noted—**Dec. 21**—and nothing written upon it.

Marley felt the breath catch in her chest. "They reserved a line," she whispered. "And never filled it."

Fenley frowned, leaning closer. "Odd. The clerk then was meticulous. He'd have inked the bride and groom even if the ceremony failed—*annulled, voided, refused.* He didn't."

Damien touched the blank with one gloved fingertip, as

if it could bruise. "Because to write *refused* is to confess. So they left a silence."

Fenley grunted. "If you want the companion ledger—filed certificates—" He had it open before Marley asked, flipping with the quickness of a man who loved order. December's tabs fanned past. No Colvin. No Callahan. Nothing.

"The certificate was never filed," Marley said, voice steady only because she had practiced steady her whole life. "They invited the town, reserved the clerk, prepared the ribbons—and never returned to make it legal."

Damien's eyes met hers. *Abandonment,* they named, without speaking it.

Fenley recapped his pencil with a weary sort of kindness. "There's your fact. Whatever else you make of it—that's between you and your bell."

When they stepped back into the square, light poured thin and bright across the drifts. The town was already stirring under its weight—shovels, laughter forced into bravery, the soft complaints of horses pulling sledges. Marley thought of that empty line, its ruled space carrying more accusation than any word would have.

"Invitations," she said. "If there was a blank, there were invitations."

Damien nodded toward the far end of the square, to the dark windows of the Colvin estate. "Let's see if they kept the guest list they pretended never existed."

—

The Colvin house had shed most of its snow but none of its distance. Inside, the air tasted of disuse and lavender left too long with its lid off. Their breath smoked in the halls despite the weak radiators. Marley moved as she always did in rooms that remembered too much—hands open, gaze attentive, listening to the way a floorboard changed its tone when you stepped on truth.

They began in the front parlor and worked outward. Drawers yielded ribbons, neat as regret. A sideboard produced a stack of folded napkins—white-on-white embroidery of bells no one dared to ring. In the library, a narrow secretary waited against the wall, its inlaid bell-flower marquetry catching the winter light.

Marley pressed the small brass button that released the hidden writing surface. Pigeonholes opened like tiny stages. Three were filled with envelopes edged in gilded frost.

Damien drew one out and tilted it to the window. Letterpress caught the light: **Amelia Colvin & Elijah Callahan**; beneath, in smaller hand, **December Twenty-First, Nineteen Thirty-Six — Brookwood**. The script wore the modesty of the era and the pride of two families sure they were binding more than two names.

"Invitations," Marley said, throat tight. "Some never sent."

Damien slid a finger under one unsealed flap. Inside, heavy card promised vows before the Winter Bell's blessing and a supper after. The RSVP card had been addressed to a post office box that now held only dust.

He set the card down as carefully as if it could bleed. "They planned every inch."

Marley reached into the paneled niche again and touched the back of the pigeonhole. It gave under her fingers—just a breath. "Help me," she said. Together they lifted the thin panel free. A shallow compartment ran the width of the desk. Within lay a bundle wrapped in rose-colored tissue, tied with faded crimson thread.

She carried it to the writing surface and untied it. The tissue unfolded like a blush being confessed.

Inside: a *seal*—a signet and its wax siblings. A small brass stamp with a carved face; half a dozen red wafers impressed and kept as proofs; a stick of sealing wax the color of fresh blood. The stamp's face bore a circlet of braided line enclosing a figure like a star with seven uneven rays, each ray pricked once near its tip—as if marked for counting.

Marley stared. She had seen that emblem once before, drawn in the margins of a charter fragment dusted out of stone in late summer, Book Three's bitter gift. She heard Damien's breath change at her side.

"The Circle of Seven," he murmured, voice gone low. "Or the sigil claimed by those who called themselves that."

He lifted the signet with a cloth between his fingers, unwilling to grease its history with his prints. "Look— there's a nick here on the lower right of the ring. The same flaw we noted on the wax impression beside the Callahan name in the Charter Fragment."

"You're certain?" Marley asked, though she already felt the certainty like a weight added to the scale.

He nodded, the scholar rising up in him in reflex. "On the fragment, the Circle's seal sat beside seven surnames in a ring—the founding families that partitioned power during lean years. One ray on the star aligned to each, if you believe in symbols behaving themselves. The nick on the ring left a tiny crescent bite in the wax—here." He held one of the preserved wafers to the light. A small crescent marred the braided border. "Same bite. Same family line, same seal."

Marley touched one of the pressed wafers with her glove. It had sealed something once—maybe an inner envelope, maybe instructions. Maybe permission granted or withheld.

"The Circle touched this wedding," she said. "Not rumor. Imprint."

Damien set the signet down carefully and drew his notebook closer, sketching the device with sure strokes. "If the Circle put its mark on the invitations—or on whatever these proofs sealed—then it presumed authority. Over a solstice union. Over the bell."

"Which the bell refused," Marley said.

He glanced toward the window, toward the tower beyond the hedges. "Because sanctity cannot be stamped."

Marley returned to the compartment and felt along its edges. Her fingers struck a thin packet tucked tight against the back—a sheaf wrapped in oilskin. She worked it loose, and they unfolded it together.

Inside lay *lists*—names arranged in two columns, with annotations in a woman's fine hand: *accepted*, *declined*, *no reply*. A third sheet bore arrangements for the church, for flowers, for the order of procession—*bell to bless—seven chimes*—underlined twice.

At the bottom of the page, in smaller script, a note: *Signet returned via Mr. E.C. per request. Seal to remain with Callahan until charter ratified anew.* Beside it, a small, hurried sketch of the seven-rayed star.

Marley felt heat rise beneath her coat despite the cold room. "Returned. As if it had been borrowed to legitimize the invitation."

"Or to coerce it," Damien said. "A seal gives a paper the weight of law. The Circle—or those in its shadow—could have made this marriage look like policy, not love."

Marley saw the scene as if the house itself projected the memory against its pale walls: men in wool coats and careful voices; a ring of red wax cooling on a letter the bride did not write; an emblem pressed to say *inevitable*.

"But the bell is no clerk," she said.

"It declined to file," Damien answered, tapping the empty space in the memory of the ledger.

They sat with it—wax cooling on a desk eighty years emptied of hands, a signet's face still cold after generations, an invitation scripted for a vow winter would not endorse.

"It's the same family line," Damien said at last, more to himself than to her. "Callahan—confirmed on the fragment. The nick in the ring betrays the seal's path. The Circle's authority ran through those seven names like wiring through an old house. If they meant to shore up their alliance with a wedding, it makes sense they'd stamp it."

"And makes sense the bell refused," Marley said. "Because a vow pressed into place by a circle of men is not a vow."

She returned the wafers to their rose tissue and folded it closed with a tenderness she did not feel for what they represented. The signet she left on the desk, face up, as if inviting the winter light to judge it.

"Let's photograph everything," Damien said. "We'll compare this impression to the rubbing we took from the Charter Fragment." His voice had steadied into the mode that had always given her comfort—the one that could read a mystery like a blueprint. "If we can prove chain of custody—the seal used here is the same used to ratify the founding compact—then we can tie Amelia's night not just to two families, but to the town's quietest government."

Marley looked from the star's seven pricked rays to the neat rows of names, to the circled number *seven* beside *chimes*. "Seven chimes for a union. Seven hands on the seal. Seven families in the ring. And none of it legal without the bell."

"Which never spoke," Damien said gently.

Marley took one of the unsent invitations and slid it into a sleeve from her satchel. "We'll return everything after we copy it," she said, aware of how often she had said some version of that sentence in the last months. "But the world needs to see what Brookwood hid."

She slipped the envelope into place, the gilt names catching briefly—**Amelia Colvin & Elijah Callahan**—before she covered them again.

Outside, a soft fall of snow began, as if the storm had decided to revise its ending. Marley lifted the signet one last time and pressed its cold face against her palm until the star's points pricked through the leather of her glove.

"Amelia," she said under her breath, a vow disguised as address, "we've found the circle that tried to write you into its ring. The bell remembered what they forgot."

Damien's shoulder brushed hers. "And we'll write it where no one can erase it."

They closed the secretary, the tiny latch catching. The room felt different—not warmer, exactly, but more honest. Evidence had a way of raising the temperature even in winter.

On the walk back to the square, Marley held the invitation close to her chest, the same way she had held Elijah's journal, the same way she held the music box some nights when the waltz finished and the silence asked to begin again. The tower's shadow cut across the snow in a clean line. She stepped over it as if crossing a threshold.

Behind them, in the quiet house, a small brass signet lay face up, its seven-pointed truth cooling slowly in the cold.

THE SNOW HAD TAPERED by the time Marley and Damien reached the bookshop, but the sky hung heavy, as though the storm had only paused to draw breath. They shook the frost from their coats, then laid their findings across the oak table: the invitation, the wafered proofs, Marley's sleeve now holding a slip of paper history had tried to forget.

For a long moment they simply stared at the objects. Each one seemed to hum with its own silence—the blank marriage ledger, the seal's red echo, the family names aligned in a circle of authority.

Marley ran her fingers lightly over the invitation. "So much effort," she whispered. "All the details, all the polish. A ceremony scripted to please the eye. And yet beneath it, a seal to enforce obedience. This was never about vows—it was about power."

Damien's jaw tightened as he spread his sketches beside the wax wafers. He angled the lamplight across them, examining the crescent flaw on each impression. "The nick in the ring is the signature, unintentional but undeniable. Whoever wielded this seal had the same authority as the hand that signed the Charter Fragment. Which means Amelia's wedding was tangled in the same net that bound the town's founding."

Marley's throat tightened. "The Circle tried to marry her not to a man, but to an alliance."

Damien looked up, his eyes shadowed. "And the bell refused. Not because it doubted her vow, but because it recognized the counterfeit nature of the authority behind it."

The silence in the room felt heavier for the truth spoken aloud.

By afternoon, Marley carried the invitation to the archive, tucked close against her ribs. She and Damien set up in the quiet corner where the fire never quite reached, the ledgers breathing dust around them.

Damien laid out the Charter Fragment rubbing they had kept safe since summer. Its edges were brittle, its ink faint, but the sigil was unmistakable: the seven-rayed star, the same crescent bite along the braided border. He placed the wafered proof beside it, tilting both under the lantern.

"They're identical," he said with quiet certainty. "The seal at Amelia's wedding is the same one pressed onto the founding compact. The Circle of Seven carried its signet across decades, stamping both beginnings and betrayals."

Marley bent close, studying the way the rays fanned from the center. Each was marked with a pricked dot, as if counting. She thought of the list of names, the way each family claimed a ray.

"Seven families," she murmured. "Seven hands on the seal. Seven rays. And when Amelia's marriage was arranged, they meant to keep the circle unbroken by stamping her name into it."

Damien exhaled. "And yet the bell broke it for them."

The phrase struck Marley with force. She turned toward him, eyes widening. "The bell broke it. That's what the silence means. Not absence. Refusal. Defiance."

Her pulse thudded in her ears as she wrote quickly in her journal: *The silence was not failure—it was verdict. The bell broke the circle's attempt to claim Amelia.*

Damien's gaze softened as he watched her. "Marley, you may be closer to the truth than anyone has dared name."

She pressed the nib to the page, her hand trembling. "Which means this isn't just a love story lost. It's political. It's spiritual. It's the town's soul refusing its own corruption."

The fire cracked in the hearth as though in assent.

. . .

EVENING FELL with a hush so dense it seemed to mute the lantern flames. Marley and Damien worked side by side, transcribing the names from the guest lists, noting which bore the margin word *accepted* and which carried *declined*.

"This one," Marley said, tapping a surname written in flowing hand. "Declined. That's one of the Circle families."

Damien leaned in. "Which means dissent within the ring. Not all seven agreed."

Marley looked up sharply. "So the silence wasn't only between bell and bride—it was within the Circle itself. A fracture."

Damien's mouth curved grimly. "And fractures spread."

They sat back, the weight of revelation pressing on them. Outside, snow slid from the roof in a heavy sheet, startling in the quiet.

Marley closed her journal slowly. "We have enough evidence to name it now. Amelia's marriage was never meant to be only hers. It was a contract drafted by a circle of families to preserve their grip. But the bell rejected their claim. And when Elijah left, it wasn't merely fear of vows—it was fear of the seal's weight."

Damien studied her, his eyes shadowed by lamplight. "You're right. And if we publish this—if you publish this— Brookwood will never be able to pretend again."

She met his gaze, her chest tight with both fear and resolve. "Then let it be so. Let truth be louder than silence."

The music box rested on the shelf nearby. Marley rose, wound it once, and let its halting waltz spill into the room. Step, step—wait. Each pause carried new resonance now.

"The wait isn't emptiness," she whispered. "It's judgment. The bell broke their circle. And it left the pause as a space for us to answer."

Damien's hand brushed hers briefly as the music

faltered and ended. "Then we must decide what to place in that pause."

They stood together in the dim light, the invitation between them, the seal's star glinting faintly like a witness.

The Winter Bell had not rung in decades. But in its silence, Marley and Damien heard the truth clear as bronze: the vow they carried now was not only Amelia's, but the town's refusal to be stamped into silence again.

THE LAMPLIGHT BURNED LOW, stretching shadows across the oak table where their discoveries lay. The invitation glimmered faintly, the gilt letters catching light like trapped embers. The wax wafers gleamed blood-red in the glow. And between them all sat the brass signet—its seven-rayed star accusing, silent, undeniable.

Marley stood at the window, arms folded, staring out at the bell tower that loomed in the night. Its shadow cut across the square, sharp as judgment. The silence pressed harder than the snow had during the storm, demanding not endurance now but response.

She turned back to Damien. "If we tell the town, we break something that has stood since its founding. Families that still hold sway—Callahans, Sanborns, Whitcombs— names stamped on businesses, on deeds, on council seats. The Circle may not meet anymore, but its line runs through everything."

Damien tapped the wafer with his pen, the crescent nick glinting. "And if we don't, we repeat their lie. We let Amelia remain a shadow, her silence mistaken for compliance. That ledger line stays blank. That invitation stays unsent. And the bell keeps tolling nothing."

Marley's hands clenched. "It isn't only her story. It's our

story now. Every candle we light, every vigil we keep, every step of the waltz we dance—if we leave this hidden, we're complicit."

Damien leaned back, exhaling. His scholar's mind weighed consequence as naturally as breath. "Exposing the Circle means naming families. Descendants who never chose the seal but inherited its silence. Some will call it slander. Some will call it treason against the town itself. And you—you'll be the one they aim at, Marley. Not me. The memoir is your contract."

Her throat tightened. "Then let them aim. Truth doesn't need protection, Damien—it needs courage."

He studied her for a long moment. "And if courage divides us?"

She met his gaze, steady despite the ache. "Then division is better than collusion."

They laid out the lists again, tracing each annotated name. Marley circled the families who bore the word *accepted* in Amelia's own hand. Damien circled the ones who declined. The pattern revealed itself like frost blooming across glass.

"Four accepted, two declined, one no reply," Damien murmured. "The Circle was already fractured."

"Which is why they pressed the seal harder," Marley said. "They needed the marriage to bind what words and signatures couldn't. But the bell saw through it. The refusal was its verdict."

Damien pressed his palms together, resting his chin on his knuckles. "If we publish this, Brookwood will have to reckon with the fact that its most cherished ritual—the solstice vigil, the bell's chimes, the candles in the window— was corrupted at its root. And yet that corruption was named in silence by the very bell itself. That is history rewritten, Marley. Not just remembered, rewritten."

She lowered herself into the chair across from him, voice soft but firm. "Then let's write it. Together. Whether the town welcomes it or not."

For the first time that evening, his expression eased. "Together," he echoed.

LATER, they carried the signet and wafers back to the Colvin secretary. They replaced them in the hidden compartment, tissue folded, latch clicked shut. Marley lingered, her hand resting on the carved inlay of bellflowers.

She whispered, "Amelia, we saw what they tried to write over you. We vow to finish what the bell began."

As they left, Damien paused in the doorway, looking back at the desk. "Seals can bind paper," he murmured, "but bells bind memory. And memory will always outlast ink."

The house groaned faintly, as if agreeing.

BACK IN THE BOOKSHOP, the air felt different—charged, as though the silence had shifted into anticipation. Marley drew her journal close, dipped her pen, and wrote with deliberate hand:

Amelia's marriage certificate was never filed. The invitation bore the Circle's sigil. The seal matches the Charter Fragment. The Circle interfered, pressed its authority onto vows it did not own. The bell refused. Our task now: to carry that refusal into light.

She underlined the last sentence twice, then pushed the journal toward Damien. He read it silently, then took her pen and added beneath:

We vow to name what silence hid. We vow to risk division rather than repeat collusion. We vow to let the bell's refusal become Brookwood's reckoning.

He signed his initials. She added hers.

The hush deepened around them, no longer accusation but witness.

THAT NIGHT, Marley dreamed again of the aisle lined with bells. But this time, when the bride reached the altar, she was not alone. Damien stood beside her, notebook in one hand, a candle in the other. And behind them, townsfolk emerged from shadows, some hesitant, some bold, carrying flames of their own.

The bells swung silently overhead. But in the pause, Marley understood: the silence itself had become their charge. To carry what the bell refused to speak. To risk what the Circle feared. To light what Amelia had been denied.

She woke with tears on her cheeks, and a strange calm. The storm was gone. The town lay under snow. And a choice lay before them that could no longer be postponed.

Marley turned to Damien, who sat at the desk, his notebook open, his pen steady. He looked up, meeting her gaze.

"No more waiting," he said.

"No more," she agreed.

The Winter Bell did not ring. But its silence had spoken, and they had vowed to answer.

11

THE FORGOTTEN BRIDE

The storm had finally broken, leaving Brookwood under a glassy, unnatural stillness. Snow shone like powdered silver across the square, and the bell tower loomed sharper for the clarity of the air. Marley, restless after days of confinement, turned her attention to the one place that had always given her both comfort and disquiet—the shop's archives.

The back storeroom smelled of dust and cedar. Shelves bowed beneath the weight of decades: town ledgers, private journals, forgotten photographs tucked into brittle sleeves. Marley had inventoried much of it since inheriting the shop, yet she knew there were corners she hadn't dared to disturb. This morning, something urged her deeper.

She lit a lamp and carried it past the first row of cabinets to the narrower set of drawers, ones her aunt had always kept locked until her final winter. Marley pulled the brass handle, heart tapping an anxious rhythm. Inside, an assortment of loose photographs slid forward, sepia-toned and stiff with age.

She leafed carefully through portraits of families long

gone, parades frozen in blur, children holding sparklers that looked like captured lightning. Then her breath caught.

A single image lay apart from the rest, heavier somehow.

A woman stood in the snow, veil trailing against the whiteness, her figure poised yet unmistakably alone. The church rose behind her—the old Brookwood chapel, its steeple sharp against the winter sky. A handwritten caption in fading ink marked the lower margin: **A.C. – 1936.**

Marley's pulse hammered.

She lowered herself onto the stool, the photograph trembling between her hands. The veil obscured much of the woman's face, but her posture carried both resolve and sorrow. The snow around her was unmarred, as if she had stood there alone for a long time, waiting for someone who never came.

Amelia Colvin.

The year of the empty ledger. The season of the unsent invitations. The day the bell refused to ring.

Marley leaned closer, tracing the faint outline of the chapel's door. Her aunt had told her once that the chapel had been shuttered in the forties, too drafty to heat, too costly to maintain. It now sat abandoned at the edge of town, its windows broken, its pews warped by time.

But in 1936, it had been ready. Decorated, perhaps. Waiting.

And Amelia had stood there, veiled, alone.

Marley pressed the photograph flat on the desk, her breath shallow. "Did you ever leave?" she whispered. "Or are you still there, waiting for the altar to fill?"

The hush of the shop seemed to listen.

· · ·

Damien found her still at the desk an hour later, the lamp burning low. He bent beside her, peering at the photograph.

"A.C.," he murmured. "Amelia Colvin. 1936."

"Yes." Marley's voice was tight. "This isn't rumor. This isn't a ledger line left blank. This is her—standing on the day she was meant to marry."

He studied the image, his scholar's eye sharp. "The chapel in the background. Look at the snowline. Heavy drift at the eaves. Midwinter."

Marley nodded. "The very season the bell fell silent."

For a long time, they simply stared. The woman in the photograph seemed to stare back, her veiled presence demanding not pity but recognition.

Damien straightened, exhaling. "This changes everything. It's not only absence—it's evidence. She went through with the procession, at least in part. She dressed. She arrived. And then—nothing."

Marley's chest tightened. "Which means she stood in that silence, Damien. Stood before the chapel door, waiting for vows that never came. Did she walk away? Did someone escort her home? Or did the snow itself bury her vow where it stood?"

The silence between them deepened, heavy as the snow in the photograph.

Marley returned the photograph to its sleeve but could not bring herself to file it away. She carried it upstairs and set it on her nightstand, as if the veiled woman deserved vigil. That night she dreamed again of the aisle lined with bells, only this time she recognized the chapel's dark wooden pews, the frosted windows. The bride stood alone at the altar, her veil stirring though there was no wind.

When Marley stepped forward to join her, the woman turned her head slightly, and through the veil Marley glimpsed her own reflection.

She woke with her pulse racing, the photograph gleaming faintly in the moonlight.

By morning she knew she would have to visit the chapel.

Damien did not argue when she told him. He only gathered his coat, notebook, and lantern. "If she stood there once," he said, "we must stand there too. To see what she saw. To ask what the bell withheld."

The square was silent as they left, the townsfolk still digging paths through snow. The photograph rested against Marley's ribs in her satchel, its presence like a heartbeat.

The road to the chapel wound past bare orchards and silent fields. Snow lay deep across the stones, muffling their steps. The chapel appeared slowly, its steeple rising stark against the grey sky. Up close, it was more ruin than refuge —boards splintered, glass gone, ivy frozen against its walls.

But Marley felt the photograph pressing harder against her side, as though urging recognition.

She whispered, "You were here."

The silence seemed to shift, as if acknowledging her words.

THEY PUSHED OPEN the warped door. It groaned but yielded. Inside, the air was sharp with mildew and time. Pews tilted, hymnals lay crumbled in heaps. The aisle stretched down the center, faint light slanting through fractured panes.

Marley stepped forward, heart thudding. She held the photograph up, aligning the image with the view before her. The angle matched. The doorframe, the steeple's shadow, even the line of drifts outside.

"This is it," she whispered. "This is where she stood."

Damien's voice was low. "And where the vow dissolved."

They moved slowly down the aisle, lantern light scattering against the broken windows. At the altar, Marley stopped. The photograph trembled in her hands.

"She was here. Veiled. Alone. Waiting." Her throat tightened. "And I can't tell if the silence drove her away or if she became part of it."

Damien set the lantern down on the altar's scarred wood. "Either way, the bell remembers. And so must we."

Marley pressed the photograph against her chest, eyes closing. "Amelia, we see you."

The hush deepened, vibrating through the rafters.

And for the first time, Marley felt not only grief but invitation—an urging to step further into the silence, to listen for what it was ready, at last, to reveal.

THE AIR inside the chapel held the chill of a place that had not known breath for decades. Each exhale from Marley and Damien rose like smoke, joining the cobweb threads stretched across rafters. Snow had forced its way through cracks in the roof, drifting against the warped pews.

Damien raised the lantern, its glow scattering shadows. The aisle stretched ahead of them like a scar down the center of the building. Marley's heart beat louder than her boots on the old floorboards. She clutched the photograph tighter, her fingers trembling against its stiff edges.

"She stood here," she whispered. "Her veil caught in the wind, her gown dragging in the snow. Waiting for someone who never came."

Damien studied the floor, crouching low. "Look. The

boards here are worn differently. Not just from age. Repetition."

Marley knelt beside him. The wood at the aisle's entrance showed deeper wear than the rest, a faint depression from countless steps paused in the same place. "Processions," she murmured. "Weddings, baptisms. And hers."

But beyond that—closer to the altar—the boards were unmarked. Clean, almost untouched, as though no bride had ever reached it.

Marley's throat tightened. "She never walked the full length. The photograph wasn't taken at the altar. It was taken just outside the door."

Damien glanced at her, understanding flickering in his eyes. "The vow halted before it began."

The thought chilled her deeper than the wind that slipped through the broken panes.

THEY MOVED SLOWLY down the aisle. Shards of colored glass crunched underfoot, remnants of stained windows that once told stories of saints and shepherds. The fragments glowed faintly in the lantern's light—reds and blues that looked more like wounds than blessings.

At the altar, Marley paused. The wooden rail was dusted with snow, the cloth covering long rotted away. But something remained—small, brittle, nearly hidden in the corner. She bent low and brushed aside dust.

A pressed flower, long desiccated, its petals flattened into paper. She lifted it carefully, heart thudding.

"A boutonniere," Damien said, leaning closer. "Winter rose. They grow even in frost if tended right. Someone dropped this here."

Marley cradled it in her palm. "Then someone reached the altar. Or nearly did."

She set the fragile flower in her journal, pressing it between blank pages as though giving it refuge at last.

THEY SEARCHED THE SACRISTY NEXT, pushing open a door warped by moisture. Inside, shelves leaned under the weight of hymnals eaten by mold. A cracked mirror hung crooked, reflecting the lantern's flame. On the small wooden counter lay a book bound in leather, its spine broken.

Damien lifted it with care. "The parish record." He opened the brittle pages, flipping past baptisms and funerals until he reached December 1936. A thin ink line marked the space reserved for a marriage. *Amelia Colvin – Elijah Callahan.* No date. No notation. Just two names abandoned mid-stroke.

"They began writing it," Damien murmured. "And then stopped."

Marley's breath caught. "As if even the priest couldn't finish the vow."

Her hands shook as she touched the page. The ink was faded but still legible, the quill's hesitation visible in the faltering line. She imagined the minister dipping the pen, preparing to witness a union, then freezing as the bell failed to ring.

The silence itself had stopped his hand.

Marley pressed the edge of the page gently. "Amelia's name written, but never sealed. Just like the certificate. Just like the ledger. Always beginning, never binding."

Her chest ached with the weight of it. "It's as if she is caught here, Damien. Trapped in beginnings that never reach endings."

. . .

THEY MOVED BACK into the main chapel, the lantern's glow growing faint against the rising dark outside. Snow began to fall again, sifting through holes in the roof like ashes.

Marley set the photograph on the altar, beside the brittle boutonniere pressed in her journal. She stood still, imagining Amelia's veil brushing against the chapel door, her breath clouding the winter air, her eyes fixed on a silence no one else dared to name.

"Did you leave?" Marley whispered. "Or are you still waiting, standing where the vow broke?"

The hush of the chapel deepened. No creak of rafters, no whistle of wind—just stillness, dense and absolute. For a moment Marley felt as though the photograph had opened a door between then and now, and that the veiled figure might step through at any moment.

Her knees weakened. She gripped the altar rail, her voice trembling. "I feel her here. Not memory—presence."

Damien stepped beside her, his hand steadying her arm. His face was grave, but not mocking. "The bell's silence has left echoes. Perhaps this is one of them."

Marley closed her eyes, pressing her forehead to the altar's cold wood. "I don't know if she ever left this place. I don't know if her vow walked away—or if it froze here, waiting for us to carry it forward."

She lifted her head, eyes burning. "But I can't leave her here alone."

Damien placed the lantern on the altar, its glow spilling over the photograph. "Then we won't. We'll keep her presence with us. And when the town finally listens, we'll make sure she is not forgotten."

Marley exhaled, tears warming her cheeks despite the cold.

The veil in the photograph seemed to stir, though no wind touched it.

And in that moment, Marley knew: Amelia's vow had never left the chapel. It remained, waiting, not undone but unfulfilled.

The Winter Bell had refused the Circle's seal, but it had not refused Amelia. It had simply left her vow suspended, aching for witnesses who would one day return to finish what silence had begun.

The snow thickened as Marley and Damien stepped back out of the chapel. The old door groaned shut behind them, muffling the lantern's glow still flickering inside. Marley paused on the steps, the photograph pressed against her ribs as if she carried not paper but the fragile weight of a life suspended.

The wind swept across the field, lifting fine powder that stung her cheeks. She tightened her scarf and looked back at the chapel's steeple, black against the pale sky. "She's still there," she said softly.

Damien adjusted his pack, his breath clouding the air. "You mean the photograph, or the vow?"

"Both." Marley's voice trembled. "The veil in the picture, the half-written name in the parish record, the boutonniere at the altar—it all says the same thing. Amelia never left. She's still standing at that threshold."

They walked slowly down the buried path, boots crunching through the drifts. The silence of the place clung to them like a second shadow. Marley could not shake the sensation that Amelia's presence trailed them, her veil stirring faintly in a wind neither of them could feel.

AT THE EDGE of the field, Damien stopped. He brushed the snow from a fallen fence rail and leaned against it, watching Marley. His expression was grave but tender.

"You're carrying her heavy," he said. "Heavier than most would dare."

Marley hugged the photograph closer. "Because I can't bear the thought of her waiting there forever. If we walk away as though nothing happened, we become part of the silence. Part of the Circle that left her vow unfulfilled."

Damien nodded slowly. "And if we carry her, we bind ourselves to her unfinished vow."

Marley's gaze held his. "Then bind me."

The words startled even her, but once spoken they felt truer than anything she had written in her journal. She exhaled, steadying herself. "I don't mean marriage vows, not yet, not even us. I mean the vow to stand with her. To not let her stand in the snow alone. If the bell refused the seal, then it left her waiting for witnesses. For us."

Damien's eyes softened, the scholar's steel in him yielding to something older, deeper. "Then we vow." He reached out his hand, palm open against the falling snow.

Marley set the photograph in her satchel and placed her hand in his. Their gloves muted the warmth, but the grip carried its own gravity.

He spoke first, his voice steady: "We vow not to leave her where she was left."

Marley continued, her throat tight: "We vow to carry her truth forward, even if the town resists, even if it divides us."

Together, they whispered the final words: "We vow she will not stand alone."

The snow seemed to pause in its fall, flakes hovering a heartbeat longer before settling. The silence deepened around them, not accusatory now but almost approving, as if the Winter Bell itself had bent closer to listen.

THEY WALKED BACK toward town as dusk fell. The road was lined with trees, their branches heavy with snow, bending low as if in witness. Marley's mind replayed the image again and again—the veiled woman outside the chapel door, waiting. Each time she saw her, Marley whispered silently: *Not alone. Not anymore.*

When the square came into view, candles already glowed in the windows of the houses. The vigil carried on, as it always did, but tonight Marley saw it differently. Every flame felt like a fragile defiance against silence. Every flicker echoed Amelia's unanswered vow.

At the shop, Marley hung her coat and laid the photograph on the oak table. Damien set the journal beside it, opening to the page where the pressed boutonniere lay cradled. For a long time they simply stood, studying the objects as though arranging an altar of their own.

"This is where we begin," Marley said quietly. "Not in whispers. Not in shadows. But here, with what we've found."

Damien nodded. "We'll need proof enough to withstand anger. Names, documents, testimonies. But this photograph... it's already more than rumor. It's witness."

Marley traced the edge of the image. "Her veil. Her stance. The snow untouched around her. She's telling us something."

"Or asking," Damien said.

Marley looked up, her eyes bright with tears. "Then we'll answer. Together."

THAT NIGHT, after Damien had gone home, Marley sat alone in the bookshop. The lamps cast a soft glow over the table where the photograph lay. She lit a single candle beside it, the flame trembling.

She whispered aloud, "Amelia, you're not forgotten. Your vow is not lost. We carry it now."

The silence of the shop deepened, wrapping her like a cloak. The flame flared briefly, bright as a toll.

Marley closed her eyes, hearing the bell not in sound but in stillness.

And she understood: the bell's silence was not a void. It was a space waiting to be filled by courage.

12

PRINT SHOP CONFESSION

The next morning, Brookwood's square was alive with the sound of shovels striking packed snow and the murmur of neighbors calling greetings through scarves. Yet beneath the everyday rhythm, Marley felt the undercurrent of the vow she and Damien had made at the chapel. Each face she passed seemed touched by a secret it refused to name, each candle in a window a fragile echo of Amelia's silence.

Her path carried her to the small brick building on the corner—the town's print shop. The scent of ink and paper wafted out as she opened the door, familiar and sharp. The shop had been in the Kinney family for three generations, its presses churning out everything from grocery flyers to solstice programs. Inside, Tessa Kinney leaned over the hand press, wiping ink from her fingers.

"Hi Marley" she said, glancing up with kindness. "What brings the Keeper to my door this early?"

Marley hesitated, then laid the sepia photograph on the counter between them. The veiled woman in the snow stared up from the paper. Tessa's face blanched.

"I've been searching," Marley said softly. "For the truth about Amelia Colvin. I believe you know something."

For a long moment, Tessa's gaze lingered on the photo. Her hands trembled slightly as she set the cloth down. "There are things we were told to let fade," she said at last. "But the trouble with ink is that it lingers, even when you blot the page."

She gestured toward the back room. "Come. If you're asking, you'd better hear it all."

THE BACK ROOM smelled of oil and damp paper. Stacks of old broadsheets leaned against the walls, their edges curled and browned. Tessa introduced Marley to John Kinney, Tessa's father who sat settled into a chair, his shoulders sagging as though he had carried the secret too long.

"I destroyed it," he said suddenly, voice raw.

Marley frowned. "Destroyed what?"

"An old flyer. One that should have never been printed. My grandfather ran this shop in '36, and he'd been commissioned to make up handbills for a special event. They called it *The Bell Bride Ceremony*." John rubbed his forehead. "It was meant to be Amelia's wedding announcement, dressed up as spectacle. Bells and vines, golden type. Grand, as if the whole town was invited to watch history."

Marley's chest tightened. "And you destroyed it?"

He nodded. "Years later, after my father passed. I found the stack in the archive. My grandfather had hidden them, ashamed. He said that ceremony had brought only tragedy, and he wanted no child of his carrying the ink forward. So I burned most, shredded the rest. I thought I was protecting us."

Marley's hands trembled on the edge of the table. "But you remembered."

John's eyes glistened. "Some ink stays under the skin, even when you try to scrub it out."

DAMIEN, who had lingered silent until now, leaned forward. "Why did your grandfather call it a tragedy?"

John's gaze drifted to the window, where snow still clung to the panes. "He said a message never arrived. Something vital. A note meant for the groom. It never reached him—or it was delayed, lost in the snow. By the time he came, the chapel was empty, the bell silent. And Amelia..." His voice faltered. "She never stood in the square again."

Marley felt the photograph's weight in her satchel. The veiled woman in the snow, waiting. A message lost. A vow dissolved by silence.

"A message," Damien repeated softly. "That would explain Elijah's sudden absence. Not abandonment, but interruption."

John nodded faintly. "My grandfather never forgave himself. He thought perhaps the shop had failed—that the messenger's instructions had been misprinted, or the words unclear. He carried that guilt until his last winter."

Marley whispered, "And so the flyers were destroyed. To bury the memory."

"Yes," John said, his hands knotting. "But the plate remained."

HE ROSE and crossed to a tall cabinet, unlocking the lower drawer. From within he drew a wrapped bundle, setting it gently on the table. He unfolded the cloth, revealing a flat piece of metal, heavy and dark with age. Its surface gleamed where it had been etched.

Marley leaned closer, breath catching. The design was unmistakable: a bell entwined with vines, each leaf curling delicately around the metal's edge. The words *The Bell Bride Ceremony* arched above in stylized script.

Damien's eyes sharpened. "This motif. I've seen it before." He reached into his satchel and drew out a notebook, flipping to a rubbing he had copied from the healer's ledger months earlier. The same vine curled across the margin there, framing a note about *winter vows sealed by the bell.*

He laid the rubbing beside the plate. The match was exact—the vine's curl, the bell's curve.

"This symbol isn't just decoration," Damien said, his voice low with realization. "It ties Amelia's wedding to the healer's bloodline rituals. What the town printed as ceremony may have been rooted in something older—something sacred."

Marley touched the plate with reverence, her fingers brushing the etched vines. "Amelia's vow wasn't only a union. It was meant to seal something larger. The town twisted it into spectacle, but the symbol betrays the truth."

John's shoulders sagged. "I kept the plate hidden all these years, afraid of what it carried. Afraid of what it might call back. If it belongs in your keeping now, take it. Better it live in the light than rot in my drawer."

Marley lifted the plate carefully, its cold weight anchoring her hands. The bell and vine glinted in the lantern's glow.

"Thank you," she whispered. "For not burning everything."

John closed his eyes, as if releasing a burden. "Tell her

story right, Miss Taylor. Tell it so the next generation doesn't have to carry ashes."

OUTSIDE, Marley and Damien stepped into the cold evening, the plate wrapped in cloth between them. The square's lamps flickered against the snow.

Marley looked at Damien, her breath misting. "The Bell Bride Ceremony. They turned her vow into a performance. And when it failed, they buried the memory."

Damien's jaw set. "But the bell didn't forget. And neither will we."

Marley tightened her grip on the cloth bundle. The vines etched into the metal seemed almost alive beneath her fingers, as though pulsing with the vow it had once been meant to seal.

She whispered into the falling snow, "Amelia, we hear you."

The silence answered, heavy but no longer hollow.

And in that moment, Marley knew the printing plate was not just evidence—it was invitation. Another step into the vow she and Damien had promised to carry.

BACK IN THE BOOKSHOP, Marley cleared the oak table and set the bundle down with care. She unwrapped the cloth to reveal the printing plate once more. Its etched lines gleamed faintly in the lamplight, the bell and vine motif holding a strange dignity—as though it had waited decades for hands willing to honor it.

Damien brought over his notebook and the rubbing from the healer's ledger. He laid the two side by side, angling the lamp until the shadows deepened the grooves of the plate. The resemblance was undeniable. The vines curled in identical loops, their stems bearing tiny leaves in the same clustered pattern. The bell hung at the center, framed like an icon.

"This wasn't ornamental," Damien murmured. "It's deliberate. The same hand, or the same tradition."

Marley traced the etching with her fingertip. "The ledger described vows sealed by the bell. The flyer called it *The Bell Bride Ceremony.* They appropriated a sacred rite and dressed it as spectacle."

Damien tapped his pen against the margin of his notes. "That changes the meaning entirely. It wasn't just a marriage. It was a ritual meant to bind more than two people—something between families, or even between the town and its own harmony."

Marley felt the chill deepen in her chest. "And when the bell refused to ring, it wasn't just a failed wedding. It was the refusal of a ritual pact."

They fell silent, both aware of how easily such a realization could fracture the town if spoken aloud.

MARLEY REACHED for the plate again, holding it up so the lamplight caught the faint impression of text around the edges. Her breath caught.

"There's more," she whispered. "Letters—too shallow to print unless you looked close."

Damien fetched a magnifier from his satchel. Together they bent over the plate. Around the rim of the vines, nearly invisible, tiny words curved in a circle:

"Seven hands bind, seven vows stand."

Damien exhaled sharply. "Seven. The Circle's number.

The same seal that tried to press Amelia's union into their ring."

Marley's heart raced. "So the flyer wasn't merely invitation. It was propaganda. A declaration that the Circle claimed the vow as its own."

Her hand trembled as she set the plate down. "They used the language of the sacred to mask control."

Damien's jaw tightened. "And the bell refused to play along."

THEY SPREAD OUT MORE DOCUMENTS: the rubbing from the Charter Fragment, the sketch of the Circle's signet, the guest list recovered from the Colvin house. Piece by piece, a pattern emerged. The Circle had tried to script a union that was both personal and political, weaving Amelia into their structure of power.

Marley pressed her palms flat on the table. "The healer's ledger spoke of harmony. The bell's chime as balance between bloodlines, between the living and their ancestors. But the Circle stamped over that, turned it into ceremony bound by their seal. No wonder the vow broke."

Damien leaned back, staring at the ceiling. "And what of the message that never arrived? If Elijah was meant to receive something—an instruction, a plea, a warning—its loss might explain his absence."

Marley's chest ached. "Do you think Amelia herself sent it?"

Damien's eyes met hers. "Or someone who loved her. Someone who wanted to free her from the Circle's grip."

The silence deepened, heavy with implication. A lost message. A vow halted. A bell that refused to ring.

Marley whispered, "If that message had arrived, the

photograph might not exist. She might not have stood there alone."

SHE LIFTED THE PLATE AGAIN, weighing its cold heaviness. "This piece of metal carried more than ink. It carried a false promise, one pressed into public memory. But beneath it lies the true vow—the one in the ledger, the one that still echoes in the silence."

Damien studied her face, his voice softer now. "Marley, are you prepared for what this means? If we reveal it, we won't just be telling Amelia's story. We'll be dismantling the Circle's legacy. Families who still sit on the council, still run businesses, still light their candles as if none of this is shadowed."

Her gaze did not waver. "Then let them face their own silence. We vowed not to leave her standing alone."

Damien lowered his eyes, nodding. "Then we follow the message. Even if it was lost, perhaps fragments remain—in letters, diaries, accounts too fragile to survive the fire of secrecy but strong enough to whisper through ink."

Marley set the plate back onto the cloth, folding the edges around it as though wrapping a wound. "The bell didn't fail. It judged. And the judgment waits for us to name it."

LATER THAT NIGHT, Marley sat by the fire, the photograph and the plate beside her. She opened her journal and began to write:

The Bell Bride Ceremony flyer was no innocent invitation. It was a mask, covering a sacred vow with the Circle's authority. The vines prove the lineage. The hidden words prove intent. The bell did not fall silent out of weakness, but out of refusal. And the message that never arrived—what truths did it carry? Whose voice was it meant to free?

She paused, the nib trembling. The flames hissed, casting shadows that curled like the vines etched into the plate.

Marley whispered into the hush, "Amelia, we'll find your message. We'll speak what silence lost."

The Winter Bell outside remained mute. But its silence now seemed less like absence and more like a pause in music—waiting for them to take up the next note.

THE FIRE in the bookshop had burned down to coals, its glow throwing long shadows against the walls. Marley and Damien sat at the oak table, the printing plate between them, wrapped once more in its cloth. It seemed to radiate a weight disproportionate to its size—not only metal but memory, not only artifact but accusation.

Marley broke the silence first. "If we bring this to the town, we risk more than whispers. The families tied to the Circle still hold sway. Council seats, business ledgers, even the library board. They'll see this plate not as evidence but as provocation."

Damien rubbed his temple, eyes fixed on the wrapped bundle. "And yet hiding it makes us no better than the Kinney's grandfather. He burned the flyers because he feared what they carried. But the bell's silence endures because the truth was buried."

Marley exhaled sharply. "The question is how to reveal it. Do we publish? Do we speak at the Winter Ball? Or do we keep it quiet until we know who lost that message—the one his grandfather said never arrived?"

Her words hung between them. The thought of the missing message, suspended somewhere in history, gnawed like an open wound.

DAMIEN LEANED FORWARD, his scholar's precision hardening his voice. "We must tread carefully. To present this plate without context would reduce it to accusation. The Circle's appropriation of the vow must be shown, not shouted. We need the ledger pages, the rubbing from the fragment, the lists from the Colvin house—all laid together. Only then can we show the continuity: the seal, the rhetoric, the intent."

Marley nodded slowly, though her hands trembled. "Evidence like a trial. But who will sit as jury? The very descendants of those who pressed the seal?"

Damien's gaze met hers. "Then let the town itself be the jury. History doesn't need permission to speak."

She swallowed hard, the weight of his certainty pressing against her doubt. "And yet..." She rose, pacing toward the window. The square below lay hushed, its lamplight glinting against snow. "If we expose this, some will turn on us. They'll call me reckless, accuse me of tarnishing traditions. They may even claim I fabricated it. The shop could become a target."

Her voice wavered, but she steadied it. "And you—you've already spoken of leaving. A fellowship in Europe, wasn't it? If you go, I'll be left to face this alone."

Damien flinched, then stood. "Marley." His voice softened. "My leaving was a thought, not a vow. But now..." He looked at the plate, the vines curling like silent witnesses. "Now I see my place may be here. If the town is to reckon with its silence, I cannot abandon you to bear it alone."

Marley turned, her breath catching. "So you'd stay? Even if it costs us both?"

He stepped closer, his hand brushing hers across the edge of the table. "Truth always costs. The question is whether we can afford to spend it."

THEY SAT AGAIN, drawing closer to the plate. Damien unwrapped it once more, laying bare the bell and vine motif. The etched letters glinted faintly, the hidden circle of words—*Seven hands bind, seven vows stand*—catching in the lamplight.

Marley touched the rim gently. "Seven vows. Seven families. And Amelia trapped in their ring. The bell refused, but she still paid the price."

Damien's jaw set. "And the town buried her with silence. That is what we must break."

Marley drew her journal close and opened to a blank page. Her pen scratched quickly, urgent. *If we reveal the plate, we reveal the Circle. If we reveal the Circle, we demand reckoning. If we demand reckoning, we may lose the town's trust—but if we stay silent, we lose Amelia again.*

She underlined the last phrase twice.

Damien leaned over, reading. Then he added beneath in his neat script: *To reveal is to risk division. To conceal is to join the Circle. Our vow forbids concealment.*

They exchanged a long look. Agreement, solemn as a pact.

THE HOUR GREW LATE. The fire dwindled further, the coals faintly pulsing. Marley rested her elbows on the table, chin in her hands, staring at the photograph of Amelia propped against the lamp.

"She stood waiting because a message never arrived," Marley whispered. "But what if that message had told Elijah to come? What if it held her plea for freedom, or his pledge to stand against the Circle? Everything might have turned different."

Damien's eyes darkened. "Which means the silence of the bell was only half the story. The other half lies in the silence of that message. If we can find it—or even fragments —we can show not only what the Circle tried to enforce, but what love or loyalty tried to resist."

Marley's throat tightened. "And if the message was destroyed, like the flyers?"

"Then we search anyway," Damien said firmly. "Ashes leave marks. Ink seeps. Words survive in echoes, even if only in margins."

He leaned closer, voice low but steady. "Marley, we vowed not to leave Amelia alone. Seeking the message is part of that vow. Until we know what it said, her story remains unfinished."

Marley's eyes brimmed, but she nodded. "Then we search. In archives, in attics, in whispers passed down in families. Somewhere, the message waits."

She reached across the table, laying her hand atop the plate. Damien set his hand beside hers, their palms touching over the vines and bell.

Together, they spoke softly, as if addressing both the photograph and the silence: "We vow to seek the message. We vow to carry it into the light. We vow the Circle will not bury it again."

The hush of the shop deepened, pressing close, almost alive. For a heartbeat, Marley thought she heard faint bells in the distance—no chime of bronze, but something softer, like memory echoing across snow.

She closed her eyes, whispering, "Amelia, we will not stop."

The silence answered, not with sound but with presence.

And in that moment, Marley and Damien knew their path was set: to confront the town not only with the plate, but with the message that had once promised to save Amelia—and might still save Brookwood from its silence.

13

WISHING WELL WHISPERS

The old wishing well stood at the far edge of Brookwood's square, half-hidden by a stand of fir trees. Its stones were slick with moss, the wooden frame bowed by years of weather. Most children knew it only as a landmark, a place for tossing pennies in summer games. But the elders whispered that the well ran deeper than memory, and that its waters sometimes carried echoes not of wishes, but of truths.

Marley had avoided it for years. Something about its stillness unnerved her. Yet this afternoon, drawn by the weight of the photograph and the printing plate still resting in the shop, she found herself standing before the well with a coin in her hand.

Snow dusted the rim, the stones cold beneath her gloves. She looked down into the shadowed throat, the water far below catching faint glimmers of light. The town's bustle dimmed here, as though even sound hesitated before entering the circle of stones.

Marley held the penny above the opening. Her voice came soft, almost reverent. "What happened to her?"

She let the coin fall.

It struck the water with a soft plink, and for a heartbeat all was still. Then, faint as a memory carried on wind, she heard it—wedding bells. Not loud, not clear, but unmistakable: the toll of a ceremony that had never been.

Her breath caught. She gripped the stone rim, staring into the darkness. The sound faded quickly, swallowed by the well, but the echo lingered in her chest.

The bells had answered.

SHE TURNED QUICKLY, half expecting Damien to be behind her. But she stood alone, the trees creaking in the winter breeze. Her pulse thudded. She whispered again, trembling. "Amelia? Was that you?"

The silence held. No voice, no shape, only the faint stir of branches above. Yet Marley felt the presence of listening, as if the well itself held her question.

She stepped back, heart racing.

The coin had not been a wish—it had been a summons.

THAT EVENING, the bookshop glowed warm against the cold. Marley closed early, her nerves still taut from the encounter. She lit the fire and set a kettle on the stove, but even the scent of tea leaves could not settle her pulse.

She sat at the desk, writing in her journal:

The well answered. A penny fell, and bells rang. Not loud, but true. Bells that have not rung in eighty years. Bells for a bride who never wed.

Her pen trembled across the page. *She heard me. Or I heard her. The silence isn't empty—it's waiting.*

She closed the journal abruptly, unable to continue. The room felt too close, shadows gathering in the corners.

NEAR MIDNIGHT, a knock stirred her from half-sleep. Soft, deliberate, against the shop's front door.

Marley rose quickly, wrapping her shawl around her shoulders. She lit a lamp and carried it to the entry, heart pounding. Through the frosted glass she saw no figure, only snow falling thick in the square.

She opened the door cautiously.

At her feet lay a bundle, small and neat, tied with silk ribbon. The fabric glistened faintly in the lamplight, as though it had waited just for her to find it.

Marley bent slowly, lifting the bundle into her arms. The snow had not yet touched it. Whoever had left it had done so only moments before. She looked up and down the street, but the square was empty, the silence unbroken.

She shut the door quickly, locking it behind her.

At the table, she set the bundle down and loosened the ribbon. The fabric unfolded to reveal lace—delicate gloves, once white, now yellowed with age. Their fingers were long, elegant, trimmed with careful stitching. But the lace was stained—dark smudges across the palms, as though ink had bled into the fabric.

Marley's breath caught.

Ink.

She lifted the gloves, turning them in the light. The stains were uneven, as if someone had pressed their hands into fresh words. She imagined Amelia herself, clutching a letter or message with trembling fingers, the ink wet and merciless.

A message that never arrived.

Her chest tightened. "These were hers," she whispered.

The fire snapped in the hearth, but the silence pressed close, listening.

Marley set the gloves beside the photograph, her hands trembling. Veil, altar, silence, and now this: proof not only of absence, but of ink, of words written and touched, of a message meant to carry her vow forward.

She pressed a hand to her chest, whispering into the hush. "Amelia, we found them. We won't let your words be lost again."

The lace seemed to glimmer faintly in the firelight, as though remembering the hand that once wore it.

WHEN DAMIEN ARRIVED the next morning, he found Marley still at the desk, the gloves laid out carefully beside the photograph. He froze at the sight, his eyes sharp.

"Where did you—?"

"Left at the door," Marley said softly. "Wrapped in silk, tied with ribbon. No mark, no note. Only this." She touched the ink stains gently. "Damien, they're hers. I can feel it. And the ink—do you see? It's not random smudge. It's transfer. As though she pressed her hands to a letter. Perhaps the very message that never arrived."

Damien bent closer, studying the stains with a scholar's scrutiny. His brow furrowed. "The spread is consistent with iron gall ink—the kind used in the thirties. And you're right. This isn't accident. It's contact." He looked up at her, his voice low. "If we can recover even a trace of what was written—"

Marley's breath caught. "Then we might find the missing words."

They exchanged a long, heavy look.

The Winter Bell outside remained silent, but its hush now felt like promise.

DAMIEN TURNED the gloves over in the lamplight, careful not to damage the delicate lace. The ink stains had bled into the fabric in irregular patterns, but some marks were sharper, more deliberate. He held them closer to the flame, his scholar's patience settling into him.

"These aren't random smudges," he said, half to himself. "The fibers absorbed the ink at pressure points. Look here—straight lines, almost parallel. Not the sweep of handwriting, but the edge of a folded sheet."

Marley leaned in, her breath catching. "So she held it. Pressed it, maybe even clutched it."

Damien nodded. "A letter. Ink still wet. She must have been desperate—either writing or receiving words that mattered more than anything. But if she pressed it so hard the ink transferred, why don't we have the letter itself?"

"Because it never arrived," Marley whispered. "Because someone stopped it."

The words chilled the room more than the draft through the shutters.

DAMIEN FETCHED A MAGNIFYING glass from his satchel and angled the gloves beneath it. He traced the stains slowly, murmuring his observations.

"Curved here...could be the loop of a letter. This darker blotch—might be from the crossing of a *t* or *f*. And here—" he paused, leaning closer. "These faint arcs. It almost looks like a bell."

Marley froze. "A bell? On the letter?"

He exhaled. "Or part of a crest. Perhaps a signature flourish. It's too incomplete to know for certain. But Marley, these gloves are more than relic. They're testimony. Someone touched a letter that should have changed everything."

Her chest tightened. "Amelia's hands. Ink on lace, proof she tried to speak. And yet the message never left her grasp."

She sank into the chair, staring at the gloves as if they could still warm to life. "Damien, what if the gloves were left for us on purpose? Not as discovery, but as direction?"

Damien looked up sharply. "You think someone in town is guiding us?"

Marley nodded slowly. "The photograph in the archives. The printing plate in the drawer. Now these gloves, delivered in the night. Each step arrives not by accident, but by placement. Someone wants us to find them."

"But who?" Damien asked. "An ally? A descendant? Someone trying to ease a conscience?"

"Or Amelia herself," Marley whispered.

The room hushed at her words. The fire snapped softly, the sound like a breath held too long.

"I don't mean ghost in the simple sense," Marley continued, her voice trembling. "I mean presence. Her vow pressing through others' hands. Someone hears her silence, and they are placing the pieces where we cannot ignore them."

Damien studied her, the skepticism in his eyes tempered by something gentler. "If that's true, then we're not only following a trail—we're being led."

Marley's gaze flicked toward the window, toward the

direction of the wishing well. She swallowed hard. "I tossed a penny and asked, *What happened to her?* Bells answered. That same night, the gloves appeared. Tell me that's coincidence."

Damien didn't answer. His silence was not dismissal but reluctant acknowledgment.

THEY WORKED LATE into the night, cataloging the gloves with careful notes. Damien sketched the stain patterns, marking where the ink spread and where it pressed sharply. Marley wrote in her journal, her words tight and urgent:

The well answered with bells. The gloves carried ink. She touched the message that never arrived. Someone placed them at my door. This is not chance. This is guidance.

Her pen dug deep into the page, almost tearing it. She looked up at Damien, her voice low. "If we follow, where does it lead?"

He paused, setting down the magnifier. "To the message itself, if it still exists. Or to the person who has been leaving us these pieces."

"Or both," Marley said.

The fire dwindled to embers. Outside, the bell tower loomed silent, its shadow stretching across the square like an outstretched arm.

NEAR MIDNIGHT, Marley stepped to the window. Snow fell softly, muting the world into stillness. She thought of Amelia, standing veiled before the chapel, ink staining her gloves, waiting for a vow to be fulfilled.

Marley pressed her palm to the glass. "We'll find it," she

whispered. "Your message. Your truth. We'll follow where the bells lead."

Behind her, Damien's voice came steady. "Then we vow again. To seek not only what was lost, but who wants us to find it. The gloves are not the end—they're the summons."

Marley turned, her eyes burning but clear. "Then let's answer."

The silence deepened, holding them in its grasp. And faintly—so faintly Marley thought she imagined it—she heard the echo of bells again, distant and tender, as though the wishing well itself had carried her words back through the snow.

MORNING LIGHT SPILLED across the square, catching the snow in a thousand sharp glints. The bookshop doorbell jingled steadily all day, neighbors coming in with cautious warmth, some carrying baked bread, others searching for candles or kindling. Word had already spread—Marley wasn't sure how—but the gloves were no longer secret.

Miriam Merrick from the council stopped by, her face pale as she gestured to the lace laid carefully in the display case. "They're saying those belonged to Amelia," she whispered, as if naming the dead woman might summon her. "That she pressed ink into them the day the bell went silent."

Marley only nodded, unwilling to spin rumor into denial or confirmation. But the weight of the stares followed her. Customers lingered at the shelves, their eyes flicking back to the gloves as though measuring whether history might yet stir to life.

By afternoon, the hush in the shop had grown too sharp. Damien appeared from the archive room, his expression taut. He leaned close and murmured, "They're restless. Not curious—restless. As though the silence of the bell is ringing in them again."

Marley's chest tightened. "And they'll look to us for answers."

Damien's gaze was steady. "Then we must choose what to give them."

THAT EVENING, after the last customer left, Marley and Damien sat together at the oak table. The photograph of Amelia, the printing plate wrapped in cloth, and the gloves lay between them, forming a constellation of artifacts that seemed to pulse with unspoken meaning.

Marley broke the silence. "Someone is leaving these for us to find. First the photograph in the archives, then the plate, now the gloves. They're not just discoveries—they're deliveries."

Damien leaned forward, fingers steepled. "Which means someone alive remembers—or knows more than they admit. Perhaps a descendant of the Circle, trying to make amends. Perhaps a keeper of their own family secret."

Marley shook her head, her throat tight. "Or someone who was silenced before, finally daring to speak. The way Amelia tried, with her letter."

Damien studied her carefully. "You believe Amelia herself is guiding this."

"I believe her vow still breathes," Marley said firmly. "Whether through hands of the living or through silence itself, she is pushing us forward. And we can't turn away."

· · ·

THEY DEBATED long into the night. Damien's scholar's caution urged restraint: catalog the artifacts, build a careful record, reveal only when evidence was irrefutable. Marley's heart pressed for urgency: to speak, to show, to give Amelia the witnesses she had been denied.

"Damien, the town already knows," she said, voice trembling. "Whispers spread faster than proof. The gloves are being spoken of whether we act or not. The danger isn't exposure—it's silence. If we don't give meaning, others will."

Damien exhaled, weary but resolute. "Then we must be deliberate. We cannot accuse without context. But yes—we cannot remain mute." He glanced toward the window, where the bell tower loomed in silhouette. "The silence of the bell has returned, but this time it's not bronze holding its tongue—it's us."

The words struck Marley hard. She closed her eyes briefly, then nodded. "Then no more silence."

THE HOUR GREW LATE. Marley rose and carried the gloves back to the window, laying them on the sill. Snow drifted against the glass. She pressed her palm beside them, whispering, "You're not alone."

Damien stepped behind her, his voice low. "The well answered you once. If we are being led, then we should return to the well and ask again."

Marley turned, searching his face. "You'd go back with me?"

"Of course," he said simply. "We vowed not to let her stand alone. If the well is a gate through which her vow still speaks, then that is where our next step lies."

A shiver coursed through Marley—not fear, but recognition. "Then tomorrow, at dawn," she whispered. "We'll return."

THE FIRE HAD BURNED to embers by the time they retired, but the hush in the shop seemed alive, almost listening. The gloves gleamed faintly in the lamplight, their stains dark as secrets, their lace fragile as memory.

Marley touched Damien's hand before they parted for the night. "We'll find the message," she said softly. "We'll follow the bells."

Damien's grip tightened in reply. "And we won't stop until the silence breaks."

Outside, snow fell steady and soft, blanketing the square. The Winter Bell stood in shadow, mute against the sky.

But within the silence, Marley heard it again—faint, like a memory carried on wind: the echo of wedding bells. Not as absence, not as tragedy, but as summons.

And she knew the well was waiting.

14

———

THE BAKER'S DREAM

By dawn the square smelled like butter and steam. The storm had passed, and people returned to their rituals as if routine itself could stitch what the bell had torn. Marley pushed open the bakery door and stepped into warmth, her breath fogging briefly before the air sweetened it away. The bell above the door chimed once—too bright a note in a town that hadn't heard the right one in years.

Ruth Bennett was already behind the counter, hair tied in a scarf, flour smudging her cheek like a careless blessing. She was boxing cinnamon knots near the ovens, face flushed with heat and worry. Mrs. Bennett looked up when Marley entered, and in that instant Marley knew she had not come only for bread.

"You're early," Mrs. Bennett said, voice careful. "Or I'm late to something I don't know yet."

"I brought you something," Marley answered, setting her journal on the counter without opening it. "An ear. If you'll have it."

Mrs. Bennett blinked once, then nodded toward the

small table by the window—the one with the cracked blue glaze in its center, a hairline fissure that had survived generations of elbows and coffee cups. "Sit. I'll bring tea."

Mrs. Bennett set down a chipped pot and mismatched cups. She poured, hands steady, then finally allowed herself to look at Marley fully, as if testing how much truth the morning could hold.

"I had a dream," Mrs. Bennett said. "Three nights running, and last night it changed."

Marley felt the room narrow to their table. Behind them, the ovens exhaled as if listening.

"A woman in white," Mrs. Bennett continued, eyes turned as if the vision hung in the flour-dusted air. "Veiled, though not like a bride on a stair. Her veil was more... river mist. She stood at the bank holding a bell in both hands, and the bell was not ours. Smaller. Hand-sized, old, as if meant for a chapel with a low roof and cold rafters. She was weeping, Marley. Not loud. The kind of crying that never learned to spend itself."

"I know dreams," Mrs. Bennett went on, "how they take shapes from what we've been carrying. Lord knows this town has been carrying its share. But there was something in this one that wasn't mine. It felt placed." She swallowed, the motion quick, embarrassed. "Last night I followed her in the dream. The woman stepped onto a bridge I know. And behind her, on the far bank, there was a green light. Not large. Not lantern-yellow. Green." She lifted her gaze to Marley's. "You've heard anything like that?"

Marley had to steady her breath before she spoke. "We've seen the color before. A motif and a mark. In the healer's ledger, in a margin where the old vows were described, the scribe drew a small flame tinted green. Copper salts—Damien thinks—mixed into the wick on solstice nights. A sign of balance kept. I still don't know all it meant."

"Would you draw it?" Marley asked, forcing calm into her voice. "The bridge. The light. What you remember of where she stood."

Ruth stood at once, grateful to have something to do. She fetched a sheet of bakery parchment and a grease pencil from the drawer where she kept tally sheets for bread orders. She hesitated, then began. The pencil moved with the speed of someone who has seen an image too clearly to mislay it: a distinct sweep of stone across water; winter-naked trees clustered like witnesses; a woman on the near side holding a bell to her chest. And there—over the far bank—Ruth shaded a small flare, rounded like a cupped flame, and in the center she left a pale streak, like a tongue of fire condensed to liquid color.

She slid the parchment across. Marley recognized the bridge before her mind agreed to it. "The Foundry Span," she murmured. "Where the river narrows by the old glassworks."

Damien slipped in then, snow on his coat shoulders, the air behind him carrying a shock of cold. He closed the door and crossed to them, reading the scene in Ruth Bennett's posture, the parchment, the tremor at Marley's mouth. "What did I miss?"

"A dream," Ruth said, "and perhaps not only a dream." She stood, pressing her palms against the edge of the table, and repeated what she had told Marley—the bell in the woman's hands, the weeping, the bridge, the green light breathing over the far bank.

Damien leaned over the drawing. Up close, he could see Ruth's hand in the sketch—a baker's certainty in measure, no flourish wasted. His eyes went to the little flame above the far bank and stayed.

"The winter vow that froze the flame," he said softly, as to himself.

Ruth's glance sharpened. "You know that phrase."

"A story," Damien answered, finding Marley's eyes across the table. "Half-lore, half-ledger. I glimpsed it months ago in the healer's book—a note crossed with later ink, as if someone argued with the original words. It spoke of a winter when a vow could not be sealed. The ritual flame was carried to the river as custom, and when the bell failed to bless it, the green fire didn't go out—it froze." He tapped the parchment where Ruth had drawn the little flare. "They said the flame turned to a bead of glass before it touched the water, as if the river itself had decided to keep what was sacred from being wasted."

Ruth stared at him, mouth slightly open. "You're telling me I drew a story older than my grandmother's hands, one I never read."

"I'm telling you," Damien said, "that your dream found a path the ledger forgot to map."

Marley's pulse climbed, not with fear, but with the fierce, familiar feeling that the town's silence had just revealed a seam. "The Foundry Span," she repeated, looking down at the rough stone arch Mrs. Bennett had captured in two clean lines. "If there was any place a flame could turn to glass at the edge of water, it would be near the glassworks. Heat and cold so close the air quarrels with itself."

Ruth exhaled. "And the green—does that mean...?"

"Balance," Marley answered. "In the old telling. Healing held between two houses. But in the ledger note Damien found, the scribe wrote that when the vow failed, the flame froze. The balance wasn't lost forever; it was locked. Their word was *rested.* As if the town put its sacred thing to sleep to keep it from being profaned."

"Amelia," Ruth said, not a question. "The woman in my dream—she held the bell like a child, and when she wept, the sound didn't reach my ears. But I felt it. The kind of grief that can only be heard with the ribs."

They fell quiet together, steam from the tea drifting between them like the ghost of morning fog on the river. Outside, a wagon passed, its wheels hissing on packed snow, a sound so ordinary it made the conversation feel more dangerous by contrast.

Ruth found her voice first. "What does it want?" She gestured to the drawing, the green flare, the curve of the bridge. "If dreams are becoming maps, what do they ask us to do?"

Marley glanced at Damien. He did not answer immediately, and in that pause Marley recognized the man who had learned the town's silence like a language. He was not withholding; he was listening.

"It wants witnesses," Marley said at last. "What the bell refused at the chapel it might be willing to show at the river. If the flame froze and was kept—by water, by winter, by hands—the river might still hold it."

Ruth let out a small, incredulous laugh. "You think a glass bead of green fire is sitting in the river waiting for us like a lost thimble?"

"I think," Damien said gently, "that the town has always hidden its truths in the plainest places. Under floorboards. Behind panels. In a secretary with bellflowers inlaid on its face. Why not at the bottom of the river where every child tosses stones?" He touched the little flame with the edge of his finger. "And if it isn't a bead, perhaps it's a story you've dreamt straight. In either case, you've given us a direction."

Ruth looked relieved, and then suddenly young, as if she had handed off a weight she didn't know she'd been carrying. "I can come with you," she offered.

"Not today," Marley said. "Let Marley and me test what we can without stirring talk," Damien added. "If there's something to find, we'll bring you first."

Ruth nodded, surrendering to sense. She poured more tea, as if ceremony could shore up courage. "I didn't mean to be part of this," she admitted, voice small. "I just wanted to bake bread and keep the east window from rattling loose in storms. But when I woke last night, I felt the same thing I feel when I pull a loaf at the exact right minute: if I waited any longer, it would have collapsed." She looked at Marley. "So I told you."

"I'm grateful," Marley said simply, and meant every syllable.

Damien studied the sketch again, then returned the parchment and pencil. "Two more things," he said. "The bell in her hands—can you draw its shape? And can you mark where on the span she stood?"

Ruth closed her eyes, calling the image back. The pencil moved again. A handbell, older style, its waist broader, lip slightly flared, handle carved with a braid. And a mark on the near bank, not the center of the bridge but close to the downstream side, where the current quickened in winter.

Marley felt her ribs ache as if bracing against cold. "The braid on the handle," she said softly. "Like the braided border around the Circle's signet."

Damien didn't flinch from the association. "But this braid predates them. The healer's sigils braided for binding balance, not for sealing power. The Circle stole the language of the braid to crown their seal. If your dream put that bell in Amelia's hands, Ruth, it may be giving her back something the Circle took."

The ovens sighed again, reminding them the world still needed bread. Ruth folded the parchment once and slid it into Marley's journal, as if trusting the book to carry what her sleep could no longer hold.

"Go before the lunch rush," Ruth said, rising. "Look at the river while it's still shy enough to keep its surface honest. If you need rope, ask Mr. Barlow at the Hardware store. He owes me five savory pies."

Marley tucked the drawing carefully beneath the elastic that held her journal closed. She reached for Ruth Bennett's flour-dusted hand and squeezed it once in thanks. Damien took the grease pencil and, with a nod of permission, traced the outline of the little green flame on the inside cover of his notebook, labeling it with a single phrase: *winter vow— frozen flame.*

As they left, the bell over the door gave another bright, ordinary ring. For a fraction of a second Marley hated the sound for how easy it was to summon. Then she remembered the woman at the river and the bell clutched to her chest, and the hatred shifted into something else—an urge to hear the right sound again, the one that would not be coaxed by pull-cords or a shop door's swing.

Outside, the air cut sharp. The river's breath drifted across the lower streets like fog. Damien tucked his scarf tighter, eyes on the direction of the Foundry Span.

"If the story is true," he said, "and the flame froze rather than died, it means the vow wasn't destroyed. It was preserved."

"Rested," Marley said. "Like a dough you let rise, covered, waiting for the right heat."

"Then the question," Damien answered as they began to walk, "is whether we're the heat."

They didn't look back through the bakery window, but Mrs. Bennett did, standing in flour and morning light, watching the two figures cross into the pale day like notes hiking toward a chord the town had long forgotten how to resolve.

THE FOUNDRY SPAN was a bridge the town rarely mentioned anymore, though everyone still crossed it. Its stones had blackened from decades of smoke when the glassworks ran hot, and now they bore moss and frost in winter, holding their silence like old workers keeping secrets. Marley and Damien walked there with the baker's drawing folded between them, the paper as fragile as the vow it hinted at.

The river ran dark and fast beneath the arch. Sheets of ice formed along the edges, white against the current's black seam. The glassworks itself loomed to the north, long abandoned, its windows shattered and its roof caved in at one corner. But Marley swore she could still feel heat rising from it—the ghost of furnaces where fire once bent sand to clarity.

She unfolded Mrs. Bennett's sketch and held it up. The lines matched: the bridge, the curve of the bank, the stand of trees leaning over the water. And there, marked with a small cross, the place where the veiled woman in the dream had stood.

Marley's pulse quickened. "This is it."

Damien scanned the scene with a scholar's precision, his eyes lingering on the far bank where the green flame had been drawn. "Mrs. Bennett's dream wasn't vague. She gave detail enough for cartography. That's not common dreaming. That's memory transposed."

Marley shivered, though the air was no colder than usual. "Memory that doesn't belong to her. It's Amelia's grief, bleeding through."

Damien crouched at the bank, running his gloved fingers along the frost-hardened grass. "If the flame froze into glass, as the tale says, it might have sunk here. Or been caught in a crevice of stone."

"Eighty years is a long time for a flame to sleep," Marley murmured. "But maybe it's been waiting."

THEY STAYED until the sun lowered, its light slicing across the river. Damien tied a line around his waist and eased himself partway down the embankment, his boots scraping against the stone. He used a small hand rake from his satchel to prod at gaps in the rocks. Marley held the rope taut, her breath sharp each time his footing shifted.

"Anything?" she called, voice tight.

"Cold silt," Damien answered, his tone clipped. "Shell fragments. Nothing that shines."

Marley's heart sank, but she steadied her grip on the rope. She looked back at the sketch again. The green flame flared above the far bank, not the near. "Damien—what if you're searching on the wrong side?"

He climbed back up, cheeks raw from wind. His eyes followed hers to the far bank. "You think the dream marked the other side?"

"Mrs. Bennett said she followed the woman onto the bridge. The flame appeared behind her, across the river. That's where it froze."

Damien exhaled, resigned but not defeated. "Then we cross."

THE FAR SIDE of the bridge was less tended. Snow lay thick on the narrow path, branches crowding overhead. They followed the curve until the water slowed into a shallow eddy against a rocky outcrop. The setting sun caught the ripples, and for a moment Marley imagined she saw a flicker of green under the surface.

She gasped, pointing. "There."

But when Damien knelt to look, the water only reflected the sky's pale fire.

"Eyes play tricks at dusk," he said gently.

Marley clenched her fists. "Or the river hides what it doesn't want to give."

She crouched beside him, touching the icy stones. "If the vow froze into flame, maybe it isn't glass we're looking for. Maybe it's story—preserved in dreams, in whispers. Mrs. Bennett didn't hand us an object. She handed us a vision."

Damien studied her face, then nodded. "Then the search isn't only with hands. It's with ears. We must listen for where the vow still breathes."

THEY LINGERED on the bank until full dark, the cold seeping through their coats. Marley closed her eyes and tried to imagine Amelia standing where she stood now, veil damp with river mist, bell clutched against her chest, tears falling silent into the current.

She whispered, "We're here. We see you."

The water gurgled softly, as if answering.

Damien touched her shoulder. "Even if we found

nothing tangible, the dream has already given us direction. The vow is tied to this span, this river, this flame. The Circle wanted it sealed at the chapel. But Amelia carried it here instead."

Marley opened her eyes, a shiver of awe running through her. "She tried to keep it from them. To protect it."

"And perhaps," Damien said, "she succeeded. If the flame froze, it was not destroyed. It was preserved, waiting for release."

They exchanged a long look, the river's hush binding them.

Marley whispered, "Then the question is, how do we wake it?"

Damien's jaw set, his scholar's mind already working. "We start with Mrs. Bennett's drawing. The bell in the woman's hands, the braid on its handle. That detail is too precise to ignore. If such a bell existed, records may remain. An heirloom, an entry in an inventory, a mention in one of the founding families' accounts."

"And the green flame," Marley added. "The healer's ledger said balance rested when vows failed. Maybe the flame itself is the key—an element waiting for witness."

They turned back toward the bridge, the night cold but their path clear. Marley folded the drawing carefully and tucked it back into her journal. "She's leading us step by step. Through dreams, through objects, through silence."

Damien glanced at her, his voice low. "Then we follow, wherever it leads."

The Winter Bell above the square remained mute, but as Marley looked back once more at the river, she thought she saw a glimmer beneath the ice—small, round, and faintly green, like a flame that had never gone out.

. . .

THE ROAD back to town was nearly silent, the crunch of their boots on snow the only sound. Yet Marley carried the river's hush with her, a pressure that lingered in her ribs. The sketch in her journal burned like a coal in her satchel, as though the dream had followed them.

Inside the bookshop, warmth and lamplight returned. Damien set his satchel on the table, rubbing his hands briskly, but his eyes were still distant, fixed on something they had left behind at the bridge.

Marley poured coffee, her own hands unsteady. "If the vow froze," she said, breaking the silence, "then it means Amelia didn't fail. She saved it from the Circle."

Damien nodded, though his expression was grave. "Yes. She took it from their grasp. But think what that implies. If the flame still rests at the river, the Circle knew—or feared—it. They must have tried to erase that version of the story."

Marley's stomach tightened. "Which is why no one speaks of the frozen flame. Why Mrs. Bennett never heard the tale awake, only in dreams."

"Exactly," Damien said. "The Circle replaced it with their own narrative: a bride abandoned, a ceremony failed, a bell fallen silent. They cast it as tragedy so no one would think to search for the vow's preservation."

He leaned forward, his scholar's intensity sharpening his tone. "If this truth comes to light, it undermines everything the Circle built. Their authority depends on the silence being interpreted as failure, not as refusal. A frozen flame kept safe at the river threatens their entire legacy."

Marley set her cup down hard. "Then we must bring it to light."

· · ·

Damien paced the shop, his steps slow, thoughtful. "If we announce it too soon, the Circle's descendants will deny, discredit, or worse. They'll call it folklore. They'll accuse us of fabrication. But if we bring witnesses—neutral townsfolk, respected elders, the very people the Circle relies upon for legitimacy—then the silence begins to break in public, not just in whispers."

Marley's breath quickened with both dread and conviction. "Witnesses. Just as Amelia lacked at the altar. That's what she's been asking all along. Not saviors—witnesses."

"Yes," Damien said, his voice low. "We return to the bridge, not alone this time. And if the flame reveals itself, if there is even a sign, then no one can bury it again."

Marley closed her eyes. She saw Amelia standing with the bell clutched to her chest, veil heavy with river mist. She imagined her turning, searching the banks for eyes that would testify. And finding none.

"We cannot let her stand alone again," Marley whispered.

Damien stopped pacing, his face lit by the fire's glow. "The Circle's suppression was deliberate. Think of the pieces: the destroyed flyers, the unfiled certificate, the hidden printing plate, the message that never arrived. Each one an erasure. The frozen flame is the most dangerous of all, because it testifies not to failure but to resistance."

"And to love," Marley added quietly. "For vows do not freeze without warmth to hold them first."

She touched the gloves on the table, the ink stains dark in the lamplight. "Amelia tried to speak. The flame tried to preserve. Both were silenced by hands that feared what they carried."

Damien studied her, his eyes softening. "And now the silence has carried long enough."

Marley lifted her journal, opened to the page with Mrs. Bennett's sketch, and set it between them. The small flame hovered on the parchment, alive despite its simple lines. "This is where we stand. At the edge of the river. At the edge of truth."

Damien placed his palm flat over the sketch. "Then we vow again. To return with witnesses. To break the Circle's silence with sight, not rumor."

Marley laid her hand atop his, steady and sure. "We vow."

THE HOURS SLIPPED PAST, marked only by the crackle of the fire. They spoke of who to trust, who might stand with them without bowing to fear. Perhaps Councilor Miriam Merrick from the council, whose hesitation earlier might hide a longing for truth. And maybe—if they dared—Mr. Barlow at the Hardware store, who owed favors and respected fire's craft.

Names built a fragile chain, each link tentative but necessary.

Damien finally leaned back, exhaustion lining his face. "We'll need to prepare. Ropes, lanterns, tools. If the flame manifests as glass, it may lie beneath ice or silt. If it is only light, then eyes will suffice. Either way, we go not as seekers but as keepers."

Marley's voice was steady now. "Amelia waited with no one. This time, she will not."

.   .   .

Before sleep, Marley carried the gloves to the window again. Snow fell lightly, muffling the square. She laid the lace against the glass, whispering, "We've heard you. We'll return."

Behind her, Damien spoke softly, almost like a prayer. "May the flame wake to witness, and may we be brave enough to stand in its glow."

The Winter Bell above remained silent, but in the hush Marley felt a shift—not absence, not refusal, but anticipation. The vow was not gone. It was waiting.

And she and Damien had pledged to answer.

15
____

THE ANTIQUE RING

The metaphysical shop on Main Street always smelled like a season trying to speak. In summer it was beeswax and clover; in autumn, bay leaf and smoke. This winter it smelled of frankincense threaded with something mineral—like clean river stone warmed in a hand. Bells never rang here; candle wicks did the talking.

Hazel, chandler and keeper of the shop's gentle order, had sent a note at first light: *Returned stock from an estate box. Something you'll want to see. Come before I cut it down.* The "estate" had not been named, but in a town of few names, silence carried its own label.

Marley and Damien arrived just as Hazel was straightening the display of taper bundles. The window burned with rows of ivory and green; the latter cast an eerie, tender glow that made even the frost look alive.

"You came quick," Hazel said, relief loosening her shoulders. "I wasn't sure if I should wait or pretend I hadn't seen it."

"Seen what?" Marley asked, already feeling the town's hush draw tight.

Hazel led them behind the counter to the workbench where she poured and trimmed. A heavy block of wax sat in a tin tray—opaque, the color of old cream. Someone had pressed a pattern along its edges long ago: a braid of small leaves, uneven from handwork. A paring knife lay beside it, wax curls like pale shavings of paper scattered around.

"This came in a crate of odds and ends," Hazel said. "House-clear. Inventory tag said *candles—misc.,* with a date that would embarrass the clerk. I planned to melt it down. Waste not. When I warmed the base to check for cracks..." She nudged the block; it knocked against the tray with a solid cluck, not hollow. "There's something inside."

Damien bent, rapped the wax with his knuckles, then glanced up at Hazel. "What estate?"

Hazel's mouth tightened. "Colvin."

Marley felt the world narrow to a point. "Show me what you did."

Hazel lifted the block and set it under a low lamp. "I only softened this side." She touched the corner with the back of her finger. "Just enough to shave. I saw metal flash and stopped."

Damien slid his notebook onto the bench as if arranging an altar. "We'll document. If this is what I think, provenance will matter."

Hazel pulled a shallow pan closer and lit the smallest burner. She set the block edge-down so the wax kissed the heat without submerging. As it softened, she shaved thin slices with the paring knife, patient, careful. The braid along the block's edge slowly blurred into plainness. With each curl folded aside, Marley's pulse climbed like someone ascending a bell ladder.

A glint again—clearer. Not brass, not the dull of tin. A

round lip emerged; then a line of engraved script, so fine it looked woven into the metal.

Hazel turned off the flame and dabbed away the melt with a cloth. "Tweezers," she murmured. Damien handed them without needing to ask which drawer. Hazel worked the fine tips beneath a narrow band and lifted gently.

The ring slid out of the wax like a secret agreeing, at last, to be shared.

No one spoke. Hazel cradled it in her palm. It was slender, old-fashioned, the rim soft from wear. The metal was warm in hue—not pure yellow, not copper—an alloy with a faint green suggestion in the shadows, as though the metal remembered fire colored by salts.

Marley leaned in. The inside of the band held an engraving in a hand intimate as breath: *Yours in time, E.C. to A.C.*

Her breath broke on the first letter. "E.C."

Hazel glanced up. "Do you know—?"

"Elijah Callahan," Marley said, the name emerging not as guess but as recognition. "And A.C. is Amelia Colvin." She swallowed and closed her eyes. The words on the ring swam with the cadence of the music box's waltz—*step, step —wait*—as if "in time" belonged to both melody and promise.

Damien lowered his head until the lens of his magnifier caught the light. "The script is period-correct," he said softly. "Hand-cut, not machine. See the slight drag at the bottom of the 'Y'? A jeweler's bur lifted there. And the serif on the 'C'—that's a local style. Whitaker Brothers used it in the thirties." He looked at Hazel. "Did your crate include any mention of who sent it? A ledger slip?"

Hazel reached under the bench, brought up the crumpled tag. Damien took a pencil tracing of the hand—just block letters, clerk's haste. But at the bottom, in smaller script, someone had added: *"for remelt—set aside until after winter."* No date. No initials.

Marley couldn't stop looking at the words inside the ring. *Yours in time.* Not *forever*, not *always*, not *until death.* Time. As if the giver had already known time would not behave for them. As if he meant not eternity but rhythm. A vow that would have to learn the town's broken cadence.

Damien cleaned a corner of the ring with a cotton cloth, the way he might have wiped a pane to see a marginalia no one had seen in decades. He held it to the light and cocked his head. "There's a hallmark near the inscription."

Marley leaned in. A tiny bellflower stamped into the band—so small you could miss it unless you were already looking for bells in everything.

"Whitaker hallmark," Hazel said. "They did wedding bands and remembrance rings both."

"Remembrance," Marley repeated, the word tasting like both comfort and warning.

Hazel passed the ring to her. For an instant Marley didn't dare touch it. Then she placed it on her palm. It was heavier than she expected, the way some truths are. The faint green cast—she saw it again when she lifted the band toward the window, a vein of color waking only in certain angles, like the green flame Mrs. Bennett had sketched above the river.

She thought of the ledger's mention: *balance rested.* Of the printing plate's hidden words: *seven hands bind, seven vows stand.* Of the music box and its companion melody, one waiting for the other's voice. *Yours in time.* If Elijah had given this ring to Amelia, did he know even then that their vow would have to pause? That time itself would be an instrument they had to learn to play?

Her hands shook. She set the ring gently on the felt pad Hazel handed over. "It's theirs," she said—then corrected herself. "It was theirs. Now it's evidence."

Damien's gaze flicked up, caution already sharpening. "And it's a grenade if handled badly. That inscription names two families. One of them still sits on the council."

Hazel's eyes moved between them, her face soft with worry. "If it's dangerous, I can—" She looked at the block of wax and the space it left behind, then back to the ring. "No, that's foolish. If it hid this long, it's tired of hiding."

"We won't parade it," Damien said, voice gentle but firm. "Not yet. Photograph, document, lockbox. Chain of custody. Marley, we'll need the journal."

Marley had already pulled her satchel in close. Elijah's leather-bound confession lay inside, the spine more cracked now than when the archive volunteer had slid it across the table weeks ago. She opened to the page she had dog-eared not for any academic reason but for the ache it held.

I bought a band before the frost took the river. I chose the old alloy the glassworkers favored, the one that shines green in certain lights. She wanted copper, she said, because copper remembers touch. I wanted time. Perhaps we were both right. Perhaps we were both fools.

Marley pressed her fingers to the line, breath snagging. "He writes about the ring," she said. "And about the alloy. 'Green in certain lights.'"

Hazel made a sound like a laugh refusing to be born. "Then it's theirs."

Damien's mouth tightened. "The journal is unpublished. Its custody is fragile. If we link it to the ring without care, we give the Callahan descendants grounds to claim both and disappear them into a lawyer's safe."

"Or we give the Colvin descendants cause to bring the town square to a boil," Hazel added, not unkindly.

Marley's grip on the journal loosened. "They'll fight over a vow they once conspired to control."

Damien nodded. "Which is why we document, then decide who sees what, and when." He turned the ring in the light one more time, the green vein glancing—like a hidden road appearing when the sun clears the tree line. "This inscription isn't simply romantic. It's theological, in the town's sense. *In time.* It claims that time is the medium of fidelity. Not instantaneous blessing, not a performance at a chapel door. Time. And that is what the bell refused: a vow stamped by a seal rather than proven by time."

Marley lifted her eyes to him. "And proven by witnesses."

"Exactly." He set the ring on the felt again and stepped back, as if acknowledging a sanctity that required distance. "But before we think of showing, we must think of harm." He hesitated, searching her face. "Marley, there are living Callahans who were children in the last years of Amelia's life. They've built their adulthood on a version of this story that lets everyone keep their seats. If we publish an inscription that romanticizes Elijah, we might be doing what he never managed to do in life: declare himself. That could break people who didn't break you."

Marley swallowed. It wasn't accusation; it was care voiced as risk. "And the other side of that caution," she said quietly, "is that leaving Amelia in silence breaks me. And the women like her who were written out to keep the minutes tidy."

Hazel reached across and covered Marley's hand. "Both can be true. That's why you two must be careful as surgeons. Cut where you must. Spare what you can."

The shop's bell jingled as a customer came in and then —seeing the closed sign Hazel had half-forgotten to flip— backed out with a polite shrug. The ordinary scrape of their boots on the step made the moment feel more dangerous by contrast.

Damien produced a velvet pouch from his satchel and, with Hazel's nod, eased the ring inside. He labeled the pouch with date, location, finder. He photographed the wax block and its emptied cavity, the shavings, the tag with its shamefaced note. He took a final shot of the inscription under the bench lamp, the letters glowing like embers: *Yours in time.*

Marley felt tears threaten and blinked them back. "He didn't write *yours forever,*" she said, half to the ring, half to the room. "He wrote *in time.* As if he knew the bell would refuse the first attempt. As if he wanted her to have a promise that could survive pauses."

Damien tied the pouch drawstring and met her eyes, something unguarded there. "That's the only kind we've had, you and I. The kind that survives pauses."

She almost reached for his hand, almost said the thing that would spill everything onto the bench beside the shavings. Instead, she lifted the journal's ribbon and marked the page, then closed the leather cover as if setting a seal of her own.

"What now?" Hazel asked.

"Now we take it to the shop," Damien said. "I catalog and lock it. Marley reads the journal again for any mention we've missed. We map Callahan descendants against what we intend to publish. And we decide—carefully—when to let the town see what it asked the chandler to erase."

Hazel nodded, relief and grief braided in her face. "Then go. And—" She touched the tray that held the block, now lighter by one secret. "I'll save the wax. We'll need every remnant."

Outside, the day had thinned to that particular winter light that makes edges look like choices. Marley tucked the velvet pouch against her heart beneath her coat and felt the metal's faint warmth through cloth. The green in the alloy seemed to hum even unseen, like a flame choosing to breathe in a small room.

As they stepped into the falling snow, Damien said, without looking away from the road ahead, "This love story is a lantern, Marley. But lanterns can blind if you lift them carelessly in a dark crowd." He glanced at her then, gentle and unsparing. "We'll carry it, but we'll shade it, too."

She nodded. The bell tower's shadow lay across the street like a bar they'd learned to step over without bowing. Somewhere behind them, in a chandler's tin tray, the emptied wax cooled into a shape that remembered keeping. In her pocket, the ring kept a different kind of heat—time's patient glow, waiting for witnesses who would not mistake a pause for an ending.

THE WALK back to the bookshop was slow, the velvet pouch heavy in Marley's pocket as though it carried more than metal. Each crunch of their boots on snow seemed to strike against the engraving in her mind: *Yours in time, E.C. to A.C.* The words clung like a refrain, their intimacy at odds with the town's refusal to let them be sung aloud.

Inside, Marley set the pouch on the oak table as if it were an altar stone. Damien unpacked his satchel with the deliberate care of a man laying out tools for surgery— camera, notebook, cotton gloves, acid-free envelopes. He spread them in a neat line, then glanced at her with a question unspoken: *Are you ready to do this properly?*

She nodded, though her throat tightened. "Let's record it before the silence tries again."

Damien photographed the ring from every angle, adjusting the lamp to catch both the greenish vein in the metal and the fine engraving. Marley transcribed aloud as he worked: "Inscription—inner band. Cursive hand. Reads: *Yours in time, E.C. to A.C.* Hallmark present, bellflower stamp. Condition—worn but intact."

Her voice trembled, but the act of saying the words steadied her. The ring was no longer a secret kept in wax; it was testimony now, written into their record.

WHEN THE PHOTOGRAPHS WERE DONE, Damien opened the journal to the page Marley had marked. He placed the ring beside the ink, so the words Elijah had written decades ago seemed to lean toward the metal like old friends.

"'I bought a band before the frost took the river...'" Marley read aloud, her voice catching on the line. "'Perhaps we were both right. Perhaps we were both fools.'"

She looked up, eyes shining. "Damien, it's not just speculation anymore. This ring proves the journal wasn't a private fantasy. He meant it. He carried it."

Damien's brow furrowed, though his tone was gentle. "Proof to us, yes. But to the town? They'll say it's circumstantial. A ring with initials. A journal with untested provenance. They'll insist anyone could have carved letters, anyone could have written a name."

Marley's frustration flared hot. "Why must truth always bow to what can be defended in court?"

"Because truth without defense gets burned," Damien

replied quietly. "The Circle taught this town that silence is safer than song. If we want the song to last, we must build its chorus carefully."

Marley pressed her palms against the table. "And what of Amelia? Of Elijah? They weren't careful enough and were erased. Do we risk repeating the same pattern by waiting too long?"

The fire snapped in the hearth, the sound like a bell struck in warning.

LATER, as night settled, Marley paced the shop while Damien cataloged. Each step across the creaking floorboards carried her deeper into the question that gnawed at her: who had hidden the ring in wax?

"Hazel said the crate was labeled for remelt," she murmured. "Which means someone in the Colvin line knew what was inside and wanted it destroyed—but not immediately. Why wait until after winter?"

Damien looked up from his notes. "Perhaps because winter is when the bell rings. Or when it should have. They feared the vow's return most at solstice."

Marley turned sharply, the idea cutting through her. "So they hid the proof in wax, timed for destruction when the town's ears were most tuned to silence. But something intervened. The crate was misplaced, or forgotten, until Hazel received it."

Damien nodded slowly. "Accident or design, it survived. Which means we must ask whether someone wanted it to survive."

Marley froze, remembering the gloves left at her door, the photograph found in the archives, the printing plate delivered into their hands. "The trail. Each piece handed to us. Someone wanted this ring found, just as they wanted the gloves and the plate found."

Damien's expression darkened, but not with disbelief. "Then we are not alone in our search. Someone alive is tending Amelia's vow. The question is whether they are ally—or manipulator."

Marley's breath quickened. "Do you think it's a descendant? Someone trying to unburden a family conscience?"

"Possibly," Damien said. "Or someone who still believes the vow must be kept hidden, but wishes us to shoulder the risk of revelation."

The thought chilled her. "Then we're pawns."

"Or partners," Damien countered softly. "It depends on whether we trust the hand that guides."

THE LAMPLIGHT FLICKERED LOW as the hours stretched. Marley sat at the desk, the ring before her on its felt pad. She reached out once, hesitated, then slid it onto her finger. It fit loosely, as though sized for another time, another hand.

For a moment she closed her eyes. She imagined Amelia slipping the band onto her finger, the weight of Elijah's promise pressing like warmth into her skin. She imagined the vow they had crafted—*in time*—a rhythm that could outlast silence, if only it were witnessed.

When she opened her eyes, Damien was watching her, his expression unreadable.

"You shouldn't wear it," he said gently. "Not until we decide what to do with it."

She slid it off, but her voice was firm. "I needed to feel what she felt. Even if only for a breath. Because we are not only keepers of artifacts, Damien. We are keepers of grief. If we forget that, then all our cataloging is nothing but dust."

Damien lowered his gaze, but his reply carried weight. "And if we let grief drive us unguarded, the Circle wins again by watching us burn."

BEFORE THEY CLOSED the shop for the night, Marley placed the ring in a small wooden box lined with velvet, the kind her aunt had once used for rare editions. She set it on the highest shelf, behind rows of leather-bound volumes. Hidden, but not erased. Waiting, like the vow itself.

Damien locked the journal away, then stood by the door with his coat half-buttoned. He looked at Marley, and for a moment the caution in his face softened.

"This ring," he said, "isn't just artifact. It's a hinge. Between past and present. Between silence and speech. If we open it too soon, the door may collapse. If we never open it, Amelia remains veiled forever. We must choose carefully when to turn the key."

Marley stepped closer, her voice low but certain. "Then let's promise one thing: we will not let the Circle decide for us again. The vow froze, but it waited. Now it's ours to carry forward."

Damien studied her, then gave a small nod. "Agreed."

The snow deepened outside, blanketing the square in quiet. The Winter Bell remained mute, its tower stark against the night. But in the hush, Marley felt the weight of the ring's words: *Yours in time.*

Not forever. Not lost. In time.

And time, she knew, was waking.

THE SNOW HAD NOT STOPPED by morning. It blanketed Brookwood in stillness, muting the edges of roofs, benches, and fences into one seamless whiteness. Marley stared out from the bookshop window, the velvet box hidden behind the highest row of books above her. The ring felt less like an artifact and more like a storm coiled in miniature—waiting, inevitable.

Damien brewed coffee in the back room, his movements precise but distracted. When he returned, mugs in hand, his face carried the gravity of decisions waiting to be spoken. He set the mugs down, sat opposite her, and opened his notebook.

"Marley," he began, "we need to talk about the families."

She turned, her breath tight. "Callahan and Colvin."

He nodded. "The initials on the ring tie Elijah Callahan and Amelia Colvin together unmistakably. The journal corroborates it. If this story is brought to light, it doesn't just rewrite history—it cuts through two living lineages that still shape this town. Both families have descendants on the council. Both carry influence in subtle, enduring ways. And both have reason to fight tooth and nail to keep this buried."

Marley clenched her hands in her lap. "The Colvins already buried Amelia once. Hid the ring in wax, labeled it for remelt. They've shown us what silence looks like when it serves power. And the Callahans—if Elijah's words ever reached daylight, their heirs would have inherited shame instead of stature. Both sides benefited from erasure."

Damien's gaze was steady. "And if we unveil it, we undo decades of carefully balanced quiet. We could fracture Brookwood's fragile peace."

Marley's voice shook, though conviction sharpened her words. "Then let it fracture. Because peace built on silence isn't peace. It's prison."

·   ·   ·

THEY SAT in silence for a long while, the fire crackling softly, the snow whispering against the windows. Damien finally spoke again, softer.

"Do you remember when we first uncovered the printing plate? You told me the silence wasn't empty—that it was waiting. I dismissed it then as poetic instinct. But now, holding this ring, I know you were right. The silence has weight because it is guarding something alive."

Marley met his eyes. "And the weight isn't ours to keep hidden. It belongs to the town. To the truth."

"But truths can wound," Damien countered gently. "Think of Mrs. Bennett's dream—the woman in white weeping at the river. Amelia's grief is no less real for being eighty years old. If we set it loose, we might make the town grieve all over again. Not only for her, but for the choices their ancestors made."

Marley's throat tightened. "And isn't that the only way healing begins? By grieving what was done, and what was denied?"

Damien looked down at his notebook, his fingers tapping against the margin. "I fear the Callahans will accuse us of tarnishing Elijah, painting him as weak for never declaring himself. The Colvins will rage at the implication that Amelia was betrayed by silence rather than by choice. Either side may try to claim the ring and spirit it away into legal oblivion."

Marley leaned forward, her voice fierce now. "Then we vow not to let that happen. We will not let this ring vanish into another vault, another wax block, another generation of denial. Amelia carried it once, Elijah inscribed it once, and now it rests with us. We will not fail them."

. . .

THE HOURS that followed were filled with names and possibilities. Who might be allies, who might resist. Councilor Miriam Merrick, perhaps, if her hesitation hid sympathy. Mrs. Bennett already drawn into the vow through dream. Tessa at the print shop, who respected flame and balance both. And others—the circle of witnesses that would be needed when the moment came to reveal.

But every name was a gamble, each one a thread that could either weave a banner or unravel into another shroud of silence.

At one point, Damien rubbed his temples, exhausted. "Do you understand, Marley? If we press this into light, we will become adversaries to half the town. Perhaps more. They will say we are disturbing the dead. That we are tearing at roots meant to stay buried. We could lose everything—reputation, shop, community."

Marley stood, pacing, her hand pressed to her chest where she could still feel the phantom weight of the ring she had tried on the night before. Her voice trembled, but her resolve did not.

"Then let it be so. Because what is a shop if it shelves only comfortable lies? What is a community if it requires us to silence the ones who loved, the ones who grieved, the ones who tried to speak? If Brookwood's peace demands Amelia's absence, then it is not peace—it is cowardice."

She stopped, turning to him, eyes burning. "I will not collude with cowardice. Not in her name."

Damien rose slowly, his eyes meeting hers with an intensity that carried both fear and admiration. "And you would risk everything for this vow?"

"I already have," Marley whispered. "Since the night the bell stayed silent, I've been walking toward this risk. Haven't you?"

His silence was answer enough.

THEY WENT to the window together, watching the snow thicken around the bell tower. Its mute outline rose above the square like a judge who had spoken once and never again.

Damien said quietly, "Then let's bind ourselves, Marley. Not to artifacts, not to families, not to councils. To truth. To vow that we will not let this ring vanish again, no matter the cost."

Marley felt her heart pound with the echo of Amelia's unheard vows. She extended her hand. "We vow."

Damien took it, his grip firm, his voice steady. "We vow."

The silence deepened, but it was no longer oppressive. It felt like listening.

Together they stood, watching the snow bury the square, knowing that when the thaw came, Brookwood itself might fracture. Yet they also knew the fracture was already there—hidden, denied, festering. Their task was not to cause it, but to reveal it.

And for Amelia, for Elijah, for the vow that froze instead of dying, they would not look away.

16

THE WINTER BALL PREPARATIONS

The Winter Ball was stitched into Brookwood's bones. Even in years when the harvest had failed, when storms had gutted the fishing docks, or when grief silenced houses for weeks at a time, the ball had gone on. Tradition demanded it, as if dancing could braid together what sorrow frayed. This year was no exception, though the silence of the Winter Bell pressed like frost against every plan.

Marley first heard the stirrings of preparation when she entered the council hall on a Monday afternoon. The air smelled of polish and evergreen sap; garlands were being tested along the beams, and the creak of ladders mixed with the chatter of townsfolk determined to ignore the heaviness hanging over them. She stood in the doorway for a long moment, half in awe, half in sorrow at the lengths people went to clothe silence in ribbons.

"Marley, there you are." Councilor Miriam Merrick, brisk as always, bustled toward her, clipboard in hand. "We were hoping you'd stop by. There's something we'd like from you this year."

Marley's heart gave a small, reluctant leap. "From me?"

"A talk," Councilor Miriam Merrick said, adjusting her glasses. "Short. Historical. Something about the Winter Ball's roots, perhaps a reminder that the solstice has always carried joy as well as mystery. With everything that's happened—the bell's silence, the unease—you could help set a steadier tone."

A murmur of agreement rose from others nearby. Marley looked from one face to the next. Their smiles were polite, hopeful, but tight around the edges. They wanted reassurance, a narrative that would smooth the jagged edges of the season.

She forced a smile. "I'll consider it. Thank you for thinking of me."

But as she left the hall, the thought needled her: what if she used the platform not to comfort, but to honor Amelia Colvin? What if she spoke the name the town avoided, gave voice to the vow buried under wax and silence?

LATER THAT EVENING, Marley shared the request with Damien. He was cataloging in the archive room, his glasses low on his nose, surrounded by the scent of paper and dust. When she told him about the talk, he paused, pencil hovering.

"And you're considering speaking of Amelia?" he asked carefully.

"I don't see how I can't," Marley replied. "She is the heart of what we've been uncovering. The ball is a celebration of vows, of continuity. How can I stand before the town and speak of tradition without acknowledging the vow that was denied?"

Damien set the pencil down, folding his hands.

"Because the town may not be ready. They asked for reassurance, not confrontation. If you speak her name there, in that setting, it will not be taken as honor. It will be taken as provocation."

Marley crossed her arms, stung. "So we keep her hidden to protect their comfort?"

"I'm not saying that," Damien said, his voice weary but firm. "I'm saying truth has seasons. Force it in the wrong one, and it dies before it can root."

Silence thickened between them. Marley wanted to argue, but she saw in his eyes something more complicated than caution. He looked tired, pulled between duty and something she couldn't name.

"Damien," she said softly, "what's wrong?"

He hesitated, then stood, pacing slowly. "I received a letter last week. From Oxford. A fellowship—three months of archival work. They want me to study ritual manuscripts in their winter collection. It's the sort of opportunity I've waited years for."

The words landed like stones in her chest. "And you didn't tell me?"

"I didn't know how," Damien admitted, his shoulders sagging. "Because the truth is, I'm considering it. I thought I could give us time—give myself time—to decide. But with each discovery here, I feel torn. As if my life is split between two callings, and I can't serve both."

Marley's throat tightened. "So while I decide whether to speak Amelia's name, you decide whether to leave?"

His gaze was pained. "It isn't abandonment, Marley. It's... an opening. And I don't know yet if I have the courage to refuse it."

· · ·

THAT NIGHT, Marley couldn't sleep. The ring in its velvet pouch weighed on her mind, heavy as a bell unmoved. She lay awake, hearing the echoes of Councilor Miriam Merrick's request, of Damien's confession, of Amelia's silence pressing against her ribs.

In the darkness she whispered, "What would you have me do, Amelia? Speak? Wait? Dance in silence while truth freezes deeper?"

No answer came, only the steady hush of snow falling outside.

By morning, the decision still loomed, unshaped. She stood at the window watching children drag sleds across the square, their laughter thin but real. The Winter Ball would go on. The town would dress its fear in finery, as it always had. And she—Marley Taylor—would have to choose whether to stand at the microphone and repeat the comfort they craved, or to speak a name that might crack their fragile peace open like ice splitting on a river.

Behind her, Damien moved quietly through the shelves, his presence both anchor and ache. He hadn't pressed her, hadn't argued further. But the unspoken truth hung in the air between them: both of them were being asked to choose.

And choices, like vows, left no one untouched.

MARLEY SPREAD her notes across the oak table, candlelight flickering over the scattered pages. She had pulled volumes from the town archive, her aunt's ledgers, even the scattered ephemera of past Winter Balls—programs, ribbon-faded invitations, yellowed clippings. The words blurred in places, not because the ink had faded, but because the choice of what to say pressed too heavily.

She dipped her pen, paused above the page, and whispered into the silence: "Do I tell them your name, Amelia?"

Her pen finally moved. She began by drafting the safe version: a history of the Winter Ball as community ritual, the solstice tradition meant to usher in light during the longest night, the symbolism of evergreen garlands, the stories of early founders who danced not for spectacle but for endurance.

But even as she wrote, her hand trembled. None of it was false, but none of it was enough. The silence of the bell hung between the lines, daring her to fill it.

She pulled the velvet pouch from the shelf and set it beside her notes. The weight of the ring felt like the weight of decision. Its inscription glowed in memory: *Yours in time.*

Marley scrawled in the margin: *To speak her name is to break the silence. To omit it is to collude with it.*

Damien entered quietly, carrying a stack of letters. He set them on his desk, not joining her at the table. His eyes lingered on her notes but did not ask.

"You're still working?" he said softly.

"I can't stop," Marley admitted. "Every draft I make feels wrong. Too shallow, or too safe."

He nodded, but his distance was palpable. He untied the letters, glanced at one, then set it aside.

"You're not really here," she said, sharper than she meant.

He looked up, startled. "What do you mean?"

"You're somewhere else. Oxford, maybe. Those archives you can't stop thinking about. Even now, when we're holding Amelia's vow in our hands."

Damien's jaw tightened. "I haven't decided."

"But you're withdrawing," Marley pressed. "I can feel it. While I wrestle with whether to speak her name, you wrestle with whether to leave me to do it alone."

He leaned against the desk, folding his arms. "It isn't about leaving you. It's about who I am if I stay. You see this place as your calling, Marley. I see it as... a crossroad. If I stay, it defines me. If I go, I risk abandoning more than I can name. Either way, it changes everything."

Marley rose from the table, her hands trembling. "And what about Amelia? About Elijah? They didn't get to choose their calling—it was stolen from them. Now we stand here with the chance to finish what they began, and you're thinking of running halfway across the world?"

Damien's voice broke, low and raw. "Because I'm afraid, Marley. Afraid that if I stay, I'll fail. That I'll dig too deep, push too far, and bring down the very walls we're trying to protect. Sometimes leaving feels like the only way to protect what's left."

The words cut her, but she saw the truth in them—the scholar's fear of becoming executioner instead of witness.

SHE RETURNED TO THE TABLE, took the ring from the pouch, and held it in her palm. "This isn't ours to keep safe. It's ours to risk. Amelia risked everything to preserve her vow. Elijah risked writing it, even if only in a hidden journal. If we hold back now, then the silence wins again."

Damien stepped closer, his expression torn. "And if we speak too soon, we may divide this town beyond repair. You think truth will heal, but truth also cuts. You know that."

Marley met his gaze, steady now. "Then let it cut. Wounds can close. But silence festers until it poisons everything."

He looked at her for a long time, the weight of her words sinking in. Then he turned away, staring into the fire. His hands opened and closed at his sides, as though grasping invisible threads of decision.

Later, when Marley sat alone again with her drafts, she sketched two versions of her talk. One that spoke of tradition, of evergreen strength, of dances held through storm and grief. The other that named Amelia Colvin—called her "the vow that froze instead of failing," invoked her as witness to the bell's silence.

She placed them side by side, candlelight flickering across the pages. The safe version soothed like a lullaby. The dangerous one ached like a wound, but pulsed with life.

She whispered to herself, "One comforts the town. The other comforts Amelia."

And she knew already which mattered more.

When the shop finally stilled, Marley blew out her candle. The drafts lay on the table, waiting. But in her heart she knew which one would follow her to the podium.

Amelia's name would not remain hidden. Not if Marley had breath left to speak it.

Snow pressed against the windows in heavy drifts, the shop groaning as if the weight of winter itself had leaned into its timbers. Marley stood at the desk with her drafts spread before her—the safe script and the dangerous one—though she no longer felt torn. Her decision had hardened like ice under frost.

"I'm going to name her," she said into the silence,

though she knew Damien was in the back room. Her voice carried anyway, firm as a vow.

He appeared after a pause, shoulders heavy with fatigue, glasses dangling from one hand. "Marley—"

"No," she cut in. "I've thought through every angle, every consequence. I've weighed their comfort against her erasure. I will not stand in that hall and speak of traditions while the bell remains silent and Amelia Colvin remains veiled. I will not pretend."

Damien's brow furrowed, but he didn't interrupt. She pressed on.

"She deserves to be named. To be honored as part of the town's history. Maybe the council will squirm, maybe the families will rage, maybe people will whisper that I've broken something fragile. But I'd rather break a fragile peace than keep holding up a lie."

The words landed between them with the weight of stone.

DAMIEN SET HIS GLASSES DOWN, folding his arms. "Do you understand what you're setting in motion? The Colvins will see it as accusation. The Callahans will feel their legacy questioned. You're not just speaking history—you're lighting a fuse."

"Then let it burn," Marley replied. "We've been walking with fire since the night the bell refused to ring. Maybe the fuse needs to burn before Brookwood can breathe again."

His jaw tightened. "And when the blast comes, do you think you'll be untouched? Do you think this shop will stand as it is? That the people who smiled at you in the market will still trust you with their stories?"

Marley's voice softened, though the conviction

remained. "No. I know I'll pay a price. But if I'm silent, the price is Amelia's eternity. I won't be her accomplice."

Damien closed his eyes briefly, then opened them with a look that was equal parts sorrow and admiration. "You've made your choice."

"I have," she whispered.

SILENCE STRETCHED. Damien paced to the shelves, running his hand along spines as if searching for steadiness in the touch of books. Finally he spoke, low and halting.

"Then I should be honest too. I've made mine."

Marley felt her heart clench. "Oxford."

He nodded. "They want me in January. Three months. It's not only the work—it's the chance to stand again in the great halls, to handle manuscripts that shaped civilizations. To see my own research in a wider frame. I can't pretend it doesn't pull me."

Marley's throat tightened. "So while I speak Amelia's name to a town that may turn on me, you'll be across the ocean?"

Pain flashed in his eyes. "Don't make it sound like abandonment. This isn't easy. Every part of me is split. A fellowship is survival for the scholar I've always been. But Brookwood—" He stopped, swallowed hard. "Brookwood is survival for something I never expected to find. You. This work with you."

Marley's eyes burned. "Then why choose leaving?"

"Because staying feels like choosing against myself," Damien said, voice raw. "And leaving feels like choosing against you. Either way, I betray something I love."

Her tears fell then, hot against the chill of the room. She pressed her palms to the desk, grounding herself. "You speak of manuscripts as if they are more alive than vows. Damien, Amelia didn't carve *yours in time* into parchment. She carved it into metal, into flesh, into silence. That's what we've been carrying. And if you leave—if you step away now —you risk repeating Elijah's silence. And I will not forgive that."

The words cut, and she knew it. But they were true, and she couldn't unsay them.

DAMIEN TURNED, bracing himself against the shelves, his back to her. His shoulders shook once, then stilled. When he spoke, his voice was hoarse.

"I'm terrified, Marley. Not of the town, not of the families —of failing you. Of standing in that hall while you name her, and knowing that all my training, all my knowledge, can't shield you from what follows. At Oxford, I know my place. Here, I feel like I'm always one misstep away from ruining everything we're trying to save."

Marley walked to him, her hand trembling as she touched his shoulder. He turned, and she saw the fear plain in his eyes.

"You don't ruin it by standing with me," she said. "You ruin it by leaving me to stand alone."

His hand covered hers, grip tight. "And what if I can't give you what you deserve? What if I falter?"

"Then falter beside me," Marley whispered fiercely. "But don't vanish."

THE FIRE in the grate sank low, shadows stretching across the shop. They stood in the half-light, two people bound by vows they had never spoken aloud but felt in every silence.

Finally Damien exhaled, long and ragged. "Then here is my vow, for now. I haven't accepted Oxford yet. I'll write them tomorrow. I'll ask for a delay. But if I feel that staying here means losing myself, I may still go."

Marley nodded, though her chest ached. "And I'll vow this: when I stand at the Winter Ball, I will speak Amelia's name. Whether you're beside me or not."

Their eyes met, the truth unflinching between them. Neither vow comforted. Both demanded cost.

That night, Marley drafted the version of her speech she knew she would give. She wrote Amelia's name in careful ink, underlined it once, then laid the pen aside.

In his own home, Damien wrote a letter to Oxford, asking for time. His hand shook as he signed his name, sealing the paper with a weight that felt like both reprieve and sentence.

The bell tower loomed in the night outside, still silent, still watching.

And two vows waited—one to speak, one to decide—both sharp as glass, both binding as rings.

The Winter Ball approached, carrying with it the risk that truth would fracture Brookwood, and the risk that silence would fracture them.

Either way, the season would not pass untouched.

17

SNOWBOUND AND STILL

The storm began in the late afternoon, sudden and unrelenting. By dusk the streets of Brookwood were near invisible, swallowed by white sheets of wind. Marley had intended only a quick stop at the print shop, but once inside, the weather decided for her. The door groaned against drifts already pushing high, and Tessa, standing behind the counter, shook her head.

"You'll not get home tonight, Marley. Not unless you fancy freezing before you reach the square."

Marley glanced at the window. Snow pressed so thick it was like looking into wool. "Then I suppose I'll keep you company."

Tessa chuckled. "No, no—I live above the shop. But you'll have the run of the records. There's a cot in the back if you need it. My father always said the print shop kept ghosts in the files; perhaps you'll make friends with them."

She left her with the key to the record drawers, a kettle, and a blanket folded neatly on the back of a chair. Then she retired upstairs, the sound of her steps fading into the creak of the ceiling beams.

Marley was alone. Alone with the howl of the storm, the scent of ink and paper, and the rows of drawers that had not been touched in decades.

She lit a lantern and wandered the narrow aisles. Dust filmed every surface, and the drawers bore labels that were barely legible: *Notices, 1920s, Marriage Announcements, 1930s, Miscellaneous Correspondence.* She drew one open at random. Inside lay envelopes with broken seals, print proofs with penciled corrections, scraps of typeface samples.

Her fingers found a bundle tied with twine. She pulled it free, brushing dust off the paper. The label scrawled on the top sheet read: *Colvin—unfiled proofs.*

Her pulse quickened. She carried the bundle to the worktable, sat down, and untied it. Inside were invitations, flyers, and handbills. Some bore the Colvin name in bold script—wedding announcements, charity events, notices of land leases. Others were half-finished, abandoned after errors.

At the bottom of the stack, folded inside a blank proof, was a letter. The handwriting was elegant, unmistakably feminine. Marley smoothed it open, her lantern throwing the ink into sharp relief.

My dearest A.,

If this finds you, then courage has outrun fear. I cannot stand in silence while the vows of men crush what breath remains in us. You are not abandoned, beloved. You are shielded. He stands because I cannot. He bears the public vow so we may keep the true one hidden. When you walk toward the altar, know it is not emptiness you meet, but the veil we built together. In another season, when time allows, we will burn away the frost. Until then, remember: love does not ring bells for witnesses. It rings in the chambers only we can reach.

It was unsigned, but the flourish at the end—a looping *M* curling into the margin—was clear enough.

Marley's hands trembled. A woman had written this to Amelia Colvin.

THE REVELATION STRUCK her like ice-water and fire all at once. Amelia had not been abandoned at the altar. Her fiancé had not betrayed her. Instead, he had shielded her. Covered for her. The silence of the bell had not been the silence of failure, but the silence of protection.

Marley pressed the letter to her chest, tears rising unbidden. All the fragments—the gloves stained with ink, the frozen flame by the river, the ring inscribed *Yours in time*—they shifted now, aligning into a pattern she had not dared imagine.

Amelia's true love had been a woman.

And Elijah Callahan, her supposed fiancé, had carried the silence to protect them both.

THE STORM RATTLED THE WINDOWS, but inside Marley felt the stillness of clarity. She read the letter again, slowly, tasting each word. *You are shielded. He stands because I cannot. Love does not ring bells for witnesses.*

The letter had never been sent. Perhaps it had been intercepted, or abandoned before posting. But it had survived, tucked among proofs, waiting for a night when the storm would trap her long enough to find it.

She folded it gently and set it beside her notes. Her mind spun with implications. If this truth came to light, it would unravel the town's entire narrative. The Colvins would be forced to face a legacy of suppression not only of vows but of love itself. The Callahans would be recast—not as betrayers, but as conspirators in mercy.

And Amelia—Amelia would no longer stand as the tragic abandoned bride, but as a woman whose vow had been kept in secret, denied not by her heart but by the world.

Marley whispered aloud, her voice unsteady: "You were never alone."

SHE SAT BACK, exhausted but alive with certainty. The cot waited in the corner, the storm wailed outside, but she could not rest. She began drafting furiously, writing down everything—her impressions, her theories, the shift this letter demanded in their understanding. Ink blotted, words sprawled across pages, but she didn't stop.

When finally her hand cramped, she leaned back, staring at the ceiling beams. She thought of Damien—his hesitation, his fear, his fellowship offer. She thought of how he would parse this letter, cautious as always, urging restraint. And yet, she knew in her marrow: this was no fragment to be tucked away.

This was a revelation.

And it would change everything.

THE STORM HOWLED against the print shop walls, a ceaseless roar that made the very timbers shiver. Marley sat hunched over the letter, lantern burning low, her mind spiraling through implications. Each line she reread pulled her deeper into a truth that unraveled everything she thought she knew about Amelia Colvin, Elijah Callahan, and the silence of the Winter Bell.

For weeks, she had wrestled with the town's narrative: Amelia abandoned, Elijah coward, the bell a mute witness to betrayal. But this letter whispered otherwise. Elijah's silence was not cowardice. It was sacrifice. He had stood in the role expected of him—not because he claimed Amelia, but because he shielded her. Shielded her love, hidden in a world that would not bear it.

Marley pressed her palms to her eyes, heart pounding. The tragedy had never been Elijah's failure to show at the altar. The tragedy was that Amelia had been forced to stand there, veiled and alone, while her truth was smothered to keep the town's order intact.

The words echoed: *He stands because I cannot.*

Elijah had carried that silence like a tombstone across his chest. Every record, every ledger, every artifact painted him as absent, weak, abandoning. But in truth, he had borne the cost of presence. He had chosen the crueler role: letting the world see him as faithless so that Amelia's beloved might remain unseen, unpunished.

Outside, the wind shrieked against the shutters, snow clattering like thrown salt. Marley rose, unable to sit still. She paced the narrow aisle between drawers, her lantern throwing shadows like broken bars across the walls.

The bell's silence—how many times had she stood beneath its tower, hearing the void where chimes should have rung? She had thought it merely a marker of vows undone. But now it seemed to carry a darker resonance. The silence had not simply recorded history—it had conspired with it. The bell that rang for weddings, for blessings, for vows sealed in daylight, had refused to ring for the vow whispered between two women in secret.

What if the town's sacred bell had always been selective? What if its silence was not absence but judgment—a mechanical witness echoing the prejudices of those who wound it, who guarded it, who claimed to keep its traditions?

Marley shivered, though the fire in the stove kept the print shop warm.

The entire narrative of the Winter Bell might be built on a lie. Not on unity, not on blessings, but on exclusion. Every peal the town celebrated could have been shadowed by another vow—unrecognized, unrecorded, unpermitted. And when the bell had finally gone silent this solstice, perhaps it was not failure at all. Perhaps it was protest.

Marley returned to the worktable, clutching the letter again. She traced the looping *M* at the end, wondering who this woman was. The town had hidden her well. Too well. Not a single ledger, not a single whispered anecdote had named her. Yet here she was, her love etched in ink, her voice breaking through decades of silence.

Could she have been a Colvin cousin? A friend from school? A woman of no family standing, invisible enough to slip between the cracks? Whoever she was, she had loved Amelia enough to write what others would not even whisper.

Love does not ring bells for witnesses. It rings in the chambers only we can reach.

Marley's throat tightened. This was not the language of hesitation—it was the language of defiance. Amelia had not stood in the snow waiting for a man to keep a promise. She had stood cloaked in a vow the town had already deemed impossible.

And Elijah, for all his silence, had been her ally.

Marley sank onto the cot, exhaustion mingling with awe. "You carried it for her," she whispered to Elijah's unseen memory. "You bore the blame so she could bear her truth. And we cursed you for cowardice."

She thought of Damien—how he wrestled with leaving, with fear of failing, with the choice between silence and witness. She thought of the parallels, sharp as frost against skin. If Elijah had chosen silence to protect, what choice would Damien make? To stand and share the weight, or to flee across the ocean and let her bear the consequences alone?

THE STORM RAGED ON, louder now, rattling the glass panes. Marley blew out the lantern, letting the firelight be her only glow. Shadows licked the corners, alive with secrets.

She lay back on the cot, letter clutched against her chest. Her mind replayed the solstice night when the bell had refused to ring, snowflakes slowing in the silence as if time itself had paused. She had thought it was omen. But perhaps it was recognition. Perhaps the bell was waiting, finally, for the vow left unfinished to be spoken aloud.

She imagined Amelia standing at the altar, the church windows frosted, her veil heavy with ice. She imagined Elijah at her side, playing his role, the town muttering of betrayal when the ceremony dissolved. But behind it all, hidden, was another woman, another love, another vow sealed without bell, without witness, without record.

Marley whispered into the storm, "Amelia, you weren't

betrayed. You were loved. Loved enough that silence became sacrifice."

The storm howled back, a wild chorus, as if agreeing.

And Marley knew: the next step was no longer only about history, no longer only about family legacies or broken records. It was about truth itself—truth that might fracture Brookwood, truth that might undo the fragile peace.

But truth nonetheless.

She closed her eyes, letter pressed to her heart, and listened to the storm's furious hymn. It was not unlike the sound of bells. Bells muffled, tangled in wind, but ringing all the same.

BY DAWN THE STORM RELENTED, not into silence but into a hushed stillness, as though the world had been remade beneath the drifts. Marley woke stiff from the cot, the letter still clutched in her hand, the ink smudged faintly against her skin from where she'd pressed it to her chest through the night.

She rose slowly, joints aching, lantern long since burned to cold wax. The fire in the stove had dimmed but not died, embers glowing like watchful eyes. Marley coaxed the flames back to life, but her mind was not on the fire. Her thoughts spun around the letter, its phrases echoing as insistently as bells: *He stands because I cannot. Love does not ring bells for witnesses.*

She sat at the worktable again, laying the letter flat before her. Morning light strained weakly through frost-rimmed windows, illuminating the words that had redrawn the story of Amelia Colvin.

This was no longer about speculation, fragments, or whispered hints. This was testimony.

And she could not keep it hidden.

HER FIRST INSTINCT was to hurry home, to place the letter in Damien's hands and watch his careful mind unravel the meaning alongside hers. But she paused, staring at the script again. She knew Damien—his instinct would be caution, analysis, warnings of repercussions. He would ask whether the letter was authentic, whether it had been planted, whether its implications could fracture Brookwood beyond repair.

All true questions. But Marley's heart already knew the answer that mattered: Amelia had not been alone in her love. That love had been hidden, shielded, silenced. And Marley would not collude in burying it again.

She touched the edge of the paper, whispering, "I vow, Amelia. Your love will not remain hidden. Not while I have breath."

The words startled her, spoken into the still air, but she felt them resonate deep in her chest. This was not research now, not history. It was calling.

SHE PACKED the letter carefully between sheets of blotting paper and slid it into her satchel, close to the pouch that held the ring. They belonged together, testimony side by side. The wind outside had softened to a mournful sigh, snow settling instead of raging. Marley bundled herself in cloak and gloves, braced against the cold, and pushed open the shop door.

Snowdrifts rose high, and she trudged through them

slowly, each step an effort. The streets were deserted, houses banked in white, smoke rising from a few chimneys. Brookwood had been blanketed into stillness. Yet in that hush Marley felt not oppression, but promise.

She paused beneath the bell tower as she made her way toward the square. The Winter Bell loomed, icicles hanging like frozen tears from its eaves. She gazed up at it, heart hammering.

"You kept their secret," she murmured. "But I won't. Not anymore."

The tower gave no reply, but a clump of snow slid from its ledge, striking the ground with a heavy thud. Marley almost smiled. Silence could answer in many ways.

WHEN SHE REACHED THE BOOKSHOP, the familiar warmth of home steadied her. She stoked the fire, shed her snow-crusted cloak, and laid the satchel gently on the desk. Her hands trembled, not from cold now but from anticipation. Damien would arrive soon—he had spent the storm at the council's records office, or so he'd said before the snow made travel impossible. She imagined the look on his face when she showed him the letter.

But she also imagined his questions, his warnings, his fear.

And still she knew: no matter his caution, no matter the town's resistance, she would not let this slip back into shadow.

She pulled fresh paper toward her and began drafting, not a speech this time but a declaration to herself. Words spilled, steady and sharp:

Amelia Colvin's story has been twisted by silence. Elijah

Callahan did not betray her. He bore the weight of falsehood to shield the truth. The vow she carried was not broken—it was hidden. It was love, and it was real, and it will not remain buried any longer.

She underlined the last line, her pen biting into the page.

THE DOOR creaked open as dusk neared, snow swirling in with Damien as he stamped his boots and pulled down his scarf. His face was tired, his hair damp with melt, but his eyes sought her immediately.

"You stayed at the print shop?" he asked, voice rough.

Marley nodded, rising to meet him. Her hands shook as she reached into her satchel and drew out the letter, still wrapped in blotting paper. She held it out to him without a word.

He frowned, took it gently, and unfolded it. His eyes moved across the lines, his brow tightening, his mouth parting slightly. By the time he reached the looping *M*, his face had gone pale.

"This changes everything," he whispered.

Marley stepped closer. "Yes. It means the vow wasn't betrayal. It means Elijah's silence was sacrifice. It means Amelia's love was real, and it's been buried under lies for eighty years."

Damien closed the letter slowly, hands trembling. "Marley... if this is true, if the town hears it, the entire narrative collapses. The Colvins will be accused of erasing a love story to protect their standing. The Callahans will be recast, their legacy rewritten. The Circle's authority will crumble. People will be furious. Divided."

Marley's eyes burned with unshed tears, but her voice

was unwavering. "Then let them be. Better division built on truth than unity built on lies."

Damien shook his head, grief etched in his features. "You'll make enemies. More than you can imagine."

"I don't care," Marley said. "I've already made my vow. Amelia will not stand veiled in silence any longer. I will speak her name, and I will speak her love, even if it shatters Brookwood's story of itself."

Damien looked at her for a long, heavy moment. Then he set the letter down and took her hands, his grip strong though his eyes shone with conflict.

"Then I will stand with you," he said hoarsely. "Even if the ground breaks beneath us."

Marley exhaled, relief and sorrow mingling. For a moment, they simply held each other, the letter lying between them on the desk like a third presence.

The storm outside had passed. But inside, a new storm had begun—one they would not hide from.

18

THE FOUNDER'S VOW

The council archives always smelled faintly of lemon oil and damp wool, as if the building had learned to polish over what it couldn't quite dry out. Marley signed the log, slipped the brass key from the clerk's hook, and let herself into the narrow room where Brookwood kept the bones of its memory. Grey winter light laid a pale band across the long table. Outside, the square exhaled the last of the storm; inside, the minutes of a century waited with their buttoned lips.

She had come because of the letter from the print shop—the one that said *He stands because I cannot.* Sleep had not held her long after that. If the town's official story could be so wrong about love, what else had its records gotten wrong? And if the Winter Ball was to proceed, and she was to stand before the town, she needed a spine stronger than rumor, braver than hints.

Damien met her at the door with his own key and thermos. He looked worn, but his eyes were awake in the way that meant the work had lit some necessary fire in him.

"You're certain we'll find something here?" he asked, closing the door behind them against the hall's colder air.

"I'm certain the minutes won't say it," Marley answered, already moving toward the shelf where the oldest ledgers sagged under red twine. "But the minutes rarely say the thing a town can't admit. We're looking for what was hidden next to what was recorded."

He smiled tiredly. "Margins. Your specialty."

She slid free a ledger labeled *Town Council—1828–1846* and another marked simply *Founders' Notes*. When she set the latter on the table its spine sighed, and a small drift of dust lifted and fell like the first breath of a long-sleeping thing.

They worked quietly, the way one reads in an empty church—out of respect rather than fear. The minutes were what she expected: votes on road repairs, ordinances on fishing seasons, three separate disputes about the color of paint for the bell tower trim. No mention, in any formal hand, of the Winter Bell Union.

But the *Founders' Notes* were different. Less tidy. A mixture of clippings, receipts, and letters tucked beneath silk ribbons that had long since gone brittle. The first envelope she opened held a map of the square as it had been laid out in 1819, with a small star drawn in the margin next to *belfry*. In another envelope, a woman's hand listed herbs said to "quicken winter lungs" in a slanting script that felt familiar—the same careful curve she'd seen in the healer's ledger months ago.

"Nye hand," Damien murmured over her shoulder, seeing it too. "Same inked flourish on the capital V."

Marley nodded, pulse quickening. The Nye family. The healer bloodline that had recorded the green flame and the phrase *balance rested*. If the Winter Bell Union had truly been a ritual between healer lines, the Nye papers were where it would breathe.

She untied another ribbon and felt the slight give a binding makes when it's been opened and closed by fingers that cared. Inside lay two letters folded together, both sealed once with wax stamped with a tiny bellflower—so like the hallmark inside Elijah's ring that Marley felt the past align beneath her hands. She eased the seals apart and unfolded the first.

Joan, the letter began, *we have agreed, you and I, that the bell is no mere call to gather but a voice that steadies the body of this place. When it rings at Midwinter with hands from our houses upon the rope (yours and mine together, as our mothers did), the river keeps her temper and the green light near the Foundry bank will take glass and sleep. Without that seal, envy kindles and wants run wild, and the breaths of our people come short. Let the Union be no spectacle; let it be vow. Two lines for the keeping of many.*

It was signed, *—S. Callahan, keeper of the bell.*

Marley looked up slowly. "Callahan," she breathed.

Damien's eyes had gone bright. "Not Elijah's generation—this is early. Silas? Seamus? But Callahan nonetheless. Keeper of the bell."

Marley turned to the second letter. This hand was Joan Nye's—there was no mistaking the sure, apothecary stroke, the way her ink sometimes flared at the start of a line the way a flame does when it remembers itself.

Silas, it read, *the Union binds blood, but not by ring alone. The bell hears breath. When the two of us pull together, the tone sets the other metals quiet in the earth, the river listens, and the children sleep. If some future eager men dress this in paper and require seven signers, remind them the number is not their making. The witness is the town itself—the shoemaker, the baker, the fishwife at the east stairs. Gifts of our houses, exchanged under the green fire, yes—but the sealing is breath and tone. If either is false, the bell refuses.*

She read the last line again, felt it settle like a stone in water. *If either is false, the bell refuses.*

Damien took the page and set it beside the first, his finger tapping the phrases as if reading out rhythm written into language. "Breath and tone. Two lines. Houses pulling together. Not a marriage only, but a harmonic binding." He looked at Marley, something fierce sparking in him. "It isn't metaphor. It's physics braided with ritual. The bell's partials —the overtones—shift depending on how it's rung, who pulls, the angle. With two pullers breathing in time, you can excite certain modes and damp others. They used that to 'set the other metals quiet,' as Joan puts it—to still, to balance."

Marley's heart pounded. "And if the breath is false—the vow coerced, or one line absent—the bell refuses."

"Just as it refused this solstice," Damien answered, voice soft but sure. "Not mechanical failure. A broken pact."

Snow squeaked under a wagon outside; the small sound felt enormous now. The bell tower trim debates in the minutes seemed suddenly obscene beside the clarity of these letters.

Marley laid the pages flat and kept going. The bundle yielded more: a receipt for copper salts "to be mixed with wick upon Midwinter, 4 measures," signed J. Nye; a diagram of the belfry's rope wheel with two notches marked *left hand, right hand* and the word *braid* inked beside them; a small card, almost a prayer, in Joan's hand: *Ring once for joining, twice for balance, thrice for remembrance; hold breath between.*

She swallowed hard. "The music boxes," she whispered. "Two melodies that become a duet only when layered.

Breath held between phrases. It's all the same language—time, not spectacle. A vow proven by rhythm."

Damien nodded, enthralled. "Their ritual assumed two bloodlines tending the bell together. The Circle of Seven commandeered it generations later, stamped *seven hands bind* into the plate, and turned the whole thing into pageant. But the founding practice is simpler and truer. Two hands, two houses, breath, tone. Witnesses not of power but of the common square."

Marley heard Ruth Bennett's name in the word *baker* from Joan's letter, and felt another seam open: the Bennett bakery line—not healers perhaps, but witnesses written into the instruction itself. The Winter Ball, then, was not entertainment; it had been built as the town's way of showing up to keep the balance.

She set the letters side by side and reached for her journal. Words spilled as fast as she could catch them. *The Winter Bell Union originated as a compact between Callahan (bell keepers) and Nye (healers). The ringing sealed more than a joining; it tuned the town. The green flame by the Foundry bank —coppered wick—sign of balance ready to sleep. The breath held between chimes.*

Damien moved to the window, stared up at the tower. "A sacred harmonic point," he said, more to the room than to her. "That's what this place is. The town's rituals made a standing wave of sorts—people, places, objects arranged to carry a tone across years. When something broke—coercion, fear, a vow shaped to please the Circle rather than the breath of two lines—the node detuned. Silence is the only honest response a bell can give when the breath is false."

Marley had to sit down. Her knees had gone weak. Elijah's inscription echoed: *Yours in time.* Not a cast-iron forever, but a vow that understood rhythm—phrases of speech and breath, pauses that meant fidelity rather than failure. Amelia's hidden letter called bells "for witnesses" the lesser sound; Joan had claimed the witness was the town's common life, not its council. All the fragments were beginning to speak the same sentence.

She read one more sheet, a small slip pinned to the back board of the binder—softer paper, later hand. *If the Union fails, carry the wick to river; flame will glass and rest. When the time returns, wake with breath before tone.* Signed in a barely legible hand: *J. Nye, 1894.*

Marley looked up sharply. "Wake with breath before tone," she repeated. "They meant: repair the relationship before you try to ring. The bell comes last."

Damien's mouth curved with a scholar's astonished joy. "It's beautiful." Then his expression sobered. "And our town's done it exactly backwards. They've performed the tone, demanded spectacle, and ignored breath."

Marley gathered the letters gently into a protective folio the clerk would allow her to copy but not remove. "This is the spine I needed," she said. "Not just for the talk. For everything. If I stand up and honor Amelia, I'm not defying tradition. I'm reclaiming it."

Damien came back to the table and placed his hand flat on Joan's letter, the way he had set his palm on the printing plate weeks before. "We still need to trace the lines. If Callahan and Nye were the original union, how did Colvin become bound up in it by the 1930s? Marriage? Money? The Circle? Somewhere between Silas and Elijah, someone braided the rope wrong."

Marley stared at the diagram of the rope wheel, at the small word *braid.* She thought of the bell-handle Mrs. Bennett had sketched, braided wood; of the Circle's signet ring, with its counterfeit braid; of the ribbon box at the bakery, satin twisted and pressed flat by years.

"We'll find the splice," she said. "And we'll show the town where the knot slipped."

Outside, a plow clanked past and broke the afternoon's hush. The square was waking, preparing evergreen and bunting for the Winter Ball, oblivious to the letters unfolding on the table like a reliquary opened.

Marley stacked the papers in order, smoothed the ribbon down, and looked at Damien. "If the bell is a harmonic point, then the night of the ball isn't a program. It's a chance to tune. We have to be ready for that."

He nodded, steady now. "Breath first. Tone after. Two hands on the rope, or not at all."

She slipped the folio into her satchel beside the velvet pouch with the ring, and the blotting folder that protected the unsent love letter. Three weights, three truths. When she stood, the bag pulled at her shoulder with the gravity of a vow.

"Let's go," she said. "We have witnesses to gather and a town to teach how to breathe."

They left the archive room as they'd found it, lemon oil and damp wool lingering. But as Marley turned the key in the lock, she felt something shift—not in the hinges, but in her chest. The bell had not spoken. It didn't have to. Joan's admonition sang in her blood: *wake with breath before tone.*

For the first time since the solstice, Marley believed the silence could be the start of music. Not absence—rest. And in that rest, a vow waiting to be struck true.

THE SNOW HAD CRUSTED by the time Marley and Damien stepped out of the archive. The afternoon light was hard and pale, sharpening the edges of the square into icy clarity. Townsfolk bustled about stringing garlands and sweeping stoops, determined to ready themselves for the Winter Ball, as if the silence of the bell were no more than a shadow to be out-danced.

But Marley carried the founders' letters pressed against her ribs. Their weight was more than parchment—it was revelation.

When they reached the shop, she set the folio on the desk and spread the documents across the table once more. Damien brewed tea, his movements absent-minded, as though his body worked while his mind still spun through harmonic theory and ritual fragments.

Marley read the letters aloud, slowly, as though intoning them might make the vow breathe again. With each phrase she lingered—*breath and tone, two lines for the keeping of many, the witness is the town itself.*

Her hands shook by the time she finished. "It was never about spectacle," she said. "It was never meant to be a ceremony for the Circle's approval. It was about balance—between families, between the river and the land, between breath and tone. Amelia's vow wasn't just a personal heartbreak. It was a fracture in the very pact that kept Brookwood steady."

Damien sat opposite her, tea untouched. "And the bell has told us so ever since. Silence, not failure. Refusal. It cannot ring false."

He picked up the diagram of the rope wheel, tracing the notches with one finger. "They built the mechanics to obey the vow. With two pullers breathing together, the tone harmonizes. With one missing, the vibration cancels. It wasn't superstition—it was engineered resonance. The silence is physics upholding spirit."

Marley's chest tightened. "And the Circle twisted it. They wrapped it in pageantry, demanded signatures, layered pomp on top of pact. They turned it into control."

Damien leaned back, rubbing his eyes. "And when Amelia stood there in 1936, veil heavy in the snow, the breath was already broken. Her vow couldn't be recognized —not because she lacked devotion, but because her partner's voice couldn't be acknowledged. The bell heard the falsehood and refused."

Marley pressed her palms flat to the table, trembling with both grief and awe. "So the silence wasn't abandonment—it was loyalty. The bell refused to bless a lie."

THE FIRE SNAPPED LOUDLY, startling them both. Marley stood and began pacing, unable to contain the energy churning inside her.

"This is more than Amelia's story," she said. "It's the story of Brookwood itself. The bell was never just a backdrop. It was the spine. Every family line that grew here, every trade, every festival—it all orbited the vow. And when the vow broke, when the ritual was hollowed, the whole town drifted. No wonder we've lived with unease, with fractures hidden beneath polite smiles. The balance has been wrong for nearly a century."

Damien closed the folio gently, as though tucking the founders' words back into rest. "The question is, Marley, what do we do with this? Do we unveil it at the Winter Ball? Do we show the town their peace has been counterfeit all along?"

Marley stopped pacing, staring at him. "Would you rather we keep it hidden? Let them dance under garlands while the ground beneath them rots?"

His jaw tightened. "You know that isn't what I want. But truth demands more than timing—it demands readiness. If we rip the veil off without preparing them, we might destroy what little harmony remains."

Marley exhaled sharply, her breath clouding in the cool air of the shop. "And yet every day we wait, Amelia's silence deepens. Every day we pretend the bell's refusal is accident instead of testimony, we collude in the lie."

SHE RETURNED TO THE DESK, fingers tracing Joan Nye's steady hand. "*Wake with breath before tone.* That's what they wrote. It isn't only instruction for the rope. It's instruction for us. We must breathe first—gather witnesses, find those who can bear the truth—before the tone is struck before the whole town. Otherwise the sound will shatter, not steady."

Damien looked at her for a long time, then nodded slowly. "Then we must decide who we can trust. Who will hold this with us until the time is right."

Marley thought of threads, fragile but real. The common witnesses Joan had named—the shoemaker, the baker, the fishwife—still lived in Brookwood. Perhaps the founders' vow had not died; perhaps it simply waited for ordinary hands to wake it again.

She whispered, half to herself: "Maybe we don't need the council at all. Maybe we need the town."

DAMIEN POURED THE TEA, finally sipping, though his eyes remained fixed on the rope diagram. "A sacred harmonic point," he murmured again. "Brookwood itself is tuned to this bell. If the tone has refused for eighty years, it isn't just tradition we've lost. It's resonance. No wonder people feel restless. No wonder dreams bleed across generations. The bell's silence is a broken chord humming under everything."

Marley sat, hands wrapped around her mug. The heat seeped into her palms, anchoring her. "Then we must restore the chord. Not by spectacle, not by council decree—but by vow. Two lines breathing together. Witnesses not in office, but in life."

Damien met her gaze, something resolute flickering there. "Then perhaps, Marley, the question is this: whose breath will the bell accept now? Which lines are willing to braid their voices again?"

The air between them tightened, weighted with both fear and possibility. Marley thought of her aunt, of her own blood she had barely begun to trace. She thought of Damien, torn between Brookwood and Oxford, his silence heavy as Elijah's. She thought of Amelia and the unnamed woman who had written *love does not ring bells for witnesses.*

Her voice came out quiet, steady. "We'll find them. The living heirs of the vow. And we'll breathe before tone."

Damien nodded once. The fire snapped again, this time not startling but affirming.

The Winter Ball would come soon. The garlands would be hung, the floor waxed, the music tuned. But Marley knew now that the dance was not the true ceremony. The true ceremony waited above them, in the tower, silent but listening.

And when the time came, the bell would not be forced. It would not be fooled. It would either refuse—or it would sing.

THE FIRE in the hearth had burned low, but neither Marley nor Damien moved to replenish it. The room felt taut, like the air just before a bell's strike, their silence threaded with unspoken recognition.

Damien spoke first, his voice measured but weighted. "If the vow was meant to be kept between the Callahans and the Nyes, then we need to know where those lines are now. Without them, the bell may never ring again."

Marley traced the faded ink of Joan's letter with her fingertip. "The Nyes scattered generations ago. My aunt used to say they drifted north, some marrying into Colvin blood, others into families no one remembers. And the Callahans... well, Elijah was the last name I've found tied to the bell."

"Which means both lines are blurred," Damien said, eyes narrowing. "Heirs hidden in plain sight. But if the blood remains, even diluted, the vow could still live through them."

Marley nodded slowly. "That's why the Circle fought so hard to keep the record tidy. If they acknowledged the truth —that the vow wasn't theirs to control—they would lose their grip on the town."

Damien leaned forward, intensity sparking in his gaze. "So the question is, Marley, where do you fall in this braid? You've been uncovering these threads as if they were written for you to find."

The words startled her. She sat back, heart hammering. "You think I'm—"

"Connected," he interrupted. "I've suspected since the first music box. Your aunt didn't keep these things by accident. She believed you would carry them forward."

Marley wanted to deny it, to push the weight aside. But in her chest, something deep resonated, like a struck chord she had felt before but never named. "And you?" she whispered. "You speak of resonance as if you've heard it in your bones. Where do you fall?"

He hesitated, looking down at his hands. "The Callahan name doesn't run through me, not directly. But there's a reason I stayed, Marley. Every rational bone in me told me to take the fellowship, to walk away. But something here pulled me back—like the bell refusing silence, like a node in a song that won't release. I don't know if that makes me heir, but it makes me bound."

THE FIRE CRACKED SOFTLY, punctuating his words. Marley stared at him, feeling the truth of it even as fear prickled her skin.

"If the bell needs breath before tone," she said, "then maybe that's what we are. Not founders' blood, perhaps, not directly. But breath. Two lines braided—not by blood, but by vow."

Damien lifted his eyes, and the weight in them nearly broke her. "Do you know what you're suggesting?"

"Yes," Marley whispered. "That it could be us."

The silence that followed was heavier than the storm's howl the night before. It wasn't romance she spoke of, not only. It was responsibility, legacy, danger. To step into the braid would mean claiming a vow that the town itself had forgotten how to honor. It would mean standing against the council, the Circle, perhaps against families who had built their identities on lies.

Damien stood and walked to the window, his silhouette cut against the snow-glow outside. "If we step into that rope, Marley, we bind ourselves not just to each other but to the town. If the vow fails, if the bell refuses again, we'll be blamed for undoing what little peace remains. And if it rings—" He turned, eyes burning. "If it rings, nothing will ever be the same."

Marley rose too, her legs unsteady but her voice firm. "Maybe that's the point. Nothing should be the same. Not after Amelia. Not after Elijah. Not after all this silence."

SHE MOVED to the desk and picked up the velvet pouch. The ring glimmered as she tipped it into her palm. *Yours in time.* The inscription felt like a question, one that had waited decades for an answer.

"Amelia's vow was hidden," Marley said softly. "Ours doesn't have to be. We can choose to step forward. Not to dance at the Ball, not to please the council—but to restore balance."

Damien's gaze fixed on the ring, then on her. "And if the town refuses us?"

"Then let it refuse," Marley replied. "The bell will decide. Breath first, tone after. If we're false, it will remain silent. If we're true, it will sing."

The words settled between them, terrifying and undeniable.

DAMIEN CROSSED THE ROOM SLOWLY, stopping just before her. His voice was low, rough with conflict. "You're asking me to vow with you. Not in romance, not in convenience. In covenant."

Marley met his eyes, unflinching. "Yes. Because without us, the bell may never wake. And without the bell, Brookwood will keep living in shadow."

He closed his eyes briefly, then opened them with something steadier in his expression. "Then I vow this: I won't leave you to bear it alone. If the rope calls for two hands, mine will be one."

Her throat tightened. She slid the ring back into the pouch, her hands trembling. "Then I vow this: I'll stand with you, Damien. No matter what the council says, no matter who tries to silence us. We'll braid breath before tone."

THE MOMENT BROKE when the church bell—one of the smaller, lesser-used ones—tolled the hour outside. It sounded thin, metallic, but to Marley it carried a deeper resonance, as if the town itself had overheard and was waiting.

She turned back to the documents, stacking them neatly. "We'll need witnesses. Ordinary ones, like Joan said. The baker, the smith, the fishwife. The town itself must hear us breathe before we strike the tone."

Damien nodded, though the weight of what they had spoken still hung heavy in his eyes. "We'll gather them. Quietly, carefully. No council edicts, no Circle signatures. Just lives bound by truth."

Marley tightened the ribbon around the folio, sealing the letters once more. Her voice steadied as she said, "Then it's decided. Whatever the cost, we will not let the founders' vow remain buried. Even if it means defying the council, even if it fractures Brookwood. The bell will hear the truth, or it will refuse forever. But it will not be mocked again."

Damien exhaled, long and slow. Then he reached for her hand and held it, firm and steady. "So be it."

And for the first time since the solstice, Marley felt the silence of the Winter Bell shift—not into sound, but into waiting.

19

THE BELL'S CURSE

The storm had left Brookwood muffled in white, but the snow had already begun to soften in the midday light. Marley walked slowly along the shoveled path toward the cottage at the edge of the square, her satchel heavy with the folio of founder letters and the velvet pouch with the ring. Damien walked beside her, his breath fogging the cold air, his silence thoughtful.

They had come at the invitation of Ruth Bennett's grandmother, Lenore Hart—a woman who had seen nearly nine decades and still carried herself with the erect posture of someone who remembered when the town truly listened to its elders. She had sent a note on stiff, yellowed paper: *If you want to understand why the bell refused, come. I will tell you what others will not.*

The cottage door creaked open before they knocked. Lenore Hart stood framed in lamplight, a shawl wrapped around her shoulders, her sharp eyes catching both of them at once. "Come in," she said briskly. "The cold doesn't wait for hesitation."

They obeyed, stamping snow from their boots. Inside, the air smelled of dried lavender and wood smoke. Every surface was crowded with small objects: ceramic jars, brass candlesticks, bundles of herbs. A house of memory, Marley thought.

Lenore gestured them to sit at the hearth. "You've been stirring the silence," she said without preamble. "The bell doesn't stay quiet without cause, and the cause is older than any councilman's decree."

Marley leaned forward, clasping her hands. "We found letters—proof that the bell was part of a vow between families. The silence this solstice was no accident. It was a refusal."

Lenore's eyes narrowed, as though testing whether Marley's conviction was genuine. Then she nodded once. "So you've heard what the records tried to smother. Good. But there's more. The bell doesn't only speak for vows. It speaks for grief."

Damien frowned, pulling a notebook from his coat pocket. "Grief? You mean in a metaphorical sense, or—"

"In sound," Lenore interrupted. Her voice had an edge, sharpened by memory. "I was a girl when my brother died. The winter of '46. He was only twelve. Pneumonia took him fast. The church had scheduled a single toll at dusk, to honor him before the evening prayers. But when the rope was pulled, the bell struck twice."

The room seemed to contract. Marley shivered though the fire burned strong. "Twice?"

Lenore nodded, her gaze unwavering. "Two clear tones, one after the other. I was there. The whole town was. People gasped, crossed themselves, whispered that the ringer had erred. But he swore his hands only pulled once. I believed him. I still do."

Damien's pen hovered over the page. "And what did people make of it?"

"They said it was omen. That the vow had been undone somewhere, that grief had slipped loose. And indeed, that year we buried three more children, two women in childbirth, and my own cousin in a sawmill accident. The bell had warned us."

MARLEY FELT HER HEART POUND. The founders' letters echoed in her mind: *If either is false, the bell refuses.* But what if refusal was only one side of its language? What if excess sound—an extra peal, unbidden—was its other?

"Are you saying," Marley asked softly, "that the bell can mark more than marriages? That it can mark death itself?"

Lenore's eyes glinted. "It has always marked death. The Circle just trained the town to listen only when it suited them. But those who lived before the pageantry knew. My mother told me of a wedding in 1911 where the bell rang once for the vow—and again, unsummoned, before the groom collapsed of fever three weeks later. She said the families whispered of curse, but the healers said it was truth. The bell never lies."

Damien scribbled furiously, but his face was pale. "That would mean the bell isn't just an instrument of ritual. It's a recorder of balance, perhaps even a barometer of life and loss. Its harmonics might resonate with events—like a sympathetic vibration to grief itself."

Lenore leaned closer, her shawl slipping. "Do you see, children? The silence this year was not only about Amelia. It was warning. *When the vow is undone, grief returns.* That's what the elders always said. And grief has been piling like snowdrifts ever since her veil froze in the chapel."

Marley's throat tightened. She remembered the storm, the way snowflakes had seemed to fall in slowed rhythm as the bell refused to toll. "Then this solstice silence isn't just refusal," she whispered. "It's omen."

THE FIRE HISSED, spitting a small spray of sparks into the hearth. Outside, the wind moaned faintly, as though agreeing.

Damien set his notebook down, his hand trembling slightly. "If that's true, then every peal we've counted as blessing might have carried another meaning. Weddings blessed—but also lives marked for grief. The town has been hearing only half its language."

Marley turned to Lenore. "Why tell us now? Why not sooner?"

The old woman's expression softened, though her eyes stayed sharp. "Because no one asked. Because people feared to know. But you—" she pointed to Marley with a gnarled finger—"you've already pulled the veil off Amelia's truth. You're not afraid of what it costs. So I'll tell you plain: if you step into the vow, you're not only risking your hearts. You're risking the bell calling grief into the square. Can you bear that?"

The question hung heavy, colder than the draft seeping under the door. Marley met Damien's gaze. His eyes were haunted, but steady.

She answered for them both. "We can bear the truth. What we can't bear is silence."

Lenore leaned back, satisfied. "Then mind yourselves. The bell does not forgive. But sometimes it warns so that the living may do what the dead could not."

· · ·

THEY LEFT the cottage as dusk fell, the square hushed beneath the fading light. Snow crunched underfoot, each step sharp in the quiet. Marley carried Lenore's words like stones in her chest: *When the vow is undone, grief returns.*

She looked up at the tower, its dark mouth gaping against the twilight. For the first time, she wondered if the silence had less to do with refusal and more to do with mercy. What if the bell had stayed quiet not only because the vow was broken—but because sounding again might have unleashed grief too great to bear?

Beside her, Damien scribbled one more note, his face taut. "If the bell's language includes death, Marley, then every mystery we've been chasing—Amelia, Elijah, the veil bride—might be only pieces of a larger warning. We're not just historians anymore. We're interpreters of an omen."

Marley's breath fogged in the cold. "Then we had better listen. Because if the bell speaks again, Brookwood may not be ready for what it says."

The tower loomed silent above them. But in Marley's chest, the echo of Lenore's story beat like a phantom chime —one strike too many, one warning too late.

THE STREETS of Brookwood were eerily quiet when Marley and Damien left Lenore Hart's cottage. Even the crunch of their boots against the snow seemed subdued, swallowed by the vast silence that hung over the town like a heavy cloak. The lanterns in windows flickered weakly, as though the houses themselves felt wary of the elder's words.

They walked in silence until they reached the bookshop, its familiar windows fogged with warmth. Once inside, Damien threw more wood on the fire while Marley set Lenore's warning to paper, her handwriting fierce, every phrase carved into the page: *When the vow is undone, grief returns. The bell rings not only for vows but for death.*

She stared at the words until they blurred. "Damien," she said finally, voice tight, "if she's right, we've been blind. We've treated the bell's silence as mystery, but what if it has been shielding us from something worse?"

Damien sat opposite her, rubbing his temples. "It would explain anomalies I've seen in the archives. Records that didn't fit the neat story the council promotes."

Marley leaned forward. "What kind of anomalies?"

He opened his notebook, pages filled with small, precise script. "I noted years when the bell seemed to ring outside of scheduled ceremonies. Sometimes only once, sometimes twice. The official records always called it error—'mis-pull of the rope,' 'wind interference,' 'mechanical slip.' But the patterns never convinced me. They clustered around deaths."

He flipped to a page near the back. "Here. 1911—the wedding Lenore mentioned. Bell struck an extra note, and within the month the groom was dead. 1923—a funeral for a miner; the bell rang twice before the procession even began, and two more men from the same shift were killed in a landslide weeks later. 1946—Lenore's brother. You heard her account. And then..." He hesitated, his eyes shadowed. "1972. The records claim a 'weather-induced double strike' during a spring dedication. That was the year the Colvin factory fire killed seven."

Marley's blood ran cold. "So every so-called error was warning. The bell has been speaking all along, and we dismissed it."

"Worse," Damien said quietly, "we silenced it. The Circle and the council made sure to file these incidents under 'mechanical issue.' They trained the town to hear only what fit their narrative—marriages and ceremonies. They erased the bell's language of grief."

THE FIRE POPPED, sending sparks up the chimney. Marley rose and paced the narrow shop, her heart hammering.

"Then the silence this solstice wasn't just about Amelia," she said. "It was about us. A warning that grief has been waiting to return."

Damien nodded grimly. "The founders may have built the bell as a harmonic point, tuned to vows and balance. But if the pact fractured, the resonance could warp—its tones no longer marking harmony, but imbalance. Death as well as life."

Marley stopped pacing, her hands trembling. "That would mean Brookwood has lived under a slow unraveling for nearly a century. Amelia's frozen vow didn't just silence her—it broke the chord that steadied everything."

The thought pressed on her like ice. Memories of the town surfaced—neighbors lost young, sudden accidents, tragedies that always seemed too frequent for a community so small. She had never connected them to the bell. No one had. But now, the pattern felt undeniable.

She turned back to Damien. "If the bell has been echoing grief across time, how many warnings have we ignored? How much of Brookwood's sorrow has been the echo of that broken vow?"

Damien's expression was grim. "Too much. Far too much."

MARLEY RETURNED TO THE DESK, shoving aside her notes to clear space. She spread out the founders' letters again, reading Joan Nye's words in the flicker of the firelight: *Ring once for joining, twice for balance, thrice for remembrance; hold breath between.*

Her throat tightened. "What if those instructions weren't metaphor? What if the bell's tones really did mean different things—joining, balance, remembrance? And what if remembrance doesn't mean honoring the dead, but warning the living?"

Damien leaned over the page, his finger tracing the ink. "Then every unscheduled strike we've dismissed as accident was a remembrance toll—a grief-note sounding to warn us. And when the vow was broken, those tones became scattered, uncontrolled. The harmony fractured into omen."

Marley pressed her palms to her eyes. "No wonder Lenore called it curse. To live in a town where joy and sorrow sound through the same voice, where blessing is always shadowed by loss—it would feel like doom."

"But not doom," Damien said firmly. "Warning. The bell has never lied. We just refused to listen."

THEY SAT in silence for a long while, the only sound the crackle of fire and the faint hiss of snow sliding from the roof outside.

At last, Marley spoke again. "If the founders' vow was meant to bind the town in balance, then perhaps only a new vow can repair it. Not a spectacle, not a Circle pageant—but a true braid. Breath before tone."

Damien studied her, his eyes dark with both fear and recognition. "And if we fail?"

Marley met his gaze, unflinching. "Then the bell will refuse. Or worse—it will warn again. But either way, Brookwood deserves the truth. They deserve to hear the bell's language, not the lies of the council."

DAMIEN ROSE and moved to the window, looking out at the tower in the square. Its silhouette cut sharp against the darkening sky. "I keep thinking of Elijah," he said quietly. "We've all called him coward. But perhaps he understood the bell better than any of us. Perhaps his silence was an attempt to spare the town from grief it couldn't bear."

Marley's throat tightened. She thought of Amelia's letter, the way it spoke of love hidden, shielded. "He carried silence so we wouldn't have to hear the curse," she whispered. "But in shielding us, he let the imbalance fester."

The fire groaned low, its wood collapsing into glowing embers. Marley crossed to Damien and stood beside him at the window. Together they stared up at the silent bell, its dark mouth gaping in the tower.

"The town thinks it is mute," Marley said. "But it isn't. It's been speaking all along, in tones we refused to hear."

Damien nodded. "And if we don't restore the vow soon, the next sound may be grief greater than Brookwood can survive."

Marley placed her hand against the cold glass, her breath fogging it. In her heart, she felt the phantom chime again—the echo Lenore had described, one toll too many.

"We have to be ready," she whispered. "Because the bell will speak again. And when it does, it will not be ignored."

THE NIGHT DEEPENED, snow muffling the square outside the shop, but neither Marley nor Damien lit the lamps. They sat in the glow of the fire, the founders' letters spread across the desk and Lenore's warning heavy in the air.

Marley broke the silence first, her voice low but determined. "If the bell has been speaking all along—blessing and warning, joy and grief—then we need to know every word it has spoken. Every anomaly. Every strike that was explained away. We can't rely on half-remembered stories. We need a record."

Damien closed his notebook with a decisive snap. "Then we trace it all. Line by line, year by year. Church logs, council minutes, family diaries. Every time the bell rang outside of ceremony, we mark it. We'll build a ledger the Circle couldn't erase."

Marley exhaled, relief threading through her. "And then we'll see the full pattern. We'll know if Lenore's warning is just story—or if the bell truly echoes across time."

Damien met her gaze, steady. "And if it proves true?"

"Then Brookwood has been living under a curse of its own making," Marley said softly. "And we'll need to tell them."

THE FIRE HISSED, and the wind rattled faintly at the shutters. Damien stirred the embers, his face flickering in the glow.

"Marley, do you realize what it would mean?" he asked. "If we tell them the bell has rung for death as much as for vows, every memory tied to it will be recast. Weddings remembered as omens. Funerals as warnings of more to come. It will shatter their sense of history."

Marley leaned forward, her hands clasped tight. "It's already shattered. The silence proved it. People are whispering in the streets, wondering what it means. Better they know the truth than live in fear of shadows they don't understand."

Damien shook his head slowly. "But fear can unite as much as truth divides. If we expose this too bluntly, they may turn against us—against the very vow we're trying to restore."

Marley rose, pacing the narrow shop, her heart pounding. "So what's the alternative? Pretend we didn't hear Lenore? Pretend the founders' letters don't exist? If we stay silent, we're no better than Elijah."

The words hung sharp, and she regretted them the moment they left her lips. Damien's face tightened, but he didn't flinch. "Perhaps Elijah wasn't coward," he said quietly. "Perhaps he understood the cost of speaking too soon. Perhaps his silence bought Brookwood time."

Marley stopped pacing, her throat tight. "And yet here we are, decades later, still paying the price. His silence may have spared them then, but it left us with rot. I won't let us make the same mistake."

Damien's gaze softened, though the weight in it remained. "Then we need a middle path. Not silence, not blunt revelation. Preparation. We trace the anomalies, gather the witnesses, and when the time comes, we speak. Not as alarmists, but as keepers of the vow."

MARLEY SAT AGAIN, the fight in her easing into resolve. "You're right. Breath before tone. We must prepare ourselves —and the town—before the bell speaks again."

She pulled a fresh sheet of paper toward her and began drafting headings: *Year. Occasion. Scheduled Strikes. Anomalies. Correlated Events.* The first column she filled easily—1911,

1923, 1946, 1972. The rest would take time, searching, patience. But the act of writing steadied her.

Damien watched her for a long moment before speaking. "Do you ever wonder, Marley, if we're not just researchers but heirs? That the founders left these threads not only to be studied, but to be carried?"

Her pen stilled. She looked up, heart hammering. "I've wondered," she admitted. "And it terrifies me."

"It terrifies me too," Damien said. "Because if the vow needs living heirs to braid breath and tone again... it may be calling us."

The words landed like the toll of a bell, vibrating in her bones. Marley's throat tightened. "If it does, Damien—if it truly does—then we must be ready. Not for spectacle. Not for pageantry. But for truth."

THE FIRE DWINDLED, shadows lengthening across the shelves. Outside, the tower loomed, silent against the night sky.

Marley closed her notebook and looked at Damien, her voice steady now. "Then let's vow this: we will trace the bell's full history, no matter how long it takes. We will gather those who can bear witness. And we will be ready when the bell speaks again—whether it blesses or curses."

Damien held her gaze, then nodded slowly. "Agreed. We prepare for both. Because the next chime may be the town's salvation... or its grief."

They sat together in the dimming light, their vow spoken not with ceremony, but with conviction. And though the bell in the tower remained silent, Marley felt its presence heavy above them, waiting.

Waiting for breath before tone.
Waiting for truth before sound.
Waiting for Brookwood to listen.

20

THE MUSIC BOX'S SECRET TUNE

By the time the sun fell, Brookwood had that particular winter hush that feels like a held note. Marley kept the lamps low in the shop and worked by the fire's steady amber; the light turned the windowpanes to dark mirrors. On the table were the founders' letters, the ledger Damien had started for the bell's anomalies, and—set slightly apart as if it required its own climate—the second music box they had found in her aunt's locked drawer.

She hadn't meant to open it. There was tea to drink, records to cross-check, a speech to finalize. But the solstice was close enough to taste, and the box felt heavier tonight, as if it had swallowed a season.

She lifted the lid.

The melody that rose wasn't the same hesitant waltz she'd heard before this long unraveling. That tune had been familiar but slowed, a consonance bent just enough to ache. This one arrived like a breath that breaks, a shape she'd never heard from it—a small, melancholic phrase that curled back on itself and then, astonishingly, lifted with tenderness. The first four notes were the old pattern, but the fifth waited a heartbeat too long, and the delay sweetened the entire line.

Marley didn't move, afraid to knock the moment loose. The tiny comb teeth glittered in the lamplight; the cylinder turned, pin by pin, as patient as snowfall. The music felt not like a song being played but like a thought remembering itself.

"Damien," she called, but softly. "Come here."

From the archive room came the scuff of his chair, then his quiet footfall. He stepped into the doorway, pushing his glasses up with the back of a knuckle. "Did you find—"

She tilted her head toward the box. He took one step, then another, and the line on his brow eased in spite of himself.

"That's new," he said.

"Yes." Her whisper almost broke. "It's the same melody —but it isn't. Listen to the delay in the fifth. And how the lift at the end feels like... like someone asking and then choosing to stay anyway."

He crouched, hands braced on his knees, face close to the small mechanism. "Tempo is down a fraction. Ornamentation added in the repeat. It's... tender." He glanced up. "It's the solstice. The box is responding."

Marley swallowed. "Or we are."

They let it play through twice before she dared move. When the cylinder reached its runout, the tune bled into the soft tick of its winding spring. Marley closed the lid as if closing a book on a secret, then reached for the older box— the first one, from the beginning of this whole series of mysteries; the one her aunt had shown her like a bedtime lantern the winter after Marley's mother died. She had kept it wrapped in a scarf inside the locked cabinet by habit if not superstition. These two had always felt like siblings separated by a story.

She set box beside box. The first was etched with a bell and vine motif, the second with the same design—fainter, as if time had thumbed it. She wound the old one, the melody she could hum in her sleep, the one that had threaded itself through an entire year of searching. When she released its spring, the familiar waltz stepped into the room like someone returning from a long walk, warm and sure.

"Again," Damien said, voice even quieter now. "Play the new one. Then the old. Let your ear put them together."

Marley obeyed. She started the second box. At the fourth note she set the first to spinning, letting the older melody come in behind the newer one as if answering.

What happened then wasn't harmony in any clean sense. The two tunes lapped and braided, sometimes parting, sometimes finding a unison that made Marley's skin prickle. The delay in the fifth note of the new box created room the first melody slipped into. Integrated, the pair sounded less like waltz and more like a conversation where both speakers were learning to trust their turn.

"It's a duet," Marley said, breath fogging the cool in the air above the table. "It was always a duet. One voice slowed to make space for the other."

Damien stood. "We need to capture this properly. The room is coloring the sound." He vanished into the archive room and returned with his small recorder and the battered laptop he used to catalog oral histories. He set two pencil microphones on small stands and angled them toward the boxes. His movements were deft, automatic, but his face had a softness she rarely saw when he was using machines.

"Let me place them," he said. "Two sources, stereo field."

He shifted the boxes a few inches apart and angled their lids as if they were singers turning toward each other.

Marley smiled in spite of herself. "Breath before tone," she murmured.

He flinched slightly—she knew the phrase had become prayer and pressure both—but nodded. "Always."

They recorded the new melody alone. Then the original. Then the two together, first with the new one beginning, then with the old. Damien watched the waveforms bloom on the laptop screen, the combs and cylinders writing their tiny teeth into digital light. He wore his headphones only half on, one ear always in the room with her, which made her love him a little more in a way she couldn't say out loud yet.

"Let me try a simple overlay," he said when the takes were done. "No compression. No correction. We'll just hear what they do to each other."

He dragged the tracks into alignment, fingers steady on the trackpad. On the screen the two songs lay like river currents, similar but offset. He nudged the newer tune fractionally forward, then back, eyes narrowing as the peaks kissed. "There," he said softly. "There's the delay."

They listened. Through the headphones the duet was clearer. When the old melody's lift met the new melody's held note, a third sound—neither note, not exactly— breathed in the seam between them. It was an overtone, a harmonic that came only when breath was held right. It sounded like the way a winter room feels when someone chooses to stay.

Marley didn't realize she was crying until a tear darkened the lacquer on the second box. She dabbed at it with her sleeve, embarrassed, then decided embarrassment had no place in a room where dead people were singing.

"It says stay," she whispered. "It says stay and I stayed."

Damien paused the track and stared at the waveform as if it might answer him. "You're hearing words?" he asked, not skeptical, simply startled.

"No," Marley said, and then corrected herself. "Yes. Not words with vowels and consonants. But intention shaped into sound. Like the bell's extra strike at funerals. Like the way silence can be a sentence if you know the language."

He didn't argue. He rewound. "Again. This time I'll shift the old box late by half a beat. See if the overtone holds or breaks."

They listened again, leaning toward the laptop as if it were a hearth. The harmonic shivered—and held. Not as strong, but present, like a thread that refuses to snap even when pulled.

"It wants to be heard," Damien said.

Marley stared at the boxes, at the etched vines that had outlived their owners. "Or she does," she said. "Or they do. Amelia. And the woman who wrote that letter. Whichever of them stayed, or both."

He didn't say *Elijah,* and she didn't either. Both of them carried the suspicion that the line *I stayed* belonged to the one the town had never rightly seen. There was tenderness in the new tune that felt like a hidden life finally letting itself speak. There was also a steadiness in the old melody that felt like a hand offered: I walked with you while the world looked away.

Damien removed one earcup and passed the headphones to her. "One more," he said. "I want you to feel the room around the sound."

She put them on. The shop fell away. There was only the minute scrape of pins on teeth, the tiny rush of springs unwinding like lungs. The two melodies reached for one another, met, and the overtone knit them together, and in that binding she heard—not language, exactly, but syllables that leaned toward meaning. A long inhale, and then the smallest exhale, like a person speaking two words too softly for anyone but a beloved to hear.

"I stayed," Marley said, not to Damien, but to the space above the table, to the air whose job it was to carry vows.

Damien, without prompting, hit record again. "Say it," he murmured. "Say what you hear. The microphone will hear you say it, and maybe the room will answer."

She felt foolish. She did it anyway. "I stayed," she said into the music. "I stayed."

The overtone flared, almost too bright through the headphones, and then in the faintest whisper—that could have been camphor in the room, could have been winter in the flue, could have been her own blood answering—she heard the phrase return to her, not from her own mouth, not from the laptop, but from the seam where the melodies kissed.

I stayed.

She ripped the headphones off, breath gone, heart tripping. "Did you—"

"I saw the meter jump," Damien said softly, not moving. "Not from your voice. After."

They didn't speak for a while. The boxes played themselves to stillness. The only sound left was the small fast sound of Marley's own pulse and the crackle of a log shifting its weight.

Finally Damien closed the laptop and set his hand flat on the table between the boxes, the way he had done with the printing plate, the founders' letters, the ring. "We'll do more analysis," he said, but the scholar had left his voice. "But I think what matters more is what it means."

Marley nodded. She slid the second box a little closer to

the first, their lids almost touching. "It means she didn't run. Whoever wrote to Amelia—whoever loved her—she stayed. Maybe not at the altar, maybe not where the town demanded witnesses. But at the river. At the vow. In time."

Damien's gaze moved from one box to the other, then up to the dark window where the bell tower's shadow lay like a held line. "It also means the town is about to hear something it cannot unhear."

Marley drew a breath she hadn't realized she was holding. The found letters swam in her mind—*breath before tone*—and the ledger Damien had built with its columns for *anomaly* and *correlated grief*. The duet in her ears felt like both prayer and loading lever.

"We'll finish the overlay," she said. "We'll shape the two tunes into one track the town can hear without straining. We'll bring the witnesses to the bridge. And then we'll teach Brookwood how to listen."

Damien reached and took her hand, not to comfort, but to anchor. "And when they ask, we'll tell them what we heard."

"What did we hear?" Marley asked, though she already knew.

He didn't hesitate. "We heard a vow speak back."

THE DUET LINGERED in Marley's bones long after the boxes stilled. It was not silence that followed but resonance—like a bell tone fading in the rafters, long after the hammer rests. She wiped her face with the sleeve of her cardigan, not embarrassed this time but steadied. She had heard something that wasn't supposed to be heard. That mattered more than appearances.

Damien closed the lid of the laptop gently, as though it

might shatter. "We'll need to analyze it properly," he said, though his voice was hushed. "Spectrograms, overlays, phase correlation. If there's a whisper in there, the frequencies will show it."

Marley shook her head. "I don't need a spectrogram to know what I heard." She pointed at her chest. "It's here. It wasn't my imagination. It was intention. Someone was telling us—'I stayed.'"

He nodded slowly, eyes searching hers. "And we have to decide what to do with it."

THE SNOW outside shifted against the shutters, a gust reminding them of the solstice pressing closer. Marley wrapped her arms around herself, pacing the narrow strip of floor between desk and shelves.

"Think about it," she said. "All this time, we've been told Amelia was left. That Elijah abandoned her. That her vow froze in the snow because she was betrayed. But what if that's only half the story? What if she wasn't abandoned at all? What if someone stayed with her, unseen, unheard?"

Damien leaned back in his chair, fingers steepled. "It would change everything. The narrative of abandonment has shaped Brookwood for generations. Amelia as the frozen bride, Elijah as coward—it's myth. But a vow shared, even hidden, means the bell didn't fall silent because of absence. It refused because of concealment."

"Concealment," Marley repeated, tasting the word. "The town has been living with a lie, Damien. And now the music itself is telling the truth."

. . .

HE STOOD and went to the shelves, pulling down the folio of letters. "If this is more than melody, then it belongs with the other artifacts—the ring, the photograph, the letter you found in the print shop. Each one has been a piece of Amelia's voice returning. The music is no different."

Marley's eyes followed him, but her heart pulled toward the two boxes still resting side by side. "Except this one speaks in the present tense," she said. "Not 'I loved,' not 'I vowed.' It says 'I stayed.' It's happening now, Damien. The vow is breathing now."

He didn't answer immediately. Instead he sat again and opened his notebook. "Then we need to treat it like the bell itself. A voice of witness." He jotted a heading: *Music Box Duet – Solstice Alignment.* Beneath it he wrote, *Message: I stayed. Intention: presence across time.*

Marley returned to the table, leaning over him. "You believe it."

"I believe we recorded something that exceeds mechanics," he said, without looking up. "And I believe if the founders built the bell as a harmonic instrument, they could have entrusted smaller instruments—music boxes, journals, rituals—to echo its vow. These boxes may be miniatures of the bell itself. Portable witnesses."

Marley's chest tightened. "Then we're carrying the vow in our hands."

THE FIRE DIPPED LOW. Damien rose to tend it, and in the pause Marley's thoughts spun. She pictured Amelia standing at the bridge, lace gloves stained, veil heavy with snow, but not alone. She pictured another woman—a face never painted in records—her hand steady on Amelia's, her voice weaving the second melody.

That was the image the duet carried: one voice making room, the other voice stepping into it.

Marley turned back to Damien, the words rushing. "We have to play it for others. Not just in here, between us. The town has to hear the duet. It's proof Amelia wasn't forsaken."

Damien added a log, sparks lifting. "Proof—or provocation. Do you understand what will happen when we present this? Families with names in the Circle will feel threatened. Descendants of Elijah Callahan will call it fabrication. And the council may forbid the Winter Ball entirely, fearing uproar."

Marley came to stand beside him, firelight painting both their faces. "Then let them forbid. The truth doesn't need their permission."

His jaw tightened, but there was no denial. He closed his notebook and set it on the mantel. "If we reveal this, Marley, we'll be doing more than honoring Amelia. We'll be forcing Brookwood to see itself. Every myth will crack. Every carefully tended silence will break."

"Good," Marley said fiercely. "Let it break. Because silence is the real curse."

He turned to her then, sudden, urgent. "And us? What of us, Marley? The vow is not history anymore—it's present. If we play these boxes before the town, if we claim them as witness, we will be binding ourselves to it. To each other. Are you ready for that?"

The question stole her breath. She looked at him, at the fire's glow caught in the curve of his glasses, at the weariness in his shoulders and the steadiness in his eyes.

"Yes," she whispered. "Because the vow was never meant for one voice. It needs two."

His gaze held hers, searching, then softened. "Then we prepare. We document every anomaly, every strike of the bell, every artifact, and now—every note of this duet. And when the solstice comes, we bring it forward."

Marley nodded, her throat tight. "And whatever it brings —blessing or curse—we will stay."

THE FIRE ROARED as if in answer, and for a moment Marley thought she heard the faintest overtone again, not from the boxes this time but from the air itself, a harmonic woven through the winter silence.

She closed her eyes and let it settle into her bones, not as fear, but as promise.

The bell would speak again.

And this time, Brookwood would hear.

THE NIGHT PRESSED close to the bookshop windows, black and still. The duet between the two music boxes seemed to hover in the air even after Damien powered down the laptop. Marley sat at the table, her hands resting on the polished lids of the boxes as if to anchor herself. For the first time since Amelia's veil had appeared in her dreams, she felt both certainty and dread braided together.

"They'll want proof," Damien said quietly, staring at the fading fire. "The council, the families—they'll demand authentication. Dates, signatures, mechanical explanations. And if we fail their test, they'll dismiss it as fancy, or worse —as fabrication meant to stir division."

Marley shook her head. "This isn't about the council anymore. It never was. The bell has always belonged to the people, not the Circle. The vow is ours to keep, not theirs to police. If we share this duet, it won't be in their chambers. It will be at the Winter Ball, before everyone."

Damien looked at her sharply, firelight flickering across his glasses. "That's reckless. You'll have no allies, no protection."

She lifted her chin. "Then I'll have the truth. And the truth is all I've ever wanted."

THE FIRE COLLAPSED INTO EMBERS, shadows lengthening across the walls. Damien rose, restless, and began pacing the length of the shop. His boots made dull thuds against the floorboards. "I've seen this before," he said. "In archives across Europe. Families clinging to myths because the myth protects them. Shatter it too abruptly, and they'll turn on the messenger. I don't want that for you."

"For us," Marley corrected softly.

He stopped, his back to her. She saw the way his shoulders tightened, the way his hands curled. "You think I'll stand beside you when you play those boxes for the whole town?"

She stood too, heat rising in her chest. "You've already stood beside me, Damien. Every letter, every artifact, every time I doubted myself. You're here because you believe too. Don't tell me now that you'll retreat."

His head bowed. The silence between them stretched taut. Then he turned, and in his eyes she saw not cowardice but fear—the kind that knows what devotion costs.

"If I stand with you," he said, voice low, "I bind myself to the vow. Not as historian, not as archivist. As heir. Are you ready for that, Marley? For what it will mean if we claim this as ours?"

She crossed to him, her hand trembling but steady when

it found his. "Yes. Because vows only live when someone speaks them into the present. And if it has to be us, then let it be us."

THEY SPENT the next hours preparing. Damien digitized every take of the duet, layering and cleaning the audio until the overtone shimmered audible even without headphones. Marley drafted her words, not as a historian's lecture but as a witness's confession: *Amelia was not left. She was accompanied. The vow did not fail because love faltered, but because it was hidden. And love hidden cannot ring true.*

Each time the overtone flared in the track, Marley wrote the words "I stayed" into the margin of her notes, circling them until the page looked like a palimpsest of one phrase.

When she faltered, Damien steadied her. When his doubts surged, she reminded him of Lenore's warning—*when the vow is undone, grief returns.* If they did nothing, the silence would remain a curse. If they dared to act, perhaps the duet could begin the repair.

BY DAWN, exhaustion weighted their limbs, but resolve steadied their voices. Marley set both boxes back in the cabinet, locking them with her aunt's brass key. She turned the key slowly, reverently.

"Tomorrow night," she said. "The Winter Ball. We unveil the duet there. Not as spectacle, but as witness."

Damien nodded, though his mouth tightened. "Then tonight, we make a vow of our own. Because once we share this, there will be no going back."

Marley closed the cabinet and leaned against it, her heart hammering. "Say it," she whispered.

Damien stepped closer, the firelight catching the edge of his profile. "We vow to let the music guide us. To follow where it leads, even if it brings both blessing and curse. We vow to stay."

Her throat ached, but she found the words. "We vow to stay. To keep the vow alive, not hidden. To face whatever grief or grace the bell demands."

He reached for her hand, and when their fingers laced, Marley felt the overtone flare again—not in the room, but in her chest, a harmonic only vows can make.

Outside, Brookwood slept beneath its hush of snow, unaware of the song waiting to break its silence.

But inside the bookshop, two voices had braided into one.

And when the Winter Ball arrived, the town would finally hear them.

21

A BELL RESTORED

The snow had begun to crust over the rooftops of Brookwood, layering the town in white silence. On the eve of her next research trip to the archives, Marley found herself pulled instead toward the square. The Winter Bell stood there, silent sentinel, its iron-dark weight framed against the sky. For weeks, she had passed it without stopping, her eyes trained on documents, journals, music boxes—but tonight the moon was high and bright, and something in her stirred.

She walked across the square, her breath clouding in the frigid air. The bell tower loomed, its base catching the silver light. Marley tilted her head back and felt the same shiver she had felt as a girl when her aunt told her the bell was older than any living soul in Brookwood, older even than the chapel ruins.

She touched the stone foundation. At first, it was simply cold and solid. But as her hand shifted, the moonlight revealed something she had never noticed before—a thin fissure, jagged but deliberate, running along the base. In the day it might look like a trick of weathering. But under the moon, it glimmered faintly, as though inviting her closer.

Her pulse quickened. She knelt, fingers tracing the crack. It wasn't wide enough to force, but she felt a hollowness behind it, a cavity hidden in the bell's base.

"Damien," she whispered, though he wasn't with her. The urge to call him rose instinctively, but this moment felt meant for her alone.

She reached into her satchel and drew out the small brass lantern she had taken to carrying—an old habit from late nights in the shop. She lit it, shielding the flame with her glove, and held it close. The fissure widened in shadow and revealed itself not as random but as intentional, a seam crafted to conceal.

Marley pressed gently, and the stone gave. A small panel shifted inward with a reluctant groan, like a hinge long unused. Her breath caught. She angled the lantern, its light spilling into the hollow.

Inside lay a single object: a folded parchment, edges brittle, bound with a faded ribbon. Across its front, written in a hand both graceful and urgent, were the words: *To Whom the Bell Speaks.*

Marley's throat tightened. Her gloved hands shook as she drew it out, cradling it as if it were a newborn. She stepped back, closed the panel with trembling fingers, and sat on the steps of the tower, lantern at her side.

The parchment was stiff but intact. Carefully, reverently, she untied the ribbon. The fold opened with a whisper of dust. Inside, the ink had faded to sepia but remained legible, a script flowing and strong.

She read.

To Whom the Bell Speaks,

If you have found this, then the bell has chosen you. You will hear what others have silenced, and you will bear what others denied. They called me bride, but I was not. I did not vow myself to marriage. My vow was to peace. I wished not to be wed, but to be keeper of balance. They placed a veil on me, but I carried light. They bound my hands in lace, but I held a lantern for all. When the bell was struck, it was not for rings of gold but for the covenant of harmony. Remember me not as forsaken bride. Remember me as keeper. If you keep this vow alive, the bell will speak again, and Brookwood will rest.

The words blurred as tears filled Marley's eyes. She pressed the letter to her chest, the parchment cool against her wool coat.

Amelia herself. Not myth, not rumor. Her voice carried across decades, across the silence of the bell.

Marley closed her eyes, the words searing into her: *I did not vow myself to marriage. My vow was to peace.*

She sat in the square for a long time, moonlight etching the bell above her. She thought of the music box duet, of the phrase "I stayed," of the overtone that had spoken through her. She thought of Damien's fears, of the town's fragility, of the Council's silence. And she knew that Amelia had never been the abandoned figure the town mourned—she had been more. She had been the vow's truest voice, and her story had been buried to protect a myth of marriage that was never hers.

Marley folded the letter gently, placed it back in her satchel, and rose. The bell loomed silent still, but now its silence felt less like absence and more like waiting.

"Keeper of peace," Marley whispered into the winter air. "We will not forget you again."

. . .

SHE RETURNED to the bookshop just before dawn, her lantern still faintly glowing. Damien was asleep in the archive room, slumped over his notes, his glasses crooked. Marley laid the parchment on the desk before him and touched his shoulder. He stirred, blinking at her, and she placed the letter in his hands without a word.

He read, and his face softened with something between awe and grief.

"Marley," he whispered, "this... this changes everything."

"Yes," she said. "It restores everything."

And as the first light of morning touched Brookwood, Marley knew the bell was no longer just silent metal. It was alive with a voice that had waited decades to be heard.

THE PARCHMENT LAY SPREAD across the desk, anchored at its corners with ink bottles and Damien's brass letter opener. Marley leaned close, tracing the loops and angles of Amelia's hand with her eyes, committing every stroke to memory. The fire crackled low, but the silence between them was taut with reverence.

"She called herself *keeper of peace*," Damien murmured, adjusting his glasses. His thumb brushed the margin of the page as though he were touching something alive. "Not bride, not wife, not abandoned woman. Keeper. That language echoes the founders' letters we translated last month. Remember the phrase about the Winter Bell Union —'to bind the hearth and the river, the hand and the song, for the keeping of harmony'?"

Marley nodded, her heart still racing. "Yes. They described the vow as a covenant for balance, not just a marriage contract. Amelia must have understood it. Maybe she was chosen—or chose herself—to continue it."

Damien opened his notebook, flipping to the page where he had sketched the bell motif. He underlined a line in his neat hand: *Harmony requires guardianship; the vow is not for one alone.*

"See here?" he said. "This matches Amelia's letter almost word for word. She wasn't improvising. She was quoting, or at least inheriting the founders' language. That means she wasn't an anomaly—she was the rightful vessel of the vow."

Marley exhaled sharply. "Then the whole story we've been told—the frozen bride, the broken engagement— wasn't just a distortion. It was a theft. They buried her role as keeper under the weight of a narrative they found easier to control."

Damien rubbed his forehead, the weight of the revelation visible in the set of his shoulders. "The Circle of Seven would have had every reason to suppress this. A vow to peace, kept by a woman who refused marriage? It under- mines the patriarchal authority they built. Easier to brand her as tragic, forsaken, than to let her stand as a leader in her own right."

Marley felt anger flare in her chest. She rose, pacing the narrow aisle between shelves. "All these years the bell has been silent not because Amelia failed, but because the town refused to honor her true vow. We've been mourning a false story while ignoring the real covenant."

Her steps slowed as fear crept in alongside fury. "Damien, if we tell them this—if we reveal Amelia rejected the role of bride—they'll accuse us of rewriting history. The families who've built their reputations on the myth of her abandonment will resist."

He tapped the parchment with his pen, his expression

steady. "Then we don't present it as rewriting. We present it as restoration. The founder's vow has always been about harmony. Amelia's words prove continuity, not rupture."

Marley returned to the desk, leaning over the letter again. The ink was faded, but the lines vibrated with clarity: *They placed a veil on me, but I carried light.* She whispered it aloud, tasting its defiance. "She wanted them to know. She wanted us to find this."

Damien's voice softened. "She trusted the bell would choose someone. That phrase—'to whom the bell speaks.' It implies succession, a passing on of guardianship. You, Marley. You were the one who found it."

Her throat tightened. She pressed her palm to the parchment, not to claim it but to steady herself. "It feels too heavy for me alone."

"Then let it rest on us both," Damien said.

THEY STUDIED the letter line by line. Damien cross-referenced passages with the founders' correspondence, circling key words—*balance, peace, keeper, covenant.* Marley drew connections aloud, mapping Amelia's phrases against the oral traditions she had gathered from elders who remembered snatches of story.

"It was always about keeping the town in harmony with itself," Marley said. "Not celebrating weddings, but binding families, mending rivalries, carrying grief as well as joy." She looked up sharply. "That explains the anomalies Lenore told us about—the bell ringing for her brother's death. The bell wasn't malfunctioning. It was keeping its vow, acknowledging grief as part of harmony."

Damien's pen froze above the page. "Which means silence—our current silence—is not neutrality. It's imbalance. The bell refused to ring because the vow was hidden, falsified. The silence is judgment."

Marley sank into the chair across from him, her body suddenly heavy. "So if we reveal Amelia's letter, we're not just offering a new story. We're calling the whole town to reckon with the silence as curse. And they'll have to admit they've lived in imbalance for generations."

The thought pressed on her chest. The Council would deny it, families would resist, even her own aunt's friends might call it blasphemy. Yet as she looked at Amelia's words, she knew silence was no longer an option.

DAMIEN LEANED BACK, eyes fixed on the ceiling beams. "We must choose carefully how to share this. If we simply read the letter aloud, they'll dismiss it as forgery. If we confront the Circle directly, they'll bury it again. But if we weave it into the Winter Ball, where memory and ritual converge..."

"...then the bell itself might answer," Marley finished for him.

The idea sent a chill down her spine, but also a spark of hope. "We let the town hear her words in the moment the bell was always meant to speak. If the bell responds, no one can deny it."

Damien nodded slowly. "But it means risking everything. If the bell stays silent, they'll call us frauds. If it speaks, they'll be forced to confront truths they've avoided for eighty years. Either way, Brookwood will not be the same."

Marley looked down at the parchment once more. Amelia's hand curved across the page, certain, unflinching. *Remember me not as forsaken bride. Remember me as keeper.*

"She was brave enough to defy them then," Marley said quietly. "We must be brave enough to honor her now."

Damien's gaze met hers, steady but shadowed. "Then we vow together: we will share Amelia's letter at the Winter Ball. We will risk silence or sound. And we will carry the vow forward, whatever it costs."

Marley nodded, her heart trembling. She reached out, and their hands touched over the parchment. The vow was not yet spoken aloud, but it thrummed in the space between them.

And somewhere above them, though the bell did not stir, Marley thought she felt the faintest vibration in the beams—a resonance waiting to be claimed.

THE FIRE HAD BURNED itself into a quiet bed of embers by the time Marley and Damien moved from the desk. The letter lay between them still, weighted by the letter opener, but its presence felt almost like a third voice in the room—silent yet insistent. Marley tightened her shawl around her shoulders, though she knew it wasn't the cold that made her shiver.

"We can't simply walk into the Winter Ball and read this aloud," Damien said, pacing the narrow stretch between shelves. His voice was calm, but the rhythm of his steps betrayed unease. "We need to prepare for the storm that will follow."

Marley nodded. "They'll call it forgery. They'll say I wrote it myself, or that we're misinterpreting it. The Circle will fight hardest—they've lived off Amelia's silence for decades."

"Which is why we need corroboration," Damien replied, pausing to adjust his glasses. "We bring the music boxes, the ring, the ledger entries, the printing plate. Each artifact sings the same refrain: Amelia was never what they said. Together, they become undeniable."

Marley looked down at the letter again, her throat tightening. "And yet the truth itself is what frightens me. Amelia refused the veil. She chose to be keeper of peace, not bride. That overturns not just myth, but identity. Entire families pride themselves on having 'descended from the bride betrayed.' What happens when we tell them there was no betrayed bride at all?"

Damien returned to the table, his presence steadying. "Then we remind them the vow was larger than marriage. It was about balance, reconciliation, peace. Amelia wasn't less than they believed—she was more. If they can't bear that truth, it says more about them than about her."

Marley swallowed hard. "And if they turn on us?"

"Then we stand together," Damien said simply.

THE WORDS SETTLED BETWEEN THEM, and Marley felt a warmth unfurl in her chest. She had feared that Damien, always cautious, might shrink from the risk. Instead, he was steady, as though he had been waiting for this crossing point.

She leaned back, her eyes searching the ceiling beams. "We should plan for questions. If they ask why the letter was hidden—"

"We tell them the truth," Damien interrupted. "That Amelia placed it there herself, knowing they would silence her, and trusting the bell would someday choose someone to uncover it."

Marley's gaze snapped to him. "You think she meant me?"

His eyes softened. "The seam only revealed itself under moonlight. You were the one who went to the tower. You were the one carrying the lantern. If the bell didn't mean for you to find it, then why else wait eighty years?"

Her chest ached. "I don't know if I can bear that weight."

"Then let me bear it with you," he said.

THEY SPENT the next hour listing possibilities: the council accusing them of fabrication, families refusing to attend the Ball if they suspected controversy, even the possibility of the Circle seizing the artifacts outright. For each scenario, they spoke through their response.

"If they claim forgery, we present the handwriting comparison," Damien noted, flipping to a page in his notebook where he had already collected samples from Amelia's journal. "It matches. Same loops, same slant."

"If they threaten to confiscate the letter?" Marley asked.

"Then we've already copied it," Damien answered, sliding a carbon duplicate across the desk.

She blinked. "You've been preparing for this all along."

"I've been preparing for the day the truth would resist silence," he said quietly.

Marley touched the duplicate, her heart catching. "Then tomorrow we don't just reveal the letter. We reveal everything. The duet. The ring. The ledger. One by one until the town has no choice but to see."

"And if the bell stays silent?" Damien asked.

Marley drew a breath, steady but fierce. "Then we will be its sound."

.   .   .

THE EMBERS DIMMED, the shop cloaked in quiet, but they remained awake, shoulders brushing as they leaned over the table. Marley thought of Amelia writing the words by lantern light, tucking them into the hollow of the bell, trusting strangers across decades to bear her vow.

"What if the vow was never meant for a single keeper?" Marley murmured. "What if it always required two voices— one to carry, one to witness? She had someone. The duet proves it. Maybe the vow only lives when shared."

Damien's hand rested on the parchment, firm. "Then we share it now. Not just with the town—with each other. If Amelia vowed to peace, then let us vow the same."

Marley felt her throat tighten, tears hot behind her eyes. "Damien—"

He shook his head gently. "Not a vow of marriage. A vow of keeping. To stand as guardians of balance, as Amelia wished. Whatever else comes of us, we hold this."

She reached across the desk, laying her hand over his. "Then say it with me."

He nodded, and together, in the quiet shop, they spoke.

"We vow to keep the peace Amelia carried. We vow to let silence hide nothing. We vow to listen for the bell, and to answer it, with courage and truth. Whatever grief or blessing it brings, we will remain."

The words settled like a mantle over their shoulders. Marley felt it in her bones—the bell's resonance answering, not in sound but in presence. The embers in the hearth seemed to glow brighter for an instant, as though bearing witness.

WHEN AT LAST THEY ROSE, exhaustion weighted them, but a strange clarity steadied their steps. Damien rolled the parchment gently, sliding it into a protective tube. Marley returned the music boxes, the ring, and the gloves to the cabinet, locking it tight. They stood a long moment before the closed door, as though sealing not just objects but intention.

"Tomorrow," Damien said, his voice low, "Brookwood will begin to change."

"Tomorrow," Marley echoed.

But as they extinguished the lanterns and climbed the stairs to rest, both knew the change had already begun. For they were no longer merely seekers of the vow. They were its keepers.

22

DAMIEN'S DILEMMA

The email arrived before dawn, when the streetlamps still painted the snow a weak gold and the bookshop smelled like banked embers and paper. Damien woke to the soft chime of his phone and, for a moment, he thought it was the bell in the square speaking inside his head. Then the screen stunned him awake: a subject line that had lived in him since he was ten years old, when a library atlas first taught him the shape of Italy.

Final Offer – Archive Fellowship, Florence

The body of the message was brief and formal, bracketed by signatures and seals: a three-month appointment with option to extend, a stipend that would let him forget rent, supervised access to a private collection rumored to contain letters whose ink had outlived empires. They wanted him in the reading room by the first week of January. They wanted his answer by Friday.

He lay there, the phone's blue light staining the ceiling. The word *final* felt like someone placing a hand on his back and urging him toward a door he had always wanted to open. Yet all he could see was the bell tower in the square, the seam Marley had found in its base, the parchment addressed *To Whom the Bell Speaks.*

Damien dressed and headed downtown. He arrived at the bookshop; snow pressed thinly at the windowpanes, and the stove ticked like a small heart. He set water to boil and read the email again at the counter, his breath fogging faintly. Florence rose in him—stone arches and worn steps, afternoons steeped in dust and citrus oil, a language that felt like song even when ordering coffee. Childhood dream. University aim. The idea that the world could be arranged by shelves and finding aids, and that a man might spend a life coaxing order from the past.

He poured hot water over grounds and said aloud, to no one, to steady himself: "I wanted this long before I wanted anything else."

A floorboard creaked above. Marley. He shoved his phone in his pocket as if it might betray him by glowing too brightly, then reopened it at once—he was no longer built for hiding. They had vowed as keepers, not co-conspirators in silence. Still, the email felt like a lit match cupped in his palm.

Marley came down wrapped in her sweater, hair hastily knotted, the unguarded soft of morning still on her face. When she saw him in the half-light, her mouth almost smiled, then paused, reading the room.

"You're up early," she said.

"So are you." He offered her the mug he'd already poured for her without thinking. The gesture felt intimate in the way habits do.

She curled her fingers around the heat. "I dreamed the bell had a heartbeat," she said, and then half laughed at herself. "And when I woke up, I knew you weren't upstairs."

He nodded at the laptop. "Email from Europe."

Her gaze flicked to the screen and returned to him. In the silence between them, he could feel the bell phrase they'd adopted—*breath before tone*—waiting like a metronome on a conductor's stand. Tell her, he ordered himself. Speak the breath before the sound of your leaving becomes rumor.

"It's Florence," he said. "The archival post. They've... made the final offer."

Marley did not flinch; he watched admiration and grief arrive together in her face and settle, civilized, at opposite chairs. "Your dream," she said simply. "Since you were a boy."

He swallowed. "Yes."

"How long?"

"Three months. With...possible extension." The words tasted like treason, though the offer had landed in the very life he'd built to receive it.

She nodded once, thinking. Her fingers lifted and fell on the mug's handle. "And the reply?"

"Friday."

They stood in it together, the quiet a tight braid. He should ask her, he knew—come with me. But the instant the thought formed, he saw her face under the bell tower, lantern in her hand, the letter spread between them, the two of them speaking a vow not of marriage but of *keeping*. To ask her to leave now would be to pull at the braid they had only just begun. He loved her enough not to ask. He feared losing her enough not to ask. And somewhere between those two truths stood the cowardice of letting the choice look noble.

"I'm not asking you to come," he said, careful. "I don't want you to feel obliged—or torn."

A small movement crossed her mouth, too quick to read. "You're not asking me."

"I—" He looked down, fingers tightening on his own mug. "I can't put that on you. Not with the Winter Ball upon us. Not with Amelia's letter. Not with the bell."

"The bell," she echoed, and no mockery touched it. But a breeze of distance moved through the word, like cold air under a door.

He loved her steadiness, the way she could hold two truths without forcing them to fight. But in that moment he wanted anything other than steadiness. He wanted her to say *stay*. He wanted her to catch his sleeve. He wanted to be let off the hook of a dream by someone he trusted more than himself.

She did not. She sipped, eyes on him as if measuring whether he would save himself.

"I haven't accepted," he said too quickly, as if the speed of his denial could make it more true. "I don't know if I will."

"What does your desire say?" she asked, and there it was: the question that made boys into men and scholars into keepers. "Not your fear. Not your sense of duty. Your desire."

He closed his eyes. Florence rose again—reading rooms, vellum, evening walks along the river. But then Brookwood pressed back—the bridge where they had heard the music say *I stayed*, the bakery where dreams drew green flame on paper, the elder's warning that the bell speaks grief when vows are undone. Desire, it turned out, had learned harmony.

"I want both," he said, and laughed hoarsely at himself. "I want the archive and the bell. I want to keep the town and touch the pages I've chased since I was ten. I want the quiet of Florence and the noise of our square when truth floods it."

She set her mug down gently. "You can't be in two rooms at once, love."

He absorbed the word—*love*—and filed it away like a rare scrap he would not risk touching twice. "No," he said. "I can't."

They worked the morning as they always did, because ordinary work is how people survive extraordinary thresholds. Marley re-read the letter from the bell's base and copied phrases onto notecards for her talk. Damien cleaned the audio of the duet until the upper harmonic—her *I stayed*—rose like a thread of light. They spoke logistics: who would steady the projector, who would cue the track, which witnesses would be invited nearest the bell rope so that if the tone came it would not be claimed by the Circle as spectacle.

But the conversation lay under every movement, like a low organ note under a hymn. By noon Marley's questions slipped between tasks: practical at first, then tender, then edged.

"If you go," she asked, labeling a card *keeper of peace*, "what happens to Amelia's exhibits? The ribbon box, the gloves?"

"I'll document them exhaustively," he said. "You'll present them. They're yours."

"And the ledger of anomalies? The grief-notes?"

"I'll finish indexing and leave the crosswalks."

"And if the bell rings while you're gone?"

He hesitated. "Then you will have done it. We will have done it. Distance doesn't erase a vow."

She nodded, but her mouth tightened the way it does when a splinter will not free itself. "Vows ask for presence," she said softly. "Even when presence is costly."

He almost said, *Come with me,* and almost said, *I'll*

stay, and said neither, because the boldness of either sentence would throw everything off the rails they'd carefully laid toward the Ball. He told himself *breath before tone* meant caution. Some cowardice wears the clothes of wisdom and hopes not to be recognized.

In the afternoon, townsfolk stopped by with gossip disguised as purchases. Each visit made the town feel like a body taking breath, a chest rising in expectation.

When the bell tower's shadow advanced across the square and reached the shop's stoop, Marley closed the ledger and said, simply, "Walk?"

They circled the square once, boots knocking old snow off new. The sky was the color of pewter, and the bell's mouth looked darker than usual, as if storing speech.

"Say you take it," Marley said. "Say you go. Not forever—three months, or six. What do you fear most?"

"That I'll miss the note we've spent all year listening for," he said, before he could make the answer pretty. "That the bell will speak and I won't be here to answer."

She thought about that, and he loved her for thinking rather than consoling. "And if you stay?" she asked. "What do you fear then?"

"That I'll resent the stillness," he answered. "That I'll blame the town for a dream I didn't even let test me."

They stopped at the edge of the square where the snow had been churned into sugar by the baker's deliveries. Marley turned to him and, for the first time that day, did not look like a historian or a keeper or a woman trying to save a town. She looked like Marley, who wanted and feared as clearly as he did.

"Then tell the truth," she said. "Not the noble version. The true one. Do you want to go?"

He was tired of evasion. "Yes."

"Do you want to stay?"

"Yes."

She laughed once, not unkindly. "That's the problem with vows and dreams. They both think they're music, and they both expect to be the melody."

He covered his eyes with his palm and let the cold bite him. "I don't know how to choose without betraying something that doesn't deserve betrayal."

Marley stood very still. When she spoke, her voice was gentle and iron both. "You won't ask me to come. I won't ask you to stay. So we'll have to ask something else to answer us." She lifted her chin toward the tower. "We built our lives this year around listening. Let's listen now."

They stood there, breathing steam into the winter. No sound came from the bell. A sparrow hopped along the eave and shook snow onto Damien's shoulder. A dog barked twice and then thought better of it.

"The town is choosing its breath," Marley said quietly, as if narrating for the air. "Maybe that's all the answer we get today."

They started back. Inside the shop she wrote two headings on a clean page and slid it to him: **If You Go** and **If You Stay**. Under the first, she wrote *Letters you'll bring back. Archives we'll gain. Distance we'll practice that won't undo us.* Under the second, she wrote *Bell we'll hear together. Anger you may feel. Rooms you'll have to forgive for being small.*

He added lines of his own, each one a concession and a mercy. It didn't make the decision simpler. It made it honest.

When dusk fell hard and took the color from everything, he looked up from the page and found Marley watching him in that way she had: a gaze that could pass through falsity like light through glass.

"We're still walking the same path, aren't we?" she asked, not quite a plea.

He wanted to say yes as easily as a man wants to breathe. Instead he reached across the table and covered her hand with his. "We are," he said, and knew the truth inside the sentence was not a map but a vow: not a guarantee of geography, but a promise about the direction they would face, even if oceans insisted on that thin blue between.

Outside, the bell did not ring. Inside, they listened anyway.

The days leading toward Friday moved with the slowness of snow falling against glass—every flake separate, visible, and yet building into something impossible to ignore. Damien carried the fellowship letter in his pocket like contraband, folded so tightly the crease deepened each time he thumbed it open. He told himself he would decide soon, but every hour the deadline grew closer, he found himself tightening the fold and tucking it deeper into his coat.

Marley noticed. She noticed everything.

On Wednesday morning, she found him at the back of the shop, shoulders hunched over the ledger of bell anomalies. His pencil lay unused; he was staring at the same page he had been staring at for fifteen minutes. She leaned on the doorway, arms crossed.

"You haven't written a single word," she said.

He blinked as if pulled back from far away. "I was thinking."

"About Florence?"

He hesitated, then nodded. "Yes. About Florence."

She stepped into the room, her boots whispering against the worn floorboards. "You keep saying you haven't decided.

But your body already has. You lean toward the window when you speak of it. You fold your arms when you mention staying. I've seen you argue with yourself more clearly than with anyone else."

His throat worked. "You read me too easily."

"You read the town too easily," she replied. "And yourself not at all."

Damien closed the ledger and pressed his palms flat against its cover. "I'm trying not to hurt anyone. Not you. Not Brookwood. Not the vow. But I don't know how to carry both paths without breaking."

She studied him. "You think leaving is betrayal. You think staying is cowardice. Perhaps it's neither. Perhaps it's simply choice."

The word struck him like a bell tone—clear, resonant, undeniable. Choice. He had spent his life imagining archives as destiny, Brookwood as detour. But what if it was reversed? What if the bell itself had intervened, not to derail him but to show him that vocation was never a single corridor but a braid of paths?

That afternoon, townsfolk came and went with the hush of anticipation. Winter Ball preparations filled the air: swatches of fabric, trays of candied walnuts, questions about whether the bell tower steps had been cleared. Damien stood behind the counter, answering absently, while Marley carried the rhythm of interaction.

He caught glimpses of her—laughter at the insistence on adding lavender to the mulled wine, patience as a young boy begged for permission to polish the brass lanterns. Each gesture reminded him that Brookwood's pulse did not come from the Circle or the Council, but from people like her, weaving daily kindness into ritual.

And the more he watched, the heavier the fellowship weighed. Florence promised access to manuscripts older than the bell itself. But what use were manuscripts if he lost the living vow before him?

THAT EVENING, Marley joined him in the reading nook, both of them wrapped in blankets. The snow outside fell steadily, muting the world to silence. Between them on the table lay Amelia's letter, still in its protective tube.

"You still haven't asked me," Marley said quietly.

Damien turned his head. "Asked you what?"

"To come."

He inhaled sharply, then exhaled. "Because I won't bind you to my uncertainty. If I ask, you'll feel pulled, and you'll choose me over Brookwood. And you'll resent me for it. And I'll resent myself."

Her eyes softened but did not yield. "You've built the argument so neatly, you've convinced yourself it's noble. But it's only another way of deciding without speaking the decision."

He shut his eyes, leaning back. "You deserve better than my torn loyalties."

"And you deserve better than silence," she answered.

The words hung between them, echoing Amelia's own refusal to be silenced.

THURSDAY CAME, and with it the unmistakable sound of preparations in the square—wooden stages creaking into place, lanterns being tested. Damien walked the perimeter at dusk, needing space, and ended up at the base of the bell tower. The fissure Marley had found was invisible now, hidden in shadow. He placed his palm against the cold stone anyway.

"Keeper of peace," he whispered, repeating Amelia's self-description. "How did you choose? Did you want both, too?"

The tower did not answer. But the silence pressed back with the weight of expectation, as if even indecision had consequence.

When he returned to the shop, Marley was upstairs. He opened his journal and wrote furiously, lists colliding with confessions:

If I go—proof I was worthy of my dream, but risk of losing the vow. If I stay—proof I can keep the vow, but risk of losing myself. What if the vow and the dream are the same thing in different languages? What if Florence and Brookwood are both archives, one of paper, one of people?

He closed the journal, his hand aching. He wanted to run upstairs, to tell Marley everything, to beg her to choose for him. But the vow of keepers meant they bore truth together, not shifted it like a burden.

THAT NIGHT, they sat at the table again, fire low, both tired. Marley studied him, her expression unreadable.

"You're leaving pieces of yourself scattered everywhere," she said finally. "In your journal. In your pockets. In your silence. Damien, I don't need you to stay or go. I need you to stand. To be whole in whichever you choose. Because if you divide yourself, the bell will remain divided too."

He felt the words strike true. For days he had been folding the letter tighter, as though compressing his dilemma into a shape that might vanish. But nothing vanishes when silence carries it. Amelia had proven that.

He reached across the table, covering her hand. "Then tomorrow," he said, "I will answer. Not with silence. With choice."

Her fingers curled into his. "That's all I ask."

FRIDAY DAWNED BRITTLE AND BLUE, the kind of winter light that seemed too sharp to belong to earth. Damien woke before the church clock struck seven, the fellowship letter on his desk like a sentinel. He had dreamed of Florence again—sun-warmed courtyards, the smell of vellum and lemon oil—but the dream had been overlaid with the bell's heavy silence, as though Brookwood itself had leaned into the dream to remind him he could not leave unmarked.

He sat at the desk in his undershirt, fingers hovering over the laptop keyboard. The email draft waited with two words typed: *I accept.* Nothing more. He had hovered over those words three times in the night, once at midnight, once at two, once at five. Each time, he had closed the machine and retreated into pacing, as if motion could delay the inevitable.

Now the deadline ticked toward him like a slow, steady drum.

Marley's footsteps creaked overhead. He did not move the laptop away this time when she came down the stairs. She stopped at the sight of the glowing screen, her hair loose, eyes still shadowed from sleep.

"You've written it," she said quietly.

"Half," he admitted. "But half feels like betrayal already."

She crossed the room, set a mug of tea beside him, and

studied the words on the screen. Then she pulled out the chair opposite him and sat, folding her sweater tighter.

"Tell me everything," she said. "No lists. No ledgers. No noble evasions. Just your truth."

Damien gripped the edge of the desk. His throat ached, but the words came.

"I have wanted Florence since I was a boy. Before I knew what love was. Before I knew what vows were. I wanted to spend my life in manuscripts, in order, in the quiet logic of archives. When the offer came, it was like someone reached through time and handed me the shape of my oldest dream."

He stopped, his eyes burning. Marley did not move, her silence steady, urging him on.

"But then Brookwood happened. Jackie and Sophie happened. The bell happened. You happened. And now I can't separate my desire from my duty. Florence is a dream I longed for. But Brookwood feels like a dream that longed for me."

Her breath caught faintly, but she said nothing.

"I fear leaving," Damien continued, "because I fear I'll miss the bell's voice. That it will ring, and I will be across an ocean, holding papers while the town heals without me. I fear staying because I fear I'll lose myself, that I'll resent the quiet for stealing what I worked my whole life toward. And then I'll become bitter, and bitterness is a worse exile than distance."

Marley reached across the desk and laid her hand over his. "And so you've been carrying both like stone weights, hoping one would fall away on its own."

"Yes," he whispered.

"And has it?"

He shook his head. "No. They've only grown heavier."

She squeezed his hand. "Then let us lay them down together. Tell me your choice, Damien. Not the choice that pleases me. Not the one that pleases the Council or the Circle. Not the one that rescues your boyhood dream. The choice that tells the truth of who you are now."

THE SILENCE STRETCHED, thick and fragile. Damien looked at the laptop screen again, at the two words: *I accept.* He thought of Florence's river, its bridges arching like spines. He thought of the tower outside, the fissure in its base, the letter addressed *To Whom the Bell Speaks.*

And he knew.

Slowly, deliberately, he backspaced. The words vanished. He closed the draft without sending. He shut the laptop, the click sounding like a bell tone of its own.

"I cannot go," he said. The words were heavy, but they settled like stones forming a foundation instead of a grave. "Not now. Maybe not ever. The bell chose us. Amelia chose us. I cannot leave before we've answered."

Marley's shoulders sagged, not in relief exactly, but in release. "You chose presence," she whispered.

He nodded. "And if someday the archive calls again, then I'll answer it with different ears. But right now, my vow is here. With you. With the bell."

Her hand tightened over his. Tears glimmered in her eyes, but she blinked them back. "Do you realize what that means? The Circle will see you as threat, not ally. The Council will resent your influence. You've tied yourself to a fight that may undo us both."

"I know," he said. "And I choose it anyway."

·   ·   ·

THE DAY unspooled around them with a strange lightness. For the first time in weeks, Damien's body did not feel split in two. He worked beside Marley in the shop, cataloging artifacts with steady hands. When customers asked about Winter Ball programs, he answered without distraction. Each act of presence confirmed his choice.

Marley, too, seemed changed. She laughed more easily that afternoon, her smile not shadowed by the fear of distance. Yet under the ease, Damien sensed something deeper: she was testing his resolve, waiting to see if his choice would hold when the evening came and the email remained unsent.

At dusk, he walked her to the square. The lanterns for the Ball were being lit, strings of golden light cascading from the tower to the bakery awning. The bell loomed above, its mouth open to the winter sky.

"Keeper of peace," Marley said softly, looking up at it. "That's what Amelia called herself. That's what we've vowed. Today you kept it, Damien. By staying."

He exhaled, the cold biting his lungs. "But staying is not enough. Keeping requires more than presence. It requires courage. The Ball will test that vow. The Council will resist. The Circle will fight. Are we ready?"

Marley turned to him, her eyes bright in the lamplight. "We weren't chosen to be ready. We were chosen to be faithful."

Her words steadied him more than certainty ever could.

THAT NIGHT, after the shop closed and the lanterns outside glowed steady, they sat again with the parchment between them. Damien unrolled it, reading aloud Amelia's words: *Remember me not as forsaken bride. Remember me as keeper.*

Marley took the parchment when he finished and rolled it carefully, sliding it back into its case. "Tomorrow we begin preparing the town for the truth. And when the Ball comes, we will speak it."

Damien nodded, his hand covering hers. "And whatever happens after, we will keep it together."

A stillness filled the shop, not emptiness but a kind of resonance, as if the vow itself had settled into their bones. Damien felt no less afraid—of failure, of resistance, of betrayal. But for the first time, fear no longer divided him. It only sharpened the vow he had chosen.

Above them, the Winter Bell did not ring. Yet Damien thought he could feel it tremble faintly in the night air, as if acknowledging the sound of a decision finally spoken.

23

FOUND IN LACE AND DUST

The attic above the bookshop's appartment was a place few had entered since Marley's aunt passed. Its beams were low and crooked, the air faintly sweet with the residue of wax and lavender. Dust lay thick over every trunk and crate, as if decades of forgotten ritual had gathered here to wait.

Marley climbed the narrow wooden ladder first, lantern balanced in her hand. Damien followed, the boards creaking under his weight, his breath visible in the draft that wound through gaps in the roof.

They had come searching for more context—records, remnants, anything that might explain the silence of the bell. What Marley did not expect was the sight of a single box set apart from the clutter, placed squarely in the center of the attic floor. Unlike the surrounding trunks, this box was free of cobwebs, its wooden sides gleaming faintly beneath the dust as though someone had polished it long after everything else had been abandoned.

She knelt before it. A label had been tacked carefully to the lid:

A.C. – Keep Closed Until Peace Returns

Her fingers trembled as she traced the initials. "Amelia Colvin," she whispered.

Damien crouched beside her, his eyes narrowing. "Why here? Why would your aunt keep it hidden above candles and not in the shop archives?"

"Maybe she didn't know," Marley murmured. "Maybe someone before her placed it here. Maybe she was guarding it in silence."

The words on the box pressed into Marley's chest like weight: *Until Peace Returns.* The attic seemed to grow colder, the lantern flame flickering as if in sympathy. She lifted the lid slowly, the hinges groaning.

Inside lay layers of fabric, carefully folded though time had yellowed their edges. Marley lifted the first sheet of muslin and uncovered a dress—the unmistakable cut of a bridal gown. Its satin shimmered even beneath the dust, sleeves puffed in the style of the 1930s, the train edged with delicate lace. But the dress had never been worn; its folds remained sharp, uncreased by movement.

Damien inhaled sharply. "Unworn," he said, his voice hushed.

"Yes." Marley touched the bodice, the fabric cold beneath her fingertips. "She never walked in it."

Beneath the gown lay other treasures, arranged with the precision of a time capsule. Dried evergreen leaves, pressed flat, their scent still faintly sharp despite the decades. A small leather-bound booklet tied with twine. A folded sheet of paper sealed with wax that had long since cracked.

Marley lifted the booklet, and the title on its first page froze her breath.

The Winter Vow

Written in slanted, feminine script.

Damien leaned closer, his eyes widening. "Amelia's hand?"

Marley compared the strokes with those she had seen in letters preserved in the archives. "It matches. This isn't hearsay or rumor. This is her own story."

She opened the booklet carefully. The first line burned itself into her memory:

I was never meant to be a bride of man. I was meant to be a keeper of peace.

The words echoed Amelia's letter from the bell's hollow base, but here they were expanded, deliberate, clothed in her own telling.

Damien's hand shook as he reached for the booklet. He did not take it immediately, as though fearing his touch might erase the ink. At last he closed his fingers around the leather cover, holding it as if it were both fragile and eternal.

"Marley," he said, his voice thick, "this is her truth. All these years, all the silence, and she left her vow written."

Marley swallowed hard. The evergreen leaves, the sealed envelope, the bridal gown unworn—they were relics, but not of failure. They were evidence of a woman who chose differently than her town had allowed her to.

Her throat tightened. "Brookwood built its solstice on her silence. And now she's speaking again."

The lantern light flickered over Damien's face as he turned the booklet in his hands, reverent. He pressed his palm over its cover, as if promising Amelia herself: *We will not let this be lost again.*

Marley lowered her gaze to the gown, spread delicately across the attic floor. In its lace, she saw not absence but resistance. And in its dust, she felt the stirrings of something unfinished, something waiting for them to carry forward.

"Her deepest truth," she whispered. "It was never told."

Damien's answer was steady. "Then we'll tell it. At any cost."

THE ATTIC SEEMED to contract around them as Damien untied the thin twine and opened the booklet. Dust sifted from its spine like faint incense, and the lantern light caught the uneven strokes of Amelia's handwriting. Marley leaned in, the air thick with the hush of revelation.

Damien began to read aloud, his voice low, reverent:

"The bell is no ornament. It is a covenant. When it rings at solstice, it does not call two into union for themselves alone. It calls families, fields, waters, and winds into harmony. We stand beneath its voice not as lovers only, but as guardians of balance. The vow is not for the heart alone, but for the village entire."

Marley drew in a sharp breath. "She understood it as ritual. Not romance, not pageant. Something binding."

Damien nodded, his finger tracing the lines. "Listen to this: *'I was chosen to stand, not to be adorned. The gown they pressed upon me was a costume for a play I did not believe in. I wished not for veil, but for vigil.'*"

The words shivered through Marley. She thought of the untouched wedding dress in the box—its satin never brushed against skin, its lace never brushed against air. It was not failure but refusal. Amelia had never consented to the story they tried to script for her.

"She left her truth here," Marley whispered. "Not at the altar, not in the registry, but in her own hand. She wanted someone to find this."

Damien turned another page. The ink had bled in places, as if written with urgency, perhaps with tears.

"Elijah tried to protect me. He bore the weight of silence so the

town would not burn me with its stares. He agreed to be the absent groom, so they might scorn him instead of me. Yet what neither of us foresaw was the way silence calcifies into myth. They needed a bride betrayed to explain their discomfort. So they invented me."

Marley's hand flew to her mouth. She felt tears sting her eyes. "She wasn't abandoned. He shielded her."

"And by shielding her," Damien murmured, "he damned her memory. And himself."

They sat in silence, the gravity of the words pressing against them like stone. Marley thought of the journal Elijah had left behind, fragments of confession scattered like broken glass. Now they saw the fuller pattern: not cowardice, but sacrifice.

Damien cleared his throat and read again.

"The vow was never broken, though they say it was. It was only misunderstood. I vowed peace, not marriage. I vowed to keep the bell's tone in harmony, not to keep a hearth in a house not my own. If the bell grows silent, it is not for my failure. It is for theirs, for forgetting the vow's true nature."

Marley whispered the words aloud to herself, as though tasting them would make them real. *"If the bell grows silent, it is not for my failure...* Damien, she's telling us that the silence we hear now is not the echo of her broken promise. It's the echo of the town's."

He nodded slowly, jaw tight. "Which means if Brookwood is to heal, it must admit that the vow was miscast from the beginning. That their entire foundation rests on a misinterpretation."

Marley looked toward the dress box, the brittle evergreen leaves beside it. "And how will they accept that? How will families built on the pride of the 'betrayed bride' yield to the truth that she never wanted the veil at all?"

"They may not," Damien said. "But truth does not wait for permission."

THEY READ FURTHER, page after page revealing layers of Amelia's voice. She wrote of walking the frozen path to the chapel, knowing her feet would not carry her to the altar. She described hearing the bell above her head, tolling once at midnight, and feeling its sound as a charge, not a summons.

"I heard it say: Keep watch. Keep peace. And so I did."

Marley felt a chill run through her. "The bell didn't condemn her. It consecrated her."

Damien's hands trembled as he turned to the final pages. They were shorter, written almost like a prayer:

"If anyone should find these words, know that I chose not silence but stewardship. I stayed, though they said I left. I remained keeper when they called me abandoned. And if the bell should fall silent again, it is because the vow awaits new keepers. Let them be brave. Let them not mistake costume for covenant."

The lantern flame bent in the draft as the words settled into the attic. Marley felt as though Amelia herself stood at her shoulder, veiled not in lace but in light.

Damien closed the booklet, pressing it against his chest. His face was pale, but his eyes burned. "This changes every-thing. Not just about Amelia, not just about Elijah. About Brookwood. About us."

Marley drew her knees to her chest, holding herself as the weight pressed down. "We've been chasing a broken engagement, a lost wedding, a myth of abandonment. But she was never lost. She was here, holding vigil, waiting for peace to return."

Damien looked at her with quiet intensity. "And she

names us. Not directly, but unmistakably. 'Let them be brave. Let them not mistake costume for covenant.' Marley, she wrote those words for whoever would uncover the vow. That's us."

The truth struck Marley so deeply she could not breathe for a moment. They were no longer just seekers of fragments, no longer archivists of silence. They were heirs to the vow Amelia had carried alone.

Her voice came hoarse. "Damien, if we reveal this, the town will fracture. The Circle will fight us harder than ever. The Ball will turn from celebration to reckoning."

He set the booklet down gently, then took her hand. "Perhaps that is what Amelia meant by peace. Not the absence of conflict, but the courage to tell the truth even when it tears. Peace built on silence is no peace at all."

Marley felt her pulse thrum in her ears. She thought of the bell, cracked but still standing, waiting in its tower for hands that would strike it again. She thought of Amelia in her unworn gown, evergreen leaves pressed around her vow.

And she thought of Damien, here beside her, steady even in fear.

"We can't carry this alone," she said finally.

"No," Damien agreed. "But we can begin."

They folded the gown back into the box, layer by layer, as though laying a body to rest. Damien tucked the evergreen leaves between its folds, reverent. Marley replaced the lid and pressed the label with her fingertips—*Keep Closed Until Peace Returns.*

"It has returned," she whispered. "At least in part."

Damien lifted *The Winter Vow* once more, holding it like a lantern of its own. "Then let's carry it into the light."

The attic around them seemed to sigh, beams groaning faintly as though the house itself acknowledged the uncovering. The lantern's flame grew steady, throwing shadows across their faces. Marley felt the resonance of the vow settle into her bones.

Amelia had not been abandoned, nor betrayed. She had been keeper. And now Marley and Damien were chosen to continue where she had left off.

THE DESCENT from the attic was slower than the climb. Marley went first, lantern swinging in her grip, the box balanced carefully in her other hand. Damien followed, carrying *The Winter Vow* against his chest as though even the faintest slip might undo all they had uncovered. The air grew warmer with each step down, but neither of them shook the chill the attic had left behind.

Back in the shop, Marley set the box gently on the long oak table where candles once had been trimmed and boxed for sale. The lantern cast their shadows across the walls, and for a long while, they said nothing. The gown's lace glimmered faintly from beneath the lid.

Marley finally spoke, her voice thin. "We can't just put this back. We can't tuck it away again and hope someone else carries it."

"No," Damien agreed, his eyes fixed on the booklet in his hands. "But telling the town will be like striking the bell itself. The resonance will break whatever illusions they've clung to. Some will call it desecration."

Marley folded her arms, leaning against the table. "Desecration, or deliverance. We've seen both responses already. The question is: when do we reveal it? And how?"

Damien lowered the booklet, his expression heavy. "The Ball. It's the one moment the entire town gathers under the pretense of tradition. But if you stand there and read her words aloud—if you say, 'Amelia never wished to marry, she wished to keep peace'—the families will fracture on the spot."

Marley looked away, watching the lantern flame. "Maybe fracture is necessary. Peace built on falsehood isn't peace. It's a mask."

He studied her quietly, hearing Amelia's own conviction echoed in Marley's tone. "You're right. But I still fear what happens after. What if Brookwood can't bear it? What if our vow to speak her truth becomes the wedge that breaks the town completely?"

She turned back to him, her jaw set. "Then let it break. Better to break into honesty than stand whole in silence."

THE EVENING HOURS STRETCHED, and the shop remained closed though customers knocked at the door, curious about the light glowing upstairs. Marley and Damien ignored them. They spread Amelia's booklet on the table, reading aloud passages and pausing after each as though sifting for gold.

"I vowed not veil, but vigil."

"They needed a bride betrayed, so they invented me."

"If the bell falls silent, it is because the vow awaits new keepers."

Each phrase sharpened the charge they already felt pressing against their hearts. Marley wrote notes in the margins of her journal, sketching the shape of how Amelia's truth might be spoken. Damien kept turning the pages back and forth, as if rereading might reveal another line between the lines.

"This wasn't just a protest," Damien said at last. "It was

liturgy. She was writing scripture for a people who never knew they needed it."

"And they still don't," Marley whispered. "That's the danger. They've carried a story of betrayal so long, it became their mythology. To undo it is to tell them their grief was never what they thought."

"Which may free them," Damien replied. "Or undo them."

Marley closed her eyes, remembering the elder Lenore's warning: *When the vow is undone, grief returns.* Perhaps the grief was not only Amelia's. Perhaps it belonged to everyone who had mistaken silence for failure.

THEY DEBATED FOR HOURS, the shop's clock chiming each quarter until midnight passed. Marley argued that truth had to be spoken plainly, Amelia's words read as she wrote them. Damien countered that context was needed—that the vow should be explained carefully, framed within Brookwood's traditions, or the town might lash out in confusion.

At last, Marley leaned across the table, her hand on the booklet. "If we dilute her words, we betray her again. That's what they did before—turned her vow into a costume. If we're to be keepers, then we keep her words as she wrote them."

Damien held her gaze. "Then we must be ready to pay the cost."

Silence fell, heavy but resolute.

TOWARD DAWN, Marley carried the gown upstairs to the guest room and spread it across the bed. She lit a single candle at its side, watching the flame quiver against the satin folds. Damien stood beside her, the booklet still in his hand.

"She wrote for us," Marley said quietly. "Not just us—anyone who would listen. But we found her. We heard her. That makes us responsible."

Damien nodded, his voice low. "Then let's speak it. Together."

Marley reached for his hand, their fingers intertwining over the candlelight. The vow Amelia had carried alone was no longer solitary. It braided itself into their lives now, binding them as keepers.

They bowed their heads, not in prayer exactly, but in recognition of a vow passed forward.

"We vow," Marley whispered, "that her words will not remain hidden again."

Damien's voice joined hers, steady, unwavering. "We vow that Brookwood will know her truth, no matter the cost."

The candle flame bent once, then grew steady. The gown lay still, unworn yet radiant, a relic not of failure but of fidelity. And in the quiet of the room, both Marley and Damien felt the Winter Bell itself shift faintly in the distance, as though acknowledging the vow's renewal.

24

ANCESTRAL REUNION

The morning after their vow, Marley woke with Amelia's words still pressed against her chest like a hidden seal: *I vowed not veil, but vigil.* The phrase threaded through her dreams and followed her into waking, a refrain impossible to ignore.

She rose, wrapped a shawl around her shoulders, and went straight to the archive corner of the shop where genealogical records had long gathered dust. Her aunt had always kept binders of family trees donated by townsfolk, stitched together from marriage licenses, obituaries, and church rolls. Marley spread them across the table, hunting for the threads of Amelia Colvin's lineage.

The Colvins were an old family—older than the bakery, older even than the lighthouse in its current form. Their name appeared across multiple branches of Brookwood's record books, woven into farming deeds and council rosters. Marley traced the line from Amelia back through her parents, then forward again through siblings.

Her breath caught when she spotted it: a great-nephew, still alive, still listed as a resident of Brookwood. His name—

Mr. Whitcomb—appeared in a faded record from the 1970s, along with notes of a current address on Ash Street.

Marley sat back, heart racing. "She still has blood here," she whispered.

Damien, drawn by her voice, came through the door holding two coffee's, then paused at the table. "What have you found?"

Marley pointed to the name. "Amelia's great-nephew. He may not even know the full story."

Damien leaned closer, scanning the faded ink. His brow furrowed. "Mr. Whitcomb. He owns the small antiques shop, doesn't he? The one tucked behind the square."

"Yes." Marley's voice trembled between awe and dread. "Her descendant is here. Living under the silence she left behind."

LATER THAT AFTERNOON, Marley and Damien walked to Ash Street, their steps muffled by the thin crust of snow. The Colvin antiques shop was small, its windows crowded with old clocks, chipped porcelain, and tarnished lamps. The bell over the door chimed faintly as Marley pushed it open.

Mr. Whitcomb stood behind the counter, a man in his late sixties with hair the color of faded pewter. He looked up, adjusting his glasses, and gave them a curious smile.

"Marley Taylor," he said, recognition dawning. "Your aunt's niece. I've heard you reopened the shop."

"I did," Marley replied, her voice steady though her heart pounded. "And this is Damien Hawthorne, working with me."

Mr. Whitcomb extended a hand warmly. "What brings you both to my little corner?"

Marley hesitated, then drew a folded sheet from her

satchel: a copy she had made of Amelia's letter from the bell tower. She laid it gently on the counter.

Mr. Whitcomb adjusted his glasses again, reading the words slowly. His brow knit as his lips shaped the lines: *I was never meant to be a bride of man. I was meant to be a keeper of peace.*

When he finished, he looked up, eyes shining with confusion. "This is Amelia's hand. I've seen samples in old family Bibles. But—where did you find this?"

"In the foundation of the Winter Bell," Marley answered softly. "Hidden away, waiting. She wanted to be remembered not as abandoned, but as a keeper."

Mr. Whitcomb sank into a chair behind the counter, his hands trembling. "All my life, I heard the whispers. That Amelia was left at the altar. That she became a ghost wandering Brookwood's winter nights. I thought it was just myth. You're telling me—she chose differently?"

"She chose peace," Marley said firmly. "And her silence has been misread for nearly a century."

Damien added quietly, "We're preparing to tell her story at the Winter Ball. But we didn't want to take that step without her family's voice. Without yours."

Mr. Whitcomb's eyes brimmed. He pressed the letter to his chest as if it might steady his heart. "She was our great-aunt, but she became a cautionary tale. No one in my family ever spoke her name without sorrow or shame. If this brings healing, then yes. Share it. Tell them who she truly was."

As THEY LEFT THE SHOP, snow falling heavier now, Damien walked in silence beside Marley. But she noticed the tightness in his jaw, the way he stared at the ground as though a weight had shifted inside him.

"What is it?" she asked, pausing under the streetlamp.

He met her eyes, hesitant. "While you were speaking, I remembered something. My grandmother's maiden name was Callahan. I never thought of it beyond casual ancestry, but if Elijah Callahan's line remained here..."

Marley's eyes widened. "You think you're connected?"

Damien nodded slowly, almost reluctantly. "I'll have to check the records, but the branch names match. If so, then—"

"Then you're not just uncovering their vow," Marley finished for him. "You're part of it."

He exhaled, the breath clouding between them. "That's what terrifies me."

Marley reached for his hand, her grip firm. "Terrifying or not, you belong to it now. And so do I. We carry Amelia and Elijah forward—together."

Damien's hand tightened around hers, but his eyes lingered on the snow-laden street as though measuring the cost of ancestry revealed.

DAMIEN SAT HUNCHED over the wide oak table in the shop's back room, sleeves rolled to his elbows, stacks of binders and loose folios spread around him. The genealogical archive smelled of dust and wax, the scent of time itself. Marley leaned against the opposite side of the table, flipping through yellowed census pages, while the lantern hissed softly between them.

His hand paused on a brittle page, finger resting against a margin note: *Callahan – branch line, Florence 1897, Brookwood return 1904.*

"There," he whispered.

Marley leaned closer, eyes narrowing on the ink. "Florence," she murmured, "and you... you were just offered Florence."

Damien gave a sharp breath, almost a laugh, but not of amusement. "The irony doesn't escape me." He traced the line downward, following the neat script of marriages and children. "Here. James Callahan, brother of Elijah. He had a son, Matthew. Matthew's granddaughter—" He swallowed. "—was my grandmother."

The silence stretched between them, thick and absolute. Marley studied his face, the flicker of the lantern light catching the tension in his jaw.

"You're family," she said finally. "Distant, but blood all the same."

He leaned back, raking a hand through his hair. "Which means this vow isn't just something I've stumbled into as an archivist. It's woven into my lineage. Into me."

Marley's chest ached at the weight in his voice. "And what does that make me?" she asked quietly.

Damien's eyes softened. "It makes you the one who uncovered it. The one who carried the silence to speech. Maybe that's what Amelia meant—that new keepers wouldn't look the same as the old ones, but they'd be bound together by choice as much as blood."

THE FOLLOWING MORNING, Marley and Damien returned to Mr. Whitcomb's antiques shop. He welcomed them into a back parlor, the fire already burning, as though he had been waiting for them. On the low table lay Amelia's letter from the bell and the copied pages of *The Winter Vow*.

Mr. Whitcomb poured tea with hands steadier than when they had first shown him the letter. He looked older, yes, but also somehow lighter, as if grief had loosened its grip after decades of being carried silently.

"I've read it through and through," he said, gesturing to the pages. "Her words cut sharper than any rumor ever did. She didn't just resist marriage—she redefined it. She said no to veil, yes to vigil. That truth can't remain hidden."

Marley wrapped her hands around her teacup, grateful for the warmth. "The Winter Ball is in two nights. If I speak her story there, it will divide the room. Some will rejoice in the truth. Others will see it as betrayal."

Mr. Whitcomb sighed, nodding. "Colvins have lived with the shame of her silence for nearly a century. If it brings healing, let it be told. But I worry for the Callahans. Their name has been lauded as the family scorned, the ones who bore Amelia's supposed abandonment. To tell them Elijah chose silence to protect her—"

"—is to tell them their pride has been built on a misunderstanding," Damien finished. His voice was quiet, yet steady.

Mr. Whitcomb's gaze shifted to him. "And yet, perhaps you're the one to tell them. Your blood carries his line."

Damien stiffened. He had not meant to reveal his discovery so soon, but the words were out. "I traced the records. Elijah's brother James is my ancestor. By some tangled branch, I am a Callahan."

The fire cracked in the hearth. Mr. Whitcomb's eyes widened, then softened with something like recognition. "Then the vow has wound you into its braid whether you asked for it or not. Colvin and Callahan, sitting together in this parlor, holding Amelia's words between you."

Marley's breath caught. The truth seemed to shimmer in the air, undeniable. Bloodlines once set at odds by silence were gathered now in the same room, the same vow hovering between them.

"Brookwood may not be ready," she said, her throat tight. "But ready or not, this is what must be spoken. At the Ball, the vow has to be restored—not just for Amelia, but for every generation tangled in her silence."

Mr. Whitcomb set his cup down, eyes gleaming with tears. "Then let it be done. And may peace finally return."

THE FIRE in Mr. Whitcomb's parlor had burned down to a low glow by the time their conversation turned to the Ball. The three of them sat in a tight circle—Marley, Damien, and Mr. Whitcomb—each cradling a cup of tea gone lukewarm, none of them willing to be the first to speak. The weight of Amelia's vow hung in the air heavier than the smoke curling from the hearth.

Mr. Whitcomb finally broke the silence. "You know what will happen if you stand at the Ball and speak her words as they are written. Some will call it blasphemy. Others will call it liberation. Brookwood has never been good at sitting between the two."

Marley set her cup down on the side table, her hands trembling slightly. "I know. But if we don't tell it now, when? If not us, who? Amelia kept her vigil in silence. If the vow is to mean anything now, we can't keep hers buried."

Damien leaned forward, elbows on his knees, rubbing his hands together as though to warm them. "It isn't only the Colvins who will feel the fracture. The Callahans, too. My name may not be spoken in Brookwood with the same weight as theirs, but it's in my blood all the same. To reveal Elijah's silence as sacrifice will unravel the story they've told themselves for generations."

Mr. Whitcomb studied him closely. "And yet you speak of it. You don't deny the bond."

Damien hesitated, then nodded slowly. "For years, I thought my life would be measured in manuscripts—words written by strangers across centuries. Now I find myself bound to words written in my own family's hand, words that demand not just reading but living. It's... not what I expected."

Marley reached for his hand, threading her fingers through his. Her voice softened. "It's what Amelia expected. She said the vow would await new keepers. Maybe she foresaw this—that her blood and Elijah's would find each other again, not in marriage, but in restoration."

Damien turned toward her, his jaw tight, eyes shining with something that looked like both fear and resolve. "Then let us speak her words, Marley. Let us become what she asked for. Not veil, but vigil."

THE HOURS PASSED as they debated how to present Amelia's vow at the Winter Ball. Marley argued for reading directly from the booklet, Amelia's words preserved in their raw truth. Damien suggested weaving context around them, guiding the townsfolk into the revelation so it did not come as a violent fracture. Mr. Whitcomb sat between them, nodding at each point, his voice steady with the perspective of one who had lived long under silence.

"People will ask," Mr. Whitcomb said at last, "why we've waited until now. Why not reveal it years ago, when records were first uncovered? Why now, in this particular winter?"

Marley answered without hesitation. "Because the bell fell silent. It called us into this moment. That silence demanded Amelia's voice be heard again. The timing is not ours. It belongs to the vow itself."

Damien lifted his gaze from the fire. "If we can convince them of that—if they can see the silence not as curse but as summons—maybe they will listen."

Mr. Whitcomb leaned back, sighing. "And if they don't?"

Marley's voice was steady. "Then at least Amelia will not stand in the snow alone anymore. We will have stood with her. That's what matters."

THE CONVERSATION DEEPENED, circling again and again around the same fulcrum: truth versus peace. Mr. Whitcomb, weary but resolute, gave his blessing for them to share Amelia's vow, even if it tore open old wounds.

When he rose at last to bank the fire, Damien lingered by the table, the booklet of *The Winter Vow* in his hands. He turned it over slowly, as though waiting for it to reveal something more. Marley joined him, her hand brushing his arm.

"You don't have to carry it alone," she said softly.

He looked at her then, and in his gaze she saw the echo of Elijah Callahan—someone who once bore silence for another's sake. "That's just it," Damien said. "For so long I've lived as though my work was about preservation, about keeping the past intact. Now I see it's about incarnation. These words aren't just records. They're a living vow."

He placed the booklet on the table, then laid his hand over it. "I vow, here and now, that I will not let Elijah's silence remain misunderstood. His choice was sacrifice, not abandonment. And I vow to carry Amelia's truth forward, no matter the cost."

Marley placed her hand atop his. "And I vow the same— that Brookwood will know her not as a ghost or a broken bride, but as a keeper of peace. Together, we'll restore what was broken."

Mr. Whitcomb returned to his chair, watching them with eyes glistening. "Then it is done. The vow has found its keepers. The rest will follow."

LATER, as they stepped back out into the night, the snow fell in slow, deliberate flakes, muffling the world around them. The streetlamps glowed like halos, and the silence of Brookwood felt different now—not absence, but expectancy.

Damien walked beside Marley, their shoulders brushing. He inhaled deeply, his breath fogging the air. "Do you hear it?"

"Hear what?" Marley asked.

"The silence," he said. "It isn't empty. It's waiting."

Marley smiled faintly, her breath catching in the cold. "Then let's not keep it waiting long."

They walked on, carrying Amelia's vow between them— not as burden, but as charge. And somewhere, deep within the tower, the Winter Bell seemed to shift against its chains, as though it, too, knew its keepers had at last stepped forward.

The revelations pressed hard against them both. Marley felt Amelia's presence in every drifting flake, while Damien walked as though bearing invisible chains of lineage.

At last, he spoke, his voice raw. "All my life I thought my calling was in archives far away—in Florence, in distant vaults of parchment and stone. But here, in Brookwood, I've uncovered something older than any archive could hold. My own blood in this vow."

Marley turned toward him, lantern glow catching her

features. "And does that change your choice? Florence, or Brookwood?"

He stopped walking, snow thickening in the lamplight. His eyes searched hers, and for a long moment, silence stretched like a rope between them.

"It changes everything," he admitted.

Marley felt the words like a toll of the bell in her chest. Whether they would bind or break, she could not yet tell. But she knew Amelia's vow had not been buried in vain.

And neither would theirs.

25

A CALL TO THE LIGHTHOUSE

Marley climbed the spiral of iron steps as evening settled over Brookwood, the sea breathing a slow, cold rhythm against the rocks below. Winter Solstice Eve carried a hush that belonged to no hour on any clock; even the gulls seemed to bow to it, wheeling wide and silent over the dark water. At the top landing, she paused with her hand on the brass latch, feeling the metal's chill press through her glove as if to ask, *Are you sure?*

"I'm here," she whispered, and pushed into the lantern room.

The lighthouse had always smelled like brine and oil and old heat, a clean, diligent scent. Tonight there was something else—the faint sweetness of beeswax from the candle she carried, and beneath that the resinous breath of evergreen from the dried sprigs tucked inside her satchel. The glass panes that made the lantern room's faceted crown were rimed with a thin geometry of frost, each triangle catching the last ribbon of twilight as it bled toward the horizon.

She set her satchel on the narrow table beside the lamp pedestal and drew out the four objects that had accompanied almost every step of the mystery: the small glass vial with its ghost of green along the seam; the antique ring engraved *Yours in time, E.C. to A.C.*; the slower, slightly discordant music box—the one that had taught her to hear a duet when layered with the first box in the shop; and the lace gloves, ink-stained at the fingertips as if truth once bled through them and never entirely dried.

"Four points," she murmured, setting each at a cardinal direction around the lamp. "Four keepers."

The vial she placed to the north, where the sea wind nosed most fiercely at the glass, remembering what Damien had said about the founders' families: one line of healers closer to river and herb, the other to forge and bell. The vial belonged with the weather and the water, with breath and remedy. The ring she placed at the east, where the earliest smudge of morning would arrive—a promise ring that never reached a finger, a circle that had waited for a dawn not yet dared. To the south she set the music box, where the sun traveled long in summer, as if to loan its warmth to a melody that had carried so much winter in it. And at the west—the direction of endings and of the sea's last light—she laid the gloves, palms up, as though they were still offering words to the air.

She pulled the brass lever that released the lamp hood and checked the reflectors, the beat of years polished into them by keepers who were more practical than mythic. The mechanism itself was fine, tended just yesterday by a contemporary blackmith, who had come with a satchel of tools and a quiet look that said he knew this vigil mattered and would speak no more than was needed. "She'll throw clean," he'd said, running a cloth once, twice along the glass, "so long as somebody keeps her fed."

Marley set the small oil tin beside the pump, then sat on the low bench and let the room's silence ring in her ears. The objects around the lamp felt less like artifacts than like companions who had agreed to sit watch with her. She reached for her journal and wrote the date with a deliberate hand. *Solstice Eve. Lantern lit at dusk.* She paused, then added: *We came to hear, not to be heard.*

The wind rose and pressed a palm along the panes; the lighthouse answered with its old bones, metal offering a soft reply. From here, Brookwood gathered itself in a shallow arc —rooftops capped in snow, the square a pale bowl, the bell tower a dark digit pointing at the sky. She could not see the fissure in the tower's base from this distance, but the seam lived in her hands now and in the folded parchment she and Damien had read until the ink seemed to warm. *To Whom the Bell Speaks.* It had spoken. They had answered. And still, some last listening remained.

She wound the music box key and set the lid open toward the south. The first notes spilled out, slower than memory, a waltz that had always carried a small sorrow in its hinge. Alone, it seemed to hesitate at the end of each phrase, as if waiting for permission to be joined. In the shop, the duet had given it courage; here, Marley let the solitary line wander the room, testing the glass, the lamp metal, the cedar of the bench. Sound finds out its space. It learns what can hold it and what cannot.

"It's just us tonight," she told the melody. "You and the bell and whatever is brave enough to carry between."

Her satchel still held more—the copy of Amelia's letter from the tower's hollow, the carbon of *The Winter Vow* in its thin leather, a twig of evergreen Mr. Whitcomb had pressed into her palm as they left his parlor. She set the twig beside the vial at north, and a faint resin lifted. Somewhere below, a wave combed rock and drew back, and the lighthouse kept its single answer: Yes.

Marley took out the ring and turned it in her gloved fingers. The engraving had become familiar enough to feel like a heartbeat. She had read Elijah's scattered confessions; she had felt their shame resolve into something steadier, not unlike the way a hand trembles until it decides to set the cup down gently rather than drop it or clutch it to breaking. *Yours in time.* Not yours in ceremony, not yours in spectacle, not yours under a veil demanded by someone else. Yours where a vow can breathe.

She set the ring back at the east and folded the gloves more neatly at the west, the ink stains dark in the lamplight, beautiful as bruises that had finally learned how to speak. She imagined the hands that had worn them—someone Amelia loved, perhaps, or someone who had written a letter with a courage the town could not yet carry. Ink is always a kind of blood; it clots or it runs, and the paper remembers either way.

The lamp's wick lowered slightly as the oil settled. She checked the valve with her fingertip, then lifted her journal again. *I believe the town can bear this,* she wrote, then scratched the sentence out and wrote, *Whether the town can bear it or not, the truth deserves air.* She liked the second sentence better; it did not make truth beg for permission.

A soft tread sounded on the stairs. Marley did not startle —only one person would climb tonight without knocking. Damien appeared in the lantern room doorway, coat dusted with snow, hair damp at the temples. He took in the circle around the lamp, then her face, and for a moment he only stood, breathing as though he had climbed more than steps.

"I won't stay," he said. "You asked to keep the watch alone."

"You can stand in the doorway," she answered. "A keeper can allow a witness."

He smiled at that, then sobered, stepping just inside. "Mr. Whitcomb sent this." He held out a small paper envelope, the kind a jeweler might use for a screw or a sliver of gemstone. Inside lay a pin—old brass, shaped as a bell threaded by a vine. The motif from the printing plate, from the healer's ledger, now small enough to wear. "He said it belonged to Amelia's mother," Damien said. "That she pinned it to her shawl whenever the town gathered for the solstice."

Marley weighed the pin in her palm. It was heavier than it looked, the way symbols are. "Thank you," she said. She set it beside the ring at the east, where morning would find it.

Damien's gaze went to the music box. The hesitant waltz unspooled another phrase, tried to bridge into something it did not yet possess, and returned to the beginning. "You brought the slower one," he said softly.

"I wanted to hear how it sounds in glass and water," she answered. "How it carries when there's nothing in the way."

He nodded, then looked down through the faceted panes toward the square. "The Ball preparations look like a field of stars. They've strung lanterns all the way to the bakery."

"Stars will help us," Marley said. "They know how to be seen without apology."

He stepped back toward the door, then stopped, as if remembering a line he had meant to say and postponed until it threatened to fade. "I'll be in the tower before midnight. Not to touch the rope. To listen. If the lamp calls to the bell, I want to be where it lands."

"Thank you," she said again, not because the sentence was small, but because the gratitude did not know how to carry its own size.

He nodded once and was gone, the stair's echo folding back into the wind.

Marley sat alone again with the circle. She lifted the vial and held it up—a small cylinder of glass capped in tin, its seam kissed by the green that had haunted the baker's dream and the folk tales the elders could not quite agree upon. The liquid was long gone; what remained was memory of tincture, a ring of color where the world had once been more fluid than it dared admit. She had learned the vial's language slowly: not potion or spell, but a tool carried by hands that tended rather than controlled. Healers made mixtures the way keepers make vows, humble and exacting.

She set it back and let the wind speak for a while. The lighthouse answered it in slow ticks of warm metal contracting, in the faint breath of the wick, in the small mercy of a room designed to throw light far enough to matter and near enough to tend.

Hour followed hour. She wrote without looking at the lines, and when the ink pooled, she blotted it and did not scold herself for the imperfect letter that emerged from a hand that had also tended candles and bells and people who did not always want to be tended. She wound the music box until it refused to wind further and then let it rest. When the silence after it felt thin, she wound it again. The melody never changed, and yet the room around it did—glass learning, brass remembering, her chest a chamber adjusting to resonance.

Close to midnight, she blew out the small beeswax candle she had brought for company, leaving only the lamp's steady heart. Her four points held—north green with ghosted remedy, east circled with a ring that had chosen time over spectacle, south listening for melody, west offering palms stained by words. Marley folded her scarf tighter and stood, stretching the ache from her back.

"Amelia," she said into the lamp's glow, not to conjure but to acknowledge, "we are here."

The panes had frosted thicker, tracing a lace more honest than the gown lying folded in the guest room, its unworn beauty now a kind of flag. The sea exhaled and inhaled, and the lighthouse did what it has always done: it kept. Marley's keeping, for tonight, was small and stubborn and necessary. She would hold the circle until morning. She would feed the lamp and listen to the wind and the distant settling of the bell's chains. She would be present with the objects that had taught her how to hear.

Down in the square, the tower did not stir. Up in the lantern room, the keeper stayed. And between them, across the dark, a thin, unbroken line of intention drew taut—the kind you cannot see, only feel when you step exactly where you were meant to stand.

She reopened her journal and wrote one line, then closed the book over it as over an ember. Not yet the last line —the last would belong to morning, or to the moment when light chose its direction. For now, Solstice Eve asked only this: hold fast; keep vigil; be ready.

THE LIGHTHOUSE GROANED as midnight crept closer, the steel bones expanding and contracting against the cold. Marley leaned against the railing that circled the lantern room, her lantern dim compared to the great light she tended. The sea below slapped against the rocks in steady rhythm, and overhead, clouds parted enough to reveal a sky strung with frozen stars.

She could feel the weight of the night pressing inward—the town's collective breath held, the Solstice Ball in preparation below, and her own vigil at this far edge of Brookwood's history. Every object she had placed around the lantern seemed to vibrate faintly, as if some hidden string beneath them all had been plucked.

The music box waltz had stopped, key refusing another turn, and the silence it left felt more like expectation than rest. Marley did not wind it again. Instead, she lifted her journal, turning to a fresh page.

Midnight is near. The bell waits. The town waits. Perhaps I wait most of all.

Her pen paused. She added beneath it: *The bride never left. She became the bell.*

The words trembled from her pen, not with uncertainty but with recognition. They had come unbidden, as though Amelia herself had leaned close and whispered them across time.

She closed the journal slowly and laid it in the center of the circle, the four relics forming a compass around it.

A sudden gust rattled the panes. The lamp flame flickered, nearly guttered, then steadied with a brighter pulse—as if it had taken breath. Marley stiffened, eyes on the glow as it seemed to gather itself, flare once, then lean. The light beamed through the frosted glass, piercing the dark, and where it landed, she saw: directly across the valley, toward the bell tower.

Her chest tightened. She rose to her feet, palms pressed

against the cold glass of the pane. "It's answering," she whispered.

The lamp's beam did not wander. It held its steady arc toward the tower as if drawn, as if the bell had called and the lamp had answered.

From somewhere below, faint as breath through stone, Marley thought she heard the creak of chain against wood. The Winter Bell was still bound, but it was not still.

She turned back to the circle and knelt before the relics. Each one seemed alive in the glow: the vial catching green along its seam, the ring glinting faintly, the gloves' ink stains darkening as though newly wet. She touched the music box gently; its lid quivered with the lamp's vibration.

"Keeper of peace," she murmured, repeating Amelia's words. "Not bride. Not veil. Keeper."

The journal seemed to pulse where it lay. Marley opened it again, writing in quick, sharp strokes, her breath fogging the page.

I see now: the vow was never about a union of two alone. It was about the town, bound in peace by the bell. The silence is not abandonment. It is waiting. The bell keeps her voice. She keeps us still.

She signed her initials beneath, as though pledging not only to Amelia but to the light itself.

The lamp's glow steadied again, its flare subsiding into constant radiance. Marley leaned back on her heels, heart pounding. She felt less alone than she ever had in the shop, in the archives, even with Damien beside her. The entire night was alive around her, every shadow strung with resonance.

Then the door at the base of the stair thudded closed. She straightened, listening. Footsteps echoed on the spiral —slow, deliberate.

Damien's voice called upward, low but sure. "It's midnight."

Relief and tension collided in her chest. "Come up," she answered.

He emerged a moment later, snow on his shoulders, eyes wide at the glow of the lamp. His gaze followed the beam out the frost-rimmed pane to the bell tower.

"You saw it too," he murmured.

She nodded, voice unsteady. "It called across the valley. The light to the bell. They're bound."

He stepped closer to the circle of relics. His eyes lingered on the journal lying open. He bent to read the words she had just written, lips moving silently over the lines. When he lifted his head, there was something fierce in his expression.

"You're right," he said. "The vow was never meant to chain Amelia to one man. It was meant to chain the whole of Brookwood to peace. She chose to carry it when the town would not. And now—" He gestured at the relics. "Now we've been called to carry it in her stead."

The words struck Marley like truth given form. She felt both the burden and the strange lightness of it, as if vows, when truly embraced, did not crush but steadied.

Damien lowered himself to the bench beside her, running a hand over his face. "Marley, when I traced Elijah's line back to mine, I felt the weight of blood. Tonight, seeing the lamp bend toward the bell—I feel the weight of choice. We're not here just because of lineage. We're here because we answered."

Marley's throat tightened. "Then what do we do now?"

He looked toward the square, the bell tower just visible beyond the lighthouse glass. "We prepare. Tomorrow night, at the Ball, Brookwood must hear Amelia's truth. Whether they want to or not."

Her heart pounded with both fear and conviction. "Then we'll be ready."

Together they sat, two figures in the lantern glow, the relics forming a compass around them, the journal carrying the words of the past and the present. Beyond, the beam still reached for the bell tower, holding steady like a line drawn across centuries.

For the first time, Marley felt the vigil was not hers alone. It belonged to the vow, to the bell, to Amelia, and now —unmistakably—to them.

THE LIGHTHOUSE HAD SETTLED into the kind of stillness that is not absence but saturation—a silence thick with meaning, every groan of the steel and every tick of the lantern flame sounding like punctuation. Marley sat once more at the narrow table, her journal open, her pen trembling with ink and intent. Damien had taken the place opposite her, the two of them braced against the glow and the beam that stretched unwavering toward the bell tower.

She dipped the nib into the small well of ink she had brought and bent to the page. Her hand moved slowly, each word a measured stone laid in a path that she knew must be walked by more than herself.

Final entry, Solstice Eve, lantern room. The bride never left. She became the bell. Tonight we have seen her vow not in books, not in relics, but in light. The beam itself chose its companion, reaching across the valley, pointing to what still waits. I vow to speak Amelia's truth. I vow to keep her vigil. I vow that silence will not win again.

Her breath fogged the page as she signed her name.

Then she hesitated, lifted the pen once more, and added: *And we vow together.*

She looked up at Damien, the invitation clear. He read her eyes, then leaned forward. His hand, larger and steadier than hers, gripped the pen, and he wrote beneath her words: *Damien Callahan. Keeper, with Marley.*

The ink bled slightly into the fibers, darker, heavier. Marley let out a breath she hadn't known she'd been holding.

Damien set the pen down carefully, his voice low but certain. "Now it isn't only history. It's covenant."

Marley closed the journal and slid it into the center of the circle, letting it rest with the vial, the ring, the music box, and the gloves. The relics no longer felt like curiosities or even clues; they were witnesses now, gathered like parishioners around a shared altar.

The beam of the lamp flared once more, then steadied, as though acknowledging the act. Damien rose and crossed to the frosted panes. "Look," he said softly.

Marley joined him, her palm pressing beside his on the cold glass. Outside, the sky had cleared almost entirely, the stars brighter than any lantern string in the square. The beam did not waver from the tower. She imagined the bell in its stillness, chains taut, iron mouth closed, yet alive with the knowledge that it had not been abandoned.

She whispered, "Tomorrow night, it will know we answered."

Damien turned his head, close enough that she felt the warmth of his breath in the cold. "And if the town refuses? If they call it blasphemy? If they turn from us?"

Her eyes did not leave the tower. "Then we still keep. Peace is not peace because it is easy. It is peace because it is chosen."

He was quiet for a moment, then he reached for her hand. "Then I choose it with you."

They stood like that for a long time, hands joined against the glass, light and frost framing them, the sea's rhythm below steady as a vow recited across centuries.

THE NIGHT LENGTHENED, and the vigil became endurance. They fed the wick twice more, wound the music box again and again until its melody became less haunting than companionable. Marley dozed once, her head against the railing, but Damien woke her gently, pressing a mug of luke-warm tea into her hands. "A keeper can't sleep through the watch," he teased, though his smile was tender.

She drank, the warmth running through her like resolve, and opened the journal again. This time she drew a sketch: the lamp, the beam, the tower, and between them a thin figure in a gown of bells. She shaded it quickly, letting intu-ition guide her hand. When she was done, she turned it for Damien to see.

"The bride never left," she said again. "She became the bell."

He touched the edge of the page, reverent. "Then tomor-row, we show them what that means."

AN HOUR BEFORE DAWN, the lamp gave a strange sigh—a draft slipping somewhere in the mechanism, or perhaps the breath of the sea sneaking in through cracks. The flame bent, then righted itself. Marley and Damien watched, hearts lurching, but the beam did not falter.

Marley rose to her feet. "It's time to seal it."

She moved to the table and lifted each relic in turn,

holding it to her heart before placing it back in the satchel. The vial first, then the ring, the music box, and finally the gloves. Each seemed heavier than before, as though the night had pressed its weight into them. She left the journal last, pressing it closed with both hands before tucking it carefully atop the others.

Damien strapped the satchel shut. "It comes with us to the Ball."

"Yes," she said. "But tonight it stays whole. The vow needs to rest with the dawn before it can be spoken."

Together they extinguished the small beeswax candle and closed the oil tin. Damien checked the wick once more, ensuring the lamp would burn clean. Then they stood side by side at the window as the eastern sky began to pale.

Snow still clung to the rooftops of Brookwood, glowing faintly in the first gray. The tower's silhouette remained stark against the sky, the beam still pointing straight toward it. Marley felt a strange tenderness bloom in her chest—toward Amelia, toward the town, toward this man beside her who had chosen to bind himself to a vow older than either of them.

She laid her head briefly against his shoulder. "Do you feel it?"

He didn't ask what. He simply said, "Yes."

WHEN THE HORIZON broke open with a streak of rose light, Marley lifted the journal once more and wrote her final line of the vigil:

We are keepers now. Dawn has witnessed it. The bell will speak again.

She closed the book, slid it into the satchel, and looked at Damien. "Let's go home."

They descended the iron stair together, their boots ringing on each step like a quiet rehearsal of the bell that waited. When they reached the base, Marley paused, looking back once. The lantern room glowed faintly above, still alive, still steady.

"Tomorrow," she said.

Damien nodded. "Tomorrow."

They stepped into the dawn together, two keepers carrying more than relics. Behind them, the lighthouse stood sentinel, its beam no longer only light but vow, stretched between the sea and the bell, between the past and the future, between Amelia and themselves.

And somewhere in the tower, the Winter Bell stirred as if it, too, had heard the words written in a journal and sealed with breath: *The bride never left. She became the bell.*

26

BRIDGE OF ECHOES

The snow along Brookwood Bridge had crusted in the night, crunching faintly beneath Damien's boots as he made his way up the slope. The lanterns strung in the square were still visible behind him, glowing like a constellation bent low over the town, but here the light thinned, replaced by the pale wash of the waning moon.

He saw Marley before she saw him—her figure drawn in stillness against the stone railing, breath pluming softly. At her feet, a small ceremonial lantern burned steady, its glass pane casting a golden oval over the snow. In her hands she cradled the bell striker, its iron polished until it gleamed like new despite the centuries that clung to it.

Damien slowed, taking in the scene. The bridge had always carried more than wagons and footsteps. Stories whispered that vows made here carried farther, that the river beneath did not so much listen as *remember*. Tonight, with the air brittle and the river half-frozen, the bridge seemed to hold its breath.

Marley turned, sensing him. The firelight from the

lantern caught her face, gilding her cheekbones, illuminating the resolve that had carried her through sleepless nights in the shop, in the archives, in the lighthouse. She didn't speak immediately, only let him approach until the hush between them was filled by the river's low churn.

He stopped beside her, eyes falling to the striker in her hands. "You found it," he said softly.

She nodded. "Restored. Hidden in the chapel's crawl space. Mr. Whitcomb's cousin remembered his grandfather speaking of it—said it was once used for the Winter Bell when the rope alone would not do."

Damien exhaled slowly. "Then it belongs here tonight."

Marley's gaze lifted to the river, to the arch of the bridge itself. She drew her scarf tighter, and when she spoke, her voice carried the same steadiness as the lantern flame. "It was never about the marriage. It was always about the vow."

The words fell into the night like a key into a lock. Damien felt something inside him give way—an opening, not a collapse. He had known it, in pieces, in the scholar's notes and the relics and the green flicker of Amelia's shadow across the stories. But hearing it aloud, spoken by Marley here on the bridge, the truth finally sounded complete.

He moved closer, so their shoulders brushed beneath the weight of their coats. The striker between them caught the lantern's light, glowing like a slender promise. "A vow to keep peace," he said. "Not just between two families. Between everyone who would call this place home."

Marley nodded. Her eyes flicked toward him, unreadable in the shifting glow. "Amelia bore that vow when no one else would. Tonight, it's ours to carry."

The wind pressed across the bridge, tugging at scarves and lantern flame. Damien steadied the glass to keep it from tipping, then looked at her again. "Are you ready?"

Her mouth curved faintly. "Are you?"

He thought of Florence—the letters waiting, the fellowship offer folded on his desk. He thought of the archives, of the dream that had once seemed his compass. Then he thought of the light in the lighthouse stretching toward the bell, of Amelia's letter, of Marley's hand pressed against glass beside his as they vowed to keep. He reached out now and covered her fingers on the striker.

"Yes," he said. "I'm ready."

They stood for a moment with the lantern at their feet, the river flowing dark beneath, the town glowing faint behind. The bridge seemed to hum with the accumulation of words spoken and withheld across decades. When Marley lifted her chin, Damien mirrored her, the two of them gazing down the length of stone as though they were not merely standing but stepping into a procession that had waited all these years.

"Then let's walk," Marley whispered.

Together they lifted the striker and the lantern and began their slow passage across the bridge. Each footfall echoed faintly, not only against stone but into memory, into silence, into the long ledger of vows Brookwood had forgotten and hidden. The lantern swung gently between them, throwing their shadows tall along the railing.

Halfway across, Marley paused, turning to set the striker gently on the stone ledge. The river below murmured beneath ice, carrying fragments of moonlight in broken channels. She placed her palm against the striker's shaft, then against the stone, as though pressing the vow into both.

"This bridge carried Amelia on the day she was meant to marry," she said. "I think she left part of herself here, when she saw the altar empty."

Damien laid his hand beside hers. The iron was cold even through his glove. "Then let's leave part of ourselves here too," he said. "Not grief. Not absence. Choice."

Marley's throat worked as she swallowed. She nodded once, then lifted the striker again. Damien steadied the lantern, and they continued.

By the time they reached the far end, the town square's bells struck the quarter hour, the sound muted by distance and snow. Marley stopped, holding the striker to her chest. Damien set the lantern at her feet again.

She looked at him, eyes bright in the moonlight. "Tomorrow, when the Ball gathers, they'll expect history. We'll give them truth."

Damien felt the weight of it settle like a cloak around them both, heavy but warm. "Together," he said.

She exhaled, a small cloud dissolving into the night. "Together."

They turned toward the town, lantern burning between them, striker in Marley's hands gleaming with a light that seemed older than flame. Without another word, they began the walk back down the hill, two keepers bearing not only relics but a vow that had waited in silence long enough.

Behind them, the bridge stood quiet, but if one listened closely, the stone seemed to echo—not with their footsteps but with a resonance deeper, older, waiting for the moment when silence would finally break.

THE ROAD from the bridge back toward Brookwood was dusted with a fresh layer of snow, the kind that muffled sound and blurred edges. Their boots pressed into it with slow rhythm, leaving twin lines of prints that shone faintly in the moonlight. Marley carried the striker close against her chest, wrapped in both arms, while Damien held the lantern aloft, its light making a small, warm circle that traveled with them through the night.

Neither spoke. There was nothing to say that the silence had not already claimed.

The relics in Marley's satchel bumped gently against her hip with each step—the vial, the ring, the gloves, the journal—each one a reminder, each one pressing its weight into her body like witnesses who refused to be forgotten. She felt them like a burden, yes, but also like guardians urging her forward. Every step seemed to echo: not only across the road but across decades of silence.

Damien walked half a pace behind, his tall frame casting a longer shadow on the snow. His hand clenched and unclenched around the lantern's handle, as though testing the strength of his own resolve with each stride. He thought of Florence—the letters, the offer, the old dream he had once believed singular. And yet, walking this road, he knew he could not measure his calling in cities or fellowships. The striker glinting against Marley's chest was proof enough that vows waited to be fulfilled here, not abroad.

At one point, the wind shifted, carrying the faintest toll of chain against metal from the distant bell tower. Marley froze, tightening her grip on the striker. Damien caught her stillness immediately and stilled too, lantern swaying softly at his side.

"Did you hear it?" she whispered.

"Yes," he said. His voice was barely more than breath.

They stood listening, but the sound did not return. Only the whisper of snow over stone filled the night. Marley exhaled slowly, shoulders stiff. "It wants to speak."

Damien moved to her side, lowering the lantern until it lit their faces. "And tomorrow, it will."

Their eyes held, and in that gaze, silence itself shifted into language. She saw his certainty, and he saw her fear, and both recognized the vow that bound them now: to carry truth into the open, no matter the risk.

They resumed walking, steps in rhythm again.

As they neared the first outlying cottages of Brookwood, windows glowed faintly with the last embers of hearth fires. A dog barked once, then fell quiet. The town was asleep, but Marley felt as though the streets were holding their breath, waiting for what dawn might bring. She imagined the families behind those windows—descendants of Callahans, Colvins, elders who had whispered away Amelia's story in fear. Tomorrow they would hear it sung aloud.

Her throat tightened. She whispered, more to herself than to Damien, "What if they turn from us?"

His reply was immediate, steady. "Then we keep anyway."

The words settled in her like warmth.

The square loomed ahead, its lanterns dimmed now to conserve oil, the great bell tower rising above them like a sentinel. Marley's eyes fixed on its dark silhouette. Even chained, it seemed awake, listening. She thought of Amelia —her gown unclaimed, her vow misunderstood, her silence carried in stone. Marley's grip on the striker tightened until her knuckles ached.

Damien noticed. He slowed, then touched her arm gently. "Share the weight."

Without hesitation, Marley passed the striker into his hands. He carried it easily, the iron gleaming in the lantern's glow. Seeing it in his grasp made Marley feel both lighter and more bound to him; the vow was not hers alone to carry.

They crossed the empty square in silence, the snow crunching softly beneath them. Every step seemed to draw them deeper into something sacred, as though the town itself had become a chapel, the bell its altar. Marley felt her fear rise again, but when she glanced at Damien—steady, lantern in one hand, striker in the other—she knew her fear was not final.

Silence had become their language. Silence said: *We keep.*

At the foot of the bookshop, Marley stopped. The lantern light pooled against the steps, familiar yet newly solemn. She turned to Damien, the night pressing close around them.

"Tomorrow," she whispered, her voice unsteady but sure, "we speak. Not just of Amelia. Of all of it. The vow, the silence, the truth."

Damien set the striker against the railing and placed the lantern between them. He took her hands in his, warming them between his palms. His gaze did not waver.

"Tomorrow," he echoed. "And together."

For a moment, the silence between them deepened, becoming vow. Not spoken, but heard. Not forced, but chosen.

They held it until the lantern's flame dipped, then both reached to steady it at the same time, fingers brushing. The gesture was simple, but in it Marley felt the whole of their resolve. They would keep.

Tomorrow, the bell would answer.

· · ·

THE BOOKSHOP DOOR shut behind them with a muted thud, and the silence of the square thickened like fog. Marley leaned back against the wood, eyes closed, the night's cold pressing in around her bones. Damien set the lantern on the counter just inside, its glow spilling over shelves that had borne witness to every stage of their search. The striker leaned against the doorframe, its polished iron catching the flame in sharp angles.

Neither spoke at first. The long walk, the bridge, the river's whisper—they all lingered between them, weight and vow made flesh. It was Marley who finally broke the hush.

"They'll resist us." Her voice was low, almost fragile, but steady. "Not because they doubt the truth. But because they fear what it will do. Amelia wasn't only silenced—she was erased. And we're about to give her back her voice."

Damien crossed the space between them, his boots soft against the wooden floor. He stood close enough that she felt his warmth, but not so close as to crowd her. His jaw worked as though he were chewing down words before letting them escape. "I've thought about it all night," he admitted. "The council, the families, the descendants of those who covered this up. We'll be accused of stirring ghosts. Of dividing a town already frayed."

Marley's eyes lifted to his. "And you?"

His gaze flicked toward the striker, then back to her. "I fear not their anger. I fear their disbelief. That they'll look at us and see not keepers, but fools chasing shadows."

Marley reached for his hand. Her palm was cold, but her grip was fierce. "Then we give them more than shadows. We give them light. We give them vow."

The words echoed in the space, heavy with promise. Damien drew her hand closer, pressing it briefly to his chest.

"Then tomorrow, no matter what they say, I'll stand beside you."

THEY MOVED through the shop slowly, Marley lighting two more candles until the room glowed soft and steady. The relics were laid out once again on the central table: the vial, the ring, the gloves, the journal. The music box sat slightly apart, its key turned just enough to hum faintly, as if even it could not resist speaking.

Marley brushed her fingers over the satin gloves, the ink stains stark even in candlelight. "Every one of these carries a cost. Amelia's silence. Elijah's sacrifice. Even the town's fear, layered across decades. Tomorrow, when we bring them together, those costs will surface again."

Damien traced the edge of the ring, its engraving catching the light. "And what about us? What will it cost us to tell it?"

Marley swallowed hard. She thought of the publishing offer that still lingered, of how easily the town might brand her opportunist rather than keeper. She thought of Damien's fellowship—of Florence waiting like a dream half-unfolded. "Maybe everything," she admitted. "But if we do not keep, then the silence wins. And the bell... stays mute."

The music box finished its hum with a tender note, the sound curling through the air like benediction.

Damien straightened, shoulders taut, and turned to face her fully. "Marley, I need you to hear me. If tomorrow they turn us out, if they call us liars, if they sever ties... I won't leave. Not for Florence. Not for anything."

Her breath caught. "You'd give it up?"

His expression softened, grief and resolve mingling. "It isn't giving up. It's choosing. This vow has claimed me more deeply than any fellowship could. And you—" His voice broke, but he steadied it. "You've claimed me too."

Marley's throat tightened, tears stinging. She stepped into him, pressing her forehead against his chest. His arms circled her instantly, solid and sure, and in that embrace she felt both the fragility and the strength of what bound them.

"It's the same for me," she whispered. "Whatever tomorrow brings, I will not walk it alone."

THE CANDLES BURNED LOWER as the hours crept toward dawn. They spoke little, but when they did, their words were spare, sharpened by the weight of what lay ahead. Marley confessed her fear that Mr. Whitcomb might rescind his support, that his family might waver when faced with the crowd. Damien admitted his dread that distant cousins might brand him betrayer for embracing Elijah's bloodline instead of burying it.

But each fear they named, they countered with vow. Marley would not yield to erasure. Damien would not yield to silence. Together, they repeated the phrase that had followed them from the bridge, letting it anchor their resolve:

"It was never about the marriage. It was always about the vow."

Near the hearth, the satchel waited, packed once more with the relics. Marley slid the journal inside last, her hand lingering on its cover. She glanced up at Damien, who nodded silently. She tightened the strap, sealing not only objects but intent.

The striker leaned by the door, its presence a quiet sentinel. Marley and Damien approached it together, each laying a hand along its length. The iron was cold, but in their joined touch, it seemed almost warm, almost alive.

"Tomorrow," Damien said softly.

"Tomorrow," Marley echoed.

Their eyes met, and in the candlelit silence, they sealed the vow not with words but with the simple act of not letting go.

WHEN AT LAST they parted for sleep—Marley retreating to her small room above the shop, Damien heading home—they did so with the knowledge that night had ended one chapter and begun another. The bell tower loomed outside, dark against the paling sky, waiting for its keepers to speak.

And as Marley drifted toward restless sleep, her final thought was not fear but resolve:

We are the bridge now. Between silence and sound. Between grief and peace. Between vow and its keeping.

The town slept, but the vow had already awakened.

27

THE BELL RINGS ONCE

By twilight the square had turned to amber. Lanterns strung from bakery eaves to the town hall glowed like a net of small suns, and the snow beneath them took on a honeyed tint, as if warmth could be painted on with light. Fiddlers tuned on the temporary stage, their bows whispering over strings; the scent of cinnamon and clove drifted from trestle tables where steam rose from cups like the breath of patient horses. People arrived in layers—wool and velvet and old lace pressed from trunks—eyes bright, voices low. The Winter Ball had always asked Brookwood to touch its own oldest story and dance with it. Tonight, the town had come to see whether that story could bear the truth.

Marley stood backstage with the satchel and the striker and the small ceremonial lantern that had burned beside her on the bridge. She could feel the circle of the relics even before she laid them out: the vial in its tiny tin cap; the ring engraved *Yours in time*; the ink-stained gloves; the booklet of *The Winter Vow* wrapped in thin leather and twine. Damien stood shoulder to shoulder with her, his coat open despite the cold, his breath fogging steady and slow. Mr. Whitcomb, trim and gray, waited just off to the side with both hands clasped before him, gaze quiet, resolute.

The mayor made careful remarks about tradition, and the council chair added her own measured gratitude, and the fiddlers played one sweet set to draw people closer. Then the mayor turned toward the wings, lifted a hand toward Marley, and stepped away.

It was time.

Marley's knees wanted to fold. Her hands did not. She stepped into the light that made the square itself a room and the town her congregation, if it wanted to be. She set the lantern on the podium's small shelf, then opened the satchel and placed each relic where all could see: vial, ring, gloves, the leather booklet. A murmur ran through the front rows; even those who had harbored doubts knew their shapes.

She lifted her eyes and found faces: Hazel with her lavender-scented shawl; boys from the school holding hats stiff in their hands; Mrs. Bennett from the bakery; Lenore, Mrs. Bennett's grandmother, the elder with her cane planted and her gaze unflinching; several of the councilors near the back; and three from the Circle of Seven, not robed, not named, but obvious in the way they watched without blinking. Mr. Whitcomb stood near the stage edge, head bowed.

Marley let the silence settle. She had learned, these past months, how silence can be cudgel or cradle. She would make of it a cradle, if the town allowed.

"My name is Marley Taylor," she said, voice low but clear. "I keep the bookshop that belonged to my aunt. That is how most of you know me. But tonight I speak not as a seller of stories, but as a keeper of one that has waited almost ninety years to be told."

The words moved through the cold like breath. She touched the leather booklet with the tips of her fingers.

"Amelia Colvin wrote these pages. Not rumor. Not hearsay. Not campfire tale. Her own hand. Mr. Whitcomb stands here tonight and has given his blessing for her words to be read."

Heads turned toward Mr. Whitcomb. He lifted his chin, eyes shining, and nodded once. A few people applauded; many more simply folded their arms tighter or pressed lips together, bracing.

Marley untied the twine. The paper had a faint scent of cedar and time. She did not clear her throat, did not apologize. She began:

"The bell is no ornament. It is a covenant. When it rings at solstice, it does not call two into union for themselves alone. It calls families, fields, waters, and winds into harmony. We stand beneath its voice not as lovers only, but as guardians of balance."

A ripple moved through the crowd—some in recognition, some in confusion. Marley let the words rest before she continued.

"I was chosen to stand, not to be adorned. The gown they pressed upon me was a costume for a play I did not believe in. I wished not for veil, but for vigil."

One of the Circle men shifted, whispering into a gloved palm. Marley did not break.

"Elijah tried to protect me. He bore the weight of silence so the town would not burn me with its stares. He agreed to be the absent groom, that they might scorn him instead of me. Yet what neither of us foresaw was the way silence calcifies into myth. They needed a bride betrayed to explain their discomfort. So they invented me."

A low hum ran through the square, a hive beginning to

wake. Marley closed the booklet, not because she feared the next line, but because she had learned how to pace revelation so a heart can receive it. She lifted the gloves, holding them so the ink stains showed beneath lamplight.

"These were left at my shop door weeks ago, wrapped in silk ribbon. Ink on the fingertips. Words do not always reach their destination, and sometimes they stain what tries to carry them. Amelia's truth did not arrive where it needed to. Tonight, it will."

She set the gloves down and lifted the ring, letting it turn once between finger and thumb so that the engraving caught the light.

"*Yours in time, E.C. to A.C.* We thought it meant inevitable marriage. We were wrong. It meant a vow that did not need an altar to be holy."

Someone in the back scoffed; someone else hissed the scoff down. Mrs. Bennett leaned in; Lenore's eyes did not waver. Damien, at the wing, lifted his chin slightly—an almost invisible sign: Keep going.

Marley placed the ring gently beside the gloves and lifted the vial, green seam catching the stage lantern. "Healers kept these," she said. "Not to command the body, but to tend it. Our founders understood that the bell's voice tended the town the way a remedy tends fever. That is what the Winter Bell Union once meant—two families standing watch over the village's peace."

She returned the vial to the cloth and reopened the booklet, voice steady as granite.

"The vow was never broken, though they say it was. It was only misunderstood. I vowed peace, not marriage. I vowed to keep the bell's tone in harmony, not to keep a hearth in a house not my own. If the bell grows silent, it is not for my failure. It is for theirs, for forgetting the vow's true nature."

A woman near the front began to cry—quietly at first, then with shoulders shaking. The man beside her reached, then withdrew, then finally placed his hand over hers and held.

"This is not accusation," Marley said into the hush. "It is invitation. Amelia did not ask us to punish ourselves for what we misunderstood. She asked us to remember. To keep."

She glanced to the right, found Mr. Whitcomb's face— wet now. He nodded. Marley breathed once, the cold burning her throat, and read the closing lines Amelia had written for whoever would someday be brave enough to find them:

"If anyone should find these words, know that I chose not silence but stewardship. I stayed, though they said I left. I remained keeper when they called me abandoned. And if the bell should fall silent again, it is because the vow awaits new keepers. Let them be brave. Let them not mistake costume for covenant."

When Marley looked up, the square was a field of faces held in the same expression—something between grief and relief, old pain loosening its fist. One of the Circle men had set his eyes on the snow; another stared at Marley with a fury that was really fear.

Marley lifted the lantern from the shelf and set it on the podium's corner, flame a small, steady heart. "Tonight I am not asking you to trade one myth for another," she said. "I am asking you to let a woman speak in her own words at last. I am asking you to hear the vow she kept for you when you would not keep it for yourselves. And I am asking whether, after all these years, Brookwood is willing to be brave."

She closed the booklet and laid her palm atop its cover. "Amelia was never the bride we made of her. She was, and is, a keeper of peace."

Silence held. Someone sobbed. A child, carried in a scarf, hiccuped against a mother's chest and went still. Marley's throat thickened. She glanced once toward Damien. He nodded.

"Now," Marley said, voice barely above the hush, "we will listen."

She lifted the slow music box—the one whose melody had taught her to hear a duet—and set it open on the podium, its tiny gears catching. The first notes rose, intact and halting, and drifted across the square like breath in winter.

The fiddlers behind her lowered their bows. People leaned forward. The melody wandered to the edge of its phrase and almost faltered, as it always had, as if waiting for a partner. Marley let it hang there.

"Not veil," she said softly, almost to the box itself, almost to the bell. "Vigil."

The last note hovered—then resolved. The square held its breath with it, all the way to the edge of what it thought it knew.

And then the music wound on, seeking the place where something more could join.

The melody lingered in the square like the last ember of a fire. For a heartbeat, for two, no one moved. And then—so softly it might have been imagined—the bell tower above them quivered.

Not a toll. Not a full strike. Just the faintest tremor, a bronze breath caught in the throat of the Winter Bell.

Marley's hand froze above the music box. The crowd stiffened. Children clutched mothers' skirts, elders reached for canes as if bracing for quake. But the tremor passed, and silence settled again, heavier, expectant.

Then, without warning, the bell rang once.

Not pulled, not commanded. It rang itself.

The note poured into the air like molten gold, resonant and round, flowing into every ribcage, every throat. It was not loud; it did not need to be. It was exact.

And with it, the silence of years cracked.

MARLEY'S KNEES WENT WEAK. She gripped the podium, steadying herself. Her chest thrummed with the sound, as if her own bones had become a bell frame.

Gasps surged through the square. A woman sobbed aloud. A man dropped his hat, forgotten on the snow. Somewhere in the back, someone fell to their knees.

The music box, still open, harmonized faintly—the tune aligning, for one fleeting instant, with the tower's bronze voice. Then its gears ran down, and only the bell remained, its single note lingering impossibly long before fading like breath in cold air.

And then—silence again. But not the same silence.

This was a silence changed.

TEARS BLURRED MARLEY'S VISION. She blinked them clear, unwilling to let this moment slip past. She raised her voice, low but certain:

"You heard her."

Her words trembled, not with fear but with awe. "Amelia has spoken. She was never gone. She was never abandoned. She remained."

The crowd shifted, rippling like wheat in sudden wind. Murmurs rose—confusion, grief, relief, denial. A man near the front demanded, "How—? Who pulled it?"

"No one," another woman answered, eyes wide and wet. "It rang itself."

"It can't."

"It just did."

Marley steadied her breath. "The vow is not broken. It waits for us. And tonight, it was answered."

She looked toward Mr. Whitcomb. The old man had tears streaking his cheeks, his head bowed, shoulders shaking. He pressed his hand to his chest, unable to speak.

DAMIEN STEPPED FORWARD from the wing, his presence a steadying hand though he did not touch her. His voice carried, firm, resonant:

"You all know the history. You know what we've discovered—the letters, the gloves, the ring. But this—this is not artifact or rumor. You just heard what has been denied for nearly a century. The bell rang because the truth was finally spoken aloud."

The Circle men stirred, their faces masks of restraint, but their eyes sharp as knives. One of them muttered, "Coincidence. A quirk of metal in the cold."

But no one answered him.

Because everyone in the square still felt the vibration humming through their ribs.

. . .

THE FIDDLERS, shaken, had lowered their instruments. One of them—an older man with trembling hands—lifted his bow as if to test whether music could still matter after what they'd heard. He drew a single note across his fiddle, and it harmonized faintly with the memory of the bell. The crowd exhaled. Someone began to clap, hesitant, then more joined, not for the fiddlers but for the sound itself, for the release.

Marley closed the booklet gently and placed it atop the other relics. She touched the lantern flame, steady as heartbeat, and whispered so only Damien heard: "It's lifted. The silence is lifted."

He leaned closer, murmuring back, "For now. But silence always waits to return. We must guard it."

A GROUP of young people pressed forward—the same students who had whispered uneasily when she spoke of the veil bride. One girl, scarf crooked around her head, called out, "Does this mean Amelia was never betrayed?"

"It means," Marley said carefully, "that the story you were told is not the story she lived. And the bell has just told you which story is true."

The girl nodded, face shining.

Behind her, an older man muttered, "Dangerous nonsense." But even he did not raise his voice. The bell had left no room for scoffs to sound brave.

THE MAYOR APPROACHED THE PODIUM, face pale but composed. She spoke into the hush, choosing each word as if it could ignite or soothe:

"The bell has spoken tonight. No hand touched its rope.

I cannot explain it. But we cannot deny it. What remains is what we do with it."

Her gaze swept the councilors, the Circle men, the townsfolk huddled together. "We have heard a story buried too long. We have felt the silence shift. Brookwood must decide how to live with this truth."

She turned to Marley, voice soft but carrying: "Thank you for giving Amelia her voice."

Marley bowed her head, overcome.

Tears fell freely now, not just hers. Neighbors embraced. Families clasped hands. A child asked his mother in a whisper, "Was it magic?" The mother answered, "No. It was memory."

Damien's hand brushed Marley's at the podium edge— light, grounding. She met his gaze, saw his own eyes glistening.

"It was never about the marriage," she whispered, echoing her words at the bridge. "Always about the vow."

He nodded once, firm. "And now it's ours."

The lantern flame flickered as if in assent.

The fiddlers found courage. They began to play—not a reel, not a jig, but a slow air, tender and clear, threading through the crowd like balm. People swayed, some humming, some weeping. The snow caught the lantern light and the music both, and for the first time in years, Brookwood felt whole.

The bell did not ring again. It did not need to.

Its single note hung in memory, strong as iron, soft as

breath, promising that silence had been broken, if only for tonight.

And in that breaking, something new could begin.

THE APPLAUSE FADED INTO A HUSH, leaving the square drenched in something deeper than celebration. It was reverence, mingled with fear, threaded with awe. For the first time since the silence had begun, Brookwood's people looked not at the bell but at one another, as though each face carried a fragment of Amelia's vow, restored in their shared hearing.

Marley stepped back from the podium, her chest rising and falling quickly. She felt hollowed, as if the bell's note had rung straight through her and left her ribs humming. Damien moved close, steadying her with the warmth of his presence.

The fiddlers began a softer air—no dance tune, no march, but something plaintive, reverent, coaxed from strings as though the music itself were trying to match the bell's resonance. People swayed together. Families who had not spoken in years clasped hands. Two elders—descendants of rival lines—leaned on one another's shoulders, their tears flowing freely.

It was, Marley realized, the first breath of harmony.

But harmony, she knew, could be fleeting.

THEY SLIPPED AWAY from the stage's edge as the crowd slowly shifted into murmurs and embraces. The relics—ring, gloves, music box, journal—remained on the table, guarded now by Mr. Whitcomb himself, his hand resting firmly over them. Marley saw in his eyes not only grief but determination. He would not allow them to vanish back into silence.

In the shadow of the bookshop steps, Damien leaned against the railing. His expression was not triumph but something heavier, contemplative.

"It rang," Marley whispered, still hardly able to believe it.

"It rang," he echoed. Then, after a pause: "But once only."

She frowned, startled by his choice of emphasis.

"One toll can be a beginning," she said. "A promise."

"Or a warning," Damien countered. His eyes, dark and steady, met hers. "The elder's words—we can't forget them. When the vow is undone, grief returns. What if this was not only release, but reminder?"

Marley's breath caught. She thought of the double ring Lenore had confessed, of death and vow entangled. For a moment, fear threatened to hollow her chest again.

But then she shook her head. "No. It was Amelia's voice. It was her choosing to stand with us. She wasn't warning. She was keeping."

Damien studied her, and slowly, something softened in his gaze. "Then it falls to us to keep with her."

The lantern flame between them flickered in the draft. Marley reached out and cupped her hand around it instinctively, shielding it. Damien's eyes followed the gesture, and he smiled faintly.

"That," he said quietly, "is what we'll be. Shields. For the flame. For the vow."

Her throat tightened. She nodded, unable to speak for a moment.

Then, gathering her courage, she whispered, "Will you keep it with me? Even if the town turns, even if it costs us Florence, or peace, or..."

"Or each other?" Damien finished, his voice raw.

The silence after his words was heavier than the bell's. But then he shook his head firmly.

"No. Not each other. That cannot be the cost. If we are to keep, it must be together. Or not at all."

Marley felt her breath shudder out of her, relief and fear braided together. "Then let us vow."

THEY CLASPED HANDS, not ceremonially, but with the rawness of people who had borne silence and would now bear truth.

"I vow," Marley said softly, "to guard the vow Amelia could not speak. To let the bell ring, even if it breaks the peace built on lies."

Damien's grip tightened, steady as iron. "And I vow to keep with you. To carry the striker when your arms grow heavy, to shield the flame when your strength falters. To keep the vow not only for Amelia—but for us."

The lantern's flame steadied, as if sealed by their words. Above them, the bell tower loomed, silent now, but no longer cold. It seemed to watch, to listen.

BEHIND THEM, the crowd began to stir into celebration again. Children twirled in the snow, echoing the fiddlers' tune. Elders pressed forward to touch the relics with trembling fingers, as though contact with Amelia's story might restore something in their own.

And though suspicion lingered in some eyes—though

Circle men still stood grim-faced at the edge—the greater current was unmistakable. It was release. The silence that had haunted the solstice had lifted, if only for this night.

Marley turned back to the square and saw it: the dawn of a new harmony. Fragile, tender, but real.

She whispered to Damien, "This is only the beginning."

He squeezed her hand once more. "Then let's begin."

THAT NIGHT, as the Winter Ball carried on into candlelit hours, as music and tears and embraces filled the square, Marley and Damien remained at the edge—keepers not only of relics, but of vow.

They knew the road ahead would demand more than one ringing, more than one vow spoken aloud. But tonight, they had crossed the threshold. Tonight, the bell had answered.

And in its single note, the town of Brookwood heard both its past and its promise.

28

PROPOSAL UNDER THE BELLS

The Winter Ball had spilled into the streets, its music and laughter rising like breath into the night. Candles glowed from every window and doorway, each tiny flame flickering in response to the miracle that had unfolded only hours before. Brookwood, for the first time in living memory, was awake to itself. The silence that had shadowed its heart was lifted, if only by one toll of the bell, and the air pulsed with a fragile but undeniable harmony.

Marley slipped away from the warmth of the square, her steps slow, deliberate, as though she were following a rhythm deeper than the fiddlers' tune. She found herself on the hill just beyond the bookshop, where the bell tower loomed above and the stars seemed to scatter themselves generously across the sky. Here, the noise of celebration softened into a murmur, carried by the wind like a distant tide.

She sank down onto the stone bench that had been carved into the hillside generations ago, a place where watchers of the solstice once gathered to keep vigil. The cold pressed into her, but she wrapped her shawl tight and let the silence wrap her tighter still. A lantern rested on the bench beside her, its flame steady, warming the small circle where she sat.

Her heart was still vibrating with the toll. The single, impossible toll that no rope had summoned, no hand had pulled. It had not been chance, nor accident, nor trick of echo. It had been Amelia—or perhaps something greater, carrying Amelia's vow into the present. Marley closed her eyes, her palms pressed together as though in prayer, whispering words she could not name.

When she opened them, Damien was there.

He had come quietly, his boots leaving crisp prints in the snow, the glow of another lantern held low at his side. His breath clouded in the air, but his eyes held steady light, reflecting not only the stars but something within him that Marley recognized instantly.

"You always find the high places," he said softly, breaking the hush without shattering it.

"And you always find me," she replied, her voice no louder than the wind.

He set the lantern down on the stone, then eased onto the bench beside her. They sat together, shoulder to shoulder, the two lanterns casting overlapping halos of light around them. From below, the sound of fiddles rose again, weaving with laughter and the shuffle of boots on snow-packed earth. But here, above the town, it was still enough to hear the river moving under its crust of ice, still enough to hear the soft crack of branches in the cold.

For a long while, neither spoke. Their silence was not emptiness now, but fullness. It was the silence of two people who had carried stories too heavy for words, who had kept when others would have turned away, who had listened until listening became vow.

At last Damien turned, his face caught between lantern-light and shadow.

"Tonight changed everything," he said quietly. "The bell... it answered. The town—it's different already."

Marley nodded, her throat too tight for words.

"But for us," Damien continued, his voice dropping lower, "tonight did something else." He paused, searching her eyes as though the stars themselves had written something there he needed to read. "It showed me that presence is what keeps. Not promises of what might be, not plans drawn on parchment, not dreams of Florence or of elsewhere. Presence."

He shifted, one hand moving toward hers, tentative but steady. "Marley, I can't offer you certainty of what the town will do tomorrow. I can't promise peace will be easy, or that Brookwood will thank us. But I can offer you this: myself. Here. Beside you. One chapter at a time."

The words sank into her, not as surprise, but as recognition. As though she had been waiting not for a proposal of marriage, but for a proposal of presence—for someone to stand beside her as she bore the vow of the bell.

Tears blurred her vision, but she did not look away. Instead, she lifted her hand, slow, deliberate, and laid it gently over his heart. She felt its beat beneath her palm, strong, steady, and real.

"Yes," she whispered, her voice catching on the word. "Not with a promise. But with this."

Damien's hand came up to cover hers, pressing it more firmly against his chest. His eyes closed briefly, as if to let the vow sink deeper. When they opened again, there was a quiet fire in them, the kind that would not waver even when winds turned fierce.

"Then let us keep," he said.

They sat together, her hand over his heart, his hand over hers, the lanterns burning steady around them. Above, the bell tower stood silent, but it was no longer absence. It was witness.

The stars seemed closer now, as though leaning in to bless the moment. And far below, Brookwood's celebration carried on, unaware that on the hillside, two keepers had sealed a vow of their own—not bound by rings, but by presence.

The night stretched before them, vast and clear, and Marley knew: the chapters ahead would be written together.

THE LANTERNS between them burned steady, their small flames holding back the sweep of winter night. Marley let her hand remain over Damien's heart, the beat beneath her palm a tether that anchored her more deeply than any bell-strike had. The stars were bright but cold, strewn above as if eternity had scattered itself across the heavens. Here, on the hillside above Brookwood, the night was not an end but an unfolding.

Damien leaned back slightly, his gaze lifting skyward. "It feels strange," he said after a pause. "All these years, I thought presence meant staying in one place—roots, archives, pages bound and kept. But tonight, with you, I realize it isn't about the walls around us. Presence is being where the vow calls you. Being beside someone when the silence presses hardest."

Marley followed his gaze, tracing constellations she remembered from childhood. Her aunt used to tell her that the stars were not just lights but watchmen, reminders that vows made in silence were still recorded above. She breathed out slowly, her voice carrying the memory.

"My aunt used to say the stars keep the stories we're too afraid to tell. Maybe Amelia's story was always written here, waiting for someone to speak it aloud."

Damien turned, his features softened by the mingling glow of lantern and starlight. "And you did. You've carried her voice into this town's heart, even when it resisted. Marley, I've seen you bear silence heavier than iron, and still you chose to speak. That's presence too."

Her throat tightened. She looked down at the lantern, its flame steady despite the wind. "But it's fragile, Damien. This —us, the town, the bell. It feels like if I breathe too hard, it could all scatter."

His hand found hers, the one still pressed against his chest. He wrapped it fully, holding it as though he could absorb her trembling into his steadiness. "That's what vow is," he murmured. "Not the absence of fear, but the choosing in spite of it. Presence isn't a fortress—it's a fire you guard with your whole being, even when you're shivering."

Marley let the words settle. Her mind returned to the moment the bell had tolled without rope or hand, the miracle that had shaken Brookwood awake. It had been a gift, but also a demand. A sign that silence could not rule forever.

"What if the town isn't ready?" she whispered. "What if telling Amelia's truth, honoring her vow as keeper and not bride, divides us more than heals us?"

Damien drew in a breath, the weight of his own history in the sound. "Then we'll stand in the division together. I've carried archives across continents, Marley—parchments and scrolls older than nations. I've seen how truth breaks before it heals. Always. But without the break, there's no room for new harmony."

His voice faltered slightly, and she caught it—his vulnerability, the part of him that still feared. "You're not just speaking about the town," she said gently.

He hesitated, then nodded. "No. I'm speaking about us too. Because choosing you, here, means I set aside a path I've chased since boyhood. Florence. The fellowship. The dream of building archives that would outlive me. That was always my vow—or so I thought."

Marley felt her chest ache, the truth pressing on them both. "And now?"

"Now," Damien said, his hand tightening over hers, "I see that presence is its own archive. That being here, keeping with you, writes something no library could hold."

The confession was both gift and cost, and Marley felt the weight of it. She leaned closer, her head against his shoulder, letting the warmth of him seep into her. The silence stretched again, but it was alive, filled with the rhythm of breath and the beating of hearts.

"Presence," she whispered, testing the word as though it were new. "After so much silence, after so many broken vows... it feels like the most fragile, the most dangerous choice."

"And the only one worth making," Damien answered.

They sat until their lanterns burned low, the wax dripping, the flames bending but not extinguishing. The music from the square drifted up faintly, laughter carried on the wind, yet none of it intruded on the space they had carved together.

Marley lifted her head at last, her eyes catching the silhouette of the bell tower against the sky. "The vow was never about the marriage. It was always about the keeping.

Amelia knew that. She became the bell, because no one else would."

Damien followed her gaze. "And now it's us. We've been asked to keep where she was silenced. To stand where others faltered."

The vulnerability pressed heavier now, not just in their words but in their unspoken knowing: the town's future hung in the balance, and their presence together would either anchor it or make them outcasts.

Marley felt fear rise in her chest, but she placed it in the same space as her choice. She touched her palm to Damien's heart again, steadying herself. "Then let us keep. No matter the cost."

His eyes closed briefly, his hand covering hers once more, and when they opened, the stars reflected in them were steady.

They lingered under the stars until the first hint of dawn paled the horizon, two lanterns burning low, two keepers holding a vow that was both fragile and unbreakable.

THE LANTERNS GUTTERED into low embers, their flames reduced to flickers that licked faintly at the glass, and Marley felt the hush of the night settle over them like a benediction. Above, the bell tower loomed—its dark shape both sentinel and shadow, keeper of a silence that had weighed on Brookwood for generations. Now, in the quiet of the square beneath it, she and Damien stood together, not as speaker and archivist, not as seeker and skeptic, but as something new.

Damien's hand lingered in hers, strong and steady despite the cold. His gaze drifted upward, past the stone base of the tower, to the crown where the Winter Bell slept.

"We've walked the roads of silence," he murmured, almost to himself. "We've uncovered secrets, broken seals, touched the edges of grief. And now here we are, beneath the thing itself. It feels like... like we're standing at the edge of the vow."

Marley followed his gaze, the weight of the tower pressing into her chest. The bell was there, hidden in darkness but present, immense. It had spoken without hands, answered questions no one dared ask, carried voices across generations. And now, it seemed to wait.

"Not the edge," Marley said quietly. "The heart. The vow isn't in the bell alone. It's in us. In what we choose to keep."

She felt Damien's eyes turn toward her, the weight of his presence grounding her in a way nothing else could. "Then let's speak it," he said. "Not with promises that can fracture, but with presence that endures. Let's seal it now, beneath her bell, before the town demands anything more from us."

Her breath caught, but she nodded. They moved slowly to the center of the square, lanterns in hand, until the shadow of the bell tower fell fully over them. The cobblestones glistened faintly with frost, catching the weak reflection of stars, as though the heavens themselves leaned low to watch.

Damien set his lantern down first, then hers beside it, their twin lights merging into a single glow. He drew in a long breath, his voice low but unwavering. "Presence over promise. To stand, even in silence. To keep, even when the keeping costs."

Marley closed her eyes, the words threading through her like music. She echoed them, her own voice carrying across the stones. "Presence over promise. To keep where others broke. To remain when silence tempts us to flee. To be the bell, not only the ones who hear it."

Their words lingered in the night, neither ritual nor prayer but something deeper—a vow spoken into the marrow of their being. The air seemed to thicken, as if the bell itself absorbed their voices. Marley felt the weight of it, not crushing but consecrating. She opened her eyes and found Damien watching her, the stars mirrored in his gaze.

"You've given me more than archives ever could," he said, the rawness of truth breaking through. "You've given me the courage to stay. To stand in one place long enough for presence to take root."

"And you've given me more than the town ever could," Marley answered, her chest aching with both fear and fullness. "You've given me the courage to speak. To believe my voice belongs in the keeping."

They stood in silence then, not the silence of fear or suppression, but the silence of completion. The vow had been spoken—not in the pages of ledgers or the toll of bells, but in the lives of two people who had chosen each other in the face of division.

Above them, the bell shifted faintly in the wind, its iron groan like the exhale of history itself. Marley shivered, but not from cold. "Did you hear—"

"I did," Damien whispered. His hand tightened in hers. "It heard us."

The town around them slept, unaware of the covenant being sealed in its very heart. Tomorrow, the Winter Ball would gather everyone, stories would be told, truth would press against old fractures. But tonight was theirs.

Marley felt the urge to write, to record the vow before dawn stole the moment. Yet she resisted. Some things were not meant for parchment. Some things lived only in the keeping.

Instead, she leaned into Damien, her head against his

chest, and let the steady beat of his heart mark the vow into her memory. His arms came around her, a shelter against the cold, and together they faced the tower that had once held their dread but now bore their promise.

"This is enough," Damien said at last, voice steady. "We don't need the bell to ring again to know it's alive. We've rung it ourselves."

Marley nodded, a tear sliding down her cheek. "And when it rings again, it will be because presence has filled the silence—not because rope or hand forced it."

The lanterns burned lower still, until only a soft glow remained, a circle of fragile light in the frost. They did not move, did not break the silence, until the first faint shimmer of dawn touched the eastern sky.

As the light grew, Damien turned her gently, so they faced each other fully. His expression was solemn but certain, the kind of look she imagined Amelia had once longed for but never received. "One chapter at a time," he said, repeating the words he'd spoken under the stars. "Together. Not because of promise, but because of presence."

Marley lifted her hand again, this time placing it over his own heart without hesitation. "Yes," she said, the word carrying the full weight of vow. "Together."

The bell above remained still, yet Marley felt as though it had answered. Not with iron or sound, but with a quiet resonance in the marrow of her bones. The vow was sealed —not just in them, but in the silence that would never again be empty.

29

COMMUNITY CELEBRATION

The morning after the vow beneath the bells dawned clear and brittle, the sky a pale wash of winter light. Brookwood stirred slowly, as though waking from a long-held dream. Marley rose early, her breath fogging in the chill of her shop, and for a moment she stood at the window, watching the square gather frost as it had for generations. Yet something was different. The silence was no longer a shroud but a waiting canvas, and she felt in her bones that the town's story had turned a corner.

The Winter Ball was scheduled for that evening, a tradition both festive and solemn, and already preparations spilled into the streets. Children ran errands for their mothers, carrying armfuls of greenery; the bakery's ovens sent the scent of spice into the cold air; the old church hall glowed with lanterns being strung along its eaves. Marley could feel the hum beneath it all, a current not just of anticipation for a celebration, but of relief—like a town finally ready to breathe again.

Damien arrived just as she finished arranging the shop's front display. He carried two things: a carefully wrapped bundle and a face taut with both determination and apprehension. "I thought we might add this tonight," he said, setting the bundle on the counter. He unwrapped it slowly to reveal the printing plate they had recovered weeks ago—the bell and vine motif etched deep in its metal face.

Marley's breath caught. "You're sure?"

He nodded. "If this celebration is going to mean anything, it needs to hold all of it. Even the parts that were buried."

They stood together in silence, gazing at the plate. Its metal gleamed dully in the morning light, not as an artifact of shame but as a testament to truth reclaimed. Marley felt her heart tighten with both gratitude and fear. The town was gathering tonight to celebrate, yes—but celebrations could turn to reckoning in an instant. Still, she knew Damien was right. The archive she was building could not begin in half-light.

By afternoon, the hall transformed. Candles lined every sill and beam, their flames flickering like stars drawn down to earth. The scent of evergreen boughs mingled with beeswax, warmth battling the crisp draft that seeped through the old wood. Tables groaned with food prepared by every family, dishes set down like offerings. A string quartet rehearsed softly in the corner, their music twining with the rustle of dresses and boots as townsfolk moved about, their voices carrying a cautious brightness.

Marley felt herself being carried along in the tide of preparations. Women pressed ribbons into her hands to weave into wreaths; children tugged her sleeves to ask about stories she might tell later; elders paused to thank her quietly for her work, though their eyes still held questions. She moved through it all with a mixture of awe and trepidation. It struck her that the Ball was no longer only tradition

—it was becoming something else. Something like a gathering of witness.

As dusk fell, the hall filled. Light pooled in golden rivers across the wooden floor as candles were lit one by one, passed hand to hand. Music swelled gently, and people began to dance, hesitant at first, then freer as laughter rose. Marley stood near the edge, watching, her heart tugged between the joy of the scene and the memory of Amelia's silence—the bride who had never danced, the vow that had never been sealed.

Damien found her there, slipping into the crowd at her side. "They're ready," he murmured, his hand brushing hers. "Maybe more than we are."

She smiled faintly, nerves knotting in her chest. "Then let's give them what they came for."

At the signal, the music softened, and the hall quieted. Candles flickered, casting halos of light across eager, uncertain faces. Marley stepped forward, the weight of her role pressing hard on her shoulders. She felt the eyes of Brookwood settle on her, not as judge but as witness. She opened her hands, palms up, as though to offer not just words but herself.

"We have kept silence long enough," she began, her voice low but steady. "And yet the silence has not left us. It has followed us through winters and bells, through memory and forgetting. Tonight we gather not to erase that silence, but to listen to it. To remember whose voice it carried."

She drew from her satchel the folded parchment—Amelia's letter—and set it gently on the table before her. Murmurs stirred, hushed quickly. "Amelia Colvin was not lost to us," Marley continued. "She was here, always. She chose not the role of bride, but of keeper. And it is because of her that we stand here tonight with the chance to be more than heirs to silence. We can be keepers too."

The words echoed in the rafters, and she felt them tremble in her chest. Damien stepped beside her then, holding up the printing plate, its surface catching the candlelight. "We found this buried," he said. "A symbol of vows meant to bind two families and a town together. But symbols mean nothing if they are hidden. Tonight we bring it into the light, not as proof of failure, but as reminder of the cost of forgetting."

The silence that followed was different than the one that had haunted Brookwood. This was silence as listening, as the gathering of breath before something greater.

Then it happened. Slowly, hesitantly at first, people began stepping forward. An elder woman placed a faded lace kerchief on the table. A young man set down a tarnished pocket watch. A mother carried forward a bundle of letters tied with twine. Each item was offered quietly, reverently, with words of explanation whispered to Marley as she received them.

"This was my grandmother's," one said.

"This was hidden in our attic for years."

"My father never spoke of this, but I think he wanted it remembered."

The table grew heavy with heirlooms, a patchwork of memory and sorrow, of stories long suppressed but now given breath. Marley felt tears prick her eyes as she touched each item, not as possession but as offering to the Living Archive she was building. It was no longer hers alone—it belonged to Brookwood, to all who dared to bring their silence into the open.

The quartet struck up a melody then, and Marley stiffened. It was faint, hesitant, but unmistakable: the tune of the music box. One violin carried the first line, a second joined with the counterpoint, and slowly the duet unfolded in the air. The room held its breath as the melody filled the hall, not mechanical now but alive, human, trembling with beauty.

Marley's throat closed as she realized what was happening. The town was not just remembering—they were sanctifying. What had once been bedtime legend, hidden artifact, forbidden song, was now lifted as sacred.

Damien's hand found hers, steadying her, anchoring her to the moment. "They've chosen," he whispered, his voice thick with awe. "They've chosen to carry it with us."

And as the final note lingered, the candles were raised, one by one, until the hall shimmered with a constellation of flame. The procession began, a line of light weaving out into the square, candles held high, melodies carried on the cold night air. Marley walked among them, the music box tune echoing through the streets as though the town itself had found its voice at last.

THE PROCESSION WOUND from the hall into Brookwood's square like a ribbon of fire against the night. Every hand carried light; every face was illumined not only by the candle they bore but by the trembling hope that had begun to take root. The music box melody, reborn in the quartet's strings, had given them a rhythm, and now the whole town seemed to breathe in time with it.

Marley walked at the center, not as leader but as one among many, her candle flickering as snowflakes drifted down in soft spirals. The square had been cleared of ice earlier in the day, yet the ground still held a sheen that mirrored the flames, as though the earth itself reflected the vow that hovered in the air.

She looked around and saw the change. Houses that once seemed shuttered in suspicion now glowed with windowlight, candles placed in rows, as though every home had become a shrine. Families who had avoided speaking of Amelia now walked side by side, their heirlooms offered, their silence lifted. Children clutched parents' hands, wide-eyed, too young to understand the depth of the night but sensing instinctively that they were part of something larger than themselves.

Marley's chest ached with the weight of it. This wasn't just a celebration—it was a risk. Unity so fragile could crumble at a single harsh word, a single memory too raw to be borne aloud. But for now, the silence of years was breaking, and she felt Amelia's presence in every footfall.

At the far edge of the square, the procession paused. By unspoken agreement, they gathered around the bell tower, its dark silhouette rising against the winter sky. The Winter Bell loomed above them, its voice still absent, but no longer an emblem of despair. It was waiting, as they were, for the next note in the story.

Marley stepped closer, her candlelight glancing against the old stone. She laid her free hand on the wall, cold and rough beneath her skin, and whispered almost without thinking, "She stayed."

Damien heard. He came to stand beside her, his own candle casting his face in shadow and gold. "The music told us," he murmured. "Now the people are telling us too."

She turned toward him. The lines of exhaustion on his face seemed softer in the glow, his usual guardedness stripped away by the sheer vulnerability of the night. "Do you feel it?" she asked.

He nodded slowly. "Hope—and fear, braided so tightly I can't tell one from the other. But yes, Marley. I feel it."

The crowd shifted, expectant. Someone began to hum the music box tune, tentative at first, then joined by others. The melody wove through the air like thread pulling them all together. Marley felt her throat tighten. This was not rehearsed. It was not planned. It was a town making its own liturgy, turning loss into song.

Damien leaned close, his voice nearly inaudible. "They're taking it from us now. From Amelia. From Elijah. It's not ours to keep anymore."

His words stung, though not unkindly. Marley knew he was right. Everything they had unearthed—the letter, the journal, the gloves, the vow—had led to this moment when Brookwood itself would decide whether to carry the truth forward. She felt both pride and a tremor of fear at letting it go.

A voice broke through the song then. Old Mrs. Callahan, her hands shaking with age, stepped forward, her candle dripping wax into the snow. "We kept too much in shadows," she said, her voice raspy but clear. "It cost us more than we ever admitted. Tonight I give this light for Amelia— and for all we silenced along with her."

Her words rippled outward. One by one, others began to speak as they placed their candles in the snow at the bell's base. "For my brother." "For my mother." "For those who never came home." The circle of flame grew, each offering a vow not of perfection, but of remembrance.

Marley felt the fragile unity deepen. These were not rehearsed speeches, nor forced reconciliations. They were confessions made holy by their honesty.

She glanced at Damien, and the look in his eyes told her he understood what she could not yet say aloud. They had been afraid the truth would divide Brookwood. But here, in this cold square, the truth was becoming the very thing that bound them.

Yet beneath that hope, Marley sensed the risk. If tomorrow, doubts crept in—if whispers of the Circle of Seven returned, if old rivalries reasserted themselves—the unity could fracture. This night was both miracle and test.

As the circle of candles brightened, Damien touched her arm lightly. "We have to stay with them," he said. "Not above them. Not outside. With them. If we falter, so will they."

Marley swallowed, the weight of his words settling deep. She thought of Amelia's letter, her declaration of wanting to be not a bride but a keeper of peace. That mantle now rested on all of them, but especially on her and Damien. To keep peace was not to avoid conflict, but to walk into it with courage, to hold truth steady even when the town wavered.

The song ended, but the silence that followed was alive, full, almost tender. Marley raised her candle, the last unplaced. Her voice carried across the circle: "This light is for Amelia Colvin, who stayed. And for every vow yet to be kept." She placed it at the bell's base, the flames now forming a ring of fire at its feet.

For a moment, the square seemed to breathe as one.

Damien reached for her hand, not to claim or steady, but to join. Together they stood, watching the fragile unity take root, knowing it was no guarantee but also no illusion. This was Brookwood choosing, candle by candle, to bind itself to a story long denied.

A cheer rose then—soft at first, then swelling as children laughed and couples embraced. The Winter Ball had become something else: not a retreat into nostalgia, but a step forward into memory restored.

Marley felt the fragile hope take root in her chest. And

she knew, with a certainty that ached, that whatever storms still waited, they had crossed a threshold. Brookwood would never again be the town of silence alone.

THE WINTER BALL had begun with caution, even tremor, but as the night stretched onward it blossomed into something Brookwood had not seen in a generation: unguarded joy. The circle of candles at the bell tower's base still flickered like a second hearth in the heart of town, but now laughter wove through the cold air as freely as the music. The quartet's instruments carried the melodies of both past and present—first the solemn strains of the music box waltz, then lighter dances that drew couples and children alike into motion.

For Marley, it was like standing inside a dream. All around her, townsfolk who once turned away from questions about Amelia now brought forward pieces of their family histories as if offering fragments of a broken mosaic. One woman approached with a handkerchief embroidered with initials too faint to read; another carried a diary missing half its pages but filled with pressed flowers. A fisherman came with an old pocketknife etched with the year of his parents' wedding. Each item was not just an object but a confession, an admission that silence had once weighed too heavy, and that now it was time to set those weights down.

She had not expected it. She thought she would have to beg, persuade, or plead for the beginnings of the Living Archive. Instead, it was as though Amelia's vow had cracked the dam, and memory poured forth in a flood.

Damien, standing close beside her, took the items carefully one by one, setting them on the long oak table that had been placed near the bell tower. His hands were steady, reverent. "We'll catalog them," he told each person, his tone solemn, almost priestly. "We'll preserve the stories that go with them. Nothing will be lost again."

Some wept as they handed things over, as though the act of release brought both grief and relief. Marley touched their hands, listened to their words, wrote quick notes on scraps of parchment. She knew she would spend weeks piecing the details together, cross-checking dates, teasing out truth from rumor. But that was not tonight's task. Tonight was about gathering what had been hidden, gathering the courage to begin again.

At one point, Mr. Whitcomb approached, holding a thin silver locket. His eyes, so often shielded by pride, glistened now. "This was hers," he said, and Marley understood he meant Amelia. "It came to me after my father passed, and I locked it away. I couldn't bear to see it, knowing all it represented." He placed it into Marley's hand, fingers trembling. "But if she stayed, as you've shown us, then perhaps she meant for us to stay with her."

Marley closed her fingers gently around his. "We will keep it safe," she said, her voice steady though her throat burned. "And we will keep her story alive."

As Mr. Whitcomb stepped back, the music shifted. The quartet began to weave the twin melodies of the two music boxes into a single, layered piece. Marley froze as she recognized the duet, that tender call-and-response of "I stayed... I stayed..." The townsfolk recognized it too, not with their minds but with their bodies. Couples swayed closer. Mothers drew children into their arms. Old rivalries dissolved as neighbors clasped hands. The duet was no longer haunting. It had become invitation.

Marley felt tears sting her eyes. She glanced at Damien, whose lips moved silently with the words he had once coaxed from the recording. His gaze found hers, and for a moment the square vanished, the town vanished, and it was only the two of them, holding the vow of presence between them like a flame they must never let die.

When the song ended, applause rang out—not the polite clapping of an audience but the jubilant rhythm of a people who had rediscovered their voice. Someone shouted, "To the bell!" and laughter followed, but it was not mocking. It was celebratory, hopeful, daring.

The bell, silent above them, seemed to listen.

Marley and Damien stepped together onto the dais where the heirlooms now lay in a careful heap. Marley raised her hands for quiet, and the square hushed almost instantly. "This," she said, gesturing to the growing pile of artifacts, "is only the beginning. These items, and the stories that come with them, will form Brookwood's Living Archive. No longer will we hide what hurts us, nor bury what binds us. Tonight we begin again—not with silence, but with memory."

Her words were met with cheers, with tears, with nods of solemn assent.

Damien added, his voice rich, resonant, carrying across the square, "We are not only keeping Amelia's vow—we are making our own. That when the bell rings, whether once or a hundred times, it will ring for truth. For love. For peace. For us all."

The crowd erupted in applause, the sound echoing up into the cold night sky, as though testing whether the bell itself might answer.

But the bell did not move. And yet Marley knew—it didn't need to. The vow was already alive in them.

As the night deepened, the Winter Ball transformed. Children darted between candles, laughing. Couples danced in the snow. Neighbors who had not spoken in years shared bread and mulled cider. The air grew thick with warmth despite the frost, a warmth born not of fire alone but of hearts unburdened.

Marley found herself standing at the center of it, Damien at her side, their shoulders brushing. They said little, because little was needed. They watched as Brookwood began to heal itself, not by forgetting, but by remembering together.

She thought of Amelia—standing in snow in her photograph, veiled, alone. And she whispered into the night, *You are not alone anymore. We are here. We stayed.*

Damien reached for her hand, threading his fingers through hers. He squeezed once, gently, as though echoing her vow. And Marley knew, with a certainty that made her breath hitch, that they were exactly where they were meant to be: not as historians, not as leaders, not even as lovers alone, but as keepers—keepers of memory, keepers of peace, keepers of the vow that would carry Brookwood into its next season.

The bells above remained silent, but Marley felt no dread in the quiet. For the first time, the silence was not emptiness but fullness—like a held breath before the dawn.

And together, she and Damien stood at the heart of a town finally beginning to heal.

30

THE BOOK OF WISHES BEGINS

By morning, the candles at the base of the bell tower had melted into shallow halos, amber pooled in the snow like coins left by pilgrims. The square wore the soft disarray of joy—the chalk scuffs of dance steps, a child's mitten rescued and set atop a post, sprigs of evergreen shaken free of their twine. Brookwood's air felt rinsed, the way the river smells after ice breaks and moves on.

Marley woke before the sun fully softened the roofs. She boiled water on the shop's small stove and laid her tools out on brown paper as carefully as a surgeon: bone folder, awl, waxed linen thread, binder's needles, soft cloths, a pot of archival paste, a ruler nicked from years of measuring spines. Damien came down the stairs a few minutes later, hair damp from a too-cold wash, carrying two mugs and the leather roll of his own instruments—the calipers, the tiny square, an old embosser he'd rescued from the town hall basement and oiled back to life. He set the mugs by her elbow and met her eyes; neither of them needed to name the work.

"The cover first," Marley said. "It should feel like a door you want to open, not a lock you can't."

Damien unrolled the leather and considered the pieces she'd gathered. "Cloth or leather?"

"Cloth," she decided. "Winter green. And a band of linen along the spine. It needs to survive a century of hands."

He nodded. "And the paper?"

She lifted a stack—creamy, thick sheets she'd kept for years without a reason good enough to use them. "Cotton rag, heavy enough to hold ink and tears." She glanced up at him and smiled. "We'll need both."

They worked in the wordless accord that had become their truest language. Damien cut boards; Marley stretched the winter-green book cloth over them, smoothing the stubborn air from beneath with the bone folder until corners lay clean as vows. He marked sewing stations along the signatures; she pierced them with the awl, steady and measured. Linen thread, waxed and warm from her fingers, slid through holes with a soft, intimate sound—the sewing of a spine like the lacing of a bodice, except this one would never constrict, only hold.

While paste cured and linen set, Marley drafted the page that would precede all others. She did not call it an introduction—Brookwood had had enough introductions to pretty lies. Instead she titled it simply:

To the Keepers of Brookwood, On the Winter Solstice
Her pen moved slowly; each sentence had to belong.

Let this book be a door we open together once each winter, not to escape what is, but to speak what we hope will be. One wish per person, per solstice. Not a list for gaining, but a ledger for keeping. You may sign or remain unnamed. Write for yourself, or for another who has no hand left to write. Write in ink that will outlast us, but know that wishes are not contracts—they are breath we share.

Damien read over her shoulder, the warmth of him steady at her back. "Add this," he murmured. "*A wish is no command to the bell, which is no servant. It is a promise to one another to listen for what the wish asks of us in return.*"

She wrote it exactly as he spoke it, the line fitting the page as if it had waited there. When she finished, she dated the page and left, centered beneath, a small space into which she pressed the shop's round seal—the one that had been her aunt's. The wax took the impression of a sprig of fir and a bell. It cooled to a dull red the color of the circle on an old map that says *you are here.*

"Cover motif?" Damien asked, setting the embosser near the cooling seal.

Marley ran her fingertips over the winter-green cloth and closed her eyes until the image rose. "Not a bell," she said. "A wreath. But not closed—one place left open at the bottom. A doorway for wishes to enter."

He sketched on scrap, quick and economical, the vine and bell motif from the printing plate transformed into a laurel that did not circle back upon itself. Marley nodded. Damien heated the brass die and pressed it gently against the cloth. The wreath appeared in low relief—elegant, restrained, a promise that did not pretend to be complete. In the empty gap at the bottom he stamped a faint star.

"For the one we forgot," he said.

Marley swallowed. "For the ones we will not forget again."

By noon the binding had set. They turned the book in their hands—the weight of it honest but not onerous, like a baby carried home the first time. Damien measured margins and ruled a faint line at the top of each page: **Wish,**

Winter Solstice, with the year left open. He'd argued for no lines—wishes, he said, should not be caged—but Marley insisted on a single one across the top, not to constrain, but to teach the hand where to begin. Between them they struck the right balance, as they always did.

A knock rattled the glazed door. When Marley looked up, the bakery sisters stood there, cheeks pinked from the cold, a basket between them emitting a saintly steam. "We brought sustenance," Sophie announced, bustling in as if she'd been summoned by scent alone. "And ribbon."

Behind them came Mr. Whitcomb in a proper coat despite the hour, Lenore with her cane and her eyes cutting like truth into everything they saw, and a pair of teenagers who had spent the night pretending they hadn't cried when the bell rang. Word had gone out—quietly, across stoops and counters—that Marley was making something for the town. Brookwood had come to help without being asked, the way people show up to move a heavy sofa or carry a casket.

They gathered around the table as Marley laid the book down. No one spoke for a long moment. Even Sophie, indefatigable as a stoked oven, pressed a hand to her mouth.

"It smells like my grandmother's wedding chest," she whispered. "Like cedar and the inside of a hope."

Mr. Whitcomb took his time. "Where will it live?"

"In the front of the shop," Marley said. "Under the east window. But tonight, it should be here." She lifted her chin toward the square. "At the bell."

Lenore tapped her cane once. "Rules?"

Marley handed her the prefatory page. Lenore read, lips moving faintly just once where Damien's line sat. When she finished, she nodded. "Good. A wish that returns to the one who wrote it and asks, *What work will you do to greet me?*"

One of the teenagers—Freya, a girl with ink on her fingers and a voice that had been the first to hum the night before—raised her hand as if in school. "Can we draw instead of write?"

"Of course," Marley said. "A wish can be a picture when words won't do."

"And can the first page stay blank?" Freya asked, eyes flicking to the front. "I mean—leave it for whatever wants to arrive."

Marley smiled. "The first page will not be mine."

The bakery sisters exchanged a look, then set their basket on the counter and drew out a roll of satin ribbon, a length of narrow gold thread, and a sprig of preserved ivy. "For the bookmark," Sophie said. "So we never lose our place."

Damien threaded the ribbon through a slit he cut in the headband, tied the gold around it, and tucked the ivy into the knot so its leaf lay like a small hand on the page.

By late afternoon, the square began to swell again with people—less formal than the night before, faces a little sleep-soft and second-day tender. Children dragged their sleds to the hill by the church, teenagers pretended not to wait to see who would show up, and elders held their coats close at the throat the way wise birds tuck their heads against weather. A table had been set under a canopy— sturdy, plain, the oak from last night now draped with a linen runner Damien found in the archive and laundered back to life. On it they placed the Book.

Marley did not stand behind the table like a registrar. She stood to the side, one hand on the cloth as if steadying a boat. Damien took up station at the other edge, enough presence to say *this matters*, not so much as to say *this belongs to us*. The music box melody threaded lightly from the quartet warming fingers; the bell tower kept its own counsel.

The mayor came first, not for theater but to cover those who would hesitate. She signed with a simple hand, then stepped aside without speech. A shoemaker followed, then a child who wanted to draw a star "for a grandpa in the sky," then two men who had not spoken in years and did not speak now but stood shoulder to shoulder while one wrote. The line lengthened.

Marley watched the procession begin as if the town were learning a new gait—awkward at first, then more certain. Wishes arrived shyly, bravely, crookedly, beautifully. Some were sealed with names, others anonymous; one was only a pressed fir tip leaving its soft green stain. The shop's clock struck, unnoticed, and shadows stretched across the square like the underlines of sentences.

In the press of hands, Mr. Whitcomb waited at the edge, the silver locket in his pocket like a second heart-beat. Lenore watched from her cane, eyes wet and fierce. The bakery sisters whispered a prayer they would later deny was a prayer. Freya sketched her star with a sure wrist.

And still the first page remained blank, face-down beneath the cover like a held breath. Marley kept her palm on the cloth and did not urge or prompt. Wishes arrive when they are ready; the keeper's work is to hold the door open.

As dusk slid toward evening and the candles from last night were lit again one by one, Damien leaned closer, his voice a thread meant for her alone. "Look at them," he said. "They're writing a town into being."

Marley nodded, throat burning, the weight of the book a warm gravity through fabric to skin. "Let the next season know where to find us," she whispered, to the bell, to the book, to the wind. "Let it find us here, with our hands open."

The line continued, breath clouding the air, ink darkening the pages. The first entry—the one that would set the tone—had not yet arrived. But Marley felt it moving toward them already, the way one feels a ringing through stone before a sound is heard.

She kept the cover lifted, the green wreath open at its base, and waited with all of Brookwood for the book to speak.

THE SQUARE GREW QUIETER as the evening deepened, though the air itself seemed full, as if holding its breath for what might emerge. Lanterns burned low, wreaths shivered against the windows, and the bell above loomed—silent, yet different now, less a sentinel of grief than a patient witness.

The Book of Wishes lay open, its first pages already trembling with fresh ink, the faint ribbon marking the place where the town's voice had begun. Each entry carried its own weight: the child's star for a lost grandfather, a widow's wish for gentleness in the coming year, the shoemaker's hope that his daughter might be bold enough to leave and return with stories.

But the first page remained untouched.

Marley noticed how eyes flicked toward it and then away, as if the blankness unnerved them more than any words could. The cover's open wreath seemed to beckon. Yet no one had dared to be the first to set down a line that would anchor the tradition.

She felt Damien's glance at her side. "It's waiting," he said softly.

"For who?"

He shook his head. "Not for us to say."

And so they let the page breathe, unfilled. Wishes need not be summoned. They arrive in their own hour.

LATER, after the crowd thinned and only the elders and a scatter of children remained, the baker's youngest sister stepped forward. Her apron still dusted with flour, she placed a slip of paper on the table, then hesitated. "May I?" she asked Marley.

"This book belongs to Brookwood now," Marley said.

The girl lifted her chin, slid the paper beneath the cover, and copied the words carefully onto the first page. Her hand was not steady, but her letters sang with sincerity:

May forgotten love always find the voice to speak again.

She set down the pen and blew gently on the ink. Around her, the square stilled; even the children hushed. Damien exhaled slowly, as though a string long wound had loosened.

"There," the girl whispered. "Now it has a beginning."

Applause did not follow. What came instead was something far older—a collective bowing of the head, the silence not empty but sacred. The wish had been written for Amelia, yes, but also for every silence that had ever bruised Brookwood. It was for the bell that had tolled when it should not, for the letters never sent, for Elijah's sacrifice, for the secret love folded into lace and hidden in an attic. It was for Marley and Damien too, standing together at the table.

THE BOOK REMAINED in the square long after the lanterns guttered. Townsfolk came and went in the dim hours, each bringing their offering. Some wrote in small, cramped hands; others spilled across the page as if afraid the ink might fade. A boy scrawled simply: "Snow." A seamstress wrote: "Enough bread for every table." An elder, her hands shaking, pressed the outline of her palm. Wishes rose like notes in a song, separate yet woven.

Marley watched, moved past words. She did not speak, though once she reached out and rested her fingertips lightly on the book's cloth, not to claim it but to honor it. She had known Brookwood's silence, had studied it in archives, in photographs, in half-burned notes. Now she was watching it learn to speak again, not with one voice, but with many.

Damien stood beside her. His posture was quiet, but the pulse in his jaw gave him away—this was as much a vow to him as any they had spoken aloud. For a man who had weighed leaving, this was proof that staying meant something.

AT LAST, when the square emptied, Damien lifted the book carefully, as though cradling an infant. "Where does it rest tonight?" he asked.

Marley hesitated. "It began at the bell. Let it remain there until dawn."

He nodded. Together, they carried it across the snowy square to the tower door. Inside, the air smelled of old wood and iron. The bell above seemed to lean into their presence, its silence a listening rather than an absence.

They set the book on a low stand, lit a single candle, and left the door unlatched. Not unlocked—never careless—but unlatched, so that anyone with a wish heavy on their heart might enter before morning.

On the threshold, Damien paused. "Do you think Amelia would have wanted this?"

Marley answered without hesitation. "She did not wish to be a bride. She wished to be a keeper. This is her keeping."

His gaze softened. "And now it is ours."

WHEN THEY STEPPED BACK into the night, the bell tower's window glowed faintly with the candle they'd left inside. Snow fell again, fine and feathery, dusting their coats. For the first time in years, Marley felt the solstice not as a season to endure, but as a threshold to cross.

Damien offered his hand—not in promise, but in presence. She took it.

Together they walked home through the hush of Brookwood, carrying the knowledge that the town's voice had begun again on a single page, with a wish that belonged to all of them.

And though the bell did not ring that night, its silence was no longer grief. It was expectancy—the breath before a word is spoken, the pause before harmony is struck.

Brookwood, for the first time in nearly a century, was listening to itself.

THE NEXT NIGHT, Brookwood gathered again, though no formal summons had been issued. It was as if some invisible current had pulled every household toward the square, each resident sensing that the story had not yet finished. Candles glowed in windows, lanterns swung from porches, and the air carried that expectant hush that precedes revelation.

The Book of Wishes rested in its place at the bell tower's

base, its pages already filling with inked hopes. Marley had traced them earlier: the blacksmith wishing for warmth in every hearth, the seamstress for reconciliation with her estranged sister, children sketching stars and sleds and improbable dreams of flying. Yet what lingered most was that first wish—"May forgotten love always find the voice to speak again"—because it had planted a seed not just on paper but in the marrow of the town.

Damien stood with Marley near the edge of the square. His coat brushed hers, his presence steady. Neither spoke. It seemed words might disturb whatever fragile promise hovered between the houses and the snow.

When the clock struck nine, the lanterns dimmed—not extinguished, but as though some unseen hand had laid a veil across them. The townsfolk turned their eyes upward, toward the tower where the bell hung in shadow.

A hush deeper than silence followed. Even the wind stilled. Marley could hear the soft draw of Damien's breath, the faint shifting of boots on packed snow. All eyes fixed on the bell rope that dangled untouched.

And then it happened.

The bell tolled.

Not thunderous, not triumphant, but clear and resonant, a single note that rolled across the rooftops and down the lanes. It was unmistakable—yet no hand had pulled the rope, no mechanism had stirred. The sound was its own, arising from a place beyond the visible.

Gasps broke the silence. A child clutched his mother's skirts. An elder pressed her hand to her lips, tears springing unbidden. Some crossed themselves, others simply bowed their heads. But none turned away.

The bell rang again, softer this time, almost tender, like a benediction rather than a summons. Marley felt it vibrate through her chest, a resonance that belonged not only to her body but to something larger, something that held the whole of Brookwood.

Damien's eyes found hers. In them she read awe, relief, and that steady devotion that had carried them through silence, storm, and doubt. For once, neither needed to interpret. The bell had spoken; they had heard.

As the final note faded into the night, the townsfolk did not scatter as they might have in past winters. Instead, they drifted toward one another, murmuring, embracing, sharing fragments of memory as though the sound had unlocked not only the bell but their own guarded hearts.

The elder Lenore, who had once warned of curses, leaned on her cane and whispered, "Grief kept it silent. But love has given it voice."

A cluster of children ran to the Book of Wishes, tugging at Marley's sleeve. "Read them aloud," they begged. And so she did, her voice carrying through the square—hopes simple and profound, laughter threading through tears as each wish became a shared inheritance.

By the time she closed the cover, the bell tower's candle glowed steady, a sentinel of peace rather than sorrow.

Later, when the crowd thinned and only the most steadfast remained, Damien drew Marley aside to the base of the tower. The snow glowed faintly under the lanterns, the night air crisp and waiting.

"Do you feel it?" he asked.

"Yes," she said. "It's not just the bell. It's us. All of us."

He nodded. "And yet—there will be resistance. Truth always unsettles. But tonight proved it. Brookwood is ready to heal."

Marley placed her hand against the tower's stone. "Amelia never left. She became the bell. But it will not keep her alone anymore. We will keep her vow."

Damien covered her hand with his. Together, they stood there as if sealing something larger than themselves, a charge passed across time.

The bell did not ring again that night. It did not need to.

WHEN DAWN CAME, the Book of Wishes was carried to the bookshop, where Marley placed it in the window for all to see. Already there were whispers of making it a yearly ritual: one page for every solstice, one wish per soul. A living testament, not to silence or secrecy, but to harmony and hope.

Marley read the first line again—**"May forgotten love always find the voice to speak again."**

This, she thought, was no longer just Amelia's story. It was Brookwood's. It was hers. It was Damien's.

The bell had spoken. And so had they.

The season of harmony had begun.

EPILOGUE: THE WINTER BELL

The snow in Brookwood did not vanish overnight. It lingered, a quiet shroud across the rooftops and the silent lanes, but something in its presence had shifted. It was no longer heavy with dread. Instead, it glistened with the kind of brightness that suggested possibility, as if the season itself had been unbound.

Marley rose early the morning after the bell's second toll. The Book of Wishes rested in the front window of the shop, catching the first rays of sunlight like a beacon. She had turned the key in the lock with a sense of reverence, realizing that the book had already become something larger than she could contain. It was no longer hers, no longer even Brookwood's—it was the voice of all who had been forgotten, and of all who dared to dream anew.

Damien found her at the window. His hair was mussed, his scarf hastily knotted, and he carried the unmistakable weariness of someone who had wrestled with choices deep into the night. But his eyes held something steadier than they had before—a clarity, a rootedness that had not been there when Florence's letter first arrived.

"The bell tolled twice," he said quietly, as if testing the words aloud.

Marley turned to him, folding her arms. "It did."

"Once for the vow restored," he said. "And once for what comes next."

Marley searched his expression. "Do you believe that?"

"I do now," Damien answered. His hand brushed hers, lingering. "I don't think we're done. Not with the bell, not with Amelia, and not with each other."

BY MIDMORNING, townsfolk streamed to the shop to add their wishes, their faces softened by the miracle they had witnessed. Some wept; others laughed; a few still looked wary, as though uncertain whether the silence would return. But the air held a freshness, like soil turned after winter frost, waiting for seed.

Marley watched them carefully. She had learned enough to know that peace did not come without tension, that truth never arrived without resistance. Yet something deep within her told her that the bell's voice was not an ending but a beginning.

It was Lenore who pressed her gnarled hand over Marley's on the counter and whispered, "The vow is not kept by one ringing, child. It is kept in every season, in every root that grows and every stone that is turned. The bell only told you where to look."

Marley nodded, though the words unsettled her. Where to look. She felt Damien shift beside her, his scholar's instinct stirring.

That night, when the square grew quiet again, Marley and Damien returned to the bell tower. They stood beneath it, the great iron shape looming in the pale light, and felt the weight of what had passed. Damien unrolled Amelia's letter once more.

"She called herself a keeper of peace," he said. "That wasn't just a refusal of marriage. It was a role. A charge."

"And a charge doesn't end with one night," Marley added. "It passes forward."

They were silent for a long time. Then Damien asked the question neither had yet voiced: "If the vow passes forward, are we the ones meant to carry it?"

Marley reached for his hand. "I think we already are."

THE FOLLOWING WEEK, snow softened into rain. The hills glistened, and rivulets carved new lines through the meadows on the town's edge. Marley and Damien walked often, needing the open air to sort through the magnitude of what they had uncovered.

On one such walk, Damien carried a folded map from the archives, its edges brittle with age. "This was drawn by the founders," he explained, pointing to faint inked lines beyond the current boundary of town. "Look here—past the mills, where the land slopes down toward the river bend. There's a grove marked with a circle. No name. Just the emblem of two entwined branches."

Marley traced the faded mark. "The Circle of Seven."

"Or older," Damien said, voice low. "Maybe the Green Healers. The records are scarce, but I've seen fragments—a place of gathering, a grove used for rites of renewal."

Marley felt a shiver run through her despite the mild air. The phrase *keeper of peace* rang again in her mind, linking Amelia's choice to something much deeper. Perhaps the bell had not simply tolled for a broken vow, but for a forgotten sanctuary.

They walked on in silence until they reached the river bend. The land there was choked with brambles and the skeletal remains of long-fallen trees. But beneath it all, Marley saw what Damien had described: the faint impression of a circle, stone markers jutting like old teeth from the earth, half-buried by time.

"This was a grove," she whispered.

Damien nodded. "And it's been hidden. Or abandoned. Perhaps both."

They stood there, the sound of the river rushing behind them, the damp air heavy with a sense of presence. Marley felt the same pull she had felt at the bell tower—that uncanny weight of history pressing forward, demanding not simply remembrance but restoration.

"We can't ignore this," Marley said finally.

"No," Damien agreed. His voice was firm, but his eyes carried worry. "But remember what the bell taught us. Revealing truth can divide as easily as it heals. If the grove was part of the founders' pact, unearthing it could unsettle the balance all over again."

Marley looked at him, the wind catching her hair. "Then we'll face it together. The bell was Amelia's vow. The grove —maybe this is ours."

THAT EVENING, back at the shop, Marley placed the map beside the Book of Wishes. The juxtaposition struck her: one a record of what had been forgotten, the other a living testament to what was being born anew.

She sat at her desk, the lamplight warm against the growing dusk, and began writing. Not research notes, not archival summaries, but her own entry in the Book of Wishes. Her hand trembled as she pressed the pen to paper:

"May what is buried rise again in peace, not in conflict. May we have the courage to keep what was once kept, and the wisdom to let it root where it belongs."

When she was done, she slid the book across the desk to Damien. He read the words, his expression unreadable at first, then softened.

"You've already chosen, haven't you?" he said.

"I think the choice was made for us," Marley replied. "All we can do is answer."

Damien bent his head, resting his forehead against hers. "Then we answer together."

THE NIGHT before the new year, Marley and Damien returned to the bell tower one last time. The snow had crusted firm again, and the stars stretched clear across the sky. Brookwood lay hushed, not in fear, but in rest.

At the base of the tower, Marley opened her journal. On the last page she had written: *The bride never left. She became the bell. And now the bell has become the town.*

Damien added his own words beneath hers: *And the town must become the grove.*

They exchanged a glance—no hesitation, no uncertainty, only the steady recognition that their lives were no longer their own. They belonged to the vow.

IN THE WEEKS TO COME, word of the grove began to stir. Not loudly, not yet, but in whispers carried between families, in hints that the land beyond the mills might hold something more than overgrowth. Some welcomed the possibility, speaking of a return to healing traditions. Others frowned, wary that old secrets unearthed might fracture the fragile harmony.

Marley and Damien knew the debate would come. They knew resistance was inevitable. But they also knew that their charge as keepers was not to silence fear, but to carry the truth forward until it found its voice.

On the morning of the solstice's close, Marley placed the Book of Wishes on the shop counter and whispered to Damien, "This is where we begin again."

He smiled faintly. "Not alone."

Together, they stepped into the dawn, their footsteps carrying them toward the hidden grove.

The bell no longer tolled with silence. The vow no longer lingered unspoken. A new season awaited—one rooted not only in memory but in return.

Brookwood's harmony had been restored. But in the shadow of the river bend, the grove stirred, waiting to test what it truly meant to be a keeper.

And so, as the last snow melted into earth, the story turned.

The next mystery awaited.

AFTERWORD

A Reflective Legacy

The Brookwood Mysteries begins, as so many stories do, with silence.

It was the silence of a bookshop whose shelves held more than novels—the silence of Clara's vow, of words written in margins, of echoes that could only be heard when someone dared to listen. Marley stepped into that silence not as an intruder but as an inheritor, though she did not yet know it. *The Bookshop Secret* showed her—and us—that history breathes through the most ordinary doors, waiting for hands brave enough to turn the lock.

From there, the path winds into resonance. *The Bridge of Echoes* carries voices across time, testing whether past promises could be trusted in the present. Each echo reminds Brookwood that memory is never idle—it insists, it demands, it shapes. Marley and Damien began to realize that listening was not passive but covenant: if they carried the echoes, they must also answer them.

The Lighthouse Prophecy shifts the gaze outward, to signals cast against darkness. It asked: what do we guard, and what do we guide? In that season, the town learned that prophecy is less prediction than mirror. The light did not foretell what must be—it illuminated what already was: a community standing on the threshold of its own forgotten story.

The Winter Bell gives voice to stillness. A bell that should have rung but didn't, a vow that had been broken, a bride whose absence echoed for decades. Silence again—but this time charged, asking whether absence could be as loud as sound. Marley and Damien discover that love and loss, entwined, toll not as ending but as call.

And finally, *The Hidden Grove* reveals itself as culmination, not simply continuation. The stones, the spirals, the ledger, the seed—all mysteries unfolded into memory, and memory unfolded into inheritance. What began as secrecy becomes community. What began as whispers becomes vows. What began as one woman's step into a bookshop becomes an entire town's covenant with its own roots.

Brookwood's Legacy

The mysteries are not puzzles to solve, nor riddles to conquer. They are invitations—to listen, to remember, to rise. At every turn, Brookwood asked its people a single question: *Will you keep what was entrusted to you, not as possession, but as promise?*

Marley answered yes. Damien answered yes. The townsfolk, hesitant, divided, afraid—they too answered yes.

And so the series does not close on a solved case or a quiet conclusion. It closes on a circle, still widening. Children's hands pressing seeds into soil. Elders whispering names into bark. A grove alive with bloom and resonance.

The mysteries of Brookwood will always remain, not

locked in secrecy but alive in inheritance. And so, the circle holds:

We remember. We root. We rise.

Brookwood Mysteries
   Book 1 - The Bookshop Secret
   Book 2 - The Bridge of Echoes
   Book 3 - The Lighthouse Prophecy
   Book 4 - The Winter Bell
   Book 5 - The Hidden Grove

ABOUT THE AUTHOR

Jordan Jace is a Pacific Northwest author whose mysteries and heartwarming tales are set against stunning landscapes. With a deep connection to the PNW region's natural beauty, Jace infuses each story with the magic of misty mountains, lush forests, and tranquil coastlines. Jace believes that joy can be found in the smallest moments and the most unexpected places. When not writing, Jace is exploring the world, seeking inspiration in every corner for the next unforgettable story. Discover more at visionsinprint.com

www.ingramcontent.com/pod-product-compliance
Lightning Source LLC
Chambersburg PA
CBHW031243310726
48971CB00004B/1147